Martha lister!
Her mother

"It's my fau

"No, sweetheart." Duke's voice was tender. "It's mine. I shouldn't have let her grow up like a boy around the mining camps."

"I knew she'd have that kind of life when I married you," Em answered. "But I knew you'd be a good father—and you are."

"She just reminded me that I'm not her father at all! That she's a senator's daughter."

"And that's where I made another mistake," Em said. "I should have told her that my first husband was not her father and that he committed suicide. She's built him up, idealized him as the perfect parent. What if she takes after her real father, whoever he was! A cold-eyed killer or a drunk Mexican boy!" Em's voice rose in hysteria. "And I don't even know which one it was. They took turns! They took turns!"

As her mother's voice echoed in her ears, Martha fled to her room. Now she knew. She was a *bastard!* Duke and Mama had lied to her. They must have been waiting for her bad blood to show. Well, to hell with them. From now on, she could do what she wanted, be what she wanted to be—and as bad as she wanted to be!

Books by
Aola Vandergriff

Wyndspelle
Wyndspelle's Child
The Bell Tower of Wyndspelle
The House of the Dancing Dead
Sisters of Sorrow
Daughters of the Southwind
Daughters of the Wild Country
Daughters of the Far Islands
Daughters of the Opal Skies
Daughters of the Misty Isles
Daughters of the Shining City

Published by
WARNER BOOKS

Daughters of the Far Islands

Aola Vandergriff

WARNER BOOKS

A Warner Communications Company

WARNER BOOKS EDITION

Copyright © 1979 by Aola Vandergriff

All rights reserved.

Cover art by Jim Dietz

Warner Books, Inc., 75 Rockefeller Plaza, New York, N.Y 10019

W A Warner Communications Company

Printed in the United States of America

First Printing: June, 1979

Reissued: October, 1982

10 9 8 7

FOR HELEN
My husband's mother;
my volunteer publicity agent.
Thanks, for both roles.

Daughters
of the
Far Islands

Foreword

The islands of Hawaii are enchanted. Any tale told of them is a fairy tale. Yet this much of it is true.

The Big Island, in 1868, felt the fury of Pele, quaking for days, finally erupting in flame. Much of it sank into the sea; perhaps a gift to Pele's elder brother, Pali Kapu o Kamohoali, the shark god.

The small town of Lahaina, its whaling era ended, dreamed at the foot of the red hills of Maui. Offshore lay the islands of Lanai, and of Molokai; the lonely isle, where by royal edict, lepers were banished to hell in the midst of paradise.

On Oahu, in the city of Honolulu, lived a king. Kamehameha, Fifth, was descended from the conqueror of all the islands. It is said that he loved his brother's wife. He never married. His dream was to hold his country for his people. Here also, were two women destined for greatness. Liliuokalani, wife of John Dominis, would someday be queen. During her reign, she threatened to behead the leaders of a group pressing annexation. She, too, wished to keep the country for its own.

Her sister, Bernice Pauahi Bishop, half-sister to Kamehameha, or Lot, as he was known, was a far-sighted woman. She worked to educate her people

9

so their culture would not be lost. Today, schools and museums are founded in her name; her gentle spirit lives on.

Transplanted Americans, in those years, were crying for annexation. Though it would not come until later, it is possible their pleas reached the ears of a man slated to be President. Railroads, needed to expedite sugarcane to harbor and factory, were talked of, though did not become an actuality for years. It is possible that the seeds were germinating.

The natives walked two paths. They attended mission churches and called upon their own *Kahunas* to situate their homes, heal their sick, and remove the curse of *kapus* they might have violated.

In the same space of time, there was a brief period of peace in China, the country beginning to acknowledge the existence of others. It was not impossible that a Chinese warlord would appear in the city of Washington, with his wives and concubines.

In the green China sea, at the northern tip of the Pearl River, entrance to the Tiger's mouth, Sir Richard MacDonnell and his lady occupied Government House on Upper Albert Road. Here, Prince Alfred, Duke of Edinburgh, was to visit after leaving the Hawaiian Islands on his tour of the world.

These are the truths, the possibilities and the probabilities I have used in creating this book. If I have taken liberties in the use of historical figures in the story, I will say, in the words of King Lot, Kamehameha, Fifth, *"It is only a legend."*

But it could have happened this way.

In the drowsy, fragrant atmosphere of the Islands; among the exotic wonders of the bottle-green China sea, truth becomes legend and legend becomes truth.

IN THE BEGINNING

1

The sun had gone, and the mountains beyond Barkersville reared in monstrous silhouette. Still, a late light lingered, enough to show the blasted slopes above the roaring mining town. A cluster of buildings huddled against a hill, denuded of its proud forest. Standing starkly outlined against the skyline, only stumps and a few trees plundered of foliage remained.

There was nothing left to stop the wash of mud in the rainy season, or the deluge of snow in winter. Branches had been burned as protection against the mosquito, the black fly, and the bitter, biting cold. Tall trees were felled and cut into logs or rough lumber for the building of sluice boxes, dams, for the shoring up of mines. Still others were used for the building of shacks, stores, and the one or two really fine homes of those who struck it rich in the once golden riverbed.

It was before one of the larger homes that Dan Courtney stopped, releasing the arm of his rebellious stepdaughter. He had just dragged young Martha out of Frye's place, the most disreputable bar in town, the final straw in a year of outrageous behav-

13

ior. He intended to settle things before they went in to Em.

Martha had a cold knot of fear in her stomach that she tried to melt with an anger of her own. He had no right to act like he did, grabbing her without a word, yanking her through the streets like a wayward child.

"And just what was that all about?" She spoke in a haughty voice that trembled at the edges.

"I think you know."

"It was uncalled for," she raged. "I was visiting with friends! And you walked in and made a scene. I'll be damned if I—"

"That's enough!" He cut her short. "Friends! Carriebeth Frye? You know what she is! And Fargo Gilles—a goddam pimp!"

"Carriebeth's the only girl my age in town! And Fargo—He loves me!" There, she'd said it! Duke uttered a shocking oath but Martha continued, on the edge of hysteria.

"Just because you struck it rich, you think our family's better than anybody else! You don't remember how we worked together, you—me—Mama—," her voice broke. "It was fun. And if we're all that good, what about Aunt Tamsen? You know she was a—"

"Martha!" Duke's roar stopped her. She tried to quell her shivering and went doggedly on.

"I know what Tamsen was. And you and Mama are always telling me how wonderful she is. How she danced in a cantina, and ran a house for men to come to, to take care of her and Aunt Arab. Well, maybe that's why she did it! But I'll bet she had some *fun!* I look like her. Maybe I'm more like her than you know."

Duke's hands twitched at his sides. In a minute,

he would be tempted to turn her over his knee. "Go in the house," he rasped.

She jerked her chin up. "You have no right to give me orders!"

"I have the right of a father—"

"You are not my father. You're only a man who happens to be married to my mother. A miner, like Fargo Gilles. My father was Senator Alden. But I'll go in. Because I want to."

She tossed her head, ran up the steps and into the house.

For a time, Courtney stood as if rooted. Her last words hurt him more than she would ever know. Worse, was the fear growing in him. Facing him as she did, chin tilted, Martha was the image of a young Tamsen; impulsive, headstrong, dark hair flowing down her shoulders; and eyes a man could drown in that were set in an oval face.

And Tamsen had gone through hell. What was in store for the child he'd thought of as his? The girl who had just reminded him that he was not her father.

His own hurt was unimportant. What really counted was Em, Martha's mother, and his beloved wife. He'd left her crying when he went to get Martha. And she was not well. After the two younger girls, Cammie and Vickie, were born, she'd lost a baby. And now, she was pregnant again. The worry over Martha's behavior wasn't helping her. Nor the actions of the younger sisters, who tried to emulate Martha in every way.

He shook his head, and walking as heavily as an old man, went into the house.

Martha had hurried straight to her room. When she reached it, the euphoria of having bested Duke wore off. Everything in it spoke of his love for her.

He'd made the canopied bed with his own hands, carving its posts intricately. On her dresser sat a Russian doll, twin to the one he'd given her long before he married her mother. She went to it, touching it with loving hands, a sob caught in her throat.

How could she have said such awful things to him? And how could she have disobeyed Mama? She didn't understand herself at all lately. One part of her wanted to be part of a warm and loving family. The other wanted to kick over the traces; to swap bawdy jokes with Carriebeth. To feel Fargo's arm around her shoulders, his hands touching her in a way that said she was desirable. She didn't really love Fargo, she admitted to herself. But she'd enjoyed the new sensation of power, and no longer wished she'd been born a boy.

She hadn't meant to go this far. She would go down and explain to her folks that she'd had a kind of sickness, like cabin fever. That, if they'd only forgive her, she'd do anything they asked. Terrified at the sudden enormity of her sins, she washed her tear-stained eyes at the basin on her washstand, and prayerfully and contritely, went downstairs.

The parlor door was closed, but she could hear voices inside, and they were talking about her.

"We've done wrong in making such a heroine of Tamsen," Duke was saying. "Em, Martha looks so damn much like her, it scares me."

"I know," Em answered. "It's my fault—"

"No, sweetheart, it's mine. Letting her grow up like a boy around the mining camps."

"I knew she'd have that kind of life when I married you, Duke. But I knew you'd be a good father. And you are."

"She just reminded me I'm not her natural parent. That she's a senator's daughter." Martha could hear the hurt in his voice, and wished she could take her words back. Then Em's answer struck her dumb.

"And there is my other mistake. I should have told her the truth. I should have told her my first husband was not her father. Since she's been at odds with us, she's been idealizing him, building him up in her mind. He was a good man, Duke—But he was a coward. Only a coward would commt suicide."

Martha absorbed the information, her mind reeling. *Donald Alden was not her father! He had killed himself!* She shut her eyes, remembering a white-haired man who tossed a giggling child into the air.

But if not he, then who?

That question, too, was answered. "You said you were scared," Em said, voice choked with tears. "Well, I'm terrified! And not because Martha looks like Tamsen. What if she takes after her real father? And I don't even know who he was! A cold-eyed killer—or a drunk Mexican boy. It could be either. They took turns, Duke! They took turns!"

"Em!" Duke's voice cracked like a whip. Only once since their marriage had she disintegrated like this, blue eyes dilated as her mind went back in time. It happened the day their baby was born dead.

"Em, you promised me! Forget the past! It's all over now."

"It isn't, Duke. The way Martha's behaving—don't you see? It could be bad blood! I can't stand to watch her turning against the kind of life we've tried to make. I don't know what to do."

"I do," Duke said grimly. "I think it's time to send Martha off for a visit. Let her go see her Aunt Tamsen, who is a most respectable lady by now. I have an idea she'll know how to deal with our way-

17

ward daughter. And you can have this baby in peace."

Em's eyes glowed with relief. "I think that's a good idea. Tamsen has always been able to handle everything."

They stepped into the hall, Duke's arm about his wife's thickening waist. The hallway was empty. At Martha's door, Duke tapped. She answered in a small voice. "I've gone to bed."

"Are we friends again?"

Martha, standing at the window, her face wet with tears, clenched her hands until her nails made half-moon prints in her palms. "Yes," she said.

Putting the jumble of facts she'd learned together, the girl had come up with an incredible story. Aunt Tamsen hadn't been so lily-white, but then neither had her mother. Two men at the same time, one a cold-eyed killer, and the other a drunken Mexican! And Mama, pious as all get-out, forever mouthing platitudes!

Damn her! Oh, Damn her!

Now even the parentage of Donald Alden was denied her. And he had killed himself. Because he'd learned she wasn't his child?

At least, she knew now why she'd been so mixed up lately. Why she was drawn to Fargo and Carriebeth. She had a heritage of badness. She was a bastard. How they must have watched over her, waiting for her bad blood to show!

Well, to hell with them! From this time forward, she would be nobody's child. She would do as she wished, go after what she wanted. She would prove she could be somebody in her own right.

Exhausted by emotion, she let her mind go blank. But for a long, long time, she stared with unseeing eyes at the blasted trees against the night horizon, pointing bleak and accusing fingers toward the sky.

Emmeline Courtney, unable to sleep, rose and tiptoed into her small dressing room. There, by candlelight, she composed a nervously written, almost incoherent letter to her sister, Tamsen.

When it was completed, she returned to her bed to lie beside her sleeping husband. It was the first really restful night she had enjoyed in months.

2

At the Rancho TN, outside Los Angeles, owned by Dan Tallant and operated by his brother-in-law, Juan Narvaéz, Tamsen Tallant entered her room and slammed the door. Her small olive-complexioned face was flushed with anger, a red spot staining each cheek.

The quarrel with her sister had begun over such a small thing. Arabella was disciplining her daughter, Ramona, for breaking a vase she'd been told not to touch, and Tamsen intervened. "It doesn't matter," she said, placatingly. "Remember you're pregnant, edgy—"

Arab had turned on her. She knew what was best for her own child.

Tamsen, startled at her sister's vehemence, tried to apologize. "I'm sorry, Arab. I've been with the girls since they were born. I suppose I feel like they're part mine—"

Once started, the red-haired Arab was not to be stopped. Before she finished, she had accused Tamsen of using the girls as an excuse to hide herself here in the walled hacienda. If she were any kind of a wife, she would have gone along with Dan to the south where he was working in rebuilding its railroads after the war. Now that he was finished, and planning to take them all to Hawaii, she'd been balking.

"You're scared," Arab said. "Scared to get out in the world! Afraid your wicked, wicked past will catch up with you! And you're being a fool! Nobody really gives a damn! And if you don't watch out, you're going to lose your husband! Look at you, dressed like an old crow, your hair pulled back like somebody's maiden aunt!"

"You don't know what you're talking about," Tamsen said stiffly. "Dan and I have no problems."

"I think you do! Dan's a man. And he's not the kind to want a prissy-proper wife. I'll bet you even wear a flannel nightgown to bed."

Tamsen's face flamed. Arab had hit too close to the truth. She turned on her heel and walked away, Arab's voice following her. "I heard Dan talking to Juan before they left for Washington. He was talking about the beautiful southern belles, and how much he admired them, still giving balls, making over old party dresses. They aren't hiding, Tam—"

The door shut out her voice.

Tamsen stood for a time, her hands pressed to her face. Finally her anger faded, but the hurt remained. Arab was wrong! Wrong!

Had she used Arab and her daughters as an excuse to remain behind while Dan went on? She closed her eyes, remembering her words before Ramona was born. "Arab's pregnant, Dan. I'll stay with her until the baby is delivered." Then, Arab had needed her during that first year. And again she was pregnant. Finally Dan had stopped asking—

As for moving away, leaving this home, she had grown to love the house, built in two sections, divided by a wide hall leading from front to back.

21

Heavy-beamed, built in the Spanish style, with vast airy rooms, it suited her.

And especially, she liked the distance from town, the wall that surrounded the immediate property—

Yes, she was hiding.

But she had reasons, reasons Arab would never be able to understand. Her past as cantina entertainer, as madam of a house of pleasure in San Francisco, and a bawdier establishment along the Fraser River in British Columbia, had returned to haunt her—and had hurt Dan. Their return from Dan's mission in Alaska had not gone unnoticed by the San Francisco papers. The article, written by a reporter who recognized her, hinted at all kinds of debauchery. And somehow, he'd gotten hold of a photograph that revealed too much.

They had purchased the rancho, and for a time she was able to forget, and to find happiness behind these walls. But Dan was an active man, unused to sedentary life. When the excitement of stocking the ranch wore off, he was restless. The summons to Washington, hinting at a post in the reconstruction of the south, delighted him. He'd insisted Tamsen accompany him to the capital city.

"When they see my lovely wife," he laughed, "it'll be a sure thing!"

They had seen his wife. All was going beautifully until they attended a gathering of prominent legislators who wished to meet Dan. Among them was a man Tamsen recognized from the days when she ran Madam Franklin's Parlor for Gentlemen. He was one of a party of visiting politicians brought for some out-of-town entertainment.

He whispered into another man's ear. Tamsen, helpless, felt the atmosphere change as the word passed through the room. Eventually, it reached one of the ladies present. There was a definite chill to the gathering.

"I don't know what happened," a bewildered Dan said as they rode back to their hotel. Tamsen, sitting in stunned silence, finally began to cry, pouring out the truth.

He put his arms around her. "Don't, sweetheart. It doesn't matter."

But it did. That she was forced into her occupation in order to care for her orphaned sisters was not taken into account. She was a millstone about her husband's neck.

Dan did receive the appointment, but only after some months. And in those months, she'd been determined he would never be hurt through her again.

So she was hiding. That part was true. Maybe she did use Arab and her daughters as an excuse. But the rest of it, what Arab said about losing Dan— Ah, God! It wasn't so!

She closed her eyes, remembering his last visit home, before he and Juan went to Washington. "Why don't you wear your pretty gowns anymore?" he'd asked. "I remember you had a red thing that made you look—" He made descriptive motions with his hands, and she had blushed.

"I'm not a girl anymore," she said. "I dress to suit my age."

He looked crestfallen. "You don't look any older to me," he said. "Maybe if you'd loosen your hair a little—"

"Don't you like me this way?"

"I'd love you any way," he groaned. "But, dammit, Tamsen, sometimes I feel like I'm married to a goddam virgin."

"I'm only trying to look respectable."

23

"I didn't marry you because you were respectable. I want my girl back!" He'd caught at her, pulling the pins from her hair, his mouth hot on hers. For a moment it was almost like it used to be, until she caught sight of Ramona and Missy.

"Stop, Dan! The children—"

He had said, "Oh, hell!" and walked away.

Maybe Arab was right on all counts. Maybe in trying to be a lady, she'd forgotten how to be a woman. *Please God, let it not be too late—*

She turned to her wardrobe, pushing all her new dark gowns to one side. In the darkened corner, the colors of her old ones glowed like jewels. She selected one of turquoise, its bosom cut low, removed the drab dress she was wearing, and tossed it across the bed. She was dressed when the messenger arrived.

The rancho TN subscribed to a service whereby all incoming mail was brought direct from Los Angeles by a mounted messenger. The man who carried Em's letter to Tamsen in his pouch stopped for a moment to marvel at the immense wall surrounding the house, then rode on to the gate where he refused to give the message he carried to the gatekeeper.

"I must take it to the señora, herself," he said positively.

Actually, he was under no such restriction. But his curiosity was overwhelming. A palm-lined drive led to the structure. Ivy climbed its walls; a background of greenery for masses of golden-throated roses. The house stood dreaming against a blue November sky, with only a faint wind trembling among the leaves.

Many had asked the messenger about the rich occupants of the large rancho. For five or six years, they had been here. No one knew much about them.

Only old Carlotta, who boasted of her years in San Francisco, provided a clue. Seeing them in a carriage, the dark girl and the red-hair, she had said, "I have seen the little dark one somewhere. I cannot remember—"

But then, Carlotta was given to untruth. She'd claimed to be a dancer in the city. Yet everyone knew she worked the cribs. Some people would say anything to get attention.

His knock at the door brought a black-browed haughty Mexican maid. Again, he refused to relinquish his message. The maid, shrugging, called the señora. As the messenger, Diaz, waited for the small dark woman who always dressed in black, he amused himself by peering through the open door. On the far wall, another door stood open on a courtyard with a velvet carpet of grass. He could hear a splashing fountain, and the shouts of children at play.

He was so engrossed that he was jerked up short at the sound of a woman's voice. "Yes?"

He opened his mouth and closed it, his voice caught in his throat at the sight of the girl who stood before him. Clad in a gown of turquoise, dark hair falling loosely to her waist, she was a vision. A full moment passed before he could identify her as the drab señora who had accepted a letter from him only the day before. This was the most beautiful woman he had ever seen, her body vibrant with the juices that stirred a man to desire. What a story he would have to tell! "Bonita," he would say, "now that she dresses like our Rosa."

Rosa would preen, and he would perhaps gain her favor.

Tamsen Tallant's head jerked up. She had been intent on the letter. Seeing his expression, the knowing leer of a man who senses a woman may be open to his advances, she went cold inside. It had been a long time since she had been exposed to such attention.

"I'm sorry," she said. "I forgot you were waiting. Here." She gave him the generous fee he'd come to expect, and he backed away, smiling. It was a long time before he turned toward his destination.

Tamsen entered the hallway and walked to the part of the house that was her private domain. She studied Em's letter, a perplexed frown between her brows. Forgetting their differences, she went in search of Arabella.

She found her younger sister sitting on the lawn beneath a ginkgo tree, watching her children at play. Dressed in sunny yellow cotton, Arab looked like a child, but an unhappy child. Her skirts were spread about her, her small chin resting on one hand in an attitude of moody thought.

"Arab?"

Arab looked up, her eyes widening. "Tam! You're beautiful!" The slanting green eyes filled with tears. "Oh, Tam, I'm so sorry for the things I said! So sorry!"

Tamsen sat down beside her. "It's all right, Arab. Forget it. I—I have a letter from Em."

"It's about time! What does she have to say? How is she? Duke, Martha, the girls—?"

"I don't know. She's pregnant—"

Arab's face lit with a warm smile. "She must have my letter by now. Wouldn't it be wonderful if our babies have the same birthday? Especially, if they were both boys—"

"I would be happy with either." Tamsen's eyes were shadowed.

26

"You'll have a baby someday, Tam."

"I'm getting close to forty, Arab. It doesn't seem likely."

"Em's older than you are," Arab pointed out. "And look at you! You don't look a day over eighteen when you dress like that. You've kept your figure. I—I'd trade places with you."

"I don't believe that for a minute. But I didn't come out here to talk about children. This letter doesn't sound like Em. One minute she says Martha is a good and wonderful girl, the next she mentions that she's giving her trouble. I can't make out whether she's asking me to invite her here; has already planned to send her on a visit—or is handing her over as a lost cause. Read this."

Arabella read. "It's beyond me. Maybe Em's upset about something. She *is* pregnant." She reddened as she recalled Tamsen had used those same words to describe her at the beginning of their quarrel. "It's probably blown over by now. Anyway, it will change things if we move to Hawaii."

"Yes."

"You are going along with the move," Arab persisted.

"Dan's letter said a man would be coming to look at the place this evening. If he decides to buy it, I suppose I have no choice."

Arab's hand reached out to grip Tamsen's. "Go along with what Dan wants, Tam. You won't be sorry—"

"Don't worry, Arab." Tamsen smiled painfully. "I will. And—thanks."

Rising, she went into the house. She would have to begin to get things in order for the prospective buyer. She opened the drawer of her small secretary

27

to put Em's letter away for answering at a later time. Then she paused, reading it once more. It did not make sense.

She folded it thoughtfully, then noted a postscript she had missed, on the back of the last page.

Martha has always worshiped you, the letter read. *I think her desire to be like you has led to our present problem. We've made a mistake in trying to explain your actions were dictated by circumstance. Please try to convince her that doesn't make it less wrong. Arab writes that you have become very staid and respectable these last years. I'm praying that you can show Martha how much you regret your past misdeeds. Please! Please!*

Tamsen's anger flared, and she crumpled the letter in her hand. Then she smoothed it out and reread it, her eyes wet with tears.

"Not the sins of the father, but the sins of the aunt," she whispered. Carefully, she folded the letter away. She would answer it tomorrow.

Turning to the mirror, she looked at her reflection. She saw a slim, defiant figure in a deliberately seductive gown. Through the simple act of donning it, she had changed, becoming once more the girl who reveled in her power over men, taking what she could get, giving nothing in return. Though she had been shocked at what she saw in the messenger's eyes, God help her, she had enjoyed the sensation of mastery it gave her—

Ripping off the brightly colored gown, she hung it back in the wardrobe, donning one of black. As she redid her hair, pulling it tightly in a matronly fashion, her face was only a blur in the mirror.

3

As if Em's postscript had precipitated them, the remainder of the day was marred by a series of upsets and calamities. Arab's six-year-old Ramona broke a window. Little Missy, who was four, developed a rash and a fever, and was sick all over the carpet.

Nell, the obese old card-dealer and cantina manager, who had been with Tamsen through most of her checkered career, came waddling in from her quarters in the wing at the rear of the courtyard. Dusty had got hold of a bottle, and was drunk as a skunk. "How the hell you going to show the man our place?" she wanted to know.

Tamsen was wondering, too. Dusty was her oldest and dearest friend. He'd been a friend of her father. And he had stayed with her through all kinds of trials and tribulations. But sometimes he was exasperating beyond belief. It was bad enough that he and Nell maintained some sort of irregular relationship without benefit of matrimony, but he'd been drinking more and more of late.

Now, the problem was that of arranging things so they would appear in their best light, when the buyer, Mr. Hobson, arrived. "We'll put him to bed,"

Tamsen said wearily. "Missy's sick. We'll say he is, too."

"That Hobson feller'll think we oughta be quarry-teened," Nell observed. But it was the only solution. Together, Tamsen and Nell managed to get the frail little man into bed, drawing the covers up under his chin.

"Cute l'il feller, ain't he?" Nell asked fondly. "Looks like a gawdam angel, don't he?"

Tamsen bit her lip to keep from laughing. Dusty —William Winston Wotherspoon, expatriate Englishman—was hardly a saintly sight. His faded blue eyes were hidden beneath wrinkled lids; his white hair stood on end spreading across his pillow. An open mouth revealed the two missing front teeth beneath his wispy moustache. Yet she loved him. She touched his cheek tenderly. "Sleep well," she whispered.

With a dusting of powder to conceal the smell of alcohol, there was nothing more to do. Tamsen left, followed by Nell's complaints. *Hell, it didden seem right for strangers to come trompin' through somebuddy else's goddam house!*

At least, things were reasonably under control, Tamsen thought as she entered the wide hall from the rear. A window broken, a stained carpet, a sick child, an intoxicated man in the rear wing. Surely nothing more could happen—

In that, she was mistaken. The ornate knocker at the front lifted and fell with a series of resounding bangs. Tamsen hurried to answer, certain that Mr. Hobson had come at last. But the figure confronting her, although clad in flannel shirt, corduroy trousers and heavy boots, wasn't that of a man.

For an instant, Tamsen stood frozen, looking

into a face that was almost an exact replica of her own.

"Well, Aunt Tamsen," a girl's voice drawled, "this is a damned poor welcome! Aren't you going to ask me in?"

"Martha?" Tamsen reached for the girl with shaking hands. "Martha? It can't be!" Her mind was in a spin of confusion. Her last sight of her niece was that of a small girl, standing between Em and her new husband on a ship that sailed away. A small girl with shining eyes and a bright face.

This was not a child, but a young woman. A woman with cool, assessing eyes.

Tamsen drew her into her arms, to kiss a smooth cheek. She could feel a stiffness, a lack of response to her embrace and drew back in confusion. "I wouldn't have known you," she said, faltering a little. "You've changed! Grown up!"

Martha's amused eyes took in the somber garb of her aunt. "We've all changed. It's hard to think of you as growing old."

Her remark, delivered with scarcely veiled insolence, made Tamsen gasp. Her moment of shock was covered by Arabella's arrival. Arab was delighted to see her niece and the girl seemed to respond with equal pleasure. Tamsen stood by, red spots of humiliation in her olive cheeks, while the reunion took place. Small Ramona came running in, and Martha dropped to her knees to hug the child. Then she allowed herself, laughing, to be hauled off to see Missy in her sickbed.

She hates me, Tamsen thought, dazed. But why? What have I done? Or had Em, in her efforts to tame the girl's spirit said something that would induce this—contempt?

31

Martha, returning, had an attitude of polite deference. "Yes, ma'am." She would like a bath after her journey. "No, ma'am." She had no clothing suitable for this climate. And she would gladly accept the loan of something from Tamsen's wardrobe—if she had anything that was suitable for her age.

"Take anything you like," Tamsen said tartly. She stood with her fists clenched as Martha left the room, not hearing Arab's approach in a flurry of skirts.

"Tam, she's a darling," Arab exclaimed happily. "The girls love her. Do you suppose she can stay with us—and go on to Hawaii? How could Em think a girl like that could be a problem!"

"I haven't the slightest idea," Tamsen lied. Her days as the operator of a house of pleasure in San Francisco had taught her a lot about women. And her intuition told her that the coming of Martha spelled trouble. This was not the baby she'd held in her arms and thought of as her own. This was a woman, determined to compete with her on any terms. A child-woman, who, for some reason, hated her.

A further shock was in store for Tamsen that day. Mr. Hobson, accompanied by his large, overbearing wife, arrived quite late. And she knew him! Dear God, she knew him! He had come, several times, to visit her parlor many years before. But from his puzzled expression, she could see that, though her face might be familiar, he couldn't place her. Not among these unfamiliar surroundings.

The Hobsons had approached the house at sunset, when it was at its loveliest, its dusty-pink exterior touched with rose. Clarice Hobson, from a poverty-stricken childhood that she desired to forget, was impressed and ready to purchase the property on sight. Though she was a large, bullying woman, he had the shrill testiness of a small, unprepossessing man. If Clarice wanted the place—he didn't. It gave him a sense of power to overrule her in most things. But since they were here, they would see the house.

Upon meeting the mistress of the place, he began to have some odd misgivings. He had met her before. He was sure of it. But where? As she showed them through the rooms, he alternated his complaints about the structure with covert glances at his hostess. Before he married Clarice, he'd fancied himself as quite a ladies' man. Surely, he'd met this woman in the past—

Having a phobia of germs, he refused to enter the room where little Missy lay abed. A sick man in the rear wing? It wasn't necessary to see it. He was not that interested.

They returned to the living room in the Tallant side of the building where he and his wife engaged in what amounted to an argument. Clarice loved the house. It was what she had always wanted. It was perfect.

He pointed out the flaws. The window that was broken. The grass in the courtyard was Bermuda, and he was allergic to it. It was too far from any city.

Clarice Hobson was close to tears as the small man swaggered about, giving reasons against the purchase. Tamsen was sorry for her, despite the fact that she seemed as unlikable as her husband.

The tirade he was delivering stopped as a door opened. Young Martha Courtney stood revealed in the aperature. She had found an old gown of Tamsen's, of a tawny orange color. Above the gown, her face and shoulders were creamy gold, her cheeks glowing with a flush of color as she stood poised, confident, exuding a hypnotic magnetism.

Tamsen went cold all over. It was her own self, stepping out of the past.

An odd gobbling sound broke the silence. Tamsen looked at Hobson. His face was turkey-red as he turned the sound he'd made into a cough, running his finger inside the rim of his collar.

"My niece," she said to the Hobsons, introducing them. Then, with a direct look at the man, she said, "She looks very much like me, doesn't she?"

Frank Hobson knew who she was, now. His only impulse was to leave the premises and keep on going. His main hold on his wife was her background, and that might be lost if his came to light. He began to make their excuses and edged toward the door.

Tamsen followed.

"I do hope you will reconsider on the purchase of the house," she said sweetly. "Your wife likes it very much. And it might be a wise buy for a gentleman with a reputation to consider."

Her veiled threat reached its mark. Mr. Hobson hastily agreed to buy the house, did not quibble on the price, mumbled something about letting his attorney handle the details, seized his wife's arm—and fled.

I've done it again, Tamsen thought. Despite her outer facade of respectability, she had reverted to type. It had been blackmail, pure and simple. She knew it, and Hobson knew it. Strangely enough, it didn't bother her conscience a bit.

But she was tired. So tired—

After a brief meal, meant to be considered as a sort of celebration, but wasn't, due to Arab's concern over Missy and Martha's determination to hold center stage, Tamsen excused herself. She intended to write Em, telling of Martha's safe arrival. Then she would go to bed.

Martha, after being shown the room in Tamsen's quarters that would be hers, had other ideas. She intended to slip out to the wing at the rear, and surprise Nell.

Nell was not only surprised, but, as she put it, "Plumb dumbfounded." She hugged the girl to her vast bosom. "Migawd, fer a minit I thought it was Tamsen standin' in the door."

"Still the same old Nell," Martha murmured, her eyes shining with tears. "Oh, Nell, I've missed you so damn much!"

"Don't cuss," Nell admonished her. "Sounds like hell, a-comin' from you!"

"And how does it sound coming from you?"

Nell reddened. "Don't sass me, young-un! I kin still smack yer butt! I talk like that cause I've allus talked like that. It don't mean nuthin'. Yer Aunt Tamsen don't cuss."

"From what I know of Aunt Tamsen, swearing would be the least of her vices," the girl shrugged.

Nell turned purple. "I ain't sure what you said," she growled, "but you be careful when you talk about yer betters."

"Betters!" Martha laughed, sharply. The two of them, the elephantine old woman and the young girl, glared at each other for a moment. Then Martha relaxed.

"I was just teasing, Nell," she said in a sweet voice.

Nell pondered for a moment, then she grunted. "I figgered you was."

The rest of the visit progressed happily. Nell had always been fond of Martha as a child. She'd been a cute little tyke, reminding her of Tamsen who was like her own. But when the girl left to return to the house, Nell watched her go, pulling at her lower lip. She didn't know of the letter Tamsen had received, but she'd already come to a few conclusions. Martha was a mighty unhappy little girl. And from her tone, she'd guessed she was on the outs with her ma. But what in the hell did she have against Tamsen?

As she made her way across the courtyard, Martha wondered, herself. There were times when she missed her mother so much she thought she would die. For a moment, when she arrived, she'd felt like responding to Tamsen's embrace and sobbing her heart out in her arms. Then she would remember Duke's awful words—"*We've done wrong in letting her think Tamsen was right in everything she did.*" The memory of hearing about Donald Alden's suicide would flood back and, finally, Em's statement, the most painful of all—"*I'm afraid she'll take after her father—whoever he was.*"

Now Martha was nothing, a bastard, a nobody. She had been shipped off like a package nobody wanted. And because she hurt so much inside, she wanted to hurt back.

A light in Tamsen's room was still burning. Martha entered the wide hall from the rear and stood for a moment, irresolute. She didn't want to go in. Tamsen might be tempted to come to her guest room for some girl-talk. To hell with it!

She continued on through the front door and stood breathing the perfume of a California night. She moved along the wall of the house, and bent to pick a rose, cupping it in her hands as she thought about the conversation at table tonight. When the family moved to Hawaii, would they take her with them? Or ship her home again?

Daniel Tallant, too, was enjoying the softness of the scented night. After the hubbub that was Washington, he was glad to be coming home, even though it would be home for only a little while. He had left Juan Narvaéz in Los Angeles, to make arrangements for a ship to carry them to Hawaii, and it had been a long and lonely ride.

Outside the wall that served as perimeter to the house and its immediate grounds, he slipped from his horse, removed his saddle, and rubbed the animal down before turning it loose to graze. He deposited the saddle in a shed and made his way on foot past the gatehouse, his pace hurrying as he thought of his wife. A day early, his coming would be a surprise.

And then he saw her.

His heart lifted as the moon revealed her form. The gown she wore was not black, but of some unidentifiable color, and her long hair streamed to her waist like ebon silk. He suppressed a groan of pure need at sight of her. Dressed like that—perhaps it was an omen. Maybe she had really come back to him. The old Tamsen, as she used to be.

She bent to pick a flower, the fluid motion of her body pure poetry, then stood, hands cupping it, her back to him, oblivious of his approach.

He went toward her on silent feet, catching her from behind. She turned with a little scream, resisting, then as his hot mouth closed over hers, she melted into his arms.

Tamsen had heard Martha leave by the front door. A sudden, dry-mouthed fear possessed her. It was clear the girl wasn't happy at being sent here. What if she decided to just walk away? She was supposed to look after her. She owed it to Em.

Leaving her half-finished letter, she hurried to

the door. And there, in the moonlight, she saw Martha tightly clasped in a man's arms, holding to him—

Someone who had followed her from home? Someone she'd met on the way? Em was right. The girl was a problem.

And then the man turned a little, and she recognized the beloved, familiar features. She couldn't restrain the sound that issued from her lips.

"Dan!"

Dan Tallant turned, the glow of love in his eyes fading as he caught sight of the woman in black standing in the doorway, face pale below the pulled-tight mass of dark hair. His expression was replaced by a look of amazement and incredulity. "Tamsen?" he said to the figure in the door. Then, "Tamsen?" to the woman in his arms.

Then he leaped backward, releasing Martha as if he had been burned. "What the hell?" he said hoarsely. "My God! Oh, my God!"

Much later, after being reintroduced to his wife's niece, an embarrassed Tallant lay beside his wife, holding her in his arms. Everything had been explained, over and over, but he still had a feeling all was not well.

"She's just a child, you know," he said, a little foolishly. "She's only a child."

She's more than a child, Tamsen thought. She is trouble. And she had a strong suspicion that they would be taking trouble with them to Hawaii.

In the guest room, Martha lay smiling at the ceiling. For she was truly in love. Not like it was with Fargo Gillis, but really, *truly* in love. She thought of the dark face that had bent above her, eyes deep with emotion; the hot mouth that burned against her own, the feel of his lean strong body, aroused and surging with passion.

38

Tamsen had made a profession of helping men cheat on their wives, so turnabout was fair play. She could take him from her. It would be easy. She had everything on her side—

With a small secret smile, Martha made her plans. It was a wonderful way to get even with Tamsen, and with Em.

HILO

4

On the last week of November, a ship left Los Angeles harbor, bound for the port of Hilo on the large island of Hawaii. It carried the Tallant family, Dan and Tamsen; the Narvaéz family, consisting of Juan, Arabella, two daughters, and a baby yet unborn. The other members of the party were Nell, Dusty, and young Martha Courtney.

The ship, provided by Dan Tallant's mysterious employers, carried no other passengers. There were three cabins in addition to the captain's own. Dan and Tamsen occupied one of these, Arab and Juan another. The last, a barracks-like affair, housed Nell, Martha, and the Narvaéz children. Dusty insisted on bunking down with the crew.

Below decks, the ship carried the structure that would be erected at Hilo, in the form of pre-cut siding, beams, studs, roofing, and flooring. There would be no glass needed for windows, Dan explained. The climate of Hilo was soft and gentle, with much rain and no wind. The walls would be erected above head level, then open to the eaves. It would be a primitive structure, not the luxurious home they'd all been accustomed to—

He looked worriedly at Tamsen, and she said, "I'm glad, Dan! I'm glad!"

They left California in an unseasonal rain which persisted for the first two days at sea. During that time, the travelers were forced to keep to their cabins, and Tamsen welcomed the opportunity to be alone with her husband. Martha had behaved most circumspectly since the night Dan mistook her for his wife, but she'd seemed ever-present. She plunged into the packing with enthusiasm, taking it for granted that she would accompany the party, always at Dan's side, speaking to Tamsen with a polite, "Yes, ma'am," that made her feel like Methusaleh.

Tamsen had sought her out, once, determined to convince her she should go home—back to Em and Duke. But she found her sitting in a window seat, staring out into the night with such a sad and haunted expression that her intention fled her mind.

"Martha," she said, "what is it? What's wrong?"

Martha leaped to her feet, a bright and determined smile in place. "I was just resting a minute, Aunt Tamsen. Now, what can I do to help?"

Tamsen hadn't had the nerve to continue. Instead, she'd given the girl some task to do. And she had to admit that Martha worked hard and most efficiently and was wonderful with the little girls, Ramona and Missy. Arab adored her. Dusty was a fatuous old fool where Martha was concerned. And Dan, after he recovered from the embarrassment of that first encounter, treated her like a beloved daughter.

That left only Nell. Tamsen had caught the big woman looking at the girl with something like suspicion in her snapping eyes, half-hidden in rolls of flesh. A gambler and a madam, Nell, too, was wise in the ways of women.

She must not think of Martha and the problems

she posed. Not now. Not when she lay beside her husband in a narrow bunk after a session of love-making that had burned them out, like a cleansing flame, leaving only two drowsy bodies, holding, touching, satisfied—

She looked at the sleeping man beside her, his rugged features belied by the lashes that curved against his cheek, the dark hair that tumbled over his forehead, the sweetness of his mouth in repose.

Gently, she touched his bare, brown shoulder, letting her hand slide along the hard-muscled arm that immediately tightened around her. He could be so easily aroused—

But she didn't want that. Not now. She just wanted to lie there and think of how exciting it was to be married to this wonderful, complex, yet simple man.

They had lain together like this on their honeymoon; on a ship bound for Alaska. There, Dan was to work as an adviser to the Russian Court at Sitka, as an expert on transportation and communication. In reality, he played a double role, gathering information that would promote the sale of Alaska.

They had their trials and tribulations, there. For a while, she'd thought he was lost to her, and she'd returned to her old trade, running a gambling house and brothel in the gold fields along the Fraser . . .

The Civil War had intervened, and the Alaskan sale had been shelved. But Dan had succeeded in the end, she thought exultantly. He had succeeded! President Andrew Johnson had summoned him to Washington to thank him in person!

On October 18th of this year, 1867, Alaska had become a possession of the United States. And Dan, her husband, had a hand in it.

Her grip had tightened in an agony of love and

pride. Dan opened his eyes. "I thought you would surely be sleeping," he teased.

"Just thinking. Thinking about Alaska, and now Hawaii. Dan, please explain what you're going to do again. I'm confused."

Tallant sighed. His lovely, forceful wife had lived in the background for some years, but she hadn't changed. If he believed in reincarnation, he'd say she'd been the mistress of some royal figure, the power behind the throne. Who would believe that in that small, slim, lovely body, there was such power, such tenacity and stubbornness, such ambition?

"Which point isn't clear," he asked, his hand teasing her.

She slapped it away in mock frustration. "All of it. Tell me all of it again."

He turned on his back, his hands folded beneath his head, and she caressed his tanned chest as he talked, her mind only half on what he was saying.

"After the audience with the President," he said, "I was summoned to a conference with General Grant. He is an old friend of mine. I was with him at Molino Del Rey, when he was made first lieutenant. Again at the battle of Chapultepec for which he was brevetted captain. He remembered me, and this thing about Alaska brought me to mind. He needed someone for a mission."

Dan continued with the conversation. There were those who believed that Grant would be the next President of the United States, and it was known that he favored expansion. Grant had received a letter from a coalition of sugar planters in the islands, begging that they be annexed through any means.

He went on to explain the history of sugar as it affected the islands of Hawaii. In 1850, the Hawaiian government passed laws permitting aliens to buy lands in fees simple. Investors went heavily into debt, gambling on westward expansion. The gamble paid off as plantations delivered sugar to the gold fields in California, then reversed itself as the gold fever moved to Australia. Hawaii found itself in the midst of a depression. The Civil War brought another boom as southern sugar disappeared, the end of the war bringing ruin. Though conditions were improving, many planters looked to the United States as their only hope.

"These people are Americans," Dan said. "Some of them descendants of missionaries, some of them relative newcomers. They need the protection of our country—"

"But what about the Hawaiian people? Don't they have a say? It doesn't seem right!"

"The race, as a people, is dying out, I understand. Washington, however, only hears the side that will benefit, that has an ax to grind. Grant wanted to send someone to look things over. Someone who would be impartial, and present the situation as it is. He's sending me. And if you ask me, it's going to be one hell of a job!"

"You can do it, Dan!"

"Can I? I don't know."

He rose, pulled on his trousers, and went to a small stand, filling a bowl with water from a pitcher. Then he turned to face her. "You know the rest. Grant has a friend in the islands, name of Wilder. He's got a bee in his bonnet about building short spurs of railway on the cane-growing islands. Transportation has become one of the most expensive and time-consuming items. The growers have imported immigrants, but there's still a shortage of labor. Wilder thinks railroads are the answer.

47

"So we are going as a surveying team. I've got the knowhow. Juan will learn to use a transit. Dusty can help when we use a compass and Gunter's chain —if we can keep him sober. I'll have the chance to talk to the planters, workmen, natives—"

"I still hope you'll decide against a take-over," Tamsen said in a small voice. "It's wrong."

Exasperated, he plunged his hands into the washbowl, splashing water over his face with both hands. Then he reached for a towel and faced her once more, his black hair sparkling with drops of moisture like diamonds.

"Goddammit, Tam, don't make judgments when you don't know what you're talking about! Kamehameha the Fourth tried to give the damn place to the British! He was impressed by France! Hell, he might have turned the islands over to China or Japan before he let them go to the States. The new one, Kamehameha, Fifth, is a different kettle of fish. He's a monarchist. He is strong for home rule by his own people, and he's bringing back a lot of the old ways."

"I don't see anything so bad about that!"

"Oh, hell," he groaned. "The way women think! Listen, there's more than sugar at stake, a damn sight more! What if the ruler thinks along the lines of what's-'is-name; the Fourth? What if he sells out to someone else? Or what if some power decides to take over the west? Good God! These islands lead to our shores just like stepping stones!"

In the next cabin, young Martha lay with her ear pressed to the wall. She'd been able to hear only a mumble of words until Dan's final explosion. Then his tone had raised, and she'd been able to pick out a few. He was swearing at Tamsen, she thought gleefully.

Her concentration was broken when an irate

Nell appeared beside her bunk, jerking her away from the wall. "What the hell you think you're doin'?" the old woman rasped.

"Just trying to sleep," Martha faltered.

"Looked to me like you was eavesdropping," Nell said, giving the girl a fisheyed stare. "If I thought you was, I'd kick yer butt t'hell an' back."

Martha rolled to the outside edge of her bed and stared primly at the ceiling. She didn't hear Dan say, "I'm sorry, sweetheart, I didn't mean to raise my voice. Guess you and I are a lot alike. We try to feel responsible for the whole damn world—in different ways."

Tamsen smiled and held out her arms. Dan smiled back, removed his trousers, dropped them to the floor and came toward her. "I guess I wasn't ready to get up, after all—"

5

Two days out of Los Angeles, the rain ceased and the skies smiled down upon calm blue waters. The weather induced a sort of euphoria in the travelers, and they poured out upon the sun-dried deck to take advantage of the mild breeze. The children were enchanted. Juan and Dan brought rugs and spread them in the sun to recline upon. Arab lay beside Juan, Tamsen beside Dan. And Martha paced along the rail, pretending not to notice the closeness of the latter couple.

The sun felt good to Tamsen. She hadn't realized how her bones ached from the frantic packing she'd done. She commented on it to Dan. "I suppose I'm getting old," she confessed.

"Nonsense," was his reply. "You haven't changed since I married you. I don't think you ever will!" There was a pause, and he asked, "Tamsen, why don't you wear bright colors anymore?"

She turned her head. His eyes were fixed on Martha at the rail, attired in a gown the color of flame. It had once been Tamsen's.

Aware of her gaze, Dan flushed. "Martha looks so much like you in that dress," he said, stumbling a little.

"That's because it's mine," Tamsen told him evenly. "When the girl arrived, she had nothing fit for a warmer climate. She is using all my old things."

"I see."

She didn't tell him that she had intended abandoning her sedate clothing once they were on their way from California—but that Martha had anticipated her. "I took everything that was bright and *young*," the girl said. "I hope you don't mind."

Tamsen imagined it would have made no difference if she had. But now she looked at Dan, levelly. "Does what I wear matter that much to you? Does it make me a different person?"

"I much prefer you with nothing at all," he said with a lewd wink.

"Then I shall have to go native when we reach the islands," she said, smiling. But the smile did not come from deep inside. She was beginning to see Martha as a real contender for Dan's affections. If Dan loved her, Tamsen, he must love her as she was. She would not compete with Martha on her terms.

"Dan," the girl shrieked. "Oh, Dan, come here! I see a big fish! I think it's a whale!"

With an apologetic grin at Tamsen, Dan rose and went to the girl's side. Tamsen felt a cold hard knot of fear in her chest.

"Aunt Tamsen, why do you look so worried?"

It was little Ramona, Arab's oldest child. She'd been watching little Missy like a hawk to keep the ecstatic toddler from falling overboard, or down a hatch. Now the younger child had gone to Juan who lay on his back, alternately tickling her and tossing her in the air. Free of her charge, Ramona had sped to Tamsen, whom she adored.

Tamsen forced a smile as she looked down at

the small concerned face. Ramona was considered the ugly duckling of the offspring of the McLeod family, her eyes too big, too far apart; a button nose, and an enormous mouth like some elfin creature. Only Nell saw any potential in the little girl. She kept insisting she'd outclass every damn one of them someday.

Tamsen put a finger to the small nose, teasingly. "I'm not worried. Just tired from moving. What about you? Are you happy?"

"Awful happy." Ramona's huge brown eyes roved her surroundings for something to be happy about. "I'm happy that it quit raining, and the sun's shining. And I'm happy that we're going to Hawaii. I'm specially happy," she added candidly, "that Martha come, too. She's awfully nice. But sometimes she looks worried. I think she misses her mommie. I know I would."

Tamsen pulled the little girl close as she watched Dan and Martha. Martha was openly flirting, she was certain of that. But Dan's attitude toward her was that of a father—no more, no less.

Watching the man she loved with her sister's daughter, she hugged the little girl at her side.

If she and Dan had only had a child!

The days passed, each exactly like the one before. The dreaming waters were tinted rose in the morning, gold with the setting sun. The air grew softer, and sometimes Tamsen thought it held a scent of flowers. The party was overcome by a kind of languor, a sense of being suspended in time.

On the ninth day, they sighted several white sails in the distance. On the tenth, a mass of clouds, seemingly spooned into the sea like whipped cream. As they drew nearer, Tamsen could see an island's spreading shores beneath the cloud formation. This confection, created by nature, was to be their destination.

When the ship was close enough that the distant shores were no longer an amorphous shade, but a definite verdant green, the waters near the shore were filled with dancing dots that proved to be boats of some type as they neared the incoming vessel.

"Outrigger canoes," Dan explained. "They are coming to greet us."

Indeed they were. When the ship dropped its anchor, a rope ladder was lowered. Slim brown boys scrambled up and into the vessel, each carrying an object: a small stalk of red bananas, a pineapple, papayas, guavas, mangoes. These were presented to the newcomers with a flourish.

Martha was clearly stunned by the sight of so many beautiful young men. But it was Nell they clustered about, highly vocal in their admiration in a strange tongue. "Alii," one said excitedly, pointing at the bewildered woman. "Alii!"

Nell turned to Dan, a suspicious expression in her small eyes. "What the hell did he call me?"

"The Alii are the royalty," Dan explained. "For many years, a woman who was—" he hesitated in confusion, "—not *thin* was most admired. Like the queen bee—"

He needed go no farther. "Well, I'll be damned," Nell cried. "You hear that, Dusty? These folks know a real woman when they see one!" She elbowed him in the side and chortled. "Better watch yer P's an' Q's, you leetle bastard! I might just see sompin' a damn sight better, an' throw you back."

Dusty was stone sober. That unusual condition,

coupled with this new eventuality, was too much for him. He looked frightened. "My word," he whispered. "Oh, my word!"

Nell beamed at him, fondly. "You know I don't mean that, you leetle sonofabitch! You're the only feller I—" She was interrupted as a smiling Hawaiian boy thrust a pineapple into her hands. She looked at it for a moment in dismay, then at Dan Tallant.

"Do I pay him? Or what?"

"Say, *mahalo*," Dan said into her ear.

"Mahal-o," she repeated, and the boy's face fairly glowed with happiness.

Nell turned again to Dan, but he had moved away. "Dusty," she said in a fierce whisper, "what in the hell did I say?"

Tamsen, too, was having her problems. She had been cornered by a young man in a bright shirt, a flower behind his ear. "Keokolo," he said, pointing to his chest. "Keokolo speak haole talk. Go mission school. You teacher da kine?"

After a while it dawned on her that her sober garb had led him to think she was a missionary.

She was even more uncomfortable when they stepped ashore at Hilo to be met by a bevy of girls carrying leis, and crying, "*Aloha.*" All of them were dressed in loose garments of bright material, their flowing black hair decked with blossoms. Martha moved among them as if she belonged.

Tamsen shut her mind to everything but her surroundings. Hilo was not a city at all. There were a few stores along the beach, a sprinkling of other frame buildings, and running away from the sea, peeping from masses of bamboo, tree fern, banana, and mango trees, were other frame homes with lattices, and grass houses with deep verandas. And everywhere flowers, gigantic blossoms that were unfamiliar, other blooms that Tamsen recognized, but which grew in unbelievable profusion. Behind the settlement was the forest, dense and green beyond comprehension. It was as if a painter had daubed a canvas with primary colors; the people in their gaudy garments, the flowers of brilliant hue, bright birds flashing among the trees—

Fragrant air stroked Tamsen's cheeks like silk. And suddenly, it began to rain.

The newcomers were overwhelmed by offers of hospitality from both natives and their fellow countrymen. A storekeeper offered them the warehouse-like building in which he kept his surplus. A dignified Hawaiian gentleman, with a dark square face crowned with a silver lion's mane, courteously indicated there was room in his house of woven grass. The most insistent hospitality came from the Reverend David Lyman, of the Lyman Mission House.

"Gawd, no," Nell said, tugging at Dan's sleeve. "If I had to be perlite an' ladylike, I'd prob'ly bust a gut!"

In the end, they did as they'd planned. They erected tents where the sea curved inward and the forest encroached, near the mouth of the Wailuku River. Apparently a Hawaiian home had once stood here, for there seemed to be a natural clearing in the midst of towering trees bearing every conceivable kind of native fruit.

As Tamsen worked beside Dan, she was soaked to the skin. Whether it was due to the rain, or perspiration, was a difficult question. At a slow pace, the humid heat wasn't noticeable. Exertion made one uncomfortable. It was difficult to breathe.

"Perhaps we should have accepted the Reverend Lyman's invitation," Tamsen sighed. When Dan said nothing, she looked up to see Martha standing beside her, lips parted in a malicious smile.

"Do you really think so? It would hardly be fair. I wonder if he would have been so prompt to issue it if he'd known—all there is to know about us."

Tamsen straightened. "Young lady, I don't know what you are implying, but there will be no gossip—"

Martha's eyes rounded. "Why Aunt Tamsen, is there anything to *tell?*"

Dan came around the tent with a few more stakes he'd hacked from the surrounding vegetation. "Something wrong?"

"Nothing at all," Tamsen said shortly.

But, intuitively, she knew that Martha, all sweetness and light until they reached the islands, a point of no return for her, had just declared war. She was sure of it that night when Martha, complaining that her tent leaked, joined them in their own. Lying between the girl and her husband, hearing the rain on the canvas, Tamsen wished passionately that Em had kept her problems at home. Dan's hand reached to touch her in the darkness, and she suppressed a shuddering sigh of need.

In the morning, they found Martha's shelter to be beyond repair, filled with a number of slashes and small holes that puzzled Dan. The damage had probably occurred aboard ship, during transportation. But Tamsen knew better. She thought of the small pair of gold-handled sewing shears that Martha owned, but said nothing. The house would soon be built, and she would have her husband to herself.

The building took a little more than a week. Though the materials had been pre-cut, ready to put together, they were hampered by the incessant rain. Oddly enough, the moment it was done, the skies cleared and a rainbow arched across the horizon. With the coming of the sun, the tropic growth began to steam, bringing out the heavy scent of flowers and ripe fruit. With the evening, the small clearing was bathed in golden light that cloaked the newness of the raw wood, gilding the long roof that united the four units. A room for Martha, one for Dusty and Nell, stood at opposite ends. Centered were two room groupings, one for Juan, Arab, and the children, the other for Dan Tallant and his wife. The hallways between the units were to serve as cooking areas.

"It's primitive as hell," Dan said, apologetically.

"It's beautiful," Tamsen said, her eyes misty. "I love it, Dan!"

That night, Dan watched his wife cooking over an open fire. She had opened the throat of her high-necked dark gown, revealing a creamy expanse that he knew would be velvet to the touch. Her hair, during the day's exertions, had tumbled down, and she had left it. Her gown, still damp, clung in all the right places. She looked as she did when he first saw her, so many years ago. Innocent, yet with a wanton look to her—His body ached with memory. She was so delicate, so small—yet she had stood up to hardships a man could not endure. What had happened to them in these last few years? God, how he'd wanted her, needed her all that time he was working in the south! He'd driven himself, not looking at other women—Then, when he came home, what did he find? Except for a few brief moments when he caught her unaware—a wife. Not a lover, but a *wife*.

Perhaps, he thought moodily, all married women became only wives. But he never thought it would happen to his Tamsen.

Tamsen served up the meal. The combined assembly ate in companionable silence—except for Martha, who retired, sulking, to her room. Then, one by one, they drifted off to their quarters. Tamsen remained to clear up, taking a long time over it. Finally Dan, sighing, took himself to bed. Apparently she didn't share his desires tonight.

He didn't know that she had been trembling inside all evening. That the feel of his dark eyes on her sent her pulses racing; the firelight flickering on his bronzed chest, revealed in an open-throated blue shirt, had aroused her to a peak of feverish need.

When she finally followed him to their private rooms, she shed the dark gown. And with it, she shed the years of trying to become someone else. Leaving the gown on the floor of the outer room, she took up the lamp Dan had left turned low, and entered their sleeping quarters. She stood for a moment, looking down at him, her mouth curved in a tender smile. She was the old Tamsen once more; the girl who knew how to please a man.

Putting the lamp in a far corner, so that it shed only a faint flickering glow, she approached the bed, sitting beside her sleeping husband, bracing herself with one hand, the other stroking the dark, hard-muscled strength of him.

"Dan?"

His eyes opened, blank at first with surprise, then beginning to smolder as he saw the expression in her dark eyes, the glow delineating creamy curves, turning them to rose, the dark hair that fell, brushing his face like a whisper.

"Tamsen! Oh, God!"

He reached for her, and they made love frantically, passionately, unable to get close enough to each other. And later, their bodies dewed with their exertions, they loved again, this time tenderly, sensuously. Through the open space between the roof and half-walls, they could see stars in a velvet sky. A scent of flowers filled the room. And somewhere in the far distance was the sound of a soft guitar, accompanied by a night-bird's call.

The islands had cast their magic spell.

The enchantment held for the next several days. When Dan realized he must get to his work, he faced the prospect with reluctance. There was still much to do to add to the comfort of their hastily built home. Sanitary facilities, a veranda to keep the interior rooms cool. And then there were the ovens. He'd spoken to Keokolo about building Hawaiian-type ovens, but the boy had not come—

Tamsen couldn't help smiling. She understood her man very well. On the one hand, he didn't want to leave her. On the other, he was itching to get his teeth into his work. It was in his nature. He could never stay in one place for long, not when there was a challenge waiting.

"Go on," she said. "We'll be all right."

It was settled that Dan, Juan, and Dusty, would make only a short foray up the coast to the point where they would begin their survey. They would possibly be away overnight. Martha watched, brooding, as Dan kissed Tamsen good-bye.

They hadn't been gone long when Keokolo arrived. The Hawaiian youth was not alone. Nell, disconsolately shuffling cards and dealing them on a stump looked up, eyes popping. For the lady in a garish, flowered muu-muu coming down the trail with Keokolo would make two of her own ponderous self.

"Dis Pua, Keokolo muddah," the boy said importantly. What followed was a jumble. It sounded as if he wished to talk to a mission lady. Finally, he said boss-lady, and Nell thought she understood.

"Well, hell," she said. "Don't jes' stan' there with yer face a-hangin' out! C'mon in." She gestured toward the house but the two stood where they were, refusing to move.

"Dammit!" She heaved herself to her feet and went in search of Tamsen. She found her surveying her efforts of the morning. A manila mat covered the floor of the small front room, and flowers had been fastened to the wall, Hawaiian-style. She wished, wistfully, that the new wood would gray quickly, to give the place a more homelike appearance.

She welcomed Nell's news of visitors. Expert at cooking over an open fire, she still longed for an oven. She went out to meet her guests, smiling, acknowledging Keokolo's introduction to his mother. Then she waited, brows lifted.

They both began to talk at once, Pua's words almost as coherent as her son's. The house stood on land that was *Kapu*. There were old bones buried beneath this soil, and their spirits did not rest. A *Kahuna* had not been consulted in laying out the building. The doors faced the wrong way. It must be torn down, built once more in another place. And a *Kahuna* must be called to see that it was done properly, and to perform a rite of purification.

Tamsen struggled to suppress a smile. "I'm afraid that's impossible."

"My husban' good *Kahuna*. *Kahuna hoonoho*. He fix. He know."

Tamsen shook her head. Apparently, even in paradise, a family could use a little ready money. It was a form of blackmail. But it wasn't one to be swallowed by a haole. Not this one, anyway.

She repeated her offer to hire Keokolo to build ovens. It was flatly refused. No native, no Chinese, no Japanese would step foot on the Tallant property until it had been cleansed.

Taking their leave politely, they left Tamsen, but Pua paused and bent to inspect Nell's cards. The big woman had returned to her dealing. "*Hoihoi!*" she said. Then, "You *kipa mai*—come—Pua house?"

Nell got to her feet again and extended her hand. "Sure," she said. "Why the hell not?" She gestured toward the hand she'd dealt. "Mebbe I'll teach you the game."

Pua held up two fingers. "Two day. Him bring. *Ua hewa oe.* Pua teach you."

They left, trailing alohas as they went. Nell stared after them, dumbfounded. "Wha'd she say?"

"I don't know," Tamsen laughed, "but I'd watch out for the gold in my teeth."

Nell, with an expression of horror, put one hand to her pendulous jaw, and Tamsen, still laughing, went into the house. She told Arab the story, expecting her to see its humor. "It was quite an act," she said. "These people are a little more civilized than I thought. But the idea! Thinking I'd swallow that story!"

To her surprise, Arab looked at her seriously, her face a little pale. "Don't discount it completely. Tam. I remember the Gitanos in Spain. Sometimes the things they said and did were beyond belief."

61

"Don't be foolish, Arab. And don't let this frighten you. Not in your condition. It's all silly, superstitious nonsense. I can't give it any credence at all."

But that night, with the men away, camping at their surveying site, Tamsen came suddenly awake. Something had touched her! Lighting a candle, she searched her bedding. It must have been one of the small lizards that clung to the trees and walls. Well, it was gone—

She slept again, this time to waken to a hollow sound of weeping. She sat bolt upright in a silent room. It had been a dream—

The next morning, Tamsen and Arab were both pale and listless. They did not mention the visitors of the previous day, or the warning they had carried.

Tamsen wished Dan would hurry home.

6

Pua's prediction that the homesite on the outskirts of Hilo would be avoided by the native popu-
lation was correct. Gifts of fruit and flowers were
left at the edge of the path leading into the clearing,
and Tamsen had the feeling that there were eyes
everywhere, watching curiously as she set to her
work.

She built a cage of green koa twigs and used it
as a frame, fitting broken lava together meticulously,
with a plaster of crushed shell and sand. With a final
coat of plaster, it would resemble the adobe Mexican
oven, or horno. Whether her solution would work,
she did not know.

In the middle of the afternoon, four of the Hilo
ladies came to call, catching Tamsen at her worst.
Non-Hawaiians, they seemed to think it their duty
to join forces against the natives, the climate, and
the customs.

The natives were lazy, irresponsible, thinking of
nothing but pleasure. Their morals were disgraceful.
The climate was too muggy. Now in Boston—Phila-
delphia—they went on and on, sitting like a row of
blackbirds in their dark gowns, hats and gloves.

"And you, my dear, where are you from?"

Tamsen, staring at a flounce of jet bugle beads trembling on the bosom of the speaker, searched back to her birthplace. "Pennsylvania," she said.

"You're one of us! I knew it, just by looking at you! I said, 'Elizabeth, that girl comes from a genteel family.' Didn't I, Elizabeth? I shall have a welcoming tea for you! Next Thursday?"

Trapped, Tamsen mumbled her gratitude. Twittering, the local ladies took their leave, their spokeswoman turning to give Tamsen one last bit of advice.

"White women do not work with their hands here, my dear. It lowers them in the native's estimation. Shall I send a boy?"

"The place is *Kapu*," Tamsen said. "Cursed. No one will come."

"Ridiculous," her visitor gasped. But she and the others said a hasty farewell and fled. Sometimes, Tamsen thought, a curse could be a blessing.

The men of the family did not come home that night. Tamsen slept, though the sheets were damp and twisted with her tossing. In the morning, Nell appeared, dressed in her finest. A gown of shocking pink velvet, cinched to the hilt. A wide-brimmed hat of lace, dripping with feathers. A matching fan, which she kept in constant motion to cool her heat-empurpled face.

"Good lord, Nell," Tamsen gasped. "What in the world—"

"Goin' a-visitin'," Nell said, mopping at her dripping neck. "Hell, can't go aroun' alla time, lookin' like a gawdam slob."

Nell must have been lonely during those years of semi-seclusion in California. All this trouble, just to go see a native woman in a grass hut, somewhere in the trees!

"You look lovely, Nell. But—what if the woman—Pua—was just being polite. Suppose she doesn't send her son?"

"If she don't," Nell growled, "I'm gonna be sore ez a boiled owl!"

Soon, the boy appeared. He led two horses, one for himself, and one for Nell. He didn't enter the clearing, but waited for her to come to him. Nell's garments would allow her to only ride sidesaddle, and the peculiar Hawaiian saddle didn't fit her build. Finally, Keokolo removed it, and placed it carefully beneath a tree. He managed to get Nell upon the animal, at last, and she carefully adjusted her weight. She moaned with every step as the pair moved out and away.

Martha had moved to stand beside Tamsen. If she laughs at Nell, Tamsen thought, I'll murder her! But Martha didn't laugh. She wore the sad, rather lonely look that Tamsen had surprised on her face once before.

"I hope Nell has a good time," the girl said wistfully.

Impulsively, Tamsen put an arm about Martha's waist, pulling her close, sensing a need for comfort and affection. For a moment, the girl seemed to yearn for her touch, relaxing. Then the old stiffness returned and Martha stalked away.

"I'm writing a letter to your mother. Would you like to add a few words?"

Martha ignored her and went into the room that was her own.

Unable to write, knowing that Em would wonder at the absence of word from her daughter, Tamsen turned to finishing up her makeshift oven. The light was dimming, and she had applied the last coat of sand and shell, when the men of the family came home.

They were tired, dirty, their clothing torn. "It's going to be one hell of a job," Dan said grimly, after kissing his wife. Hawaii didn't lend itself to railroads, if the terrain he'd been over was representative. Most of it was slashed with gullies, torrents of water running to the sea. The cost of bridging those chasms would be prohibitive. Wilder's idea of circling the island with rails, spurs running to the big sugar plantations, wasn't feasible.

Dusty, who had gone in search of Nell, returned in alarm. The big woman was gone, clothes strewn all over the room. He was certain his love had been attacked, kidnapped, carried away—

"She's all right," Tamsen placated him. "She's only gone to see a friend."

The small man's moustache quivered. "By Jove, she meant what she said the day we arrived! She's left me—"

"She's left no one," Tamsen scolded. "I'm talking about a woman friend!"

He subsided, though he still looked doubtful. When Nell returned in the company of Keokolo, Dusty bristled like a bantam rooster.

"The woman's son," Tamsen said quickly, catching his arm.

Nell didn't need as much aid in dismounting as she did in getting on the horse. She slid to the ground, landing with a jolt, and surrendered the animal to Keokolo, who disappeared into the greenery. Then she walked toward the staring group awaiting her.

Gone was the shocking-pink velvet. Gone were the corsets and trappings beneath which Nell's flesh had heaved in a struggle for breath. Gone was the feathered, wide-brimmed hat, the ornate piled hairdo. Nell wore a simply made voluminous *holoku* of yellow, splashed with crimson flowers and green leaves. It was clear that there was nothing beneath it, but Nell. Her hair hung down her shoulders, framing a beaming face. Behind one ear was a scarlet hibiscus, around her neck a lei of frangipani. The little feet that supported her enormous frame, were bare.

She came toward them, moving with a grace and majesty Tamsen hadn't known she possessed. She looked—almost beautiful, as though she had been born to this exotic setting.

"Nell, have you been drinking?" Dusty's voice sounded scandalized.

"Hell, no, you little *pilau!* And if I did, it's none of yer bizness!" She swept past him, nose in air. Dusty looked after her in hopeless adoration.

"She looks like a queen," he said with reverence. "Jove, yes! A queen."

As they dished up the stew that was to be the evening meal, Nell confided to Tamsen. That Pua was a sharp one. And Nell should have stuck to her own game. Instead they'd played one with a big flat rock, like a table, with holes carved in it. In the holes were a number of white stones and black. "Sorta like checkers."

Nell said glumly that she had lost her shirt. Not only that, she'd lost her shoes, shift, and drawers. If it wasn't fer Pua's gift of a dress, she concluded, she would've hadda come home in her epizootic!

What's more, Nell figgered she'd lucked out, losin' them duds. She felt good in the *holoku* and was goin' to have a couple dozen made—

"Hell," she said, "ain't there a old sayin'? When yer in a room, do what th' roomers do?"

Tamsen turned her back. "That's close," she said in a voice that shook suspiciously. "That's very close."

It wasn't until they were washing up that Tamsen remembered to ask the meaning of the word she'd called Dusty.

"*Pilau?* Ain't too sure. Learned a lot of words today. It means *fool,* er *stupid,* er *stink.* Can't call ter mind which 'un. But it sounds good, don't it?"

Nell speaking Hawaiian wouldn't be less colorful than she was speaking English, Tamsen thought, visualizing a group of enchanted natives surrounding her beloved old friend as she conversed.

When the stew was set on the tables beneath a huge pandanus, Dan continued to hold forth on the difficulties of the job ahead. "To make matters worse," he growled, "we've got all sorts of damned interference. Seems like half the island is *Kapu.* I'm supposed to deal with sugar plantations, churches built in the goddamnedest places! Pay off the Kahunas—"

"These Kahunas," Tamsen pushed a plate of biscuits baked on a hot stone toward her husband. "Are you going to hire them? Do you think there's anything in what they say?"

"Hell, no! It's graft, in any language!"

Nell, down the table, opened her mouth to speak, then closed it again. Dan had changed the subject, anyway. Had anyone realized it was only a week until Christmas?

"I can't believe it," Tamsen whispered. The air was soft, scented with ginger. The Hau tree, covered this morning with golden blossoms, now was studded with dark red blooms. The flowers, lasting only a day, changing color as if changing gowns, would fall with the night.

The tree reminded Tamsen that life was all too short. She shivered now. The holiday season had come too early.

They had decided, Dan continued, that with such a gargantuan task ahead, they would wait to begin until the new year. It would not hurt to have some time with their families before they had to devote all their energies to their work.

As Dan talked, Juan Narvaéz rose and took his wife by the arm. The dark eyes in his lean, aristocratic face, tender as they rested on her.

"Walk with me," he said. An almost imperceptible signal to his daughters indicated that they should stay behind. He led her through the screening ferns and lianas, down to where the beach curved before the sea. To their right, they could see Coconut Island, favorite picnicking spot of the Hawaiian royalty. Palm trees stood there, in feathered silhouette, as if they were pasted against the sky.

To their left, dense greenery shielded the spot where the Wailuku sang its way into the sea. And before them, the great ocean swelled, folding over itself in waves that curled and broke against the shore in a froth of lace.

"The sea is timeless, is it not?" he asked in his softly accented voice. "It makes our time seem so small."

Arab leaned against her husband dreamily, not really listening. It was enough that he was speaking, in words that harmonized with the cadence of the waves. Then his voice took on a different timbre that summoned her attention.

"Dan is going to tell Tamsen, in whatever way, at whatever time he thinks best. But I can't hold things back from you. Not when you're the one it will most affect."

He went on to explain. Leaving their wives at Hilo, they would use it as a central point, returning every night at first, then at least twice a week. It had seemed simple on paper. Almost half the land area of the islands was within five miles of the sea. The farthest point inland from the sea on Hawaii, the largest, was 28.5 miles.

They hadn't counted on the intricacy of the job in store; the roaring streams that cut deep gashes in the earth; valleys that fell away at one's feet. Chasms and cataracts, beds of lava, rolled in swirls and billows—and jutting in angry, jagged points that made it difficult for a man to ride.

"You are trying to tell me you won't be coming home?" Arab's voice was flat. Dull.

"Not that. At first we'll be able to manage twice a week. Then once. Twice a month, once. I'm afraid that I won't be here when you need me. I could move you to Kohala—"

"Would you be home more often?"

He shook his head. "It is just that we will be in that area a longer time."

"This isn't a real survey, Juan! Why can't you just put a few figures down on paper—?"

"It's very real, sweetheart. Dan hopes there can be some kind of peaceful conclusion to this thing. If the States should annex Hawaii, it should be through mutual consent. If not, then it is in our interest to maintain friendly relations. There must be no hint that we're engaged in any kind of espionage."

"I see."

"The baby isn't due till May. We're going to push on, try to finish the big island by that time if we can. First, we'll get everything in order here. You will have Tamsen, Nell, Martha."

"But not you."

He gripped her shoulders. "Arab, I like this job. It is a challenge. But if you will ask me to, I will tell Dan we, you and I, must return home."

She could see the eagerness, the pleading in his eyes as he awaited her decision. The waves that had sounded so relaxing a few moments before seemed to beat in her temples like a metronome. As if to cover any tears she might shed, it began to rain.

"It's quite all right," she said. "Don't worry, Juan."

He took her in his arms.

7

Tamsen absorbed the information about the necessary absences of the men better than Dan expected. After all, she told herself. I didn't go to Atlanta or Charleston when he asked me to go. If she had, she thought wryly, she would have been much in this same position. He would have been gone at his work, leaving her to wait in a lonely room.

Still, their reason for coming here was so that they could be together. And here she was, in a tropical paradise, in an atmosphere conducive to romance, needing Dan, wanting him—It wasn't fair!

She toyed with the idea of accompanying Dan along the trail. That wouldn't be fair to Arab. Arab needed her, and would need her more, now that Juan would be away. For her to go along pregnant, with two small girls in tow, was out of the question.

Martha did not feel held back by responsibilities. "Let me go with you," she cried. "I can do it! I did a man's work in the gold fields!"

Dan touched her cheek with a teasing finger. "Not on your life, little sweetheart. You stay home and let your Aunt Tamsen teach you to be a girl."

Martha shot Tamsen a glance of pure hatred.

But that night, she rationalized Dan's refusal to let her accompany them. He wanted her to be a girl, dainty and delicate, in rustling petticoats And he had called her *sweetheart*, his name for Tamsen. She lay on her small cot, hands clasped over her heart, and a shivery feeling inside as she vowed to make him love her.

Tamsen, in her disappointment at the direction Dan's work was taking him, accepted it calmly, but she couldn't avoid a certain coolness toward him. She dressed in her best dark dress, and returned the visit of the Hilo women. The home of her hostess was quite nice; an imported piano smelling of lemon wax; gleaming floors. A number of women had gathered to greet the newcomer. She managed to endure two hours of inspection, then gladly escaped and went home.

In her absence, Dan and Juan had erected a long veranda, grass-thatched, that ran the length of the house. It was beginning to appear as if it belonged in the clearing. During that week, they brought water to the house through a bamboo conduit leading from a spring. It poured into a metal basin, another length of bamboo carrying off the overflow. Behind the main structure, they constructed small grass and bamboo houses for sanitary facilities.

As they carried on their job of making the place comfortable for the girls during their absence, Tamsen prepared for Christmas. Her jerry-built oven, surprisingly, worked successfully. She baked bread, pies from the local fruits, and finally, an odd looking goose Dan procured from a native who had trapped it in the rugged, high lava country where it originated. Called a nene, it had claws, rather than webbed feet.

73

Juan and the little girls went far afield to locate a small Cook's pine, which made a very adequate Christmas tree. It was decorated with nuts, shells, and berries. As a final touch, the tree was draped with leis, in lieu of tinsel.

It was a very satisfactory celebration, with the afternoon of Christmas Day serving as a time of open house for the people of Hilo. Many visitors came to partake of the holiday fare, displayed on long tables beneath the grass roof of the veranda. Dan and Juan didn't seem to notice that there were only white faces among the guests. Tamsen was especially glad to welcome Reverend Lyman and his family, and Father Damien, a young Catholic Priest passing through. Perhaps the house faced the wrong direction, the doors were improperly placed, and the clearing was occupied by doomed souls, but these members of the clergy seemed unruffled by it. In fact, Father Damien blessed it and its occupants.

Only Martha was silent. She excused herself early that evening, and went to her room. There she carefully put away the bolt of material Tamsen had given her; the sewing basket, adorned with shells from Arab and the girls, the ornamental combs from Nell and Dusty.

Putting the Kukui necklace Dan had given her about her neck, she slipped into bed, only to sit up, burying her face against her bent knees. For she was remembering other Christmases. One, long ago, when Duke Courtney, not yet her stepfather, had appeared at her mother's door, dressed most comically as a Santa Claus—and bearing a Russian doll for an excited little girl.

For the last several years, she'd been so anxious to grow up. Now, she wished she could grow small again. Small, and innocent of the bad things in this world, including her own beginnings.

At home, there would be snow. Cammie and Victoria would be snug in their beds. Duke and Mama would be sitting together watching the fire burn low. Did they think of her today? She doubted it. They were probably happy she wasn't around to spoil things.

Martha Courtney cried herself to sleep.

The time between Christmas and New Year's Day passed quickly. Dan and Juan built a long shelter at the edge of the clearing, and stocked it with riding horses, carefully selected for surefootedness and sensibility. The days were clear and blue, perfect for an excursion to Rainbow Falls on the Wailuku. They went at dawn, seeing the mist rise from the foot of the falls in colors of rose and gold and lavender. Another time, they picnicked on Coconut Island, playground of kings. The only problem, Tamsen thought, was that she and Dan were never alone.

Arab felt much the same on that last night of the old year. Tonight, they had sat up until very late, talking about times that were long past. She had grown overtired. In the inner room, the children were asleep the minute she tucked them in; Juan, soon after his head touched the pillow. But she had been able to think of nothing but his impending departure. Oh, he would be home at intervals, but those intervals would soon be spaced farther and farther between—

It was so hot. Or perhaps it was the stillness of the night. It seemed an effort just to breathe—

Sighing, she rose and stepped outside, lifting her face to the stars. The air was like velvet. But the horses seemed so restless. She could hear them stamping and shifting in the shed where they were sheltered. Frowning a little, she turned. And she saw the thing.

It was only there for a moment, gaping at her through eyeless sockets set in a decayed, discolored face. It garbled something at her through rotting lips, then scuttled away leaving an incredible, horrifying stench.

Arab screamed and slumped to the ground.

She woke to find herself in bed, the members of the family crowded about her, frantic with concern. It had only been a dream, she kept insisting. She had a bad dream. And she had walked in her sleep. For the remainder of the night, Juan held her close. In the morning, when it was time for the men to take their departure, she seemed quite herself.

It was only after they had gone and she was alone with Tamsen that she lost control. Clinging to her sister, eyes dilated, she began to babble out the story of the night. The creature she saw had once been human. But it was dead, decayed. Its hair! If she had touched it, it would have come off in her hand. The smell! "Oh, God, Tamsen, believe me! Believe me! We must get the Kahuna—the Kahuna! Pua was right in what she said!"

Tamsen felt cold. She did believe her. Arab had seen something that frightened her. Perhaps the play of shadows across a face would create the effect she described. But who would have come this close to the house in the night? The Hawaiians were known for their honesty and—her chill deepened—to them, the vicinity was *kapu*. The residents of Hilo were respectable people. Perhaps a sailor, who had jumped ship?

No matter. The important thing was to convince Arab that it had been a dream.

While Dan, Juan, and Dusty were away, Tamsen moved to Arab's room. She took Nell into her confidence, and Nell stayed with an irritable Martha. There was little rest for Tamsen. She found herself snapping at Martha, and the girl sullenly stored up Tamsen's words to fuel her own anger.

At first, the men came home frequently, Juan certain that Arab's nightmare was a symptom of ill health. As the blue shadows beneath her eyes seemed to be less prominent with each homecoming, he began to feel a little safer about leaving her. Dan, too, was glad to have an excuse to be with Tamsen. But his work was falling behind schedule and must be done.

January passed, and February. The women in the clearing outside Hilo and the men, having reached Niulii, had all come to terms with their way of life.

If Arab, her child quickening, made her way down to the beach to listen to the cadence of the sea, imagining Juan's voice beside her, she said nothing to Tamsen. And if Tamsen, now returned to her own bed, reached out at night, yearning toward the familiar body of the man she loved, that was her secret.

In the evenings, they sat with their sewing, while Martha watched the children at play, and Nell and Dusty played their interminable poker hands. Tamsen was making a gown in the Hawaiian style. A deep crimson shade against a lighter rose, straight in front, its fullness forming a train in the back, it would be most becoming. Let the ladies of Hilo think what they would. She would wear it when Dan came home.

77

The evening of March 23rd was no different than any other. Arab finished hemming the last of a dozen diapers, and Tamsen's dress was finally complete. Relaxed, satisfied with a job well done, they put the little girls to bed and said a yawning goodnight. It was a night made for sleeping. A slight breeze stirred among the ginger flowers, bringing the scent into the open rooms. It mingled with a smell of new-baked bread. Tamsen had lifted five loaves from her rounded outdoor oven on the way to her quarters. She put them on the table in the outer room of her unit, and went drowsily to bed.

Something woke her. She lay still for a moment, not daring to move, then identified the thing that interrupted her dreams as, not a sound, but an odor. It was faint, but definite. The soft breeze that laved the room carried the sick-sweet smell of decay.

She sat up, a knot of nausea in her throat, and listened. Did she hear something in the outer room? A slithering, scraping sound?

Cautiously, she slipped from her bed and tiptoed to the door. The scent was worse, and she put a hand to her throat, staring into the darkness. She imagined that she could see a pool of black shadow that had not been there on other nights. Though she looked at it for a long time, it didn't move.

Suddenly, her nerves snapped. She whirled, closed the door behind her, and shoved a chair against it. Then she went in search of a candle, lighting it with shaking fingers.

She had been a coward, she told herself, firmly. If there were something out there, she must discover what it was, not only for her own sake, but for Arab's.

Bracing her spine, she moved the chair and swung the door open once more, her knees going weak with relief. It had been her imagination. There was nothing there, though the dreadful smell still lingered. Perhaps there was something dead among the trees that surrounded the house. Or some tropical fruit that was tainted with a scent of decay—

Laughing at her fears, she returned to bed. It took a few moments for her heart to resume its normal pace and stop bumping in her chest. And finally, she slept once more.

In the morning, she rose early. She would begin breakfast for them all. She had managed to get some eggs, and the new bread, toasted, would be a treat. She looked toward the table where she'd left the loaves, and moaned. One loaf was completely gone, another torn, raggedly, the floor covered with crumbs. Probably one of the rats that infested the island—

She went for her broom and began to sweep the crumbs, distastefully, toward the door, the smell that had disturbed her the previous night seeming to rise in waves. Reaching farther under the table, she discovered the culprit. It was a wormlike thing, swollen and obscene, pallid with streaks of purple and—oh God! There was the remnant of a nail! It had been a finger or a toe—

Tamsen made it to the door and was violently ill.

8

Tamsen said nothing of the night's events. Without touching the gruesome object she'd found, she managed to wrap it in a piece of oiled silk cut from a slicker. It now rested in a small enamel box that formerly held pins.

She had burned the broom that came in contact with it, then scrubbed her hands with seawater and sand before returning to her original intent of making breakfast.

The family of women rose to find a table set under the trees. Breakfast consisted of the usual porridge and fruit. There was no bread. A rat had gotten into it, Tamsen told them shortly. She had thrown it away.

She was quiet during the meal. Her head hurt as she pondered the identity of the midnight visitor. It could not be a' spirit as Pau hinted. Spirits did not seek out food. The creature had to be living— and human. But living things did not leave such ghastly tokens behind. If it were not for what Arab had seen and described, she would think someone had done this deliberately, to frighten them into leaving. But perhaps what Arab saw had also been staged! A trick! Who would profit by terrifying a bunch of women?

"I'm goin' a-visitin' t'day," Nell said sunnily. "That is if nobody don't need me. Feel a lucky streak comin' on. Think I've figgered me out a system."

Tamsen looked at her, thoughtfully. Twice a week, regularly, Nell went to the home of Pua and her husband. Each time, she'd come home filled with tales of bad luck coming to people who broke a *kapu*. Pua was a smart woman. Smart enough to take Nell for almost everything she owned. Smart enough to get her husband hired to break an evil spell.

"I'm going along with you, Nell," she said.

Nell looked pleased. "Pua's sent you a invite, ever' time," she beamed. Then her face fell. She hoped to hell Tam being along wouldn't throw her off her game—

As they rode along the trail that led upward from the sea, making their way through flowering trees and tall fern mingled with bamboo, Tamsen pumped Nell for information about the family.

"Pua," Nell said, "is a eddicated woman." She went on to explain that her friend had been a student at one of the early missionary schools. "Real religious women," Nell added piously. "Religious ez all hell."

"Then how can she believe in this *kapu* thing? Surely if she's any kind of Christian—"

"Jes' hedgin' her bets, so to speak. Couple of their Gods is sompin' like ours. Hell, who knows what's right er wrong? She figgers a little of both ways, an' she's got it made. Anyways, when she took up with her ol' man, Kapiki, the church throwed her out."

"For marrying a Kahuna?"

"Nope, fer marryin' her brother."

At Tamsen's shocked face, Nell hastened to explain. "That's the way them alii done, Tam. All of 'em. Kep' the bloodline pure. These here two, Pua and Kapiki, they's royal, awright, but clean down at the tail end of the line. Their folks married wrong way back there, somm'ers. Pua and her ol' man decided t' build the line back up—"

"My God! Then Keokolo—?"

Nell nodded. "Keep it mum. It's agin th' law now. But Pua sez most folks have fergot her 'n' him er relations. Don't want t' stir up a stink."

"I won't mention it. But I don't think much of your choice of friends." Tamsen dug a heel into the side of her mount and it moved on up the trail.

"Tam," Nell called after her. "Be keerful what you say afore Kapiki. He don't talk nuthin' but High-wayan, but I have an idee he could if he had a mind."

He would understand what *she* had to say, whether he spoke her language or not, Tamsen fumed.

They were upon the native hut before she saw it, so charmingly was it hidden among the foliage of tree fern and banana trees. Pua came to meet them, huge and beaming, but possessed of a certain grace that made her seem almost beautiful. She seemed to be unsurprised at Tamsen's coming.

"*Nou ka hale,*" she said, enthusiastically, embracing first Nell, then Tamsen. Tamsen looked beyond her at the big man standing in the entrance of the hut. He had the enormous square head she had seen in pictures of the royal family. His face was dark, almost mahogany color, his lips full and well-formed, his hair was white and close-cropped, silver where it caught the sun. He did not speak, but inclined his head graciously as introductions were performed.

Massively built, with inherent dignity, Kapiki didn't fit the image of the money-grubbing fakir Tamsen expected. Setting her jaw, she approached him, reached into her pocket, and pulled out her ghastly souvenir, unrolling the oiled silk before his eyes.

He murmured something to his wife who came forward and looked at the thing, eyes round. "Kapiki say where you fin' dis?"

Nell had forced herself into the group and began to bellow. "Gawdam, Tamsen! Git rid of it! Throw the damn thing away—"

Kapiki said something that was definitely a negative sound. He took the object and turned on his heel, went into the house and closed the door.

There, he remained. Shrugging, Pua led Nell to the tablet of stone that was the game Nell had described. Tamsen was ignored as the two women played, their attention focused fiercely on the pebbles with which they gambled. Nell lost consistently. Beneath the full sleeves of the muu-muu she wore, she had clasped many bracelets about her fat wrists. One by one, they changed hands.

At noon, a feast was spread. It consisted of *laulau*, various types of foods wrapped in leaves and steamed; *haupia*, a coconut pudding, and *pia*, or beer. The older women gossiped as they ate, seeming to understand each other. Tamsen was silent. Kapiki had not joined them. Apparently, he had no intention of doing so. She wondered what was in his mind. Perhaps she had embarrassed him, presenting him with the evidence of his cruel joke.

Tired of sitting, watching the women at their

gambling, Tamsen rose. As if it were a signal, Pua rose, too. "Wait," she said.

She entered the grass hut, then returned, beckoning to Tamsen. She ushered her into the dim interior, then left her, closing the bamboo door. Tamsen was alone in the room with Kapiki. He sat before a small fire of twigs, naked except for a twist of cloth about his hips. Above the gaudy print, his body glowed in the firelight. In his cupped hands, he held a bowl.

The object she'd brought lay on a flat stone. It seemed to have a phosphorescent sheen.

Tamsen backed away. She had no intention of being taken in by some superstitious hocus-pocus! But Kapiki raised his eyes to hers, and they held her there, poised, with a compelling power.

"You come with a question." His voice was deep, well-modulated, only a hint of accent.

"A question? Yes, I do! I want to know who was in my home last night. Who tried to frighten me, and why!"

"Manu not come back. Manu die, this day."

"That—that *thing*," she choked, pointing to the repulsive remnant, "has been dead for a long time. If this is a joke—"

"Manu, leper," he said gently.

A leper? Leprosy? Dear God, she'd heard of it! Her face paled. Leprosy had been in her house! Oh, God! Arab! The girls—

"No afraid," the Kahuna said. He explained that the king had issued an edict, sending lepers to Molokai. Manu had hidden, coming here for food and medication. He had become a little *pupule*, else he wouldn't have ventured where there was a *kapu*. Still, he had gone to *Waikea*, since he had died in peace. His body was safely hidden in the cave in which he had lived, overlooking the waters. With his last efforts, he had closed the opening with a stone.

Tamsen stare at him, stupefied. "How do you know all this?"

It was simple, the Kahuna smiled. He had called upon his *aumakua, pueo*, the owl. First, he had drunk *awa*, then the *makani* had spoken to him from the roof of the hut, telling him these things—

He paused, his eyes saddened at her expression of disbelief. There was more. She and the others must leave the place of *kapu*. The Gods were angry. They were welcome to seek sanctuary in his home—

Tamsen's eyes narrowed. Now, they were getting to the root of the situation. Next, he would casually mention his fee.

"Thank you," she said, "but we are quite happy where we are. What do I owe you."

A wave of something like pain crossed his features. He closed his mouth tightly, signifying his intent to speak no more, and waved her from the room.

"Wha'd his nibs have to say?" Nell asked, curiously, as they rode down the trail that led to their home near the water.

"I haven't the slightest idea," Tamsen said, her tone cross. "A lot of mumbo-jumbo."

That night, she left her door open and placed a chair where she could see and not be seen. The leper did not return. That did not necessarily mean the man was dead, unless someone—Keokolo, for instance—had knowledge of it and told the old fraud!

In the morning, reeling from lack of sleep, she began once more to clean. Finding a trail, like that left by a California slug, near her oven, she swept

85

the area around it and packed it with clean sand. In answer to Martha's questioning about her flurry of housekeeping, she said that she expected the men of the family to return before long.

Finally, seeking to purify the oven, she built a hot fire in it, and kept adding wood. She had gone after another armful when there was a sharp crack, and the contraption exploded like a bomb.

She dropped the fuel she was carrying, and burst into tears. Then she set her teeth and doggedly began to build another. When Dan and the others came home, they would want bread.

Her days were spent in a flurry of activity, her nights, watching over her beloved family. Therefore, on the morning of March 27th, she was near exhaustion. In a state half between sleeping and waking, she sat at breakfast beneath the trees, oblivious to the female voices rising and falling about her. Suddenly she seemed to turn dizzy, the table rising, undulating. Her plate slipped away from her, sliding down the table. Then she was leaning backward at an impossible angle, staring into the branches of the tree behind her, into a sky that had turned an odd, murky yellow.

Righting herself, she stood, looking dazedly at her plate which had returned once more. She closed her eyes, then opened them to apologize for having taken leave of her senses and saw that all of the faces about the table, down to little Missy, were equally shocked and bewildered.

She caught the table's edge as the ground jolted again beneath her feet, seeming to move sideways and back, up and down, in a motion that induced vertigo. Then it settled for a moment, quivering with the ominous promise of another shock as the women stared at each other in horror.

Earthquake!

And in the distance, thirty miles to the south and west of Hilo, the crater of Mauna Loa sent up columns of smoke and steam. A red glow that intensified as rivers of molten stone poured from the volcano's throat and flowed down the mountainsides in diverging destroying lines.

9

On the far side of the island, in the Kohala District, the job Dan Tallant, Juan Narvaéz, and old Dusty Wotherspoon had set out to do was at an end. Tallant wished to recheck a last sighting, then they would be headed home. They were all exhausted, but a bit euphoric as Dusty took his appointed place with a flag and Dan, Juan beside him to transfer his figures into a notebook, settled his tripod and peered into the scope.

"Dammit, Dusty, hold still," he shouted as the small man seemed to dance before his eyes. Then the apparatus was jerked from his hands and lay on the ground, kicking and bucking like a live thing as Dan staggered backward to cling to a tree.

"What the hell!"

The earth continued its violent contortions for a few moments. When they ceased, becoming only a persistent, menacing ague, the three men ran for their horses. The beasts were rearing, terrified, eyes rolling as they were fought into submission. The men packed their gear and mounted, working silently, only one thought between them.

They had to get home.

Riding hard, they cut down toward Kawaihae,

a journey that should have taken an hour stretched
into most of a day. Parts of the trail had fallen away.
And along the coast, the sea seemed to slop and
swirl like water in a cup. Mounting a hill as darkness
fell, Dan spotted the reason for the red light bleeding through the night sky. Mauna Loa was crested
with a shower of flame.

Good God!

At Kawaiihae, oblivious to the natives who ran,
helter-skelter, in their terror at the earth shocks, the
men cut across to Waimea, to the Parker Ranch. All
along the trail, belly-deep in grass, the cattle stood
as though carved from stone, muzzles lifted to the
sky as they moaned in uneasy fear. It sounded like
the weeping of the damned, Dan thought. The ani-
mals' red and rolling eyes did little to dispel his impression. As the earth trembled, the skittish horses
danced sideways, and had to be turned with brute
force.

They rode through the night and the greater
part of the next day and were nearing Honokaa,
where they would take the coastal trail, when disaster struck. With a tremendous rolling heave of the
earth's crust, Juan Narvaéz's mount went to its knees.
Juan pitched over the animal's head, to lie unconscious as the horse struggled to its feet. Dusty's
mount slipped, slithered, and fell sideways, pinning
the small man's leg. Dan escaped only by sawing at
the reins, his horse going to its hind legs, pawing at
the air as it uttered a shrill scream. Then it was on
all fours again, and Tallant surveyed his companions with bleak eyes.

First, he caught up the horses and tethered
them, then he inspected the injuries of the men. Juan
had not regained consciousness. He put an ear to
the man's chest and checked his breathing, finally

satisfied that it was only a concussion. Dusty gritted his teeth as Dan cut away his boot and trouser leg. His leg was broken.

Trembling with fatigue, Tallant managed to set and splint the broken bone. Then he opened their blanket rolls, covering the fallen men against the night chill. Making a fire and boiling a pot of coffee was out of the question.

The earth would not hold still.

In the clearing just out of Hilo, Tamsen was having her own troubles. The several days since the quakes began had been terrible ones. The children had vomited, incessantly, their equilibrium shaken by the constant movement beneath their feet. Nell, frightened by anything that, as she said, "didn' make no gawdam sense," was reduced to quivering hysteria. Martha, too, was terrified. But having cut herself off from those around her through her rebellious attitude, she was unable to reach out for help and comfort. As a result, her attitude seemed cold and insolent, even though she was trembling inside.

But it was Arab that concerned Tamsen most. Heavy with child, she had the fixed idea that something had happened to Juan; that he needed her.

More and more, Tamsen thought of the old Kahuna and his warning. They were welcome to come to him for sanctuary.

She tossed her head. His prediction of impending disaster had been a lucky guess, that was all. Or perhaps, having lived here all his life, he was sensitive to the moods of the island.

Things were improving. Though the world still shook and quivered, the sky today had been blue, and Mauna Loa no longer shot angry flames into the sky. She washed Missy's small face and tucked her and Ramona into bed, with promises that things would be better in the morning.

Leaving the girls, she went in search of her sister. She was gone. Frowning, Tamsen made her way toward the shore. For some reason, Arab seemed drawn to the water. She had asked her not to go there—or anywhere—alone. She found her leaning against a tree at the edge of the sand, her face a white oval, her green eyes staring.

"Arab?"

When Arabella didn't move, seemingly blind and deaf to her presence, Tamsen followed the direction of her fixed gaze. A ledge of black lava had run like a pointing finger down to the water's edge. Now, with the trembling of the island, some of it had fallen away. It revealed a hollow in its depths, a miniature cave.

And there a ragged creature squatted, staring out at them through eyeless sockets, its rotting mouth falling away. Clutched in monstrous, swollen, mutilated hands was the remainder of a loaf of bread.

The earth rocked, and the thing toppled to its side. Manu the leper. Dead. Dead.

Tamsen took her sister's shoulders. "Come, let's go to the house." Receiving no answer, she shook her a little. Arab looked at her, a measure of sanity returning to her blank face.

"I can't, Tamsen. I can't walk. Something's happened to my legs. They're paralyzed."

Somehow, Tamsen summoned the strength to half drag, half carry her sister away from the dreadful sight on the beach. The earth undulated beneath her feet, and the belt of trees between the sea and the clearing seemed to jig about her as she struggled through them, her fainting sister in tow. A palm was uprooted, crashing at their heels as they emerged from the foliage.

Arab sank to the ground, and Tamsen fell beside her, covering her with her own body for protection as she called for help.

An hour later, Tamsen, Nell, and Martha stood beside the semiconscious Arab who had been put to bed. It was plain that Arab had gone into premature labor. The earth tremors were almost constant now and it was Nell who put her thoughts into words.

"Let's git th' hell out of here," she said grimly.

Tamsen started. The thought had been in her mind, but now that it was voiced she rejected it. "There's no place to go, Nell. The whole island is affected—"

"We c'd go up to Pua's," the old woman persisted. "This gawdam place hez got a curse on it. Kaniki'll help us. Hell, we got us a Kahuna, might ez well try 'im out—"

"That's nonsense, and you know it. We're having an earthquake. The volcano is erupting. No hocus-pocus is going to stop it. We're as safe here as we would be anywhere."

Her words carried little conviction. The vision of the dead leper still haunted her. Kapiki had known the man was dead; had described the location of his burial place. Tamsen shivered in the damp heat. True magical powers? Actual knowledge of Manu's death? Or a lucky guess?

"We will stay here," she said firmly.

But Arab's haunted eyes had opened. "Nell's right. All of you leave. Take the girls. Get them out of here. Please! Please! Just leave me—Ah-h-h!"

She writhed with the onset of another pain and Tamsen wiped her damp forehead. "We can't go without you, Arab. Do you think you could travel that far? The horses—"

"I'm staying here. Juan will be here soon. You know that."

"Of course," Tamsen whispered. "Of course."

Arab slept once more, and the three women stood silent. The earth bucked beneath their feet, the timbers of the structure around them popped and cracked. There was a strong smell of sulphur in the air. And finally Tamsen spoke.

"She can't be moved," she said. "But she's right. The rest of you should go. Listen."

The sound of the sea that had been a dreaming whisper in the soft tropical nights before the quake had become a frightening roar as it churned against the island's shores. Tamsen met Nell's eyes.

"Nell, wake the girls. Get them dressed. Martha and I will saddle the horses. Hurry."

Nell rushed to do her bidding and Martha and Tamsen stumbled across the trembling clearing to drag the frightened beasts from their shelter. Tamsen chose the two most tractable ones. Martha would take Ramona up behind her. Nell could hold little Missy in her arms.

"And what about you?" Martha asked in an odd voice.

Tamsen looked at her, puzzled. "I'm staying with Arab."

"I'm staying, too." Her tone was firm. "You don't need to think you can get rid of me."

"Rid of you!" Tamsen stared at the girl's expressionless face, lit with a red glow from the distant fires. "Rid of you! We need you, Martha! Nell and the girls can't make it alone—"

"I heard Arab say Juan is coming. That means Dan is coming, too. And you want me out of the way, don't you? You want me gone when he gets here! You're afraid—"

Tamsen lifted her hand and slapped the girl across the face. For a moment they stood looking at each other in a contest of wills, then Tamsen commanded, "Do as I said! Move!"

The girl turned sullenly to her work.

In a short time, the small caravan consisting of Nell and Missy, Ramona, and Martha, moved up the trail that led to the house of the Kahuna. Tamsen watched them go. Martha had delayed, deliberately, fetching a bundle of things to take with her. But at last they were on their way.

Wearily, Tamsen returned to her sister's side, her anger slowly subsiding. Martha's feelings were out in the open, now. The challenge had been made and met. At the moment, with Arab in pain, it made little difference. Very likely, none of them would survive.

All night, she sat beside Arabella Narvaéz, sponging her sister's damp forehead, murmuring soft words of comfort. At dawn, Arab resting at last, Tamsen made her way to the door. Below the clearing, the waters moaned along the shore like a lost soul, and she couldn't put the thought of the dead leper from her mind. Was his body still there, watching the destruction of the island with sightless eyes?

She leaped back as a sharp crack sounded. The long timber that supported the veranda crashed down, its thatched roof effectively barring the door.

She had little time to assess the damage, for Arab had wakened and was once more in the throes of pain. Tamsen hurried to her sister's side.

"What day is this?" Arab asked weakly.

"The second. April second. Now try to rest—"

94

"Juan is coming," Arab insisted. "He said he was coming in April."

"Of course," Tamsen said, her eyes wet. "Of course."

Inside, she was not so sure. All night she had prayed for the safety of the Narvaéz daughters, of Nell, and of their men who were somewhere on this quaking island. There seemed little chance that any of them would emerge from this holocaust alive. At last, exhausted by nerves and sleeplessness, she sat by Arabella, holding the girl's twitching hand, and slept.

She wakened to the sound of an ax. Someone was chopping at the debris that blocked the door. Leaping to her feet, her heart in her throat, she rushed to the choked opening.

"Who's there?" she called. "Dan—"

Keokolo's voice answered. The Kahuna's son assured her that he would have the doorway free in a moment. He removed a few timbers and bundles of woven thatch, and finally climbed through the door.

There was little time, he told her in his broken English. She and her sister must leave immediately and go to join the others at his father's house.

Tamsen shook her head. Arabella was in no condition to travel.

"Seestah no go, seestah die," he said simply. The earth shuddered violently as if to punctuate his words. Tamsen felt he spoke the truth.

He had come prepared, leading a small Hawaiian pony with a crude travois attached to it. He helped Tamsen place Arab on the makeshift stretcher, and then mount the animal that seemed calm despite the ravages of nature around it. Then he gestured toward the trail.

"Hele aku," he said. *"Go! Wiki-wiki!"*

"Aren't you coming with us?"

He shook his head. He was carrying a warning to Kau, south of Hilo. The earth reeled, and he slapped the animal on the rump. "Aloha."

Tamsen was far up the trail, frantic with her concern over her sister's agony, before she remembered something. Keokolo had done something unprecedented. He had violated the *kapu* that kept all natives from the clearing. She found herself shivering.

It was a long, agonizing journey. In places, trees had fallen to block the path. The wet warm air was heavy with a scent of crushed fruit and blossoms mingled with a sulphur taint. Tamsen would dismount, clear the path, and wipe Arab's pale face. Arab, past coherent thought, called incessantly for Juan.

The sun had reached its zenith when the pair arrived at the house of Kapiki and Pua. Ramona and Missy ran to greet them, screaming with delight, only to be shooed away by Nell. "Gawdamit, girls, yer ma's sick!"

Pua came forward to meet them, moving in her usual stately unhurried fashion. She lifted Arab from the litter and carried her to a small hut set away from the main house.

"This *hale pe'a*," she explained. "Woman house."

Inside, the floor was covered with *lauhala* mats. In one corner, layers of *makaloa* mats, made a bed with a rectangular pillow of *lauhala*, and spread with sheets of *tapa* cloth. Here, the big Hawaiian woman gently placed her burden. *"Keiki lohi,"* she said frowning, after a brief examination. "Baby slow, late. Much *hui*. Go, now." She gestured imperiously toward the door and Tamsen, drained of strength, meekly obeyed. Outside, she sank upon the stone that served as a seat at the game Pua and Nell had played so often, eyes blind as she felt her sister's pain.

Late in the afternoon, the surface of the island rose in one tremendous heaving gasp, then sank. Rocks were torn from their age-old moorings, mountains split and fell. In Kau, south of Hilo, an avalanche of red earth poured from the mountainside. Houses were engulfed, a village was buried. The earth yawned in a thousand places, throwing horses and their riders to the ground. In the villages, people prayed. And a wall of water, forty to sixty feet high, hurled itself against the shore.

Tamsen scrambled to her feet in horror as the world reeled around her. And in that moment, Arabella Narvaéz's baby was born.

10

For five days, the ground continued to surge and tremble. Then a hot and liquid river of fire, having traveled underground for twenty miles or more, forced its way through a fissure, boiling up in flaming fountains. Rocks were flung into the air against a background of livid lava. The river of molten rock flowed and boiled toward the sea, channeling itself into four streams that trapped all living things between them.

The land raged with fire and fury; the seas boiled and steamed. And when it was done, the pressure that had quivered beneath the earth like a trapped demon now released, the southeast coastline of Hawaii had sunk from four to six feet, and had been extended half a mile.

And it was over.

In the clearing about the Kahuna's hut, it was as if nothing had taken place. The ground stood still. A delighted Ramona and Missy had come out to play. Nell sat disconsolately at the game-rock, attempting to play a game against herself. Pua had not left Arab's side since the baby's birth. Arab had developed a temperature and her body was covered with overlapping ti leaves to break the fever. Occasionally, she was given *ko'oko'olau* tea to drink.

She needs a doctor, Tamsen thought, walking the perimeter of the clearing, the baby in her arms. She had no more faith in Pua's preparations than she did in Kapiki's charms and spells. The Hawaiian man had shut himself away.

She looked longingly toward the trail that led down to Hilo. If it were not for the baby, she would try to go for help. Surely, there was someone left alive down there, some American—

She dared not take the child, and she didn't want to leave her with Martha or Nell. Poor little unwanted mite! She lifted the tapa cloth in which the child was wrapped and looked at the tiny face; a baby-girl face, with hair and lashes like yellow silk. So beautiful, except for the mark that touched her forehead like a crimson fingerprint. But the otherwise perfect features held no expression, nor did the long silver eyes beneath golden arched brows.

Pua had studied the child. "B'long Pele," she announced. Arab, when the baby was placed in her arms, had shuddered away. "She's cursed," she said hoarsely. "Take her away! Oh, God! Take her away from me!"

The situation had not changed. In lieu of its mother's milk, the little thing was fed on poi. She seemed to be healthy enough, but she never cried. If she'd only cry just once!

I'm the one who should reject you, Tamsen thought, not Arab. For once, many years ago, she had stood like this with another baby in her arms, yearning over it, loving it. And the child had been Martha; Martha, who seemed determined to compete for Dan's affections—

99

Dan, who might even now be dead, along with Juan and Dusty.

Kapiki, coming from one of his trances, had announced that Keokolo was dead. Neither he nor Pua had seemed unduly disturbed by the news. It was as if they had always known it would end this way. Perhaps Keokolo, himself, knew it. Else why had he dared to enter a place of *kapu?*

The lovely island held dark and sinister secrets at its heart—like the fire in the depths of Mauna Loa—

Carrying the baby, Tamsen moved to sit on the stone facing Nell at her gambling game. "How is it going?"

"Hell," Nell growled. "Can't git my mind on th' gawdam thing. Keep worryin' about Dusty, the l'il sonofabitch—"

Tamsen's eyes swam with tears. They were all frantic; she, Arab and Nell. "He'll be all right," she comforted the old woman. "They should be back soon."

"Sure ez hell hope so." Nell's face brightened. "There's Pua."

The Hawaiian woman had gone to her hut and was returning to the *hale pe'a* with a coconut-shell cup in her hands, evidently some sort of witch's brew for Arab. Dressed in a flowing gown, a fresh flower tucked behind her ear, she seemed to glide despite her bulk; a study in grace.

"Looks good, don't she?" Nell said, "An', say, speakin' of looks, you look like hell."

"Thank you," Tamsen said, dryly. "I might remind you that I've been wearing this same gown since the day we arrived. Pua's clothes might fit you, but I'm lost in them."

"Martha stays gussied up," the old woman observed. "Them clothes she brought along was yers in the first place. Git a couple of 'em back."

Tamsen stiffened. "I don't want them. I don't want anything from Martha. Let's get that straight right now."

Nell's beady little eyes were speculating. "Figgered you'd say that. But one o' these days, yer man's gonna be comin' up that trail, an'—" Her mouth fell open. "Migawd!"

Tamsen followed her gaze and stood, the baby in her arms, her knees trembling. For emerging from the trees were three horsemen. Dan Tallant was in the lead, dirty and unshaven. Behind him rode Juan, his face as pale as the bandage that hid his dark hair. And finally, Dusty, clinging to his saddle, his leg sticking out at an odd angle.

Tamsen stood still, her throat filled with tears, her traitorous legs refusing to move as Dan dismounted, not seeing her, and aided his two companions, helping them to the ground. At last, she started toward them, feeling as though she were walking in quicksand.

Before she reached them, a slender figure came flying from the house. Martha, in the new gown Tamsen had made to surprise Dan with when he came home. It, too, had gone into her bundle carried from the house near Hilo—

"Dan!" Martha's voice rang like a bell. "Oh, Dan!"

She threw her arms about the neck of Tamsen's husband and burst into tears. "Oh, Dan, it was awful! I was so afraid!"

Juan spied Tamsen and came toward her, his face drawn with determination and pain. "Arab— where is she?"

101

Tamsen pointed out the *hale pe'a* and held the baby toward its father. "Juan—"

But he brushed by her and disappeared into the hut that held his wife. Nell had reached Dusty, enveloping the little man in her massive arms, weeping copious, sentimental tears that he tried gallantly to stem.

Tamsen stood in her stained and ragged gown, hair straggling from its moorings, holding a baby that nobody wanted, as a radiant Martha clung to Dan Tallant, home from the dead.

11

When Dan Tallant caught sight of Tamsen, he managed to disentangle Martha's arms and made a beeline for his wife. He tried to hug her. It was awkward, because of the baby in her arms, so he settled for taking her face in his hands, kissing her shadowed lids, the trembling mouth.

"Ah, God, Tam! I've been going crazy, wondering if you were safe! I've been through hell—"

"And so have I," she said in a muffled voice.

He looked down at her bent head, at the smooth parting in dark hair, still drawn back tightly despite stray wisps that had escaped about her face. She was so small—and silent.

Dan touched the face of the child in her arm. "Arab's? So soon?"

"April second."

"Good God!" He remembered the horrors of that day. "Is it a girl?" At her affirmative nod, he reached for the baby, holding her in the crook of an arm so that his other would be free to hold Tamsen.

Tamsen was stunned. The child's silver eyes had opened, displaying a human intelligence for the first time. The little mouth quirked in a Mona Lisa smile, so fleeting Tamsen was sure she'd imagined it.

"Let's take her to her mother," Dan said. "We're going off somewhere and be alone."

"Arab doesn't want her."

"I suppose not. Not with Juan home." Leaving Tamsen, he deposited the baby in Martha's arms, then led Tamsen toward the sheltering trees.

"I can't figure it," he said. "This place is practically untouched. Everything around it is practically wiped out—"

"Kahiki says his gods have protected him."

Dan laughed. "You don't believe that, do you?"

She stopped and looked at him, soberly. "I don't know, Dan. But there's something—Yes, I guess I do. It's different here. Can't you feel it? Dan, let's go home. Leave these people in peace. These are their islands—"

"And I have a job to do," he pointed out. "I have to do it. You know that."

They were both silent as they entered a small glade of tree fern and bamboo. A pale sun filtered through the greenery, touching the place with a finger of magic. Dan gathered Tamsen to him for a tender moment, murmuring words of endearment. Then his hands went to her hair, removing the pins that held it. Like black water, it fell in a stream to her small waist.

"I've dreamed of this," he said hoarsely. His hands went to her throat, undoing hooks and buttons, sliding the gown from her smooth olive shoulders. Then he stood back to look at her; her small figure dusted with gold from the sun's rays. Turning for a moment, he plucked a white ginger flower. Its scent filled the air with fragrance as he tucked it into her hair with trembling fingers.

"My Tamsen! My love! My wife!"

He threw his ragged shirt aside, pulling Tamsen close, lifting her so their hearts beat against each other. "I want to do this right! I always feel like we must begin from the beginning. But I can't wait. I want you!"

"Dan—please—"

He carried her to a spot of soft grass, putting her down gently, his hands going to his belt.

Then they heard a sound of running footsteps and Martha burst into the clearing. Juan Narváez had collapsed into unconsciousness, and Dusty had hurt his leg trying to help. Arab was hysterical. They needed Dan.

Dan left the girls together, with a muffled oath. Tamsen, face burning, buttoned her disheveled gown before Martha's gaze. "And the baby is wet," the girl finished, sweetly.

"You might have changed her," Tamsen said crossly. "She's not my responsibility."

"Isn't she? Arab doesn't want her, that's for sure."

"Where did you leave her?"

"I put her on a stump. Ramona and Missy are with her."

"Good lord! A six-year old? A four-year old?"

But Martha was gone, hurrying back toward the clearing. She would not admit, especially to Tamsen, the feelings she'd had while holding the small, precious bundle in her arms. For a moment, she'd pretended it was her own. Hers—and Dan's. Tamsen hadn't given him a child, but she would. Someday, he would realize it was Martha he really loved, and that Tamsen was old—

She shut her eyes against the picture she'd seen as she entered the glade; that of a slender figure touched by the sun's rays; the smooth figure of a girl, yet ripe with womanhood; dark hair tumbling like silk, a flower—

She stumbled, then clenched her fists. She would win out. She had to. Meanwhile, the clearing was in view. The baby was where she had left her.

She breathed a sigh of relief.

For a time, the small peaceful clearing surrounding the huts that made up the Kahuna's domain was in turmoil. Juan, indeed, had lapsed into unconsciousness, a condition brought on by his head injury and his delight in being reunited with his wife. Dusty, trying to go to his aid, had fallen, snapping the newly mended bone in his leg. Nell was frantic, Arab was sobbing, certain that Juan was dead.

Seeing that Martha held the baby, Tamsen went straight to her sister, calming her while Pua prepared a sedating drink. Juan would be all right, Pua said in her sparse English. Kahiki had given him *awa* to drink. He had also made a poultice of *awapuhi* mixed with a tablespoon of Hawaiian salt, applying it to his head around and on the injury.

The ailing men had been bedded down in the *hale mua*, or men's eating house. This was another small outbuilding where male members of the family took their meals before the altar of the family gods. Kahiki took his meals alone in solitary splendor, now that Keokolo was gone, and he'd been sleeping there since his grass hut was filled to bursting with women and children.

Now it would serve as shelter for all the men; Pua and Tamsen would occupy the *hale pe'a*, along with Arab, and Nell, Martha and the girls would sleep in the *hale hoa*, or main house.

Listening to Pua's arrangements, Tamsen's heart sank. She and her husband would remain separated until the other members of the group recovered enough to find new quarters. For women, the *hale mua* was *kapu*.

Arab slept at last, and Tamsen remembered her charge—the baby. In her concern over her sister, the child had been almost forgotten. Releasing Arab's limp hand, Tamsen tiptoed to the door of the hut, there to confront a heart-stopping sight.

Dusk had come, and the moon had risen. It's light revealed a composition that was poignant in its beauty. Martha, still dressed in Tamsen's bright gown, held the infant in her arms. Dan faced her, leaning toward her in conversation, one hand against a palm trunk. Behind them, the tropical jungle made a frame of flower and leaf.

As Tamsen stood, uncertain, in the doorway, Dan Tallant reached to touch Martha's cheek. She heard him laugh.

Tamsen stepped back into the dimness of the hut where she stood for a long moment, her hand at her throat.

My collar is still undone, she thought dully. And my hair still down. Mechanically, she buttoned her gown and pinned her hair back into its tight bun.

During the remainder of their stay in the clearing, Dan Tallant was unable to get close to his wife. She must care for Arab, for the baby. Most of her activities were centered in the woman's house, *kapu* to men. Out of doors, she was like a will-o'-the-wisp, appearing, disappearing, and—when caught—stiff in his arms.

He was puzzled at first, then worried—and finally angry. They had been separated for a long time. It was only through God's own luck that they'd gotten together at all. If they hadn't met the Hawaiian boy who directed them here—

Now, it would seem he had disappointed her in coming back at all.

As if his thoughts had summoned her, she appeared beside him, her face white, smudges beneath the lovely eyes. His heart gave a surge. "Tam—"

"I've got to talk to you, Dan."

"And I want to talk to you. In fact, I could do with more than talk, at this point. Tamsen—"

She put up a staying hand. "We've got to leave here, Dan."

He looked at her in bewilderment. "We are. We're going to Lahaina, as soon as we can arrange passage."

"Not just here. We've got to leave the islands. We don't belong here. Kapiki says—"

"Good God! Is that why you finally condescended to come looking for me? Why the hell should I care what an old witch doctor has to say?"

She raised her eyes, looking at him steadily. "We have had an earthquake, a tidal wave, a baby born that's not—not right. Everything's gone wrong since we came here. How much proof do you need?"

He caught at her arm. "You're coming with me!"

"I have to get back to the baby."

"The baby is Arab's responsibility! I don't know what the hell's wrong, but you're my wife, and you're going to act like it!"

"I don't know what you expect me to do," she flared. "There's no privacy—"

"Privacy, hell!" he growled. "What do you think you are? Some goddam virgin high priestess?"

She flinched and his face softened. "Tamsen! Please, sweetheart, I miss you! I want my girl back!

Look, if it's privacy you want, there's a place I know. It's up on the coast above Papakou. A horseshoe trail that loops down to the ocean and back again. There's a cave with a waterfall flowing over it, and a deep pool surrounded by flowers." He stopped, faltering a little. "When we were surveying there, I used to imagine you in that pool, your hair down—"

Tamsen swayed toward him. "Dan—"

"I would go if I were you, Aunt Tamsen." Martha had appeared like a shadow. Moving to Dan's side, she linked her arm through his and smiled up at him. "It sounds awfully romantic."

"I can't go," Tamsen said in a tight voice. "I have to take care of the baby."

She turned and walked, straight-backed, to the hut. Dan stared after her in angry confusion. For a moment there, he thought Tamsen was herself once more, but he was wrong.

"I wish I could go," Martha said wistfully. "Dan, would you take me?"

"I don't see why the hell not," Dan grated. He left her standing there and strode to the *hale mua*.

Martha watched until he had disappeared from view, then smiled.

Tamsen, in the women's hut, tended Arab's child, trying to shut out the horrid thing that was growing in her mind. She kept seeing pictures: Martha flying into Dan's arms upon his return; Martha and Dan—Martha in Tamsen's bright gown—holding the baby, Dan leaning above her; the girl linking arms with Dan so casually just now.

That Martha was infatuated with her husband, was obvious, but did Dan want her?

Hugging the baby to her, Tamsen closed her eyes with a feeling of nausea. Martha was enough like herself to be her twin—twin to the girl Dan Tallant loved and married. And Martha was young, fresh, untouched. Why wouldn't he want her?

It was true that their marriage had deteriorated for a time. But those early nights when their house was completed, all was as it had been before. She seized on those memories. Surely they proved something.

Or had he only needed a woman? Had he pretended she was Martha, there in the darkness? Once, before she was married, she had lain in a man's arms, making believe he was Dan. She had let that man love her, out of friendship and pity for his loneliness.

She did not want friendship or pity from Dan. Dear God, she wanted his love! And she was afraid.

12

Dan's words had not actually been an invitation, but uttered in anger; a lashing out at Tamsen's treatment of him. He would have forgotten it, if Martha hadn't been waiting for him when he emerged from the *hale mua* at dawn.

"The horses are saddled," she said eagerly. "And I've made your breakfast. I thought you'd never wake up!"

His first instinct was to tell her to forget it. But she seemed so much like a child in her excitement at an outing that he capitulated. Poor kid! These last days couldn't have been a picnic for her, with the world turned upside down and everyone catering to three invalids and a baby.

"I didn't think you'd be such an early bird," he teased. "Well, bring on the grub—and let's go."

They rode down the trail toward Hilo. North of Hilo, they would intersect with a passable road that ran along the coast. The atmosphere was heavy with moisture and jungle-scent as it always was on this side of the island. Martha was quiet, and Dan felt oddly uneasy. He was a married man. And he had no business being out on a lark with a pretty girl—even if she was his wife's niece. He found himself talking too much, being too jovial, self-conscious in Martha's presence.

"You should see the Kona side of the island," he said. He told of the lava flows, a tumbled mass of rusty red that covered miles, and of the white beaches rimming the sea.

He had ridden along the coast to survey the terrain, leaving Dusty and Juan behind. On one of those beaches, he had built a fire at night. He had seen what he'd thought to be a shark's white fin in the dark water. But when it came near, it proved to be a giant manta ray, four-cornered, as large as a table, with its deadly sting trailing behind. Kneeling on a point of lava, he had touched the thing. It had veered away, but returned to his hand.

"It liked to be petted?"

Dan reddened and laughed. "More likely it was after small fish attracted by the firelight," he confessed. "Though I'd like to think otherwise. It was quite an experience."

He went on to tell of how he'd traveled the road of the alii, going from Kailua to the City of Refuge, where those who were in danger, or those who had violated a *kapu* could flee to reach safety and be cleansed. There, the waters were like blue silk. It was a favorite spot of the Hawaiian kings.

I sound like a garrulous old man, he thought. *She's not even listening.* He spurred his horse ahead of her, far enough that there was no need for talk.

Martha wasn't listening, it was true. Martha was beginning to be frightened at what she planned to do. This was her last chance before they left for Lahaina; her last chance to help Dan realize it was her, Martha, he loved—and not Tamsen. Who knew, at Lahaina, they might not have a chance to be alone.

For some reason, the enormity of what she had

112

planned weighed heavily upon her. Dan Tallant was a married man, Aunt Tamsen's husband. But she doesn't love him, she told herself, And I do! She's been treating him miserably! And she has no right! She's not good enough for him! Surely, he knows what she's been.

Feeling her confidence slipping, Martha reached back into her mind, reliving the scene when she'd stood outside the parlor door in Barkersville. Her mother had admitted that the things Tamsen did were wrong. And because she looked like her aunt, she'd been watched, spied upon. She looked like Tamsen, and was the child of a mother who was no better—and one of two unknown men.

Well, she was not too good to resist taking the man she loved from his wife. But she was better than Tamsen! She was young, her reputation unsullied. She would give him children and make him happy—something Tamsen certainly wasn't doing!

The sun was halfway up the sky and they had been on the better road for sometime when she asked, "Are we almost there?"

"Almost," he answered.

In a short time, they turned down a small trail that led toward the sea. Here, there were a number of small rivers and falls. Finally they reached a spot starred with *hau* trees, their blossoms still yellow with the morning. Here and there, African tulip trees blazed with red trumpets, and a poinciana spread its flowered umbrella. A small stream flowed from a shadowy forest of tree fern. And in its dimness, a waterfall splashed silver over a grotto-like cave, spilling into a pool at its foot.

Martha caught her breath at its beauty. Dan heaved a sigh of relief. "It's still there," he said. "I was afraid it had been destroyed. Let's ride on

113

down to the beach. I want to see what's happened there—"

"You go," she said. "I want to go to the pool. You can come back for me."

"Well," he hesitated, "I suppose it's all right. There's nothing here to hurt you. The island has no snakes—"

She had climbed from her horse and was tethering it as he left her. He followed the U-shaped trail that bent at the edge of the sea. Here, there was a small beach. The waters today were limpid, blue, edged with lace frills. It seemed impossible that they had ever raged against the shore.

He wished that Tamsen were here. Everything he did, everything he saw, seemed to be in relation to the small girl-woman who was his wife. And since his return, he hadn't even been able to talk to her. The story he'd told Martha about the manta ray. He'd wanted to share it with Tamsen. Now he had narrated it, and the magic of that night was gone.

He'd understood her behavior in California to a degree. She'd wanted so much to be rid of her unsavory past that she'd swung violently in the other direction, becoming almost puritanical.

That, he mused gloomily, wasn't like his Tamsen at all. His Tamsen was the one he'd dreamed of —poised, waist-deep in that pool beneath the waterfall. And she'd refused to accompany him. He'd found himself here with a young girl, a child, really, who looked like Tamsen. And that was all.

Doubling his fist, he swung at the trunk of a palm tree in frustration. "Dammit, Tamsen," he groaned. "Oh, damn, damn, damn!"

He mounted his horse again, deciding to go back and collect his charge. All he wanted to do now was to get back to his temporary home.

As he neared the spot where he left her, he heard the sound of singing above the music of rippling water. A girl's voice. It sounded like Tamsen—when she used to sing. A ridiculous hopefulness stirred his mind. Was it possible that she might have changed her mind and followed?

He slid from his horse and walked toward the pool.

And there she stood! Tamsen! Waist-deep in water as he'd dreamed of her, the water falling silver over golden arms, black hair swinging to her waist—

He gave a strangled, inarticulate cry and she turned to face him, swinging her dark hair back to reveal her flawless rounded bosom. She beckoned—

Good God! Martha! He rubbed his eyes. He should have known, but it had been like his dream. And those arms lifted in invitation! Surely she didn't think that he—

"Get dressed," he said roughly. "It's time to start back. I'll wait for you."

He made his way through a tangle of flowering vines, blind to the beauty around him, mounted his horse and moved a way down the path, out of sight of the waterfall.

Martha joined him a few minutes later, her face demure. "It was a lovely place," she said. He did not answer.

They rode in silence, the leaves on the hau tree turning red as day deepened into afternoon. They reached the trail that led upward to Kapiki's home, and Martha suddenly reined in her mount.

"There is something wrong with his foot, I think."

Cursing inwardly, Dan dismounted, checking the animal's hooves. Martha was immediately beside him.

"There's nothing wrong," he said, after a cursory examination. He turned toward his own horse, but Martha's hand was on his arm.

"Dan," she said, "love me."

He looked at her, incredulous. "My God, Martha! You don't know what you're saying!"

"I do know," she said, her chin lifted. Then her words came out in a rush. "I love you, Dan! I can make you happy. Tamsen doesn't! I've seen how she treats you—"

"Tamsen's my wife," he said roughly. "What goes on between us is none of your business! What in the hell are you trying to do! My God! You're just a kid! I held you in my arms when you were a baby!"

"Then hold me now! You'll find I'm not a child!"

She had pressed her body to his, her lips raised invitingly. So like Tamsen! So like Tamsen! And he had needed Tamsen for so long! Had needed his wife—

He shut his eyes for a moment, sickly, then gave her a violent shove. Going to his horse, he mounted and stirred it into a canter with a slap of the reins. Let her follow as she would. She knew the way.

From behind him, he heard the sound of silvery mocking laughter. He couldn't know that tears were streaming down Martha's cheeks. She'd been so sure! So sure!

But by the time they reached the collection of huts, she'd convinced herself that, for a moment, he'd been tempted; that it was somehow all Tamsen's fault—and that she would win him in the end.

Reaching the edge of the clearing, Dan Tallant slowed his mount and waited for Martha to join him. It would look like hell, he thought, to come galloping in as if he were being pursued. He didn't look at Martha as she reined in beside him. But his expression of guilt was enough for Tamsen, who stood, holding Arab's child. She turned quietly and reentered the women's hut.

That night was to be their last on the beautiful, romantic, tortured island of Hawaii. In the morning, they would go down the trail to take ship for Lahaina, on the island of Maui. Pua had prepared a luau, an aloha celebration. A small pig had been roasted in the *imu*, the Hawaiian pit oven. There were a number of native dishes, among them: laulau, breadfruit, taro, raw fish, and kukui nut relish. A colorful tray held slices of melon, mango, and papaya.

After they had eaten, Pua danced for them, teeth flashing as she moved smilingly through the classic motions of the royal hula. Her plump hands moved gracefully, depicting rain, becoming birds in flight, poignant in a gesture of love.

"I be gawdamned," Nell whispered noisily to Tamsen. "Ef we had her at th' house, we'd a drawed 'em in like flies!"

Following the dancing, Pua issued a command. Arab's baby must have a name or the spirits would steal it away. Her name would be *Luka*. "Luka mean Ruth," she explained. And she had a reason for her choice. Ruth, in the missionary Bible, went to a strange land. And little Luka, touched by the Gods, would always be a stranger.

Tamsen felt a momentary chill at her words, but little Luka opened her long silver eyes. On her tiny face was the fleeting ghost of a smile.

Then Kapiki, in his resonant voice, began to tell tales of the Hawaiian gods. The firelight shone on his silver hair, his massive dark features alternately in light and shadow as he talked on and on. The story was about the volcano goddess, Pele; her sister, and a young man named Lohiau, whom they both loved.

Tamsen listened, without hearing, fascinated by the Kahuna's marvelous face, hypnotized by the drama in his tone—until he came to the end.

Standing at the brink of the crater where Pele simmered in anger, the sister, Hiiaka, and Lohiau, had appeared as man and wife. Pele, angered, tossed up fountains of lava, covering Lohiau, turning him to stone. And his spirit had fled.

Hiiaka, crazed with grief, began to tear open the sides of Pele's fiery pit, opening the way to the sea. Then she journeyed to the spirit land to find the ghost of Lohiau, restoring him to life.

"Hiiaka fight for Lohiau. Not give up."

Tamsen jumped. The old Kahuna's eyes were fixed on hers meaningfully, mesmerizing. He was speaking to her! And the others had gone. In the distance, she heard Martha calling goodnight to Dan.

Hiiaka had fought for Lohiau. And she would fight for Dan! Dear God, what a fool she'd been! Trying to hide under a somber veneer while that— that little ninny chased after her husband! When once she had been Madam Franklin—who could have had any man.

The past be damned, she thought fiercely. It was only the future that counted. That, and Dan. And if necessary, she'd use every trick of the profession she'd grown to know so well.

Two red spots burned in her cheeks as she rose, the old man's eyes still fixed on hers as she went toward him carrying Luka, for whom Arab would have to start taking responsibility tomorrow.

On the morrow as the little group headed down the trail toward Hilo, and thence to Lahaina, they would be presented with leis and small gifts made of shell. But Pua and Kahiki had already given gifts beyond measure. The life of Keokolo, sanctuary in time of danger, a name for little Luka—and a goal for Tamsen who had been lost for a while, trying to make herself into something she wasn't.

"Thank you," she said, formally. "*Mahalo.*"

"*He mea iki,*" he answered. "Just a trifle. You're welcome."

BOOK II
LAHAINA

13

Tamsen had no opportunity to get close to Dan the next day. In the flurry of departure, Nell burst into tears at parting from Pua. Juan and Arab were both still weak; Dusty, pale, but bristling with enthusiasm over the impending journey. Tamsen still was in charge of little Luka. Arab was in no condition to care for her along the trail. But as soon as they reached Lahaina!

They set off down the trail. Dan Tallant led the way, small Ramona with him. Martha followed close behind with Missy in her arms. Nell's mount shouldered Dusty's. The big woman determined to watch over her man, hell 'er highwater, as she put it.

Tamsen followed with her charges, Arab refusing to look at the baby Tamsen held in her arms.

Alohas followed them as they moved into the shelter of the trees. Tamsen looked back at Kapiki and Pua, envying them. Their life was one of such beautiful simplicity. They had lost their son, but they'd accepted their loss gracefully. Death was inevitable—a part of life.

Tamsen's eyes were wet with tears; the lei Pua had draped about her shoulders, crushed by the baby's small body filling the air with fragrance. Nell was bawling, unashamedly. They were halfway to Hilo before she ceased her noisy crying. Then she whacked Dusty on the shoulder.

"You little bastard," she snuffled. "Wasn't fer you, I'd a-stayed."

He winced, then looked at her with adoring eyes. "You can't mean that, old girl! A woman like you belongs to the world. You can't hide your light under a bushel!"

Nell mulled that over, then subsided. "Aw, hell," she sighed. "I guess yer right."

Martha's mount crowded close to Dan. Today, he was able to survey the girl's advances with an embarrassed amusement. After all, she was only a kid —with a crush on an older man. She had scared the hell out of him yesterday. Or maybe he'd scared himself. She looked so much like Tam that it had been a close thing there for a minute. But she wasn't Tamsen, she was Martha. As long as he remembered that, things would be all right. She'd forget all about him, once she met some good-looking young buck, closer to her own age. But in a way, it was kind of flattering, a girl like that falling for an old warhorse like him.

"Sonofagun," he said, unable to suppress a self-satisfied grin. "Sonofagun!"

Tamsen, bringing up the rear, felt a wave of nostalgia. The big island had shown her its darker side: leprosy, earthquake, volcanic eruption, and tidal wave. Still, riding through a flowering forest, brushing away lianas that touched her cheek, she felt she would never see a place so beautiful again. The blue skies smiled down, and ahead of them was Hilo with its whispering surf—and Lahaina.

Lahaina, on the island of Maui, where she

would have to face up to her problems and begin living again.

At Hilo, still shocked and crippled by the disaster, Dan disposed of the horses. A small boat, manned by a Hawaiian crew, rowed them to the waiting ship. It was an ugly little steamer crowded with passengers and gear. Chickens, pigs, and dogs set up an ear-splitting racket as they got under way.

Tamsen stood at the rail, holding Luka, and Dan moved to stand beside her. She smiled up at him, thinking how many times it had been like this. They had stood together, watching a shoreline recede, moving on—

Their moment of closeness was interrupted by a well-meaning passenger. Father Damien, the stocky little priest who had visited their home at Hilo was also aboard, and delighted at having their company. For a long time, he talked of his mischievous boyhood. It was not difficult to see the boy in the man, with his ruddy cheeks and snapping eyes. He went on to describe his transition into priest, telling how he'd come to the islands in place of his ailing brother Pamphile.

He loved the islands. Nowhere was there such need. They must be brought to the Truth, the power of the Kahunas removed—

"Are the Kahunas all so evil?" Tamsen asked in a muffled voice.

He looked startled. "No, indeed not. There are some who practice—shall we call it white magic? But it is all based on superstition and ignorance."

"I'm not so sure," Tamsen said quietly.

"Tamsen!" Dan was appalled, but Father Damien waved a placating hand.

"Sometimes, I'm not so sure either," he confessed, smiling. "And I should be."

He went on, extolling the beauty of the islands; the ease of living, with fish and fruit in plenty; the people with their gentle, generous hearts. He was concerned for them. Look at the way smallpox had devastated Honolulu some years before. Maui might have followed the same path, had it not been for the efforts of Reverend Baldwin. And then there was leprosy—

Tamsen shivered as he talked, telling of the edict forcing all lepers into exile on the island of Molokai. Superimposed against the sea, she saw a mental picture of the thing that invaded her house. Squatting in a rift in the rock, the remains of a moldy loaf of bread clasped to its bosom as it looked at her through empty eyes.

Where was it now? Now that the waters had washed the shore clean? Washed upward into the trees, to fester and spread its disease? Or into the sea, perhaps bobbing along in the wake of the ship, irresistibly drawn to human companionship.

Dear God!

Had she said those words aloud? Dan was looking at her with concern. "You don't look well, Tamsen. Perhaps you should lie down."

Ignoring her protests, he made arrangements for Martha to look after the baby. Surely, she and Arab could manage together. If not, there was always Nell. He steered her toward the small saloon, an extension of the stern cabin. It was fitted with double berths, no accommodation made in regard to race or sex.

Tamsen lay down, fully dressed. Several men had evidently decided to sleep through their journey, and their snores filled the air. She would never be able to sleep!

She hadn't taken into account her fatigue; the

fact that, for once, she wasn't responsible for Luka; the gentle swaying of the ship. She slept until morning, until Maui was in sight.

When she joined Dan and Father Damien, it was as if they'd never left their position at the ship's rail. In truth, both men had bedded down on deck. They turned at Tamsen's approach. "There is Maui, and there is Lahaina," Dan said, pointing at a cloud-crowned land mass in the distance.

Father Damien drew a small collapsible telescope from his cassock and squinted through it.

"Two whalers in the roadstead," he commented. "Several merchantmen. And an American battleship. I pray it means nothing—"

Dan Tallant was instantly alert. "Problems? What kind?"

"There are several factions in the islands. In 1866, a fight broke out on the floor of the legislature, between Hawaiians and whites. Now, a paper is being circulated: *Ka Makamae Hawaii*, The Loyal Hawaiian, protesting the American Party's return to office. The Hawaiians are afraid of being annexed, of losing their autonomy—"

"And what would you think if Hawaii were annexed?"

"I don't think I'd care to see it taken over by anyone."

Tamsen's eyes flashed to Dan. "That's because you're not an American," he said stiffly.

"Perhaps. But there's a way of life here that one finds nowhere else. It would be as if the world annexed paradise."

Dan was silent, and Father Damien uttered a cry of excitement. "Ah! Lahaina!" He passed his telescope to Tamsen, helping her position it. Before her, the landscape blurred, then came into focus.

Beyond a foaming reef and an interval of blue water lay a small town with many one-story houses; some of white-painted frame, others of grass, a few built entirely of coral. All had deep cool verandas, and were situated among dark groves of palms, bananas, *kukuis*, mango and breadfruit trees. Everywhere, flowers blazed. Behind the town, the brilliant green of sugarcane made a background. And where its growth ceased, the red Maui hills, with their pinnacles and chasms, soared to a height of more than six thousand feet, brilliant in the dawn.

It was a breathtaking sight, and Tamsen passed the telescope to her husband.

The knowledgeable little priest began to point out landmarks. The Catholic Church, erected in 1858. The courthouse, built from the salvaged material of *Hale Piula*, the former palace of Kamehameha III. Once Lahaina had been a royal court, a place of kings. And, see, there was the prison, built of coral. It was an essential building. Lahaina, at the height of the whaling era, now almost dead, had been a very wicked city.

For that matter, there was still a great deal of vice, despite the coming of law and order. With the end of the whalers, derelict sailors had chosen to remain here, homeless, jobless, content to live in a land where life was easy to sustain—perhaps believing that the days of whaling would return.

Lahaina, dreaming in the morning sun, looked very peaceful. But then, so had Hilo. "I understand there is a volcano here," Tamsen said nervously. "Do you know how long it has been since there was an eruption?"

"About 1790," the little man said pedantically. "The year Kamehameha conquered Maui, I believe. It was also the year of the Olowalu massacre, which was started by the crew of the American ship *Ella Nora*, Captain Simon Metcalf commanding. They fired on native boats after a truce was agreed upon, due to the murder of an American sailor."

He continued pouring forth encyclopedic facts to which Tamsen finally shut her ears. She wanted to absorb the atmosphere of this place that would be her new home. Unlike Hilo, there was a hint of breeze, ruffling the blue water beyond the reef.

At last, they were ferried ashore in a small dory. The American consulate had done the best he could for them. They had their choice of two places; a ramshackle warehouse building on the waterfront that smelled of fish, or a series of small grass huts in a kind of compound, situated on a defunct Hawaiian farm at the edge of town. They had once been used for visiting royalty, but had been abandoned in favor of newer, larger structures.

Tamsen opted for the huts without hesitation. Though the warehouse could be curtained off, the sharing of quarters did not appeal to her. Tonight, she would have a chance to be alone with her husband. And half the battle would be won.

She was to discover her choice had not been an inspired one. Set in a grove of banana trees, with a small spring at one side, the huts were picturesque. But they were all in various stages of disrepair. There were four of them, the largest about twenty feet long and twelve wide, the smaller ones perhaps eight by ten, the peaked roofs reaching six feet in the center. Built in an earlier day, the doors were small, only to be entered in a crawling position.

Dan entered the first, stretched his tall frame to its erect height, and hit his head on the ridgepole. The hut, perhaps for the first time, was treated to a burst of a white man's profanity. Tamsen could not help laughing, and, after a while, he joined in, sheepishly.

There was much to do. Several of the huts had settled to one side, the cage-like framework having snapped from age. The broken poles must be pulled back into place, splinted. Woven mats, covering the earthen floors, had deteriorated. Tamsen removed them, sweeping the areas clean. Dan worked frantically. Though he didn't plan to start his actual work for a week, he would be leaving early in the morning to consult with a number of planters. He didn't know how long he'd be gone, but he wanted to be sure all were comfortable in his absence.

As Tamsen worked, Ramona and Missy watched over little Luka. Dusty proved to be expert at tying thatch. Juan, Martha, and Nell made trip after trip into Lahaina, bringing back supplies: cooking pots, mats, foodstuff. Everything they'd owned had been lost at Hilo and must be replaced.

I wish they could bring me a new gown, Tamsen thought, wryly. She was still wearing the old ragged thing she had on when she took Arab up the trail to the Kahuna's home. She had been able to wash it there, draping herself in a length of tapa. But there had been no such opportunity of late.

Only Martha was decently dressed. And in Tamsen's things. She'd offered none of them back, and Tamsen would ask nothing of her. Tomorrow, with Dan gone, she would go into Lahaina and purchase material. When he returned, he would be in for a surprise.

"Surprise!" It was Nell's voice. She had panted her way back from another walk into the little whaling town. "Looky whut I brung yuh!"

She carried a covered pail of milk. Tamsen's

eyes filled with tears. It had been so long since she'd tasted it.

A scant cupful was allotted to everyone, except Dusty, who preferred his own type of liquid refreshment. Tamsen eyed the remainder, dubiously. Though it had tasted delicious, it was on the brink of turning. If the remainder could be saved until morning, she could make a milk gravy.

She set the pail in the run-off from the spring.

It was long after dark when the huts were finally fit for habitation. The larger house would be used for indoor dining, half of it sleeping space for Martha, Ramona, and Missy. The smaller huts for Dan and Tamsen; Juan and Arab; Dusty and Nell.

After a hastily prepared evening meal, Nell announced her intention of retiring. She felt like she'd beat off a bear with a switch, she complained. "Hurt all over." All present could agree with her feelings. They had worked themselves into exhaustion—all except Arab, who had spent the day napping beneath a tree. Dan's face was pale and drawn. He's worked harder than anyone, Tamsen thought. And for a long time. He'd managed, single-handed, to bring two hurt men through the earthquake's devastation. And he'd had little time to rest. In the morning, he'd be on his way again.

She spooned the last of the poi she'd brought from the big island into little Luka's mouth, a sense of desperation settling over her as she realized the supply must be replaced—and soon. She looked at Arab. Her sister had bound her breasts, but to no avail. She could care for the baby—if she would!

In the distance, she could hear Nell grunting as she negotiated the doorway to her hut. "Hell," she was saying, "them High-wayans is as big as me. Why couldn't they build theirselves a gawdam door!"

Her words brought a smile to the weary faces about the fire. Their smiles froze at her screech.

"*Mo-o*," she was shouting. "*A gawdam mo-o!*"

Dan was on his feet and gone in an instant. They heard the sounds of argument, and finally, he returned. "A lizard," he said. "Just a little lizard on the wall. It seems Pua told her the things are bad omens."

Dusty rose, a bit tipsy. "Jove! I should be there to protect her!" He wavered off in the direction of the hut.

"I'm for bed, too," Dan yawned. "Coming, Tam?"

"As soon as I finish feeding Luka."

They had all gone before the chore was accomplished. Tamsen stood, her lips tight. She walked to the little house Juan and Arab occupied, and called to them. At Juan's answering voice, she entered. The two lay on their sleeping mat, Arab's red curls spread against Juan's bare shoulder, glowing in the light of a string of Kukui candles.

Tamsen moved toward them, placing Luka in the small hollow between them. "Your child," she said. Then she turned and bent to make her way through the door, Arab's shocked voice calling after her. "Tamsen!"

Tamsen was free! Free! She would miss the baby: a hollow feeling was already spreading inside her. But now she could get on with her own affairs. She could go to Dan.

Dan was already sleeping. By the light of the Kukui, she could see the lines of fatigue and strain in his face, the new touch of silver at his temples. She undressed quietly, and lay down beside him. He moaned and turned to her, throwing an arm across her, pulling her close. But he still slept. It was an automatic gesture. And for now, it was enough. Later, he would waken. She could wait—

For a time she lay stroking the hard-muscled arm that held her, feeling the smooth skin of his tanned chest against her cheek. And finally, comforted by his nearness and dearness, she also slept.

It was nearly morning when she heard Juan's frantic whisper at the door of the hut. Disentangling herself from Dan's drowsy embrace, she wrapped a tapa cloth about her, and crawled outside.

Juan's dark Spanish face was tortured. "My God, Tamsen! We need you! Hurry! She's dying!"

Tamsen felt the night spin around her. "Arab? Oh, Juan!"

"Not Arab," he said, distractedly. "It's the baby —Luka."

14

Tamsen sent Juan back to Arab and salvaged her clothing from the hut, dressing outside in the darkness. She was still buttoning her gown as she ran across the compound to the Narvaéz dwelling. The baby's thin wail reached her ears, and her heart turned over.

Inside the hut, she found Arab frantically clutching the screaming child. Little Luka was bent backward like a bow, her tiny fists clenched, her face an odd shade of gray.

"I didn't mean to make her sick," Arab whimpered. "Oh, Tam! Have I killed her?"

Tamsen stared at her sister. "What did you do?" Her voice was low, quiet, cold.

"I couldn't stand to have her near me," Arab confessed. "When she cried, I—I gave her some of the milk Nell brought."

"The milk was already blink! Turning! Do you have any left?" She sniffed at the cup Arab proffered guiltily. "It's sour! In this climate! My God, Arab, you should have known!"

Snatching up a tapa to use as a blanket, Tamsen took the baby in her arms and knelt to pass through the door.

"Where are you going? Where are you taking her?" Arab's voice was ragged.

"To the medical mission, to see if I can find a doctor at this time of night. To see what happens to a child who's never had milk before—and then is given swill!"

"I shall go with you," Juan said, his jaw set.

Tamsen looked at him. "No. But I think Arab should. Maybe she'll learn something about being a mother." At his agonized expression, she relented. "You can come. But first, wake Martha and tell her where we are in case we're not back when Dan and the girls awaken—"

She did not wait, but hurried down the rutted cart trail that led from the compound to Lahaina. Once there, the building she sought wasn't hard to find. Father Damien had pointed it out to her from the sea.

Locating the mission, she banged at the door.

Young David Selwyn, healer of body and saver of souls, had finally managed to catch a few winks of sleep. It had been a bad night. First, a young girl with the beginning symptoms of leprosy. He would have to make the complaint that would banish her to the barbarous colony on Molokai. Then there had been a terrified native, his hands clasped to his throat. His spirit had been stolen by a *Kahuna poi uhane*, a professional spirit catcher. Now he would die. And despite the young reverend's ministrations, he did. Right there in the dispensary. And finally there had been an American sailor, knifed in a fight with a Britisher over the favors of a Hawaiian girl.

None of the incidents were unusual. It wasn't as if they hadn't occurred before. But tonight they seemed enough to try the soul of a young minister fresh from the austere rockbound New England coast. He could not see that he was accomplishing much here. The natives came to him only as a last resort, usually too late. Even those who were raised in the missionary schools, professed Christians, seemed to have tailored God to fit their heathen beliefs. He'd attempted to behave with utmost propriety, giving them a good example. But sometimes he had the feeling they watched, secretly amused at a young man who did not know how to enjoy the good things of life.

If it were not for Lani, the lovely half-caste daughter of a planter up the coast, he would chuck it all and go home; get a little office on Main Street. In truth, it was because of Lani, he *should* go home. With every smile, every unconsciously seductive movement of her body, she tempted him. He woke from sleep, his face burning from his wild and erotic dreams.

Worse, he had to face her after those dreams, since she worked with him as a volunteer during the day, boarding with a Hawaiian family nearby. Her manner was most circumspect. It was her friend, Kimo, who bothered him most. Of course, Lani's father was at fault, employing the burly young Hawaiian as his foreman, letting him run about dressed in only a twist of bright cloth unless he came to town. And allowing him to speak to Lani in such a familiar manner—

He thought of his last visit to Lani's home. Kimo, dressed in his sarong-like garment, a string of koa nuts and what appeared to be teeth about his neck, had approached them. "Lani!" he cried. "Aloha! E! You, Kimo, we go bushes! *Hana hou! Wiki-wiki!*"

He'd learned later that *"hana hou"* meant "do it again." It made him ill to think that the beautiful fragile creature, her mixed ancestry revealed in her high waist and long slender legs, might have allowed that ignorant native to touch her.

But she had only laughed, and Kimo had laughed too. He knew his face betrayed his shock, and he'd wondered, since, if they were laughing at him—

Depressed by his night's work, tormented by thoughts of Lani, he finally slept. Only to be awakened by a desperate banging on the dispensary door.

At least, these were Americans like himself. His eyes took in Arab, her glorious hair flaming above a tear-stained face, and Tamsen, the lovelier of the two, he judged, and a lady, by the clothing she wore, though it was woefully ragged. Then his glance fell upon the baby, writhing in spasmodic agony, and he forgot everything else.

Taking them into his dispensary, he placed the child on a table, his clever hands exploring its distended abdomen. He directed his questions to Tamsen, whom he wrongfully assumed to be the mother. His anger was apparent as she told him the baby had been reared with *poi*, the fermented paste of pounded taro. Until last night, when she was given milk that had gone sour.

He did not approve of the poi. A baby's diet should be consistent, any mother should know that. Milk should have been introduced in minimal amounts, and care should have been taken to ensure that it was fresh. Did she, herself, have a problem? A baby should be fed naturally. It was a wonder the little thing still lived.

He talked, not seeming to expect an answer, as he forced a few drops of something between the baby's lips. "Paregoric," he said matter-of-factly. Then he began to rub the small body with sweet oil, warmed to a comfortable temperature. Tamsen stood stiff and silent, accepting the accusing remarks directed at her, while Arab cringed.

At last little Luka was quiet, relaxed, one hand crumpled against her cheek as she slept, free from pain. "She will be all right, now," he said.

Tamsen swallowed tears of relief. "It's the first time I've ever heard her cry."

David Selwyn looked at her, an expression of consternation on his face. He reached for a small lamp and brought it close to the child's face, lifting one of the long-lashed lids that shielded Luka's silvery eyes. For a moment, he studied her, running his fingers over the soft blonde head.

"Was it a difficult birth?"

"Very," Arab said in a small voice.

"I was speaking to the child's mother—"

"I am her mother. I made her sick, and I knew better. But I was afraid of her. I thought she was cursed—"

"She was born on April second," Tamsen said hastily, "at the height of the eruption, in a place above Hilo—with the wife of a Kahuna in attendance."

"I see." David Selwyn looked at Arab with infinite compassion. "Have you taken her to a medical doctor before?"

She shook her head, and he sighed. "Then I'm going to have to tell you something you should know. The child is cursed, not by any God, but by a too-long, traumatic birth. There is a degree of retardation, how much, I cannot tell. But in my opinion, she will develop much more slowly than most children, and then only to a certain point. What that point will be, it is impossible to say."

Little Luka—Ruth—a stranger in a strange

land. Pua, Tamsen thought dazedly, knew what she was doing in selecting the baby's name.

Juan Narvaéz had been standing in the doorway for some time, unnoticed, his dark eyes filled with pain. Now, he moved forward in time to catch his wife as she wavered beneath the shock of Selwyn's pronouncement. For a moment, she leaned helplessly against her husband's chest. Then she turned, snatching the baby up, holding it in a fierce embrace.

"It's not true," she told the young missionary. "I don't believe it! I'm taking my baby home!"

She left the mission house, Juan following. When Tamsen moved to join them, David Selwyn put a detaining hand on her shoulder. "Let them go. I'd like to talk to you. Please sit down."

She obeyed. He washed his hands and prepared a pot of hot tea, pouring her a cup. She sipped at the reviving liquid, a little color coming back into her face. At his questioning, she described those last days in the clearing near Hilo; a place declared *kapu*. She told of Manu, the leper; how she had sent the others to the house of the *Kahuna*, finally fleeing with Arab, already in labor, up the long trail. And then the baby, born at the moment the big island exploded in flame.

Luka, as yet unnamed, had been given into Tamsen's hands, Arab somehow seeing the child as an inimical force.

"And the husband? Is he acquainted with all the facts?"

"I don't think so." She explained that Juan had been injured. He and Arab were both weak and ill when he returned. He'd probably thought it was natural for Tamsen to care for the child until Arab gained her strength; though lately, he'd been eyeing her with a puzzled expression.

139

"I think you should talk with him. Tell him everything. He will need all the facts to keep his family running smoothly."

"But it's all right now! She wants the baby. She's not afraid—"

"Sometimes the pendulum swings too far in the other direction. It is my guess that your sister may neglect her husband, her other children; turn into a lioness protecting one cub."

"You think she's—deranged?" Tamsen's voice quivered.

"On the contrary, I think she's a normal woman. She rejected the child, seeing it as the cause of her hurt, her terror. Now, seeing it as just a baby —who needs her—she will probably lavish all her affection on it. The little one will need special care. If the mother denies there is a problem, she may grow up like a vegetable, smothered in love. I think you can help her."

When Tamsen left, David Selwyn began clearing up after his night's work. As he replaced the paregoric and sweet oil on the shelves, his doubts of the previous night disappeared. His understanding of Arabella Narvaéz's problem amazed him. He was certain the advice he'd given her sister had not come from his mind, but God's. Perhaps he would make a medical missionary, after all.

Tamsen took the path back toward the compound. She must hurry. Dan would be ready to leave, and they'd had no time together. She reached the collection of huts to find Martha sitting by the fire. Not speaking, she passed the girl and went into her hut.

Dan was gone.

She went back to the fire, still without a word, and looked at Martha, a question in her eyes. The girl took her time, pouring herself another cup of coffee from the pot, then raising her gaze to meet that of her rival.

"Dan's gone," she said with barely concealed triumph. "One of the planters sent a messenger. He has to leave for Honolulu this afternoon, and wanted to see him before he left."

"But surely he wouldn't go when the baby—"

"He rode out when Arab and Juan came back. They said you'd stayed behind to talk to the doctor. Tell me, Aunt Tamsen," she said, her eyes glittered over the brim of her cup, "tell me, was he good looking? And what did you pay him for his trouble?"

With a muffled oath, Tamsen whirled and went into her hut. Trembling with anger and fatigue, she lay down on the bed made of mats. Because Arab was a damn fool, she'd lost her first night beside her husband in months. And because she, herself, was a damn fool, she'd stayed behind at the mission, discussing her sister's problems. "I think you can help her," the Reverend Selwyn had said.

Dear God, she'd helped everyone but herself all her life! She'd become a singer in a cantina, supporting her sisters, when she was no older than Martha! And from there, she'd gone on to become the proprietor of a house of ill fame. She'd stuck with Arab through the births of Ramona and Missy. And now she was expected to put Arab's life in order!

At one time, she'd taken a certain pride in being needed. Now, all she wanted was Dan! And it seemed her problems were multiplying as her sisters' families increased. There was some excuse for Arab, she thought, swallowing her resentment. But what about Em? Em discovered she had a problem in her daughter, and her first thought was, *Ship her off to Tamsen!*

That little ploy could work both ways! She rose from her bed and sought out the writing supplies she'd had Nell purchase yesterday in town.

"*Dear Em,*" she began.

After a dozen angry pages in which she poured out all her frustrations, she reread the blotched, heavily underscored lines. She couldn't send this! Not to her beloved sister. Wearily, she tore the paper into tiny pieces.

No, she would not send Martha home. She had to meet the girl on her own ground. This morning, she would go into Lahaina and buy material for new gowns; a comb, a brush, a bottle of scent.

And then she would wait for Dan to come home.

15

Lahaina's streets were crowded. Even in San Francisco, Tamsen had not seen such a mingling of cultures. It was a Saturday. Prosperous planters and their families drove through the streets in polished carriages. Everywhere, Hawaiians moved, tall, sturdy women in holokus of black, white, crimson, yellow, rose, and bright green. Many of them were crowned with garlands of flowers that filled the air with haunting perfume.

Their men were also birds of bright plumage, dressed in white trousers and shirts of brilliant print, opened to show smooth brown chests. They wore necklaces of shell, of polished seeds, and sometimes of braided human hair.

Beside the immense Hawaiians, the Chinese were small in their neat clothing, all looking alike with their yellow faces and braided pigtails. Where the Hawaiian people moved majestically, eyes and teeth flashing as they called greetings to one another, the little Chinese went silently about their business.

There were also a few Japanese, newly arrived. They were the *Gannen Mono* or first-year people, imported laborers, who must work in the cane fields until their contracts expired. There were people of mixed blood, a few Negroes, and a scattering of dark-skinned Polynesians. Here and there, an unshaven, drink-bloated face appeared in the crowd, and Tamsen knew, instinctively, these were the derelict sailors Father Damien had talked about. She had seen such men in mining camps, lost, unhappy. Men who would never have a home.

It cast a cloud on her day. It was dispelled when she found a wealth of materials in Lahaina's few stores. She bought recklessly, having the things she couldn't carry delivered to the compound.

She would not keep the making of these gowns a secret. She showed the cloth when the group had gathered together for the evening meal, daring Martha with her eyes. If the girl filched one of her new dresses, everyone would know. "I've decided to take your advice, Nell," she laughed. "Now, help me decide how to make them up."

Nell was unable to arouse much enthusiasm. That little sonofabitch, Dusty, had gone into Lahaina earlier in the day. "Prob'ly drunk ez a skunk," she said dolefully. "Mebbe layin' somewhere on th' waterfront, with his gawdam head bashed in."

Tamsen tried to comfort her, but it was an impossible task. Before daylight, Nell awakened her. Dusty hadn't come home all night.

"It isn't the first time, Nell."

The big woman's jaw jutted. "Fust time in a strange town. Hell, Tam, you know whut a gawdam innercent he is! I figger he's got hisself into some bad company," she added virtuously. "They's allus wimmen lookin' to pick up a slick gent like him, lead 'em astray!"

Tamsen felt like laughing at her outraged expression. Nell, former dealer in a gambling joint!

Manager of a bawdyhouse! And not even married to the man she lived with. Surely, Dusty was sleeping it off, somewhere—

But as the day dragged on, she, too, began to worry. Finally, she consented to accompany Nell into town. To hide her concern, she teased Nell. "Why don't you marry him, and make an honest man of him? Then he wouldn't dare do this kind of thing?"

Nell blinked her eyes rapidly and blew her nose. "Me? Marry that scrawny little sonofabitch? Hah! But wait'll I ketch him! I'll kick his butt up to a hunnert an' sixty!"

They searched the streets and the alleys, knocking at the closed doors of grog shops, asking tipsy grounded sailors.

Finally, Tamsen thought of David Selwyn at the mission house. A pretty half-Hawaiian girl admitted them and asked them to wait. Doctor Selwyn was with a patient. It seemed hours before a small Chinese gentleman made his exit from the dispensary, his arm in a fresh splint. Despite his injury, he bowed a number of times to the waiting women.

"He done that once more," Nell growled, "his gawdam head woulda fell off."

Tamsen's efforts to shush her were of no avail. The doctor, Reverend Selwyn, stood in the doorway to the inner room, his mouth drawn in a disapproving line.

"I will do the talking," Tamsen said fiercely. But her voice trembled as she explained their errand. Selwyn's look of concern over the missing man faded as Tamsen gave his description.

They had come to the right place, he told them grimly. He knew exactly where the man was. He'd gotten into a brawl with an Irish sailor the previous night. He had treated him for a head wound. He'd been struck with a bottle.

"Then it's awright," Nell said, heaving a gusty sigh of relief. "Little sonofabitch—par'm me, Reverent—is prob'ly home by now. Hell—Par'm me agin, Reverent—ez long ez it's his *head,* we don't have to worry none."

Nell was wrong. Reverend Selwyn had treated Dusty in the prison, where he had been taken, charged with public drunkenness, and inciting to riot. It took the combined efforts of Reverend Selwyn and the American consul to free him. Then it was only on Tamsen's promise to ensure his further behavior.

Dan will be livid, Tamsen thought as she herded a quarreling Dusty and Nell back to the compound. The success of his venture depended on the goodwill of the citizenry, both white and Hawaiian. She felt like braining Dusty herself.

But the sight of his woebegone face beneath the now stained and dirty bandage stayed her. Dusty was British to the core. If the Irish sailor had made disparaging remarks about his native country, his gallant nature would have compelled him to enter into battle, drunk or sober . . .

Doubtlessly, he had been drunk. In spite of his faults, he had always been there when she needed him.

One thing for sure, he and Nell between them had managed to change her plans. She had thought, when her gowns were completed, of trying to enter into the social life of Lahaina. Perhaps in meeting important people, such as the American consul, she might be of some help to Dan.

Well, she had met the consul, in her worn and dusty gown and in the company of a woman who swore like a trooper while searching for a man who had been involved in a drunken brawl.

She had an idea that an invitation to return her visit to the consul's home would be long in coming.

By nightfall, Dusty had managed to convert his humiliating experience into an act of heroism. The sailor who struck him attained gigantic proportions each time he related the story of his adventure. Looking back, he was certain he managed to get in a few telling blows before he was struck in such a cowardly fashion.

"Jove, Nell, I wish you had been there."

"Me, too," she said with feeling. "I'da whupped hell outta him!"

"I handled it quite well," he said modestly. "I mean, I wish you could have seen the place. You, too," he said, bowing to Tamsen. "I believe you might be able to give the owner some pointers."

He expanded on his story. He had met a sailor on the streets of Lahaina. They went to a small park, where they finished off Dusty's bottle, then his new friend had taken him to a place outside the limits of the town. It was a large house, operated by an old sea captain, called Billy Whiskers. A pseudonym, of course. There was a bar, entertainment, girls—

"I was only interested in it as a business setup," he said hastily, seeing Nell's thunderous expression. "The place has no *class*. I spoke with the owner, suggesting that you and Tamsen might be able to—"

Tamsen rose hastily. "Nell and Tamsen will do nothing," she said tartly. "And you will do your drinking on these premises, or not at all. Moreover, you are not to go into town alone. Is that clear? Now, I suggest you go to bed and sleep it off!"

She left the fireside. Nell rose too. "Come on, you leetle bastard!" She waddled toward the hut she shared with Dusty, but he remained looking forlornly into the dying embers. In spite of his head wound, his escapade had been quite exciting to him, taking him back to the old days—

He jumped a little, looking up at Martha as she spoke. He hadn't realized the girl was sitting there. "Uncle Dusty," she said, "where is this place? Tell me about it. It sounds thrilling."

He hadn't lost his audience after all. Straightening his thin shoulders, he smiled at her. He began the story again, and Martha hung on every word with rapt attention.

In the days that followed, Dusty's delinquency was almost forgotten. Dan sent a message that he would be gone longer than he'd planned. He, too, had gone to Honolulu, to confer with certain people. The actual surveying would be delayed for a short time.

Tamsen was both disappointed and relieved. At least, she would have the opportunity to complete her wardrobe. Unfortunately, she was to discover her problems hadn't ended. Arab, as the young missionary doctor suggested, had turned into a doting mother. She hovered over little Luka day and night, allowing no one else to touch the child. The doctor had lied, she kept asserting, angrily. Anybody could see that this was a perfect baby!

Juan, troubled, came to Tamsen with his concern. Arab wasn't—Arab, anymore. She had no time for him. She was neglecting Ramona and Missy—

Tamsen looked at the children. They sat disconsolately on a log at the edge of the compound. And they did look like little orphans, skirts bedraggled, hair in lumpy braids. Juan had a flush on his high Spanish cheekbones. "I do the best I can," he admitted, "but I don't know how—"

"I'll bathe them," Tamsen said. "But they'll have to have new clothes sewn for them. I'll talk to Arab."

"It won't accomplish anything. I've tried. Her preoccupation with Luka—Tamsen, it isn't normal—"

Talk to her husband, Selwyn had said. She hadn't done it, Tamsen thought guiltily. There had been too many other things on her mind. She told Juan the story of Manu, the leper; that Arab's nightmare at the *kapu* place near Hilo had been quite real. She described their terror at the quakes, telling how she'd found Arab on the beach in shock at the horror the riven rock revealed. Arab had gone into labor then. She was still in labor the next day when they'd fled to the hut of Kahiki and Pua. Tamsen described the travois-like litter on which Arab had been dragged, moaning in agony, along the trail as the earth trembled and shook beneath her.

"She didn't tell me," Juan said, his eyes haunted. "My God! What she must have gone through!"

"The baby isn't normal, you know that." Tamsen looked at him, levelly.

"Dios, Tamsen! Do you think that makes a difference? She is my child! I will love her as I do the others!"

"Arab went through more pain and fear than her mind could cope with. The leper was a—a terrible thing to see. The place we lived was *kapu.* The baby was born in a Kahuna's hut, at the moment the island erupted. You've seen the child's birthmark?"

Juan nodded. "It seems to be fading. It will be concealed by her hair—"

"Arab decided the baby was cursed. She was terrified of her. She didn't touch her until the night I brought her to your hut."

"I knew something was wrong," Juan confessed.

"But I was ill. Then I thought perhaps you cared for Luka because Arab was still weak. Oh, God, Tam! Do you think Arab has lost her mind? What can I do!"

"She's sane enough. I think she's trying to give the baby enough attention to make up for her neglect. We've got to give her all the love and understanding we can. Do you see?"

He nodded and she stood, briskly. "Now, I'll see what I can do about the girls."

One of her lengths of material would make four muu-muus, such as the Hawaiian children wore. She snipped it ruthlessly into two outfits for Ramona, two for Missy. Then she went in search of Nell and Martha, putting them both to work at stitching.

Nell groused that she hated that gawdam sewing, Martha complained that she was tired.

She did look bad, Tamsen thought as she watched the smooth dark head bent above the bright material. These last few days, she'd been dragging about, circles beneath her once sparkling eyes. Could she possibly be ill? More likely, she thought bitterly, she was pining for Dan.

Pushing the notion from her mind, she said, distractedly, "This is going so slowly. We'll never get done. Perhaps I should try to get Arab to help."

"She won't leave her baby," Martha said, "and I don't blame her. I'll always hold my baby when I have one."

Tamsen jabbed her finger with a needle. The girl's remark—the way she'd looked, especially in the mornings—*Was it possible that she and Dan . . . ? Dear God, no!*

Two of the gowns were soon finished, one for each child. Tamsen heated water on the outside fire, bathed the children and washed their hair. Clean, dressed in the comfortable little gowns, they were beautiful—even Ramona, the family's ugly duckling. Her big wide-set eyes were shining, the button nose pink at the end with excitement, her wide mouth elfin as she smiled. "I want to show Mommy," she said.

"Wait!" Tamsen plucked two hibiscus blossoms, tucking them behind each small girl's ear. Elated, they ran toward the hut where Arab tended the baby, Tamsen following.

They entered, giggling, and Arab looked up. "Sh-h! You'll wake Luka."

"Look at us, Mommy! See our new dresses? And we've had a bath!" Ramona was dancing in her excitement.

"Very nice." Arab's glance swept over them and back to little Luka's sleeping face. "You know, Tamsen, I think this baby is going to be the beauty of the family. She's even prettier than Missy."

The light went out of Ramona's eyes and she stood stolidly as Tamsen put an arm around her. "They're all beautiful," she said, her voice tight. "You're very lucky, Arab."

"I know," Arab said mechanically. Her mind wasn't on what she was saying, for little Luka had moved a hand.

Taking the girls with her, Arab went in search of Juan, who was properly appreciative, picking up each girl, tossing them in the air, tickling them until they squealed.

"Daddy's fun," Ramona said wistfully when he had gone. "I wish we could sleep with him and Mommy, so we wouldn't be so scared."

Tamsen stopped in her tracks. "Scared? What are you afraid of, Ramona? Martha stays with you, and she's a big girl."

"She did for awhile," the little girl said. "But now, she's always gone. Sometimes, Missy cries. I don't cry, though, because Missy would get more scared." She looked up at Tamsen pleadingly. "Don't tell Martha I told."

"I won't," Tamsen said in a stunned voice. She knelt beside Ramona and tried to question her. The little girl had nothing more to offer. Martha got dressed up and went out after they were in bed. She came home before daylight. That was all Ramona knew.

"Your Uncle Dan's away," Tamsen told her. "And I've been lonesome. Tonight, you can spend the night with me."

The children were ecstatic and Tamsen laughed with them, but her laughter didn't reach her eyes.

Dear God, what kind of a problem faced her now!

16

Tamsen's first instinct was to go to Martha and face her with what she'd discovered. She quelled it, knowing that she would probably learn nothing, and that the girl would ignore anything she had to say. If Dan were here, he might have some influence over her, but he was away. Juan? No, Martha's trampish behavior would be beyond the comprehension of the well-bred Spaniard. Besides, he had problems of his own.

She stitched away, hemming a third gown for herself, a dark crimson that would be the loveliest of them all. But her mind wasn't on what she was doing. Martha was a strange girl. She adored the little girls. Why on earth would she leave them? Maybe it was all Ramona's imagination. Martha might slip out at night for a brief walk around the compound. To a child's mind, it could appear she was gone for hours—

That night, Ramona and Missy asleep in the security of her hut, Tamsen slipped out, going to the larger structure that was allotted to Martha and the children. It was empty. Martha was gone.

She returned to her bed to lie wakeful the remainder of the night, her mind going back to the time when Martha was a baby, when she had loved her as her own. Then the little Martha she knew in the gold fields along the Fraser River—a spunky, sturdy child, always laughing, loving—

What had happened to change her?

Sleep was impossible. Toward dawn, she tiptoed from the hut once more. Martha had not yet returned. Then what Ramona said was true, Tamsen realized with dismay.

Her last foray, at dawn, proved more fruitful. Martha lay curled up on her sleeping mat, her clothing in a heap on the floor. In a mass of petticoats and underthings, Tamsen recognized one of her old, more seductive gowns. On Martha's bare arm was a bracelet she hadn't seen before. The jade stone studding silver, looked real. And there was a slight scent in the air, reminiscent of Dusty. The girl had been drinking.

Tamsen went to the other end of the long room and began moving pots and pans, rattling them angrily. Martha opened dull eyes. "What are you doing? It's not morning."

"It is morning," Tamsen hissed. "We're going to have an early breakfast."

"I'm not hungry," Martha yawned. She went back to sleep.

All day, Tamsen raged inside. She washed her hair and pinned it up in a softer fashion, donning her new crimson gown. She had been saving it for when Dan came home, but she felt she needed the confidence it gave her.

Even Arab was jolted from her preoccupation with Luka long enough to admire the change in her sister. Juan complimented her gravely, the little girls were enraptured, and Martha, finally awake, looked at her with envious eyes.

It was Nell and Dusty who were most delighted. "Hell, girl, yuh look like a gawdam Christmas tree," Nell boomed.

"Like old times," Dusty breathed. "My word! Just like old times!"

Tamsen's eyes brimmed for a moment. How she loved these two people! The sad-looking, tippling little Englishman; the bawdy old woman who had been with her through many trials. Here was someone she could share her worry with.

"Nell," she said, "Dusty—We've got a problem with Martha. And we've got to do something about it. We owe it to Em."

She told them what little Ramona had said, that she had checked on the girl, and that it was true. Martha was slipping out at night. She didn't know if she were meeting someone—or where she went during those hours of darkness.

Dusty fingered his scraggly moustache, recalling the girl's questions about Billy Whisker's place. Perhaps he had gone a bit overboard that night, investing the place with a glamour it lacked as he basked in the warmth of Martha's attentiveness. His face reddened as he recalled his exaggerated descriptions of the festivities that took place there. Martha had asked where it was.

"Maybe I'll walk by and see the outside in the daytime," she'd laughed.

But she wouldn't go there, he thought. Not unaccompanied. Not a young thing like Martha! Or— would she?

"I think," he said guiltily, "I may have an idea—"

He stated his suspicions and Nell went into a flaming rage. "Gawdam little eejit!" she roared. "We's goin' over there tonight, Dusty! You an' me! Ef she shows up, I'm gonna beat th' hell outten her! Kick her butt all th' way home! Em knew what she was up to, she'd have herself a fit!"

"You're not going," Tamsen said, her voice tight. "I am. I'm responsible for her. Besides, Dusty's on his good behavior. I don't want him back in jail."

Nell was crestfallen. "Aw, hell!" But she had to admit that Tamsen was right. She conceded to Tamsen's plans. Nell would stay in the large hut with the children tonight. Tamsen would wait outside Billy Whisker's House of Pleasure and watch for Martha.

If she didn't come, they could assume she was meeting some man. If this were true, they would enlist Juan's aid if necessary.

That night, Tamsen stood in the darkness outside a rambling, leaning structure that had perhaps once been a warehouse. It was built on the beach, looming bleakly against the background of the sea. Here, a scattering of koa trees and palms grew close to the water. Tamsen had found shelter in their shadow. The approach to the building, across the sand, was illuminated by a full moon that glinted on the structure's tin roof. It was an excellent spot to see—and not be seen.

Tamsen waited, hoping against hope that Dusty had been wrong; that Martha would not come. She recognized the character of the place. It was probably on a level with the cantina where her own career began. But she had not been a sulky, rebellious girl as Martha was, and she'd had Nell to watch over her. Martha had no one.

It was still early in the night, and already she could hear the sounds of breaking glass, a man's rough swearing, a girl's scream. Then a lewd remark reached Tamsen's ears above the other racket, a woman's laughter. It was all so familiar, a scene out of her own past, that she put her hands over her ears. She concentrated on the waters beyond, the gentle waves that lapped along the shore, their whispering drowned out by the noise from the structure that defiled the view.

She almost missed seeing the small slim figure that flitted across the sands. The door to the structure opened, drawing her attention, and she sensed, rather than saw, that it was Martha who entered. Then the door was closed, and she heard a chorus of male voices crying out in welcome. "Here's the little lady, now!" "Hello, sweetheart!" "Give us a kiss! Yer a sight fer sore eyes!" And a Hawaiian voice, *"Hui! He wahine u'i!"*

She had lived through this before, she thought dully. Oh, God! She couldn't go in there! Not alone! And she wasn't even sure it had been Martha.

She sat down, her head in her hands, as she heard the sound of raucous music accompanied by the noise of clapping hands and stamping feet. She finally stood, brushed the skirt of her crimson gown, and looked away, toward the red hills that soared against the horizon, black, now, except for a spot touched by moonlight. It looked like a trail of blood.

Drawing a deep breath, she walked toward Billy Whisker's House of Pleasure, opened the door and went in.

For a moment, she went unnoticed. All eyes were fixed on the girl in the center of the floor.

It was Martha.

Tamsen stood silent, swallowing her anger, surveying the girl with a cold assessment. Martha was beautiful, of course. Her voice was passable. But her inexperience and youth certainly showed in her overstated, exaggerated movements. She would like to have the chance to show her a thing or two! If she

157

were going to do something, she might as well do it right! Oh the little fool! To throw her life away like this—

Martha's song ended and a burly sailor lifted her, standing her on the bar. She threw her head back, laughing, feeling a heady sensation of success. Tamsen wasn't so great, after all! She could probably do as well, or better, already, and she'd only just begun. And if a whole room full of men admired her, wanted her, then why not Dan Tallant? If Tamsen thought—

Her eyes widened. From her vantage point, she could see the figure in the doorway, clad in crimson, like a slender flame. Tamsen! What was she doing here? How had she guessed? Her eyes narrowed. So the spying had begun here, too! Probably instigated by her mother! Mama and Aunt Tamsen, trying to make a silk purse out of a sow's ear! A lady out of a—a bastard. And they'd made her what she was.

She tossed her head and raised a hand for silence. "Thank you," she said, curtsying prettily. Then, "I have a treat for you. I'd like to introduce you to a woman who taught me all I know. She, too, was an entertainer when she was *young*. All that was years ago, of course, but I'm sure she will be able to do *something* for you—if she can *remember*, after all this time."

Tamsen stood stunned for a moment, then her lips twitched in a reluctant smile. The little cat! Well, she had two choices: to leave the place immediately and speak with Martha when she came home, or to join her in her own game.

She chose the latter.

The hem of her gown lifted in one hand, her arm crooked gracefully, she swept up the avenue formed by gawking sailors as they stepped aside. There was dead silence as the two met, the woman and the girl. Tamsen met Martha's eyes. They were defiant, but something in them was terribly young, hurt and vulnerable.

"Thank you, Martha," she said in a soft whisper. "I will try to perform, despite my advanced years." She spoke to the guitar player and his eyes widened. The newcomer was clearly a lady, and the title she mentioned was that of a very naughty song. He stirred, uneasily, certain he'd misheard, but obediently began to strum the preliminary chords she'd requested.

As he strummed, she took the pins from her hair. It fell in a silken waterfall of black, reaching her slim waist. With two deft movements, she tucked up the crimson gown on both sides, looping it into the ribbon that belted the dress, revealing segments of a shorter, ruffled white petticoat and a daring glimpse of slender ankles.

There was a gasp, then a roar of approval. The guitar player, eyes popping, stumbled, then picked up the beat as she moved outward on the floor.

And then her song began—

Where Martha's movements had been merely suggestive, Tamsen's were seductive, sinuous. No childish wriggling here. This was a woman, with a woman's voluptuous body. Every man in the room recognized it and wanted her. She could see their wanting in their eyes. An old derelict in the rear of the room choked on his cud of tobacco. His best buddy shoved him out the back door with one movement, and turned to feast his eyes on the vision before him. She was singing just for him. He knew it! And the same held true for the others in the building. Each knew the naughty words of invitation were directed at him alone. The crowd swayed forward as her hands gestured them to her, backward as she put them palms forward in a sign of mock negation.

The song ended with a gesture of surrender, a hike of the ruffled petticoat that promised more than it revealed. And Tamsen bowed her head to applause that shook the rafters.

"More!" they pleaded. "More!"

"Bigod," someone choked, "it's just like home. There's this house in Saint Louie—"

"Shaddup," another man growled. "Yer drunk. Go ahead Sweetheart, give us another—"

Tamsen did as she did those long years ago. "Make them smile," she'd told Nell so often. "Then make them cry." Standing in the circle of men, her dark hair swung back as she looked upward, her face an oval of purity. And she sang her father's favorite song. *"Black is the color of my true love's hair—"* Her seductive movements were gone as she turned about to reach the ears of all who encircled her, moving with the grace of a drifting leaf, her hands clasped at her bosom.

When she had finished, there was dead silence. Then a few embarrassed sniffles signaled for even more thunderous applause. Tamsen curtsied again.

It had been an exhilarating experience, knowing that she had, once more, held an audience in the palm of her hand. The old feeling of power had returned to drum in her veins, the knowledge that she possessed a kind of magic that could reach out and touch every man present. She was dizzy with power. Drunk on it, like wine—

Then her knees went weak. She was no longer an entertainer. She was Tamsen Tallant, wife of a respected man. She had no business being here in a place of ill repute! The faces around her ranged from brutal and bearded—to senile, bewhiskered and leering. Dear God, she had to get out of here!

"Martha?" She scanned the room for the girl. Martha had gone. The other women present, a few blowsy creatures, watched sullenly from the corners of the room.

"Thank you," Tamsen said, curtsying once more. "Now, I must go—"

"Like hell, you will!" A squat stocky man barred her way. "I come ter be entertained, I'm gonna git whut I come fer. Give us another look at them legs—" He snatched at her exposed petticoat, and she jerked away, leaving a length of ruffling in his hand.

"Now, that's what I calls a souvyner," he said. "My buddy, Clem here, wants one too."

He reached for her again, this time ripping her bodice. She cowered from him, covering herself with her hands, as another burly sailor jerked him backward, crashing a fist into his jaw.

"Sorry, ma'am," her rescuer bowed. "He's drunk. Some fellers ain't got no manners. How about you come along with me? We'll have us a private—"

His sentence broke off as a bottle crashed against the side of his head. A swarthy man lifted a bench and rushed at his friend's attacker. "Sonoma-beetch!" he shouted in an unrecognizable accent. "I keel you!"

He was intercepted by someone else's fists. Soon the room was a swirl of fighting swearing men. Someone slammed into Tamsen and she was crushed against a wall. She put a hand to her mouth. Her lip was bleeding. She had to get to the door! She had to!

Moving along the walls, she ducked and flinched. The room seemed to be filled with flying ob-

161

jects. The door was open. Billy Whisker, himself, stood in the aperture. "*Pilikia*," he was shouting. "*Pilikia!*"

Unable to pass him, she managed to slide beneath his arm—and into the hands of a young Hawaiian Guard, a multitude of white-helmeted cohorts behind him.

"Help me," she sobbed. "Please—help me."

Two men were assigned to guard her, the others entered the building to quell the riot. Billy Whisker joined Tamsen, speaking to those who watched over her in a mingling of Hawaiian and pidgin English. It was not his fault the *pilikia*—trouble—had started, he told them piously. It was the woman. A common prostitute, who had wandered in and started a fight between the men. He would be pleased if they would remove her from his premises.

"It isn't true," Tamsen cried, agonized. "He's lying! Can't you tell by looking—?" Her voice halted. Her gown was still looped up, revealing her petticoat and ankles. Her petticoat was torn, her bodice ripped to the waist. Her hair was down and in wild disorder, her face bruised, her lips bleeding.

"Damn you!" she cried furiously at her accuser. Then she wished she could have swallowed her words. She'd only set the dreadful things he said in the Guards' minds. They looked at her with mingled curiosity and repugnance.

When the Captain of the Guards returned, he insisted upon knowing if she had conformed to the act requiring prostitutes to register and submit to medical inspection.

"Of course not," she said hotly.

Tamsen Tallant was marched off, along with a number of drunken, stumbling men, Guards at either side. When they reached the prison, she insisted that a message be sent to the American consul, or to David Selwyn.

A Guard snickered. She would see Selwyn in the morning.

Tamsen was thankful she wasn't thrown into a common cell with the drunken men. But after a night shut in a room with a mad woman, covered with syphilitic sores, and gibbering, she was not too sure.

17

Martha had left Billy Whisker's place at the beginning of Tamsen's song. She was furious with both Tamsen and herself. She'd thought the older woman would refuse to go along with her invitation to sing, or if she did, she'd be shown up as an aging entertainer.

It hadn't worked that way. The minute Tamsen took the floor, she'd taken control. For the past few nights, Martha had been the darling of the place. Tamsen had made her look silly! Like an amateurish schoolgirl. She'd stepped back into the circle of men, and nobody'd even noticed her. They probably didn't know she was gone—and didn't care.

Her cheeks still burning with humiliation, she entered the largest of the huts, only to find her sleeping mat occupied. It was occupied by Nell. And she was awake. She reached up, catching Martha's wrist.

"So you come home! Where the hell you been?"

Martha jerked away, rubbing her arm. "Out," she snapped. "Now, I'd like to go to bed."

"Like hell you will! You'n'me's got some jawin' to do." Nell rose, a formidable figure in her billowing nightdress. "Outside," she barked. "I don't wanna wake them kids." In the outer darkness, she said, "Awright, you little bitch! Where's Tamsen."

Martha stood sullenly quiet as Nell raged. Finally, her nerves at the breaking point, she yelled back. "All right! All right! I went to Billy Whisker's place. What are you going to do about it?"

"I dunno," Nell said glumly. "Smack yer butt, mebbe. Have to think on it. Now, where's yer aunt?"

Martha's lip curled derisively. "She's at the same place, Nell. When I left, she was singing and dancing."

"Yer joshin'," Nell said in a feeble voice. "Er liein', one." Finally, seeing the truth in Martha's face, she said, weakly, "Well, I be damned!"

Deciding to delay judgment on Martha's escapade, Nell went to her own bed. She didn't begin to worry until the next morning. Tamsen had still not come home. Finally, she pulled on a clean muu-muu and groaned her way into town, accompanied by Dusty. Puffed up with importance, he led her through Lahaina, and for some distance along a beach at the other side. Occasionally, she had to sit down and rest. "Gawdamit, Dusty, my dogs is barkin'! Ef I'd knowed it was so far, I'd of rid a horse. Ef I had me a horse," she added as an afterthought.

Dusty's injured leg was aching, but he gallantly withheld the fact. It was a man's duty to care for his lady.

After all their walking, their errand proved futile. Captain Billy Whisker's place was locked, closed for repairs. There was no answer to Nell's repeated pounding. Nell grimaced, took off her shoes, and cooled her feet in the waves at the edge of the beach as she pondered.

"Dusty," she said finally, "I dunno what the hell

to do now—less'n we go see that missionary feller—"

Painfully, they made their way back to town.

Again, the Reverend Doctor David Selwyn was not a happy man. Lani's father had come into town only this morning, bringing his foreman, Kimo, with him. "Young David here doesn't seem busy," he'd said to his daughter. "Why don't you and Kimo run along? Have a good time. Maybe David would like to talk a little man-talk for a change."

It was the first time the man had addressed him as anything but Reverend or Doctor. Selwyn supposed he should be pleased. But Kimo had made some remark in his own language as they left, something that made Lani blush and laugh; something *lewd*, the missionary was certain. And her father hadn't turned a hair.

Even worse, their conversation had been dull and quite uninspiring. The man was obviously a hypochondriac. Odd that it hadn't shown in their talks before! What were the symptoms of tuberculosis? Heart disease? Leprosy? Kidney disease? Yet he looked healthy enough.

Selwyn studied him, seeing a big man, sandy hair lightly touched with gray above hot blue eyes. He seemed in superb condition, approaching middle age. His chest was broad and deep, his waistline thickening only a little. He moved with the panther-like grace of a man accustomed to the out-of-doors. If he were ailing, why didn't he come right out and say so?

As the conversation stayed with medical subjects, David cast a furtive look at the note on his desk. Signed by a prison official, it was a request that he examine a woman now being held in custody. *White, aged 38, profession, prostitution. No record of registration or medical inspection.*

She would be held until he had given her a clean bill of health. If she were infected, she would be hospitalized. He hated this part of his job. But someone must do it. And he hated to keep anyone waiting, even an imprisoned prostitute.

"And what about cancer?" the man before him was asking now. Sighing, Selwyn gave him a textbook description of the symptoms of various types. Then, seeing that Lani's father had run short of ailments, he asked, rather tartly, "Are you interested in the effects of venereal disease?"

His companion jerked up his head, the hot blue eyes blazing. There was only a brief moment when Selwyn wondered if he would be struck down. Then his caller began to laugh; helpless, infectuous laughter that David Selwyn couldn't help joining in.

"Sorry," the man said, wiping tears of merriment from his eyes. "It's just—you never struck me as having much of a sense of humor." He reached out and shook Selwyn's hand. "I never had much use for a damn missionary, but I've changed my mind. Let's shake on it—And say, how about coming out to the plantation for dinner next week?"

David stared at Lani's father, confused. He'd never be able to figure the man out!

A battering at the outer door interrupted his thoughts. Excusing himself, he stepped into the outer office. His visitors had already entered without invitation. His eyes widened as he recognized the pair.

"You gotta help us, Doc," Nell blurted. "It's Tamsen what's missin' now. We've got one helluva mess on our hands. Looked everywhere but th' calaboose—"

"Where was she last?" Selwyn asked.

"Billy Whisker's place. We already been there. Locked up tighter'n a gawdam drum."

Suddenly the words of the note on his desk seemed graven on Selwyn's brain. Not that pretty woman, garbed so modestly in black—with so much concern for her sister! His mouth was a taut line. You could always judge a character by the company she kept. And these two were certainly unsavory, if he were any judge.

"I think I know where she is," he said. He turned to see Lani's father standing white-faced in the door of the dispensary. He looked as if he might be going to collapse. The man *was* ill. He moved toward him. "Sir—"

The sandy-haired man had been thumbing through a medical book he had seized the moment Selwyn left the room. At the name *Tamsen*, the book dropped from his nerveless fingers. For a moment, he was certain he was imagining things, then an unmistakable burst of profanity identified the speaker.

Nell!

"Nell!" He said her name now, his lips pale, the freckles that dusted his pleasant features standing out beneath his tan. He looked beyond her, seeing the little, expatriate Englishman.

"And Dusty!"

Nell looked at him, goggle-eyed with surprise. "Well, I be damned! Sam! Sam Larabee!"

The reunion was ecstatic, but stort. When Selwyn voiced his suspicions as to Tamsen's whereabouts, the others headed up the prison road so fast that he could barely keep pace. As they went, Nell tried to fill Sam in on the events leading to their search. "It was all that damn Martha's fault," she explained puffing along.

"Martha? the baby?"

"Baby, hell! Migawd, Sam! You ain't seen 'er sence the year of the Frisco fire! She's growed up

168

now. Snuck out last night an' Tamsen went to git her. Dunno whut happened after that."

Sam listened, but with only half his mind. If David Selwyn had checked his racing pulses, he would have been shocked. Tamsen, his brain kept reiterating. Oh, Tamsen! Tamsen!

He had only seen her once, since that night more than fifteen years before; the night they had spent in each other's arms before he sailed for Hawaii. He had loved her—but not as much as his freedom. She had loved him—but not enough to leave her sisters, little Martha, Dusty and Nell: all the people who depended on her.

Here in the islands, he'd met Josie; pretty Eurasian Josie, now grown thick in the waist, a comfortable woman. He'd grown to love her. But his conscience had taken him back to the States, fearing there had been some issue of that one wonderful night. And he'd found Tamsen operating a brothel, financed with the money he had left while she slept—

He'd thought Tamsen was a widow, that Martha was her kid. She'd soon disabused him of that fact. And she'd told him there was another man. She'd set him free.

Now she was here. On the island of Maui! He wondered if she'd changed, if she, like Josie, had grown placid and plump with advancing years. He couldn't imagine such an eventuality—though it wouldn't change his feelings for her. There was something in Tamsen that burned like a flame—

"Seems like her damn husband's off ever time she needs him," Nell grumbled.

He was jerked from his daydream. "She's married, then."

"Feller name of Tallant. Dan Tallant. J'ever meet 'im?"

Tamsen had clung to him. In the moment of love, she had called him Dan. Now she had the man she loved. Though the thought twisted in him like a pain, Sam was glad for her.

They reached the prison, Nell shoving the Guard at the gate aside. It might not have gone well for her, except for the presence of David Selwyn, and Sam Larabee, a well-known and respected planter of the area. They were taken to the prison office where an official knew Larabee. He also knew Larabee had connections. He was one of the oldest, best-established planters in the area, his business methods keeping his cane fields lucrative when others around him failed. It was also known that his wife was a friend of Bernice Pauahi Bishop, and Lili-uokalani, adoptive daughter of High Chief Paki, wife to John Dominis.

A mistake had been made. Someone would answer for this! The lady would be released at once.

A Guard went to fetch Tamsen, Sam Larabee insisting on going with him. Through the door of the cell, he saw the mad woman, crouched in her sores and rags, and his heart almost failed him. Then he saw the figure leaning against the opposite wall, black hair falling to reveal a slender, vulnerable neck. She hadn't changed, he exulted. She hadn't changed!

"Tamsen—"

She turned at the sound of his voice, her eyes growing huge as she rose to her feet; a slim little figure, hair wild, face bruised, her bosom barely covered by her torn, disheveled gown.

"Sam," she said. "Sam Larabee! It's you!" And then she was weeping, held close in his remembering arms.

170

18

Martha, at the compound, had been suffering the tortures of the damned. Throughout the night, she'd been angry. Tamsen, in her opinion, had come to spy on her—and stayed to show her up; make her look like a silly kid. She was still there, singing and dancing; cheered on by the patrons of Billy Whisker's place, and making a—a damn fool of herself. At her age! Probably cheating on Dan, something she, Martha, would never do—

But with the morning, her anger faded, replaced by alarm. She hated Tam, of course—but she didn't want anything awful to happen to her. She began to see the place she'd sneaked out to, where she'd had such great fun, for what it was: a sleazy, miserable place, catering to riffraff. And she began to think about what might have happened in such a place.

Maybe there had been a fight, and Tamsen was killed. Or she'd been trapped by some ugly drunk on her way home—or maybe two or three. Maybe, right now she was lying, raped, bruised, and bleeding, somewhere in the bushes. Maybe dead. Or they could have thrown her body into the sea.

If something happened to Tamsen, she, Martha, would be at fault. She was born with something evil in her—something ugly. Her own mother had said so.

The rebelliousness with which she'd layered her feelings like a shell began to crack, and she burst into tears.

"What's the matter Martha?" Ramona looked up at her with big eyes. "Are you tired of watching us? Daddy said—"

"Don't be silly," Martha scoffed. "Now, let's play hide-and-seek. You and Missy hide, and I'll close my eyes and count."

Martha closed her eyes, but she didn't count. She was wishing Nell hadn't insisted she keep the truth from Arab and Juan. If she told them Tamsen was missing, they could watch the children and she could aid in the search. Anything was better than this awful waiting.

"Here I come," she called, "ready or not." She opened her eyes to see a strange procession coming down the trail. Tamsen! She was alive! But she was being held up, supported in the arms of a strange man. Martha flew to meet them.

"Aunt Tamsen! Are you all right?"

Sam, at sight of the running girl, had almost dropped his burden. Another Tamsen! A twin to the battered girl he held in his arms. This would be Martha, the reason for Tamsen being in such a situation. His hot blue eyes changed, taking on a glacial look.

"I believe it's obvious she's not," he said. "Right now, we must get her into bed."

"I'll help her," Martha said eagerly. She took hold of Tamsen's arm.

"Gitcher goddam hands off'n her," Nell growled. She and Dusty, both limping, had caught up with Sam at last. "Hell! You've done enuf damage."

They left the girl standing. Sam carried Tamsen to the door of the hut Nell indicated, and carefully stood her on her feet. "You will be all right?" he asked tenderly.

"Of course. And Sam—thank you." She swayed toward him, and he held her for a moment, then placed a gentle kiss on her stained cheek.

"I have an appointment in Lahaina," he said against her hair. "But I'll be back tomorrow morning."

He left. Passing Martha without a word, he gave her another wintry stare. As he walked toward Lahaina, he thought of Tamsen, the girl he had always loved—a love that in no way diminished the way he felt for Josie, his wife. Her husband must be a thoughtless, inconsiderate man to leave her in such surroundings. It was no way for an American woman to live. He had an idea forming in his mind.

By late afternoon, he had purchased the property of a neighboring planter. The man had been a fool. Beginning with modest wealth, he had first built a spacious home, surrounded by smaller structures for his foreman and servants. He built a small sugar factory, and set himself up as a Hawaiian planter. Ignorant of the growing of the product, he left it to others. When Samuel Cooke, of Castle and Cooke, advocated the quota system, he'd ignored good advice, preferring to remain an independent.

The gentleman had built a showplace—a place to impress his guests from the States. And he had lost his shirt.

Sam closed the deal, ignoring his banker, who hinted he might have gotten the place for less. He grinned, as the words he'd used so often came to his lips.

"Hell, what's money for?"

Sam Larabee still had the golden touch. Every gamble he took turned into money. He'd given away fortunes in the past, and it had come back a thousandfold. He'd sometimes considered his talent a curse. But not now. Now, it was helping him gain something he wanted.

As a test of his ability, he grinned, flipped a coin, and slapped it against his waist. "Call it," he said to the banker.

The banker lost. Sam's luck was still with him. Now, he would return to the dispensary. If Selwyn were not busy, they could continue their interesting conversation. He hadn't thought to ask about diseases involving the circulation. Then there was something called gout—

Nell—bathing the fragile, bruised body of her charge and getting her bedded down on her sleeping mat—grew angrier by the minute. She administered the opiate Selwyn had prescribed, and waited until Tamsen's eyes closed in sleep. She called to Martha, sitting at the edge of the clearing with Ramona and Missy, and went on to the Narvaéz hut.

"Arab," she bawled. "Juan! Gitcher butts out here."

Both had been resting. At the urgency in Nell's voice, they emerged, Arab holding the baby, protectively. Juan's eyes went quickly toward his little daughters, assuring himself that they were not hurt, then rested on Nell. "What is it," he asked quietly.

Nell's beady little eyes shot sparks, her bosom heaved in indignation. "Hell," she growled, "Everthing! Tamsen's gonna be mad with me fer spillin' th' beans, but I don't give a damn! Martha!" She turned on the girl. "Tell 'em whut you been doin'!"

Martha's lips closed tightly, her eyes evading

Arab's, and Nell advanced on her, threateningly. "Start tawkin'! Now!"

"I've been entertaining," the girl said sullenly. "Hell, it's what Tamsen used to do."

"Watch yer gawdam mouth," Nell threatened. "Now tell 'em where!"

"Billy Whisker's place," Martha whispered.

"A gawdam dive," Nell announced. "Now tell 'em when."

"At night," Martha said wildly. "You know it all! Stop badgering me!"

"At night," Nell said with satisfaction. "Now, she done tolt you, not me. She's been sneakin' out, leaving the girls alone, and bawlin'. Ef you was any kind of a mother, Arab, you'da knowed it. How long has it bin since you tucked them kids in?"

Arab's face flamed. Before she could make an angry retort, Nell held up a staying hand. "The girls tolt Tamsen. She went to the dive to have a look-see, and, sure-nuf, this little bitch was there." She eyed Martha balefully. "So whut does Martha do? She run out on Tamsen. There was a riot, an' Tam got the hell beat outten her."

"She was singing when I left," Martha said defiantly.

Nell overrode her. "On top of that, them gawdam fancy-pants High-wayan sojers arrested her, put her in jail for prostitution. Hadn't bin fer the doc in town, and a old friend of Tam and Em's, she'd still be in the calaboose. I've got her to bed, now, an' she's all doped up—"

Arab, her face white with shock, began to move toward Tamsen's hut. Nell reached out and caught her arm. "You ain't goin' nowheres! Yer goin' t'stay here an' git a load of how the cow et th' cabbage! There's gonna be some swappin' here. You folks is goin' t'move into the big shack—with yer own kids. Try to be a gawdam fambly fer oncet! Martha, you kin move into the little hut, all by your lonesome, 'er you kin make other plans. Go home to yer folks, 'er git a job in town, I don't give a damn. Em's kids ain't Tamsen's t'raise, ner Arab's, either."

"I can get a job at Billy Whisker's," Martha flared. "He's already asked me."

"Go the hell ahead," Nell grinned evilly. "Give it a try, sis!"

She lumbered away. Her sermon was over.

Arab looked at Juan, her red hair glorious in the sun, her green eyes brimming with tears. "Have I neglected the girls, Juan? Pushed them off on Tamsen?" Her eyes widened with the memory of these last weeks. "Where are they?"

"We were playing hide-and-seek," Martha said through stiff lips. "They hid, and I forgot to go and find them."

Arab placed little Luka in her father's arms and sped off in search of her other children. Juan looked into the face of the little girl who opened silver eyes, her lips curving in a lazy smile. His heart swelled with an intense paternal emotion.

It was the first time he'd been allowed to hold her.

Martha's heart contracted at his expression. It only served to point up the fact that she had no one. She turned and went slowly down the trail that led to Lahaina. No one called out to her. By the time she reached Lahaina, she had begun to build up a case for herself, in her need for self-justification. They were all against her. All of them! It wasn't her fault Tamsen had been sneaky enough to spy on her! And Tamsen didn't have to make a spectacle of herself last night!

Nell said she'd been arrested for prostitution. Well, there would have to be a *reason!* Maybe she'd gone back to another of her old trades. She certainly *looked* like it, the way her gown was torn, her mouth all swollen. She'd returned in the arms of a strange man. Martha had seen him kiss her—

Martha tossed her head. Tamsen's story was a cover-up for her night's activities, planned purposely to get her, Martha, in trouble.

Her steps slowed as she reached the other side of Lahaina. Somehow it hadn't seemed so far to the place when she'd gone there just for a lark. Ah, there was the path where she should turn.

Forcing a bright smile, she made her way through the sheltering trees to the ramshackle structure on the sands. At sight of it, she couldn't suppress a nervous shiver. She hadn't realized it was so depressing and tumbledown. It looked so—empty.

When she reached the entrance, she found it padlocked. The sign said, *Closed for repairs.* She recalled Nell's smirk. The old woman had known it all the time.

Martha returned to Lahaina, determined to find a job. There was no work to be had, unless she wished to work in the pineapple fields, or cut cane— for a coolie's wages.

It was dark when she returned to the compound, everyone abed. She crawled into the little hut that had been occupied by Arab, Juan, and the baby. Her sleeping mats had been moved and carefully spread for her.

She lay down and cried herself to sleep, only to be awakened by a sound. It was only a small lizard moving in the thatch, but Martha didn't know that. During the remainder of the night, she was to learn what it felt like to be young, alone, and frightened

177

of the dark. Toward dawn, she remembered the frosty gleam of Sam Larabee's eyes. A killer's eyes, they became in retrospection. Nell said he'd known Tamsen and Em long ago.

She wondered if he might be her father.

19

Tamsen awoke, aching all over, but with a tremendous feeling of happiness. For a moment she was disoriented, wondering at her bruises, and the emotion that overwhelmed her. Then she remembered.

Sam!

Dear Sam, who even in his devil-may-care youth was the most steadfast man she'd ever known. He had loved her then. He loved her still, in a way that took nothing from his wife Josie. It had been good to put her head against his broad chest, yesterday. Good to look up and see the expression in his candid blue eyes—a look that told her she was beautiful to him—and always would be.

That was it. He made her feel safe and loved and beautiful. And he would never change.

She rose. He would be coming this morning. She selected a gown of deep rose that put color in her olive cheeks, wondering, as she dressed, at the mystery of love. With Sam, she would have known no jealousies, no doubts. Her past life wouldn't have affected his career. There would have been no need to try to make herself into a person she wasn't in-

179

tended to be. Their relationship would have been calm and serene.

Why, then, did her love go to Dan instead? Their life had been full of misunderstandings, a tinder box, fiery quarrels, and flaming passions.

Fire! That was the answer. She couldn't imagine living without it. But, as Sam loved her without taking from Josie, she could return it without being unfaithful to Dan.

She was waiting for him when he arrived in a one-horse trap that was narrow enough to negotiate the trail with ease—one that would accommodate a battered lady if she chose to ride.

The Tamsen who ran toward him, arms outstretched as he dismounted, was hardly battered. At least, her bruises didn't show. Her sparkling eyes bespoke her delight at seeing him.

"Sam, I could hardly wait! I still can't believe it's you! Come, you haven't met my sister Arab, yet, or Juan—"

He liked Tamsen's sister at first sight, though there was a haunted look in the girl's sea-green eyes. He liked Juan Narvaéz, too. Though Sam had been born into—and had rejected—a background of aristocracy, he still recognized class when he saw it.

Sam enchanted Ramona and Missy, picking one up in each arm as he talked with them. When he reached for the baby, Arab made a nervous move. He paused, then certain he'd imagined it, took little Luka in his arms. She didn't feel right, the small limbs too stiff and straight, unmoving. Then she opened her empty silver eyes.

He gave her back to her mother. "A beautiful child," he said. Then, "You're very lucky. I only have one daughter. I lost my two sons in the smallpox epidemic some years back."

"Oh, Sam!"

The look in Tamsen's eyes brought him as close to consolation as he'd ever come. "It's all right," he said gently. "It's been a long time."

Then he asked if Tamsen felt up to a drive, perhaps lunch with his daughter Lani and David Selwyn.

Tamsen felt wonderful. Tamsen was delighted.

As Sam handed Tamsen into the trap, he realized Martha had been conspicuous by her absence. He wondered where the girl was.

Martha wasn't far. Crouched behind a flowering bush, she was watching their departure: the way Sam's hands had lingered at Tamsen's waist as he lifted her into the carriage; how she had smiled down on him, reaching a small hand to touch his cheek.

Dan, Martha thought triumphantly, wasn't going to like this. Not at all!

On the drive into Lahaina, Sam asked about Dan's work. Tamsen, though she was tempted, evaded with a half-truth. Dan was a surveyor, here to check out sites for possible railways, connecting the plantations with sugar mills.

Sam looked pleased. "Then he's the man I've heard of! I'm for anything that will improve working conditions in the islands."

"Annexation?" Tamsen asked in a small voice.

"Good God, no! There's an American Party here, pushing for it, but I don't have anything to do with them. There's a—a kind of *magic* here." He flushed at his fanciful term, but went on stubbornly. "It isn't like anyplace else in the world. It would be like annexing the Garden of Eden."

"I agree," Tamsen said. But would Dan? When he forwarded his recommendations to Grant, what would they be? Looking at Sam's honest, open face, she felt like a traitor. She changed the subject. "Did you like my sister? Her husband?"

"Very much." His face sobered as he asked, hesitantly, "The baby, Tamsen, is she well?"

Hands clenched tightly in her lap, Tamsen told him of their stay at Hilo, the visits of Manu, the leper. His face went gray as she described the horrors of that time. Then she went on to tell the rest, their flight, the volcano's eruption, and the circumstances of Luka's birth.

"It must have been hell!"

"It was."

Sensing her memories had cast a dark shadow on the day, Sam forced a smile. "It won't happen here. Haleakala Crater has been dormant for almost a hundred years."

"I know," she said wryly. "I asked before we landed." They laughed together, but Sam's eyes remained somber. He was thinking, strangely enough, not about the earthquake, the eruption of Mauna Loa, but of the leper Tamsen described so graphically.

Lunch was a picnic on the beach. Sam had ordered a hamper made up at a small Chinese grocery. It included a bottle of wine. Tamsen adored Lani, Sam's pretty daughter. David Selwyn, away from his dispensary, seemed oddly boyish, not like a missionary at all. He talked and laughed until Kimo joined them, then became stiff and silent.

He's in love with Lani, Tamsen thought, surprised. And so is Kimo! I wonder if Sam knows, and who the girl favors. It was impossible to tell. Lani's cameo-like face showed nothing. But David Selwyn's devotion was so apparent, Tamsen felt like shaking him.

Not that Tamsen didn't like Kimo. He was a handsome young fellow, but his lack of education, his relaxed Hawaiian style of living, seemed wrong for Lani.

The others returned to their work, Lani and David to the mission house, and Kimo to his purchasing of supplies for Sam's plantation. Sam and Tamsen talked for awhile, then gathered the picnic residue, regretfully. The sun had been warm. There was a faint scented breeze, and the waters ranged from blue to indigo as they lapped against the shore.

"I'm not going to take you home yet," Sam said. "Come!"

He took her to the intersection of Front and Shaw Streets, explaining that Front had been known as *Alanui Moi*, or King's Road, while Shaw was once *Alanui Waiokama*, translated as The People's Way. There, they came to a narrow causeway leading to the island of *Moku-ula*, Sacred Island, in the pond called *Mokuhinia*.

A gate shut the causeway off to the general public, a king's sentry standing guard. The sentry smiled at Larabee, and allowed them to pass. Tamsen found herself in a miniature city of splendid grass huts, on an island studded with palm trees, and, except for the causeway, surrounded by water on every side.

"It's lovely," Tamsen whispered.

"Do you think so? You are standing on hallowed ground."

There was an odd note in his voice, and she looked at him, puzzled. "Many years ago, the King of Maui, Kihapilani, had a daughter who died. Her bones were stripped of their flesh and she was buried beneath this island. She was transformed into a mo'o, a lizard god, and was—still is—the most powerful god on Maui. The special guardian of the royal family."

Surely, he didn't believe that claptrap! Conscious of her stare, he stopped and smiled sheepishly. "Actually, I'm leading up to another story."

He told her the tragic story of the love of Princess Nahienaena and King Kamehameha, Third. Brother and sister, they would have been a perfect royal couple before the coming of the missionary. Instead, they had been forced to marry others. Nahienana had died while still very young, and the grieving king had her brought to this island where he maintained his residence, building her mausoleum above the mo'o's cave.

Tamsen followed his pointing finger and shivered. Kamehameha, Third, had died little more than twenty years before. It could not be true! Surely things were more civilized! Then she remembered Pua and Kapiki, so right for each other.

"He brought her here," Sam said slowly, "and they say he spent much time in the mausoleum. Sounds gruesome, I guess. But when I come here, I feel like maybe there's something after death. Makes me feel peaceful—"

"Sam, is there anything you haven't told me? Are you well?"

The look he turned on her was a little dazed, as if he'd been asleep. Finally, he managed a painful grin. "Hell, yes, I'm well. Healthy as a horse! Do I look sick?"

She surveyed his muscular frame and laughed. "No, you don't. But I think I'm going to be, if we don't get out of here! And I think I'd better get home."

"I'm going home tomorrow," he said. "Tamsen, I want you to go with me. Surely you can spend one night—"

Her mouth opened in shock at his words, then

closed again as he completed his sentence. "I want you to meet Josie, my wife."

For a moment, she poised on the brink of indecision. With Sam, she forgot that she spent a night in his arms. He was just a dearly beloved friend. But to meet his wife? It was a frightening thought. But this was a small island. She'd be bound to meet her sometime, Sam would see to that.

"What do you say?"

"Of course, Sam. I'd love to meet your Josie. Thank you for asking me."

They left the island, Sam saluting the sentry who responded like an old friend. Sam must come here often, Tamsen mused. He'd been happy and carefree in the old days. What Nell would refer to as a *heller*. It was odd that he seemed to have such a preoccupation with death.

Determined to shake him loose from the hold the island had over him, she began a line of cheerful chatter that set him laughing. The story of Birdie Faraday, prim little cook at her "Parlor for Gentlemen." The way she'd stirred a pot to the left, saying, "Damn!" and then to the right, saying, "Hell!" Birdie had practiced cussing so she could hold her own with Nell. And there was a tale about Nell, too. The log she'd refused to cross over a rushing stream. They'd tied ropes about her waist, the ends held by members of the party on both sides of the water-filled crevice, and still Nell had persisted in sitting down, hitching herself with her knees, gathering splinters all the way.

They were both weak with mirth when the carriage drew into the compound. Tamsen's face, as Sam lifted her down, was rosy, her eyes sparkling.

That fact was not lost on Martha. And there were others who saw it, too.

Nell was frankly worried. Those two look good together, she admitted to herself, reluctantly. But hell! So did Tam and Dan. With that snot-nose Martha hangin' herself around Dan's neck, and now Sam showin' up like this, there was bound to be trouble.

"Nell," Dusty whispered, "Sam and Tamsen—you don't think—"

"I don't think nuthin'," Nell growled. "Gitcher gawdam mind outten th' gutter. They's friends, thass all!"

"I don't think Dan's going to like this turn of events, Nell. Perhaps you should have a word with the girl."

"I'll mind my own gawdam business," Nell growled. "Mebbe this is what Dan needs t'shake 'im up a little."

Tamsen came toward them, hands outstretched, her face glowing. "Nell! Dusty! I've had such a lovely day." She stretched, yawning. "I think I'll skip supper and go to bed. Sam will be here early in the morning. I'm going to go out to his place tomorrow, and spend the night."

She left the stupefied pair and danced toward her hut. The two stared after, silent for a moment. Then Nell looked at Dusty, seeing her own thoughts echoed in his faded blue eyes.

"Gawdam," she said weakly, "Gawdam! Things is goin' t'hell in a bushel basket, ain't they?"

Nell and Dusty could not sleep that night.

In Martha's hut, the little lizard played in the thatch, making spooky sounds as he'd done the night before, but his efforts failed to produce any effect. Martha's ears were deaf to the night sounds. She lay in a half-dreaming state, her lips curved in a smile of triumph. Tamsen had shown her true colors. Dan wouldn't want a woman like that. She conjured up a picture of him; blue shirt opened to show a tanned throat; his broad shoulders, the muscles rippling in his arms. A real man! He might even kill Tamsen when he found she was cheating. The thought touched her with a thrill of horror, and she fashioned a scene to fit the occasion.

She would save her. She would say, "Dan, don't. She's not worth it!" Then he would turn to her—

That's the way it would be.

In her own hut, Tamsen was dreaming, too, but in a different way. She'd gone instantly to sleep, relaxed after a day without worry, without responsibility. And her dream was welcome. It was colorful and exciting. She was descending the stairs at the parlor, clad in a gown of black velvet gored with red. Her shoulders were bared, a necklace of rubies fastened at her throat. A sea of male faces looked up at her, eyes filled with approval.

She reached the middle of the floor and began to sing, feeling the power surge in her veins as she held her listeners enthralled. Then, at the back of the room, she caught sight of a familiar face.

Sam? Sam didn't belong in that setting, but in another place, another time. But it was he. Still singing, she moved toward him, the watchers parting to let her through.

"Sam—"

And suddenly, it was Sam no longer, but a grinning death's-head.

She screamed, and woke.

Arabella Narvaéz, up and moving about in the large hut, heard the sound and dismissed it as that of a night bird. One of the girls had awakened her, crying out. Which one? Ramona.

"Are you sick?" she asked, smoothing the little

girl's hair away from her brow. "Does your tummy ache?"

"I'm scared," Tamona whimpered. "The mo-o."

Arab followed her pointing finger. The burning candle revealed a small lizard high in the thatch. "That? Ramona, I'm surprised at you. It won't hurt you."

"It's bad luck. Pua said—"

"Pua believes one thing, we believe another. Oh, all right!" She couldn't reach the thing, she knew. She would have to wake Juan.

The lizard safely deposited outside, Arab tucked Ramona in and kissed little Missy on the forehead. It was dreadful to think of the nights they had lain in fear with no adult to watch over them. Thank God for blunt, profane, good-intentioned Nell! For a while, she'd been lost to her children. It would never happen again.

She'd been lost to Juan, too, she thought as she touched little Luka's cheek with a loving finger. Then she lay down beside her husband, her heart bursting with love as he drew her close.

20

Tamsen was ready when Sam Larabee came for her at dawn. Their road wound along the shoreline, the vegetation sparse here, with only a few koa trees and an occasional palm to inhibit the view of blue waters with Molokai like a shadow in the distance.

Sam looked a little tired this morning, and was unusually silent, a line of white running along his jawline. Tamsen thought of her dream and shivered. Then she remembered he was taking her to his home, to meet his wife. Maybe the invitation had been an impulsive gesture and now he, too, was concerned about the meeting.

"Sam—"

He jerked at the intrusion of her voice, then forced a smile. "I'm sorry. I was thinking of the thing I saw when I left Lahaina. They were taking a shipload of lepers over to Molokai, poor devils. Look, there they are." He pointed toward a small dot dancing in the distance, sails white against Molokai's shadow. It looked pretty, like a pleasure craft, from afar.

Thinking of the leper, Manu, hiding, living in a cave like an animal, having to steal in order to eat;

finally driven to a *kapu* spot to get his food, Tamsen shuddered.

"Maybe they'll be happier among their own kind," she offered.

The eyes he turned on her held a sick anger. "You don't know what the hell you're talking about," he said harshly. Then, "I'm sorry. You couldn't know. The place is a hellhole. No law, not enough food, no one to care for the sick." He glared at her. "Suppose it was discovered you had the disease in its beginning stages! Can you imagine what it would be like—tossed from the ship to swim ashore—only to be grabbed up by some insane, rotting monster—then passed on to another? Good God! And there are women on that boat! Torn from their husbands, their children—"

"I didn't know," Tamsen whispered. "Oh, Sam, I didn't know!"

His look softened. "Of course not. I shouldn't have mentioned it. I've spoiled your morning. Look there—"

He pointed inland. A mass of verdant green climbed toward the soaring Maui hills now radiant with the sun. "Cane," he said. "This isn't my property. You will see the difference when we arrive. I've experimented with new procedures and it's paying off. I would say this will bring two tons of sugar to the acre. Mine has been producing six—"

"Same old Sam," she teased. "Still making fortunes—and spending them."

He grinned as he repeated the phrase he lived by. "Hell, what's money for?"

They rode companionably, passing occasional small villages from which, invariably, a smiling native called a greeting to Sam, including Tamsen in his welcoming smile. Then the cane grew more lushly as the road climbed. To one side there was green cane rooted in red soil; to the other, the land dropped off. From the height, there was a magnificent view of small half-moon beaches of white coral sand; of points where the waves dashed against rock, throwing white spume high into the air.

"We're almost home," Sam said. Then he pointed again. "Look!"

There was a break in the cane. Symmetrical rows of an odd-looking plant curved along the hillside. Tamsen strove to find something to compare it to.

"Some sort of yucca?" she ventured.

He laughed at her. "Pineapple. There, too, I'm trying different strains."

"I never thought you'd be a farmer," she teased.

"It's a good life," he said soberly. "And I don't have an itching foot anymore. I'm satisfied. And I hope nothing ever changes."

He was silent after that, until they turned into a small trail that led between evenly spaced mango trees. The trail curved to reveal a long white ranch-type house, with smaller, similar outbuildings behind it. It had a green lawn. A flowering vine climbed the porch supports, falling in masses of fragrant bloom. Bamboo chairs and a table were placed beneath an enormous poinciana tree. And in one of those chairs, with a thronelike, woven-lace back that curved like a shell, a woman was waiting.

"Josie," Sam said simply.

"Sam, I'm nervous! She doesn't know who I am —that I was coming here—"

Sam laughed as he lifted her down. "Relax. I sent Kimo with the news yesterday."

The woman was already coming toward them, her white teeth flashing in a welcoming smile. Sam went to meet her, taking her arm, looking down at her with infinite love as he led her toward his guest.

Watching them, Tamsen felt a jolt of surprise. She had expected—Dear God, she didn't know what she expected!—But not this. Sam's wife was a pleasant little woman, a holoku covering her plump figure. she was frankly middle-aged, walking as though her feet hurt. Just a—a motherly looking housewife.

Josie Larabee moved forward, her hands outstretched in welcome. "So this is Sam's Tamsen! Sam, she's even lovelier than you described." She stopped, dropping her hands, not touching her guest. "I'm so glad you've come. I've been wanting to meet you since Sam and I were married."

Tamsen searched her face. There was no trace of irony or guile. She honestly meant what she said. Tamsen could not have been so generous. Surely she guessed there had been something between herself and Sam long years ago.

Closer up, the woman had a kind of beauty that dispelled the impression of plainness Tamsen received earlier. She had lovely eyes, huge, dark and haunted. Tamsen thought of the little boys that died in the smallpox epidemic. Josie's sons as well as Sam's.

"And I've been wanting to meet you," Tamsen said. "Now I know why Sam's such a happy man."

Josie's face glowed. She turned adoring eyes to her husband. "She'll want to freshen up. Take her to the guest room. I'll ring for Kee, and have breakfast brought out here." Again the white teeth flashed as she smiled at Tamsen. "I'm incredibly lazy. My Hawaiian blood, I suppose. And Sam spoils me."

Sam led Tamsen toward the house and Josie returned to her chair. Behind them, they heard the tinkle of her little bell.

"She's nice, Sam. You are a very lucky man."

Sam grinned. "You don't have to tell me. Hell, I know!"

He led her through the house, a place of uncluttered spacious rooms with just a few pieces of comfortable-looking furniture. The guest room was done in sunny yellow, a window opening to a view of the sea. The floor, of wide waxed boards, was covered with a creamy matting. A bamboo chair was cushioned with yellow. A nightstand, with a turquoise bowl and pitcher, stood beside a bed with a yellow counterpane.

The whole effect was one of simplicity and freshness. But to Tamsen, it was incredible luxury. Tonight she would sleep in a real bed.

Sam, seeing the delight in her face, was moved. He was feeling pretty shaken, himself. In his life there had been many women, but he had loved only two. And those two would spend the night beneath the same roof. Dammit! If a man could have two wives, it would be perfect.

"I'll wait for you," he said. The door closed behind him.

The day that followed was very pleasant. After a meal that was essentially American with the addition of platters of fruit, Sam showed Tamsen over the plantation. Here, crops were being harvested, the cane having been burned over, leaving the residue that would be converted into sugar. There, a field would lie fallow. In another spot, cane grew knee high. In still another, smiling coolies were preparing the soil for an additional crop. Cane was planted here in almost every month of the year, Sam told Tamsen. The usual custom was to take two crops, then allow the land to lie fallow for two years. Sam's procedures had changed all that on most of his land. His cane matured in fourteen months as compared with sixteen months to two years for other planters. He seemed to loom even larger as he walked his land.

He'd come a long way from his hell-raising days, Tamsen thought. But he was still the same Sam.

That evening, dinner was served. It was an enjoyable meal, candlelit, pleasant, and with easy conversation. At one point, the kitchen door opened long enough for Tamsen to see that it was filled with steam. She looked questioningly at Josie.

"We're very conscious of disease, here," the woman said, toying with her spoon. "Sam insists all utensils be sterilized."

Tamsen thought of the two little boys they'd lost to smallpox. It was odd that Sam should be so finicky. But she supposed, under the circumstances, she would be, too.

After the meal, Sam insisted that Tamsen sing for them. He called Kimo, who came with his guitar and devilish smile. Tamsen was surprised and a little embarrassed when Sam requested some of the old bawdy tunes he recalled from his salad days, but complied. Kimo was obviously delighted, and Josie clapped her hands, asking for more.

Finally, she ended with her favorite: *Black is the color of my true love's hair—*" and felt the purification of her spirit that the song always brought to her.

Watching the slim girl, hands clasped in an attitude of prayer, Josie's dark eyes filled with tears.

"She's just as you said she was," she told the husband at her side. Sam Larabee's big hand closed over his wife's in a gesture of loving affection.

That night, it was Josie who saw Tamsen to her room. "I want to thank you for tonight," she said.

"And for coming. You see—I know Sam loved you once. And meeting you—I feel even prouder that he married me. That I now have his love."

Tamsen flinched. Was the woman challenging her? No. Josie truly meant what she said. She knew there had been something between Tamsen and Sam, but she was secure enough in her position and love for him that it didn't matter.

Tamsen thought of Martha, the way she'd been running after Dan, and wished she could be so sure of any man. "I think you're a lucky woman, Josie," she said. "But Sam's even luckier to have found someone like you."

It was hard to say good-bye to the Larabee house the next morning, but once on the way, Tamsen found herself eager to get back to the compound. Supposing Dan had come home in her absence—

Therefore she was a little dismayed when Sam, upon leaving the trail that led to his house, turned the carriage in the opposite direction. "I want to show you something," he said. Then, seeing her crestfallen face, "It won't take long. I promise you."

They ascended, driving along a road that led steadily upward, and finally reached a home set on a promontory. Built of a combination of coral and frame, it was flanked by similar outbuildings, much as Sam's place had been, but this was on a grander scale.

Helping her to alight, he led her to the front, which looked out over the sea. A small path led crookedly down the cliffside, to a white sand beach curled between rocky ledges at either side where waves tossed their mains and broke like thunder.

Sam didn't knock, but opened the front door ushering Tamsen into a vast parlor, carpeted, sumptuously furnished. "Do you like it?" he asked.

"I don't understand," she whispered. "Who lives here?"

"No one at the present," he grinned. "I'm hoping you will."

She looked at him, her eyes wide with shock, her heart beginning to thunder in time with the waves that crashed against the rocks below.

21

As they drove down the road on their way back to the compound near Lahaina, Tamsen pondered on Sam's offer. He'd bought a neighboring plantation, he said, planning to develop the fields there. The house was to be Lani's when she married. In the meantime, it would go to ruin, standing empty. He would be pleased if she and the others would occupy the premises for the length of their stay on Maui. It would be a favor to him. Josie, too, thought it was an excellent idea. It would be nice to have friends near.

Knowing Sam, Tamsen didn't doubt the sincerity of his offer. She was however, dubious of his reason for acquiring the place. No doubt it would go to Lani, but she wouldn't have put it past him to have purchased it after he saw the grass huts in the compound. Somehow, to accept Sam's generosity seemed to put Dan in a bad light. It wasn't that Dan hadn't tried to provide for his family. When they came to Hilo, they'd carried a house with them, like a turtle. When they reached Lahaina, there'd been little choice—

"I will talk to the others," she said.

"And so will I. I've always been a persuasive ıofagun."

Tamsen was silent. She had reason to know.

As she had expected, Juan and Arab, Dusty and Nell, were in accord on the move. "Hell," Nell said. She rubbed her backside ruefully. "Gittin' flat ez a pancake, sleepin' on them gawdam mats."

Arab was certain that a house would be better for the baby. Even little Ramona joined in the general excitement. "Are there any mo-os in the thatch?" she asked seriously.

"None at all," Sam told her. "Because there isn't a thatch. All the buildings have roofs. One of the houses has a nice fenced yard, just right for you and Missy."

Martha said nothing. If they lived near Sam Larabee, surely Dan would notice the way the wind blew. Fate was playing right into their hands.

As if her thoughts had conjured him up, Dan Tallant appeared in the middle of the noon meal. He greeted Tamsen with a bear hug when she went to meet him, lifting her off her feet. Then he looked questioningly at the big man who seemed so at home, seated on a fallen log between Arab's children, a plate in his hands.

Sam Larabee put his plate down and stood. For a moment, the two men studied each other, taking each other's measure, the dark man, whipcord-thin, dressed in blue workclothes, a red bandana about his throat; the sandy-haired planter with hot blue eyes.

Larabee made the first move. "Sam Larabee," he said. "I have a plantation up the coast. I've heard about your survey—"

Dan's face cleared. "Larabee! Your name's on

my list of people to see. I'd like permission to look over your land—"

"Granted. And I'd like your approval of something—an idea I had. I have some buildings standing empty, and I'd like to offer them to you and your wife—and the others, of course. They are furnished, and I believe quite comfortable. Just to have them occupied would be a load off my mind—"

"Your offer is a load off *my* mind," Dan admitted with a grin. "Thanks. But I insist on paying—"

"Not at all," Sam said. "I won't hear of it. You'll be protecting the property. Empty places soon go to rack and ruin."

"It's kind of you. Especially, since we are strangers—"

"Dan," Tamsen interrupted, "Dan, listen to me! This is—"

Sam saw her white face and realized she had some explaining to do. He had told Josie about Tamsen, but it was clear Dan Tallant knew nothing about him. He would leave her to manage whatever she chose to tell in her own way.

"I must go," he said. "Nice meeting you, Tallant. Thank you for your hospitality." His nod included all present. He stepped up into his carriage, saluted with his whip, and was gone.

Dan didn't watch him out of sight. His eyes were on his wife. She wore a bright gown; her hair, though up in a ladylike fashion, was loose about her face, a tendril curling across her brow. His old Tamsen was back again.

"Sweetheart," he said, "you're beautiful! Oh, God, I've missed you!"

Her face was white and strained. "I'll fix you a plate—"

"I'm not hungry. I think I'll go into the hut and lie down for awhile. Tamsen?" There was no other interpretation for the hunger in his eyes.

"I'll go with you," she said hastily.

They disappeared into the hut. Outside, Nell lifted her head and set her jaw. "Explainin' Sam Larabee's Tamsen's bizness. You all got that? We don't do nuthin' but keep our noses clean! You, too, Martha! Keep yer damn mouth shut er I'll shut it for you—permanent-like. Unnerstand? An' that Billy Whisker's mess. Tamsen wants t' tell Dan, she will. You say one gawdam thing, an' we start tawkin', too. Dan finds out it wuz yer fault, he'll shoot you home with yer tail afire!"

"I won't say anything," Martha flared. She wouldn't need to. Give Tamsen enough rope, and she would hang herself.

The inside of Tamsen's hut was heavy with scent. During her absence, Nell and Arab had mended and cleaned the crimson gown. It hung against the wall. Little Ramona had gathered white ginger flowers and spread them on Tamsen's sleeping mat. It was a welcome-home gift for Tamsen. But how was she going to explain it?

Dan had already drawn his own conclusions. "You knew I was coming home," he said, his voice filled with wonder. "I don't know how you knew it, but you did! Oh, Tam, you can't believe how worried I've been! Bringing you to a place like this; falling asleep on you the first time we had a night together in months; leaving without seeing you! I made the man who came for me wait for two hours—

"And now I find my sweetheart here, waiting for me! Oh, God, Tamsen! It's too good to be true!" He moved toward her, taking her in his arms. She

200

felt his body throbbing against her, burning through her gown.

"Dan," she whispered. "Please listen! I—"

"Hush!" He placed his lips against her own, shutting off her flow of words, one hand going to the buttons at the throat of her gown. For a moment they swayed, mouth hot against mouth, Tamsen's body arched to his.

The gown slid from one shoulder and his lips moved on, tasting the sweetness of her soft flesh.

I've got to talk to him, she thought dizzily. I've got to explain! As her gown whispered to the floor, she said, "Dan, please—"

It was the word she'd used so often. Dan Tallant's heart thudded with emotion. He had his Tamsen back. He lifted her and carried her to the sleeping mat, lowering her gently.

"In a moment. Wait—"

He lit the string of *kukui* candles, their light enough to dispel the dimness of the room. "I want to see you." His voice was husky with feeling. "Ah, God, sweetheart, I've dreamed—"

He stopped short as he turned to her again. Tamsen lay among the crushed blossoms, her black hair spreading around her, her slender body golden in the light.

Golden, except for the bruises she'd received in the brawl at Billy Whisker's Place. A great spreading stain of purple marred her hip, its edges blurring into green and yellow. Another bruise colored the area between her breast and waist. One shoulder was black and blue. On her right arm, parallel lines looked to be the print of a man's cruel fingers.

"Tamsen! Good God!"

She raised on an elbow, following his gaze. She had forgotten the evidence of that awful night. Dan's eyes were shocked, frightened—even accusing. Dear God, what could she say? That she'd been entertaining in a house of ill repute? That she'd been mauled, arrested for prostitution? That she'd spent the night in jail—but that it wasn't her fault, but Martha's?

He wouldn't believe it. He'd never believe she was innocent. And perhaps she wasn't, she thought uneasily, recalling the surge of power she'd felt at performing in that place.

"Tamsen!" Dan's voice was hard. "Are you going to tell me what happened?"

"I fell." She closed her eyes, not daring to meet his gaze.

"A fall wouldn't do that!"

"I was standing on some rocks by the water," she improvised. "I fell and rolled—"

He touched her arm. "Those bruises—they look like a man's fingers."

"A man caught me," she said flatly. "He kept me from falling in."

"Who was he? Do you know?" His lips were tight.

Tamsen tried to think of an answer that would satisfy him and settle his doubts. She seized upon the first innocent name that came to mind. "The missionary in Lahaina," she lied. "Reverend Selwyn. Now, are you through with the inquisition? Are you coming to bed—or aren't you?"

He lay down beside her, holding her close. "I'm sorry, sweetheart. It was a shock. Why didn't you tell me?"

"I can't seem to tell you anything," she flared. "I tried to tell you Sam Larabee—"

"—has offered us a house," he finished for her. "And you're all for it. We'll take it, I promise you. Now—let's not talk anymore."

She was stiff with tension as he lay down beside her, pulling her close. He began his old, familiar routine of touching—his hands tracing her throat, her shoulders moving down. And at last she clung to him, helpless with need and desire, the tender beginnings of love forgotten in the fierce coming together, the striving to be one mind, one body, one madly beating heart.

She moaned as he moved away, and he touched her face, feeling the tears that wet her cheeks. "I didn't hurt you?"

"No," she said. She clung to him in a fit of violent weeping. "Oh, Dan! Dan!"

"I'm glad to have my little wildcat back," he teased. "It was good, wasn't it?"

"Oh, yes."

Then he said the words that put a chill along her spine. "It was better than it's been for a long time. If I didn't trust you, sweetheart, I'd think you'd been practicing—"

Dan had always been a jealous man. And she supposed her past had given him reason to be. This was certainly no time to explain about her old friendship with Sam Larabee—or anything else. As humiliating as it was, she'd have to ask everyone to cover for her until she could work something out.

Dan finally slept, weary from his journey. Tamsen slipped from the hut, and went to find Martha.

The girl sat disconsolately on a stump, her shoulders slumped. It was clear she thought Dan would be told of her misadventures. And he should have been, Tamsen thought to herself, if she'd only had the nerve. But she hadn't. She'd lied, and the lie would have to be perpetuated.

"I haven't told my husband about your visits to Billy Whisker's place, or anything about that last night," Tamsen said crisply. "And I want you to promise you'll keep your mouth shut!"

The relief on Martha's face was evident. "I won't say anything."

"I have your promise?"

The girl nodded.

"And I haven't had a chance to explain that I knew Sam Larabee before today. You will keep quiet about that, too, until I have a chance to tell him."

A light dawned in Martha's eyes. Tamsen wasn't trying to keep her out of trouble. She was protecting herself. She smiled, insolently. "And if I don't?"

Tamsen was white with anger, her hands knotted into fists at her side. "If you don't, I'll ship you back to Em so fast you won't know what happened. I will, anyway, if you don't keep your hands off Dan."

"All's fair in love and war," the girl said sulkily.

"You don't know what love is," Tamsen said in a soft, deadly voice. "You don't know what war is, either. If you want to find out, just try me a little more!"

She turned on her heel and went to find the others, asking their cooperation in keeping the news of the Lahaina incident from Dan. "I was afraid to tell him," she said frankly. "I lied. Now, the best thing to do is forget it ever happened. And about Sam—I'm going to tell him I've known him for years, but I'll have to find the right time."

Juan and Arab were skeptical. After all, Martha had caused her problems. If Dan were angry, he had a right to be—

Tamsen shook her head. "He wouldn't understand. And I've told him I fell."

It was different with Sam Larabee, Arab argued. Since he was an old family friend, Tamsen should come right out and say so.

"I tried," Tamsen exploded. "Every time I said something," her face crimsoned, "he wouldn't listen! It's too late—"

"I'm with Tamsen," Nell said. "Hell, the only way t'handle a stubborn bullheaded mule is t'be smarter'n he is."

"Nell should know," Dusty said, his cheeks pink with pleasure at coming up with a joke. "Nell mounted one in the Fraser River country. Jove! He wouldn't budge!"

Nell's eyes flashed, then glinted in appreciation of Dusty's humor. "It wasn't cause I didden have th' whip-hand, you leetle bastard! But, hell, couldn't ennything move with me on its back. Wasn't nuthin to do with *brains*."

It was settled then. Tamsen's bruises would be explained away as due to a fall. Larabee would go along with it, they were sure, seeing it as an embarrassment to Tamsen. As far as their long-time friendship, it looked like Sam handled that all right. He wouldn't mention it until he was certain Dan knew. After all, what difference did it make, whether Tamsen met the man a long time ago, or today—

It made a lot of difference, Tamsen thought. Sam had saved them all in the San Francisco fire. He had asked her to marry him, and she'd refused. But on that last night of farewell, she'd been unable to let him sail for Hawaii without something of her to remember.

There had been a time, before she and Dan married, that she tried to confess to him, but he'd dismissed her past as being unimportant. Now, she knew, uncomfortably, that he would explode in anger. He would never believe that she could still look on Sam as a friend, and not a lover.

She was beginning to believe that she and her husband were lovers—and not friends.

The next morning, Sam Larabee appeared at the head of a caravan. It consisted of his carriage and three empty wagons. He had delivered a load of pineapple to the port at Lahaina, he said. If the residents of the compound were inclined to accept his offer, here was transportation for themselves and their gear. No point in returning with the vehicles empty—

Dan accepted his offer for all of them, thanking him warmly. There was little to take. Soon the members of the group, together with their possessions, were aboard the wagons and ready to leave. Dan handed Tamsen into the carriage with Sam.

He would follow along a little later, he said. He had a few errands to attend to in Lahaina.

He talked to the man who was his contact there; a small, wizened gentleman who had been in the islands most of his life, and who had an almost fanatical contempt for all things Hawaiian. The States should take over, by force, if necessary. Put in businesses, big hotels. Run the natives out! They were godless, immoral, fornicating heathens—

Dan left his presence in a state of depression. As soon as he was convinced there was nothing better for the islands than annexation, he ran into an American who thought like this. He walked, head down in thought, to where his horse was tied, the hot Maui sun blazing on his bare head.

The sun! He remembered poor Dusty's inclination to blister. Their surveying would begin in earnest soon. It would do no harm to get some sort of protective lotion—or at least some salve to ease the little Englishman's pain.

His eye went, speculatively, toward the mission. He might find something there—and thank the Reverend at the same time.

Reverend David Selwyn, himself inclined to burn rather than tan, had mixed a special concoction. He was only too happy to share it with a fellow unfortunate. Dan watched as he packaged it. Selwyn was little more than a boy, slender, shoulders not filled out as yet. And the long tapering fingers that wrapped the package did not look capable of inflicting the bruises on Tamsen's arm.

"My name is Tallant," Dan said as he took the proffered medication. "And I really came for two reasons. I want to thank you for rescuing my wife—"

"It was an unfortunate thing," Selwyn said, after acknowledging Dan's self-introduction and returning his handshake. "I can't see how it happened. I do not exactly approve of some of her friends, but it's clear she is not a prostitute. And to be arrested as such was most degrading for her. As for rescuing her, I cannot take the credit," he said modestly, unaware that Dan's fists had clenched in shock.

"The credit goes to Samuel Larabee, my assistant's father. It seems he and your wife have known each other for years. For him to appear in her time of need—it was like a miracle."

"I'm sure it was," Dan said in a tight voice. "This Larabee—I've only met him once. What—what sort of man is he?"

"Oh, a fine man. Well thought of." Selwyn glanced toward the outer room and lowered his tone. "A bit of a hypochondriac, if you ask me, but then— we all have our faults."

"Some of us more than others," Tallant said darkly. Then, "Well, whatever part you played, I want to express my gratitude. Perhaps a donation—?" He reached into his pocket, and Selwyn put up a staying hand.

"It isn't necessary. As I told you, Sam Larabee handled the situation. Though I did manage to get the place closed, for good, I hope."

"The—place?"

"The—I suppose you would call it a brothel. Billy Whisker's House of Pleasure." Selwyn stopped suddenly, his eyes stricken. "Your wife did tell you?"

"Of course. I didn't understand," Dan said dully.

Selwyn followed him to the door. "I do hope that you will exercise your authority as her husband, convince her she mustn't attend such places, no matter the reason. Maybe we might be able to involve the women of your family in good works—the Church—"

"That would be impossible," Dan said stiffly. "We're moving quite a distance up the coast, today, into new housing. Courtesy of my wife's old friend, Sam Larabee."

Mouth set in a straight line, eyes blind with fury, he left the mission house and mounted his horse. It was time to ride out. The directions to the place were in his pocket. The house that Tamsen had somehow gotten from Larabee. What had she done to pay for it?

He didn't want to know.

22

What had she done to pay for it!

The thought kept ringing through his mind as he followed the trail his wife, Sam Larabee and the others had taken earlier. And she had lied! Why did she think it was necessary to invent that tale about a fall? And why didn't she tell him Sam Larabee was a friend from the past? Why couldn't she have told him the truth?

It wouldn't be the first time she lied! Look at the way she'd let him think Martha was *his* all those years ago! She'd gotten enough money out of him to set up her fancy Parlor. And some other sucker had put up the rest—

Sonofabitch!

A conversation came flooding back to him; the words of a girl named Katie. She was a self-professed whore, but she'd loved him. She'd been making up to him, and he rejected her, telling her he was only after some straight answers.

"Aw-w, Dan, can't it wait? It's been so long—"

Good God! He could hear her voice now!

"I'm not in the mood for games tonight," he'd told her. "Some other time. Now, tell me, where did Tamsen get the money to go into this business?"

"She got it off a man," Katie said. "Sam Larabee. Supposed to be an investment for him, but I witnessed the deed. Didn't say Larabee on it, as far as I could tell."

"Then how did she get the money?"

Katie's face was before him now in his mind's eyes; her pretty Irish face, lip curled derisively.

"The usual way, I suppose. Some of us are luckier than others—"

Sam Larabee! No wonder the name on his list had a familiar ring!

Reaching a point where the road ran high above Napili Bay, Dan Tallant dismounted, letting his horse wander freely, grazing as his master sat on a stone looking out to sea.

Below, the blue waters were gentle. A single white sail gleamed in the distance. Behind him, white ginger spread a haunting scent of memory. Gradually, he forced his temper to cool. One by one, he took the things Reverend Selwyn said.

Tamsen had been arrested as a prostitute. And the place where she had been arrested was closed down. Apparently, Sam Larabee had appeared later.

Why had she been arrested? It might be merely for being on the premises. Perhaps there had been some sort of fight. That would account for her bruises. But why would she go there in the first place?

He thought of her frantic fight for respectability these last years. When he'd left on this trip, she had still been dressed in black, her hair skinned back in an attempt to be inconspicuous. And with that look, she'd acquired an attitude of—almost primness. It had been a bone of contention between them for a long time.

He'd returned to find her attractively gowned, as irresistible as she'd been in the old days. Perhaps, with the donning of something new and bright, she'd also had a yearning to visit a public place. It made sense.

Then there was Larabee to explain away. He might—or might not—be an old friend of Tamsen's. He might—or might not—be the man Katie mentioned. It was possible that he, himself, had fitted the name into that time-blurred conversation.

He would give Tamsen the benefit of the doubt, remaining silent until she chose to tell him the truth about what happened in his absence. He'd gone off half-cocked too many times, and he'd usually been wrong.

It was a weary, beaten-looking man who rode into the yard of the house on the cliff a little later. The magnificence of the place stirred his suspicions once more, but they were allayed when Tamsen came running toward him, arms outstretched, eyes shining with excitement—and love.

His fears were put to rest the next evening. Sam had a house guest, a young Australian sailor, in port for a few days, who wished to see how a sugar plantation was operated. In addition, David Selwyn had been invited to dinner; an invitation Larabee regretted but couldn't withdraw with grace. To offset Selwyn, Lani would also be coming home for an evening. Sam decided, rather than dinner, to make it a luau to welcome the guests who occupied the new premises above his home. The Tallant and Narvaéz families, Dusty Wotherspoon, Nell, Martha, and the irrepressible Kimo.

It was a gala occasion. Dan liked Larabee's plump wife from the start. She was certainly no beauty, though sweetness seemed to shine from her. The amazing thing was that Larabee had eyes for no one else. He was constantly at Josie's side, seeing to her comfort, his face soft with genuine affection. If there was anything between Sam and Tamsen in the old days, there certainly wasn't now.

The tropic night cooperated in every way. The night sky was clear, studded with stars; a faint breeze wafted perfume mingled with the mouth-watering odor of pork from the pit where a pig was roasting in ti leaves. There was pineapple juice for the children and a concoction of coconut milk and alcohol served in pineapple shells for their elders. More important, there was good, relaxed conversation. The women grouped together, discussing new fashions, children. The men stood in a huddle, fascinated at what the handsome young Australian had to show them.

His name was Peter Channing. He'd sailed on a merchant ship in order to see the world. But rum as he'd thought it, he'd found no place to compare with his home. So he was going back—to look for *these.*

He drew several twists of paper from his pocket, and opened them to reveal a number of opals, some white, some black, some a deep, smoky gray, all with fire at their hearts.

"They're found where there was once an inland sea," he explained in his odd accent. "There's something about them that gets into a man's mind, drives him round the bend."

Tamsen, seeing the expressions on both Dan and Juan, felt a twinge of fear. She'd seen the same look on men in the gold fields. A look of hunger that could never be satisfied.

"Aren't opals supposed to be unlucky?" she called out.

Channing laughed. "Indeed not! The reverse, rather! An opal makes its owner invisible in the sight of hostile forces. He escapes the eye of misfortune."

"Would you part with one of those?" Sam Larabee asked. "I'd like to purchase it for my wife."

"Sam!" Josie Larabee, half-laughing, half-serious, tried to stop her husband as he badgered the Australian, raising his bid until the young man laughed and gave in. "You made me an offer I can't refuse," he confessed.

The feast was finally spread and they all ate to the point of misery. Following the meal, Kimo began to strum his guitar. The sea wasn't visible from Sam Larabee's home, but the wash of waves carried to blend with the music. At Josie's request, Tamsen sang a soft ballad that brought tears to the eyes of all present. Then Sam Larabee whispered to his wife, who nodded.

"Josie hasn't danced in a long time," he told them. "She's had trouble with her feet. An arthritic condition, we think. But she's willing to try, with your permission."

At the round of applause following his speech, the plump little woman stepped into the circle of firelight. She had worn Hawaiian garb, tonight, her dark hair around her pleasant face and falling to her waist. Kimo strummed and she began to sway, arms curving to form a moon; fingers twinkling, becoming stars; passing the fragrance of the ginger flower beneath her nose. As the song ended her hands reached skyward, and the movements of her hands became the falling rain.

For a moment, after she bowed, one foot pointed gracefully forward, her hands cupped together, there was a hushed silence. Then the guests stood, clapping, in appreciation of what they had seen.

Smiling, she pushed her damp hair back. And Dan noticed that her eyes seemed glassy with tears.

Beside him, David Selwyn was staring, as if he couldn't get enough of the sight of her.

Dan remarked on it when they wended their way home, preferring to walk in the deep Hawaiian night. "I thought Selwyn was interested in Sam's daughter. But it would appear to be her mother he's attracted to. I wonder what Larabee thinks of that?"

Tamsen gasped. "I never heard anything so ridiculous in my life! Dan, she's *old!*"

"How old? Forty? And you just had your thirty-eighth birthday. Are *you* old?" his tone was teasing.

"She's too old for him, and she isn't the *type!*"

"Is there a type? I was in love with a schoolteacher when I was eight. She could take her teeth out."

"Dan, you fool!"

"Seriously, Tam, I watched him when Josie was dancing. The boy's in love with her. He looked positively wretched."

David Selwyn outstayed his welcome that night. He waited until Kimo left the fire; until the big Australian had gone to bed, and Josie had excused herself. Finally Sam, yawning, asked, "Don't you think you and Lani had better be getting back? The place where she boards—they may not appreciate her coming in so late."

"When are you coming to town?" Selwyn's words stumbled over each other in a rush to be said.

"Why, I suppose any time." Sam eyed him curiously. "Do you have something on your mind?"

"I want to talk to you," the missionary said. "It's important. I want to talk to you alone."

"Tomorrow, then?"

"Tomorrow will be fine."

Selwyn helped Lani mount, and got on his own horse with an awkward motion. Sam watched as they rode off into the darkness, his face creased in a worried frown. Then he laughed. With David Selwyn, the important meeting would be due to only one of two things. Either the mission needed money—or the young missionary would stammer a formal request that he be allowed to ask Lani for her hand in marriage.

Whatever Lani wished to do was her own business. Shaking his head in amusement, Sam went toward the house—and his wife.

He erred in his belief that David would approach him first. When they reached the spot above Napili Bay, David turned his mount along a small downward path that led to the white sand bordering the whispering water. Lani followed without question. Reaching the beach, he stopped, dismounted, and lifted her down. His nice gray eyes had an odd expression; a mingling of affection—and pain.

"Lani, I have something to tell you." He looked at her for a moment, then walked away. For a long time, he stood looking out to sea, then bowed his head for a moment as if in prayer. Then he came back to her.

"Lani, I love you. I want you for my wife."

"You don't know what you're saying, Rev—David," she said. "Your church might frown on it. I'm part Hawaiian; a—a *heathen*," she mocked herself. "I like the native ways. I even believe in some of them! I'd be an embarrassment to you."

He took her flowerlike face in his hands, marveling at its serene beauty. "Nothing you could do would embarrass me!"

"I respect the *kapus*, I told you that! My mother keeps a shark's tooth in her jewelry box, her father's *aumakua*—"

"And Sam bought her an opal, to put beside it. Because an opal will help her hide from misfortune. Sam Larabee's a white man, and a Christian of sorts."

Lani was silent for a long time. "I can't let you do this to yourself," she said. "I love you too much."

David Selwyn, with a choked cry, took her into his arms. "You just said what I wanted to hear."

They sank to the sand and he held her close, telling her of his dreams, the nights of agony he'd spent, wanting her, needing her. And when he felt his passions rise to an extent that they ruled his head, he stood and took her hand, lifting her. He must get her to her boarding house. They would discuss their wedding plans tomorrow.

David Selwyn might fall in love with a girl who respected *kapus*, whose mother kept an *aumakua* in her jewelry box, but he could not allow himself to be tempted into mortal sin.

23

The next morning, Sam Larabee rode into Lahaina. His hat sat well back on his sandy hair, his blue eyes echoed the color of the placid sky, and he was whistling a soundless tune. Last night had been pleasant, something they should do more often. He'd awakened this morning with a feeling of well-being, the ride down was pleasant, and he was looking forward to an amusing interlude with Selwyn. He wondered how a missionary would propose marriage. Not the way he had, by God! He was sure of that.

Still, there was a real man under all that buttering of piety. And Lani, his deceptively sweet child, had enough of her mother in her to bring it out. So there was nothing to worry about.

He tethered his horse before the mission and strode in, sailing his hat at Lani, who had the grace to blush. A dead giveaway, he thought grinning as he went into the dispensary.

David had asked Lani to leave the mission while he spoke with her father. Wanting to obey his wishes, but nervous, in spite of her knowledge that Sam was fair-minded, she lingered, hearing only the low hum of David Selwyn's voice.

Then there was a yell of anger, a resounding

crash, and Sam rushed past his daughter, his face livid with fury, his eyes those of a crazed man.

"Papa—?"

He was gone, slamming the door behind him.

Her heart palpitating, Lani hurried into the dispensary. David lay on the floor, dazed, surrounded by broken bottles and the pills she'd hand-rolled so carefully this morning.

"David!" She dropped to her knees, seeing his swollen jaw, the imprint of Sam Larabee's fist. "Oh, David!"

Weeping, she filled a basin of water and began to wring out cold compresses, applying them to his face. Finally, he sat up, rubbing his jawline, ruefully. "What was it, David! What did he say? He doesn't want us to marry?"

"I didn't get around to asking him," Selwyn said, dully.

"Then, why—"

She didn't get a chance to finish her sentence. The door crashed open and Sam entered, still with the face of a madman. He took hold of Lani's arm in a cruel grip, jerking her to her feet. "Get away from him. You're coming home with me. I'll come back after your things."

"Papa! No! I won't! I don't know what's the matter, but—"

"Out," he roared, his eyes murderous. "Do as I say!"

"I'll be back," she called as he propelled her toward the door, "Don't worry, David, I'll be back—"

Sam Larabee didn't speak to his daughter during the two hours it took to reach the turnoff to his home. He rode ahead of her, shoulders slumped, his sandy hair showing streaks of white she hadn't noticed before. In spite of her hurt and anger, she felt a kind of pity for him. When they reached the trail that led off toward their house, he turned to face her.

"I'm sorry I was so high-handed. Please forget what happened. And forget that hymn-singing sonofabitch!"

"I'm going to marry him, Papa."

"Then I'm going to ask you this. Give me one month. Just one month. After that, you can do anything you please."

His face was gray, and she found herself promising what he asked. A month was only a little time when she and David would have a whole life together.

"Another thing," he said heavily, "I don't want to upset your mother. I'm going to leave you up at the Tallant place for awhile. Just until I can get my head straight on this. It's your place, anyway, or will be one day. Will you go there?"

"Whatever you say, Papa." Her head was high. "Just remember that it's one month, no more."

"I won't be apt to forget it." His face was grim once more as he led the way to the house on the cliff.

Tamsen welcomed Lani to the Tallant-Narváez domicile. It was already filled to overflowing, all of them but Nell and Dusty living in the main house, Nell and Dusty occupying a small neat bungalow originally belonging to an overseer. Lani was given a room to share with Martha, a fact Sam seized on in this explanation for bringing her there.

She had quit her work in town, due to overwork and fatigue. She needed to rest, and to have the company of a girl her own age. He intended to keep the news of her quitting from Josie for awhile. She tended to worry, make mountains out of molehills, and she would insist Lani come home. It was lonely there for the girl.

"Sounds gawdam fishy t' me," Nell growled to Dusty after hearing the story from Tamsen. Then her face lit up. "Hell, mebbe they's more t' that there mishunary feller than I figgered. S'pose he's bin a-gittin' there?"

"Nell!" Dusty was scandalized, and Nell subsided.

"Hell," she said stubbornly, "He's a *man*, ain't he?"

Tamsen and Dan were also perplexed. Sam Larabee's eyes were strange when he brought his daughter to them. Lani, herself, was pale and too quiet. Only Martha heard her crying in the night.

Lying in her own bed, she listened, thinking of all the nights she'd cried alone. After an idyllic childhood, she'd been shipped off to her aunt—like a bundle of laundry. And here, she'd been blamed for everything. It looked like Lani was being treated the same way. Maybe Lani would confide in her. She would have someone to talk to, who would understand. She might even tell her of her love for Dan—

Slipping from her bed, she tiptoed across the room, touching Lani's shoulder with a sympathetic hand. "Don't cry," she whispered, her own eyes filling with tears. "What's wrong, Lani? If I can help—"

"There's nothing wrong," Lani said after a moment.

"But I heard you! You were crying!"

Lani buried her face in her pillow. "Leave me alone! Just leave me alone!"

Martha, her face an angry red in the darkness, returned to her bed. She'd been a fool to think she would find friendship anywhere in this house. After this, Lani could bawl her damn head off if she wanted to. Martha would keep to herself.

But presently, she, too, was crying, muffling her sobs in her pillow. What's the matter with me? she asked herself, in agony. What's the matter with me?

She couldn't get close to anyone.

The days that followed began to assume a sameness. Each morning, the men set out to their surveying work at dawn, returning late in the evening to their home. For Tamsen, Arab, and Nell, it was a time of happiness. Dinners were taken under the night sky on a velvet lawn. Afterward, Kimo would usually appear with his guitar and his foolish clowning. It was obvious that he was there as a suitor for Lani's hand, but she remained cool and remote, unsmiling.

Only Dan received an inkling of what had happened. He was forced to make a trip into Lahaina, and Lani asked him to deliver a note to the mission house. It was in regard to some of her effects she'd left behind, she said. He delivered the thing to David Selwyn, noting with surprise that the young missionary's jaw was taped, and that bruises spread above the bandage in a colorful stain.

"My God, man! What happened?"

"It isn't wise to take the name of the Lord in vain," Selwyn reproved him. "It's nothing. I—fell."

Selwyn excused himself and returned with a folded paper, carefully sealed with candle wax. It was to be given to Lani, an answer to her missive. Tallant slipped it into his pocket, then went to inquire about his own incoming mail. There was a letter from Duke Courtney, forwarded from Hilo. Oddly, it was addressed to him.

He opened it with shaking fingers. Em had been due to deliver some time ago. Duke Courtney was not a man for corresponding. Lord, Dan hoped it wasn't bad news.

A drunken sailor, leaning against a storefront, was shocked sober at the sound of a rebel yell. Dan Tallant grabbed the man by his shirt front and lifted him into the air, setting him down and pushing a wad of money into his hand.

"It's a boy!" he yelled. "A boy! And Em's fine!"

"Congratulations," the dazed stranger finally stammered. But Tallant was gone.

He rode home at top speed, pushing his mount like a madman. David Selwyn's note to Lani slipped from his pocket and blew away on the wings of a soft Maui wind. He didn't miss it until much later; after the news had dissolved his household into a state that veered from laughter to happy tears.

He'd probably handed it to Lani during all the excitement. He dismissed it from his mind.

When the furor died down, each had time for his separate thoughts. Tamsen was delighted for Em's sake, but there was a wistful sadness as she remembered this was Em's fourth child—and she, herself had none.

Arab, cradling her baby in her arms, leaned against Juan's shoulder. More than anything, she would have liked to give him a son. But, her arms tightened fiercely about little Luka. She would not trade this baby for anything.

Martha went to her room to sit dully on the edge of her bed. She was glad Mama was over her pregnancy, and well. She'd worried more than she'd let herself admit. And the sight of Duke's sprawling writing had been almost too much to bear. But Mama had what she wanted now. A boy. And certainly legitimate. They were probably glad to be rid of her. Now they could be happy.

Nell's reaction was more explosive. "I be damned," she chortled. "A boy! Didden figger them McLeod girls ud have nuthin' but girls. Hell, that Duke-feller must be quite a man!"

Lani, set apart from all the family rejoicing, slipped away. She followed the crooked path that led from the clifftop down to the curving beach at the water's edge. The sun had set, the waters still stained with ts afterglow. At her feet, the waves lapped gently, while they threw themselves on the horns of the rocks that framed the shore with a booming sound. It was like being surrounded by a storm, with her own immediate area untouched, serene.

Lani felt anything but serene. Why hadn't David written her? She'd expected an answer.

Maybe he was through with anyone by the name of Larabee, forever.

Immersed in her thoughts, deafened by the sound of the surf to right and left, Lani did not hear Kimo approach.

"*Hui, Ipo!*" he grinned. "Dis *ol* place mek love!"

She turned on him. "I'm not your sweetheart! And I wish you wouldn't play your stupid game with me! I know you've got a college education! That you can speak English better than I can. Oh, Kimo, why do you have to be such a *fool!*"

She burst into tears, and he put his arms around her, comforting her, leading her to a stone protruding from the sand. He brushed it clean, and seated her, standing before her; his sturdy body, clad only in a length of bright cloth, seeming to belong there, framed against the darkening water.

"I'm sorry if I offend you," he said gently. "And

you are right. But I don't want to be an educated white man, Lani! I'm Hawaiian, a native! I intend to stay that way. When some of the white planters look down on me, call me boy, I can laugh at them, inside, knowing that I could meet them on their own ground, but I do not choose to. Don't you see?"

"The world is changing," she cried. "You've got to change with it! You can't always be a clown!"

"I will not change. I am a Hawaiian. My father is a Kahuna, you know that. He is teaching me his secrets, and I plan to return to the old ways as many of our generation will. The white men will go away."

"You don't know what you're talking about! Do you think my father—?"

"Your father is one of us, no matter what color his skin is. And, Lani—he wishes us to marry. We have his blessing."

Lani leaped to her feet. "No! I don't love you, Kimo! Not that way! It's David! David! Oh, dear God—"

Kimo stood, arms folded so that he would not be tempted to touch her. She stood before him, her face stricken, a slim half-caste girl in a yellow gown; the girl he had grown up with; his playmate, his little sister, and now his love—

And she loved David Selwyn, one of the breed who had changed his islands; his beloved way of life.

"*Auwe!*" He twisted his face comically, clasping his hands over his heart. "You mek all *pau!* All *pau!* We mek go house now?"

Lani was laughing and crying at the same time. "Kimo, you idiot!"

He touched a hand to his forehead. In the dusk, she could see the gleam of his white teeth, but not

224

the deep sadness that shadowed his eyes. *"Pupule,"* he agreed. "Absolutely, indubitably, and incurably *pupule!"*

A better word, he thought as he led her up the crooked path, the waves weeping behind them, would be *poho.* For he was absolutely, indubitably and incurably out of luck.

At the top of the path, he held her shoulders for a moment, looking down into her flowerlike face. *"Aloha au ia oe,"* he whispered. He kissed her tear-stained cheek, and then was gone.

24

Several days later, knowing Dan and the others would be coming home soon, Martha dressed carefully, placing a flower in her hair. Though she had been careful since her confrontation with Tamsen, there was no law that said she couldn't look her best—or that she couldn't be first to greet him.

Seeing a mounted man approach, she sped to meet him, stopping in confusion as he dismounted and came toward her. It was the young Australian seaman, Peter Channing. His look of surprise and admiration made her pulses race, and she hated herself for it. He wasn't Dan!

For Channing's part, he had never seen anything as lovely as that small flying figure, dark hair blowing in the Maui wind. As she reached him, he identified her as young Martha, Tallant's niece. That night at Larabee's, he'd lumped her in with the nippers—one of the children. But, lord, she was a dazzler—

He altered his opinion as her face fell upon recognizing him, settling into sulky lines. He followed her to the house, hurt by his cold reception, until it dawned on him that she had been expecting someone else. Just as well. This was his last leave.

His ship would be sailing in a week or two. One day, he would be back among the sheilas of his own country. Still, he couldn't keep his eyes off the small figure leading the way.

Reaching the house, he explained his errand to Tamsen. He had an open invitation at the Larabee home, and he had come to say good-bye. When he arrived, the place was deserted. He'd finally located Sam, but the man behaved oddly and he didn't look well. Was something wrong? If there was anyway he could lend a hand—

"You didn't see Josie?" Tamsen felt a twinge of alarm.

"Off visiting friends, I understand."

Lani and Martha had joined them. Lani's face paled at Channing's words. "My mother never goes anywhere. She wouldn't leave my father. She has no close friends on Maui."

Tamsen put a calming hand on her arm. "I will go down in the morning. I'll talk to Sam and get to the bottom of this. For now," she smiled at the sailor who stood awkwardly twisting his cap in his hands, "let's make Peter welcome. The men will be delighted to see him when they get home. Lani, will you and Martha set the tables—outside under the trees? We will make this a party in Peter's honor.

Tamsen was not as confident as she sounded. She'd been concerned about Sam since he brought Lani to the door. As she set about making Peter feel at ease, her mind raced with suppositions. Perhaps Sam and Josie had quarreled. It was evident Sam and Lani were at odds. Surely the Larabees wouldn't break up their marriage with a quarrel about their only child! She would see in the morning. Frantically, she wished the hours away.

Martha, spreading a cloth on a table beneath a

227

flowering tree, was angry. First, her planned meeting with Dan was spoiled. Then Tamsen had sent her off to set the tables—like a child. She wanted to be alone with Peter Channing, that was why! She had to have any man's full attention! Especially, an attractive man. Not that she cared—

"The cloth isn't straight," Lani said.

Martha, looking at the pale girl who had rejected her friendship, transferred her malice. "You've played into Tamsen's hands, haven't you? Now she's got an excuse."

Lani dropped a cup. "What are you talking about?"

"An excuse to go see your father. Surely you know what's going on. I don't blame your mother for leaving."

"I don't see—"

"You would if you had eyes. And so would Dan. Your father and Tamsen have been carrying on right under everybody's nose. Guess Josie found out—"

Martha's head rocked back as Lani delivered a ringing slap. Putting a hand to her crimson cheek, she glared at the half-caste girl. "If you don't believe me, follow Tamsen in the morning. See for yourself!"

Lani whirled and ran for the room she shared with Martha. She did not come out for dinner.

The meal was not the festive one Tamsen wished it to be. Her mind was too filled with worry over Sam and Josie. Lani refused to eat, Arab was forced to take little Luka in early, Nell was grumpy, Martha silent.

Only the men of the group were alive with interest. Peter was asked to produce his opals again, and they were passed from Dan to Juan to Dusty, all of them exclaiming over the flashes of liquid fire that came from the heart of one particularly fine stone. Peter was patient in explaining the phenomenon.

The flashes of color were caused by light interference or cracks within the opal, filled with material of slightly different optical density. He caught for a clearer way to put it. "Like a film of oil on water," he said finally. "You have a rainbow."

As he talked, Martha left the space where Tamsen sat with Ramona and Missy, crowding into the circle of men. Channing saw her hand slide possessively into the crook of Dan's arm and noticed the way she pressed her body against him.

I'll be damned, he thought. *So that's the way the wind blows!* He cast a surreptitious look at Tamsen. This little no-hoper was after Tallant, and his wife knew it. What a crook deal!

Channing turned his gaze to Martha, his eyes like cold gray stone. She flushed beneath his look, but tightened her grip. Dan Tallant, finally aware of the girl at his side, patted her hand absently. "Run along, sweetheart. We're talking man-talk."

Channing relaxed a little. The man had treated her as if she were a child. Maybe there was nothing to it, after all. Martha returned to sit stiffly at Tamsen's side, watching the play of light on Dan's beloved face as he held the opal near a candle, absorbed in its beauty.

"I'm going to go to Australia one day," he said. "There's something about these things that get into a man's blood."

"*Australia* gets into one's blood," Peter said quietly. "It's a bonzer place, these things lying about on the ground; millions of acres to be settled. I have ten thousand acres in sheep, north of the Goyder line—"

"Ten thousand! Good God!" Dan whistled in amazement.

"A small holding," Channing said ruefully. "My da left it to me. He and Mum died in the same year. The drought followed after, and I signed on ship to save the station, leaving a foreman in charge. When I go home, I plan to expand. It's a man's country, a gambler's country. Sometimes the gamble pays off, sometimes it doesn't."

Dan grinned. "Sounds like my kind of a place. Guess you've given me the fever."

"I'm suffering from the same ailment," Juan said. Dan laughed, proffering his hand, and Dusty proffered his own to each in turn, insisting on being included.

Finally, it was time for Channing to take his leave. He insisted on giving Tamsen a small smoky gem. "In memory of your hospitality," he said, "and to keep your husband's visit to my country fresh in his mind." He said good-bye solemnly to each of the little girls, shaking hands with them, touching Martha's hand in a brief farewell gesture, though his eyes were cold.

He was startled at the tingling sensation her touch produced, and knew that she had felt it, too. She jerked her hand away, and turned her face from him.

"You were surely joking about a trip to Australia," Tamsen said as she readied herself for bed that night. Dan, who usually delighted in watching the process of clothing falling in a froth of lace, hair tumbling in a silken mass as pins were removed, had his back to her.

"I would like to," he said, turning to face her. She saw what he held in his hand; the small smoky stone with fire at its heart.

"For heaven's sake, Dan! You look at that thing like it's some kind of—*aumakua!*"

"Maybe it is," he said soberly. "Good God, Tamsen! Can you imagine how *old* this thing is? Formed at the bottom of what was once an inland sea! It gives me a feeling of—of the permanence of things. Makes me feel—peaceful."

Tamsen's mouth went dry. He sounded so much like Sam, that day on the island of *Moku-ula*. Dan Tallant found his case for immortality in a gemstone; Sam, on an island of the dead.

She shivered. "Put that thing away," she said. "And come to bed."

He obeyed, a teasing light in his eyes as he came toward her, taking her in his arms, holding her, whispering words of love as he aroused her to a white-hot blaze of emotion.

He'd forgotten the opals, she thought with satisfaction when their lovemaking was over and he lay sleeping beside her, but she'd been unable to erase her worries about Sam Larabee.

The next morning, she dressed with care, putting on the mended crimson gown that was so becoming to her. It wasn't in order to look her best, she told herself, but because the dress was such a cheerful color. There was something dreadfully wrong at the Larabee house. Sam had never been morose or introspective in the old days. His words on the island of Moku-ula still worried her. And bringing Lani up here—leaving her, not even visiting—it was beyond understanding. She still had a feeling it was something to do with Sam's health, either physical or mental. And she was determined to get at the cause of the trouble.

As she rounded a curve in the path, a sea wind

caught at her hair, sending the pins that moored it flying. The only thing to do was to put the remaining pins in her pocket and let her black locks hang to her waist.

Sam Larabee, at the edge of his property, near a foot-trail that led through heavy vegetation to the sea, saw her approaching the house. He was certain he'd never seen anything so beautiful in his life as the slim girl in her red gown, her hair falling in a cloud of dark mist.

He did not want her at the house. Concealing the oilskin covered bundle he carried behind a bush, he stepped out into the open.

"Tamsen," he called, "over here."

She turned and came toward him. Again, her beauty caught at his heart. But when she was close enough, he could see a line of worry between her brows.

"You didn't come to us, Sam, so I came to you."

"I'm glad you did," he said huskily, meaning it.

"I think you owe me an explanation, Sam. Lani's obviously unhappy. You haven't been to see us. Josie seems to have disappeared, according to Peter Channing." Her eyes studied him, seeing the lines that framed his mouth like parentheses, the set of his lips, as though he had suffered pain. He had lost the slight thickening at the waist, denoting a comfortable middle age, his shoulders seeming to stoop a little with weariness.

"You are ill, aren't you? And you're trying to keep it from everyone. For heaven's sake, Sam! Don't be a fool! Go talk to David Selwyn. If he can't help you—"

"I don't want anything to do with that sonofabitch," Sam gritted.

Tamsen's heart sank. She remembered Dan's remark about the young missionary. *"I watched him when Josie was dancing—The boy's in love with her."*

Josie Larabee adored her husband. But did Sam know that? Would jealousy drive Sam to the state he was in now?

"Where is Josie?"

Her question caught him flat-footed. "Visiting," he stammered. "Visiting friends."

"If she's in Lahaina, I might ride in to see her."

"She's in Honolulu," he said too quickly. "She'll be home soon."

"Lani needs her. And she needs her father."

"I'll be up tonight," he said dully.

"I'm glad," Tamsen said. "And, Sam, share your troubles. Next to Dan, I guess I love you more than any man in the world. And Josie loves you—"

Sam's face crumpled, his breath catching in a harsh sob. Tamsen reached out to him in alarm. "Sam! Oh, Sam!"

He buried his face against her shoulder and wept; the horrible, wrenching sobs of a strong man who had never cried in his life.

On the hill above the Larabee plantation, Lani and Martha crouched, watching. "See? See how close she's standing?" Martha had pointed out.

"It doesn't mean anything," Lani scoffed. "They're just talking." She choked on the last word as Tamsen reached out to Sam Larabee and he went into her arms, his own going about her in a desperate embrace.

Lani turned, running from the sight. Martha followed, sympathetic with Lani's pain, but glad that her own suspicions had been proven. Now, all she had to do was prove it to Dan.

233

25

Sam did not offer an explanation to Tamsen for his emotional behavior. After a bit, he stepped back, worked his ravaged face into a smile, and asked her to tell Lani he would call that evening.

He came, attired in a spotless white planter's suit, freshly shaven, his hands pink from scrubbing. Lani treated him with cool politeness, speaking only when she was spoken to. Tamsen, seeing the agony in his eyes, tried to make up for the girl's lack of co-operation, unwittingly offering fuel for the girl's suspicions.

As Sam's visits continued, night after night, Dan Tallant's misgivings returned to plague him. "For God's sake," he exploded one night. "When's the man's wife coming home? When he offered us the house, I didn't know he went with it!"

"I asked him here for Lani's sake," Tamsen said defensively. "It would be nice if they settled their differences."

"Then tell him to take his daughter home. Let them fight it out, if they want to. It's none of our business—"

"Dan, I can't do that! He asked—"

"Don't you think you're going a little overboard,

Tam? Taking so much interest in the affairs of a man you've known little more than a month?"

He didn't look at her as he spoke, but he felt the impact of his words strike her. In a moment, she said, in a small voice, "He did let us have this house, Dan."

"Maybe it's costing a little too much," he said grimly. After one long level look at his wife, he went outside, going down to the shore where he sat staring into the blue waters for a long time. It was very late when he came in. Tamsen had gone to bed, but she lay huddled in a small miserable heap. She looked like she might have been crying.

Dammit, she looked so innocent!

He sat down beside her, smoothing her hair back with a gentle hand. "I'm sorry I was cross, sweetheart. There's something I haven't told you. I have to leave for Honolulu, tomorrow. A meeting of the backers of the railway system. I don't get to see you alone much anymore. Maybe I'm jealous of Larabee—"

There. He had given her an opening to say anything she had to say—

Tamsen lay quiet for a moment. Now, if ever, was the time to confide in Dan. But she had waited too long. "You needn't be jealous of Sam, Dan. He wouldn't look twice at anyone but Josie. If you want me to, I'll ask Lani to leave. But we do owe him—"

"Forget it," he said shortly. Then, with a groan, "Tam—I love you so damn much!"

"And I love you." Her arms came up, pulling him down to her. For a long time, he lay with his head pillowed against her shoulder as he held her, hating himself for his doubts and suspicions. He should come right out with what he knew, ask for an explanation. But their relationship had been so

235

fragile these last years. Tamsen's defensiveness had precluded such times as this—this warm and tender togetherness. He was certain she had reasons for anything she did, and for keeping those reasons to herself.

If only he weren't such a jealous bastard!

Her hand stroked his face, moving down his hard-muscled chest. Finally, driven out of his mind with desire, he loved her, everything else driven from his mind.

Afterward, lying close and warm, he convinced himself that all was right between them. The wish that she had told him the truth was pushed to the back of his mind. Their love was here and now, and he would have to be leaving her tomorrow.

Sam Larabee arrived on the heels of Dan's departure. He did not look well at all, Tamsen thought. Each time she saw him, he seemed to be paler, thinner. One eye had developed a nervous tic. He did not seem like the old cock-sure Sam at all.

Learning that Dan was to be gone for sometime, he put forth an idea. He owned property at Hana, on the other side of the island. Lani had been born there. Though he had a competent overseer, he must visit from time to time, to keep his affairs in order. It was a lovely place. He thought perhaps a trip, such as he and Lani had taken over the years, might help to heal the breach between them.

She would not go alone with him, he knew. Not the way things were at present. But she might if Martha went—Tamsen and the others, if they wished.

Tamsen's first impulse was to refuse the invitation. She turned from Sam's beseeching eyes and was lost for a moment in thought. If all went well, and the journey brought father and daughter together, Lani would go home. She had an idea the association with Martha wasn't good for the girl. There had been an atmosphere of tension lately that she didn't understand.

Surely, Dan wouldn't mind if she went along with a group of people. And when he came home, it would be to a peaceful house.

The small party set out the next morning. It consisted of Tamsen, Sam, Martha, and a rebellious Lani. Nell had flatly refused, saying that her backside fit a veranda better than it did a horse. Juan and Dusty had work Dan laid out before he left. And Arab, who looked forward to the outing for herself and the girls, had to beg off at the last minute. Luka was running a low temperature.

Tamsen, herself, sought vainly for an excuse to remain behind. Only Sam's crestfallen face brought her around. After all, these were modern times—and the girls would be there.

They rode toward Lahaina, reaching it with the morning sun. In addition to their mounts, there was one packhorse carrying food, cooking utensils, and a tarpaulin, since they must break their journey for a night before reaching Hana.

Martha and Lani lagged behind, not an auspicious beginning, but Sam was ebullient as they left Lahaina, traveling along a narrow lane bordered by sugarcane. He gave a running commentary on the merits of the growth about them. When they reached a small plantation town called Paia, where pineapple fields ran upward into the village of Makawao, he was still talking.

"It means 'forest beginning on the slopes of Haleakala,'" he informed Tamsen.

She tried to give an appearance of interest, but her mind was on the girls who had dropped far be-

237

hind. Their eyes boring into her back made her feel guilty at being here. Surely, it was her imagination—

They spent the night at Maliko Bay. Sam built a fire of driftwood, and Tamsen cooked a plain but hearty meal. There was to be no camaraderie about the fire. The girls retired immediately after eating, but they were still watching. Tamsen could sense it.

She cleaned up after the meal, and wished to excuse herself, but Sam reached for her hand, pulling her down beside him.

"Don't go," he begged. "Sit with me, just for a little while."

He didn't relinquish his grip, and she looked nervously toward the spot where the girls were supposed to be sleeping. "I'm very tired, Sam."

He didn't seem to hear her. "This is a very special place to me. Josie and I were married in Honolulu. We took ship immediately, and landed at Lahaina. We spent our first night together—here, on our way home to Hana."

He went on, describing how beautiful his Josie had been. She had danced for him, framed against the blue water, her long hair like a shining veil—

"You miss her, don't you?"

"Neither of us will ever leave the other again."

She finally escaped, leaving Sam with his memories. His shoulders drooped, and he looked the picture of despair. She wished she'd asked Dan to search out Josie in Honolulu, and tell her she was needed at home.

Even Lani seemed in better spirits the next morning. The air was soft, with a hint of dew, and the area they rode through had changed drastically. They had entered an area of sea cliffs, rich with pandanus and fern. The trail wound through rich valleys, fording streams fed by waterfalls, and into thickets of bamboo, giant a'pe leaves, wild ginger, kukui trees, ground orchids, hauhala, and hau trees. Along the route was an occasional grass hut; a taro patch, earth thrown up to form a square water-filled pool. Here and there, they came upon an ancient village, where life went on as it had for centuries. Larabee pointed out items of interest as they made their way toward Hana: waterfalls, blue bays dreaming in the sun, lava flows from ages past. Words fell from his lips like music.

Kaulanapueo, Kailua, Koolau: the Puohokamoa Valley, Honomanu Bay, Keanae, Punalau, Wailua; Wailuaiki, Nahiku—

They forded many streams, crossed rude bridges where falling water flung a rainbow spray to touch their faces, and climbed from the valley to the most surprising sight of all.

Here were rolling hills, fat cattle belly-deep in lush grass. An incongruous scene, belonging to the States, not a small tropical island in the middle of the sea.

"Sam, it's beautiful!"

"And it's mine," he said with boyish pride. "There is the house where Lani was born. We moved above Lahaina before the boys came." A shadow touched his face. "I like to come here where there were only happy times."

Lani spurred forward to meet an aged horseman. "Koma!" she called.

The *Paniola*, or cowboy, swept past her, turned, and put an arm like an iron band around the girl as she kicked free of her stirrups. Then he lifted her in front of him and they galloped like the wind, heading for a small, low ranch house. Her laughter trailed back to them.

239

Tamsen turned a startled look on Sam. He was smiling. "It was a game they had when she was small," he explained. "Koma's nearly eighty, now."

That slim, laughing horseman? It was difficult to believe. "A man like that will probably live forever," she remarked.

Sam's face darkened again. "I wish to God we all could," he said, his voice harsh. His mood lightened, however, when they reached the house, now occupied by his overseer, an ancient black man with close-cropped white hair.

"This is Henry," Sam introduced him with affection. The old man had been a slave on his family's plantation. After the war he had looked him up and brought him here.

"Knowed this boy all his life," the Negro grinned.

By that time, they were surrounded by a crowd of laughing, jostling *Paniolas*, greeting their boss-man, all asking where "Mama" was.

By *Mama*, they meant Josie, Tamsen discovered. Sam's answer was reluctant, and she found herself the center of curious glances, some of them not too friendly.

By evening, they seemed to have accepted her. A huge spread was prepared for the *Paniolas*, their wives, and families. Sam's homecoming was a festive occasion.

After a night in a small, but very clean room, Tamsen rose to an invigorating morning. Martha and Lani were already out and gone. Sam was in the ranch office, going over the crude books Henry kept with the aid of Paulo, a mission-educated native. Grateful for the opportunity to be alone, she walked along grassy paths, returning for a light lunch of fruit, and spent a lazy afternoon drowsing in a hammock slung between two mango trees. The heat settled around her like a warm blanket, and the flowering bushes Josie planted long ago filled the air with a narcotic perfume.

At the evening meal, Sam announced that he had a surprise for them. He had finished his work sooner than he'd expected, thanks to Henry and Paulo. He grinned at the two men who looked suddenly shy. Tomorrow, they would take a lunch and go to the village of Hana, and from there, down the Pilani trail to the Seven Pools.

Lani and Martha exchanged glances. As if by mutual agreement, they both refused to go.

Sam's face went white when he looked at his daughter who had loved this journey as a child. Then he turned red with anger. "I can't force you to go, either of you." His eyes went to Tamsen. "You will accompany me?"

She wanted to say no, but at the sight of his painfilled eyes, the white line about his mouth, she agreed. Dan, she thought disconsolately, wouldn't like this arrangement. Not at all. She could only hope Martha kept her mouth shut. Why couldn't people understand it was possible for a man and a woman to be friends?

She was still ill at ease the next morning when they set out on the trip. Sam's face was set, and she understood his feelings. He had counted on this trip to break through Lani's cold indifference.

If he'd only tell me what caused the rift, Tamsen thought, *maybe I could help*. As it was, all she could do was just be there.

The small village of Hana was still sleeping when they passed through, taking the Pilani trail. "It was built by Kihapiilani," Sam explained. "A king's son." He pointed out the small Alau Island, offshore.

Further along, they left the trail, going about two hundred yards inland, in order to see pictographs drawn under a ledge at the end of a stream. These were not carved into the stone, Sam explained, like petroglyphs, but painted with a red dye, possibly by the Alii, who frequented this trail.

Returning to their path, Tamsen was surprised to see the big island of Hawaii looming in the distance, its peaks, Mauna Loa and Mauna Kea visible, though the distance was some eighty miles. They paused at Muolea Point, where the ruins of ancient royal summerhouses stood beyond a verdant meadow. A little further, the road turning into Wailua Gulch, two roaring waterfalls could be seen at the back of the valley.

There was too much beauty to absorb all at once. Tamsen felt dazed with it as she followed Sam along the turning trail to reach another crude bridge.

"Here we are," Sam said simply.

Tamsen put a hand on his arm. "Oh, Sam!" Below them, a rushing river of silver dropped into a basin of water, clear as crystal, only to overflow again, into another pool, and yet another. The banks of the river that fell into tiered fountain-like pools, were bordered with trees and a profusion of flowers, blurred in the mists of falling water.

Above the bridge was yet another pool.

Sam dismounted and helped Tamsen to alight. Without a word, he led her beneath the bridge and upriver, passing a fifth pool, a sixth. They finally came upon the seventh pool. It lay in a deep gorge beneath a two-hundred-foot waterfall.

"Oheo Gulch," Sam said reverently. He pointed out the tropical plants growing lushly in the gorge. Almonds, Java plums, mango, guava, sisal, all introduced to the islands within the last sixty years. The other trees and plants, such as Kukui-nut, banana, breadfruit, hau, ti leaf and coconut came with the Polynesians; possibly from Tahiti and the Marquesas.

"I can't understand why you left here," Tamsen breathed. "I've never seen anything so lovely."

Sam's eyes were fixed on the falling water. "I thought it would be better for Josie and Lani," he said in a pitiful tone. "Better? Hell!"

"If you're ready to talk about your problems, Sam—"

"And put them on your broad shoulders?" he teased, putting his hands on her shoulders, his big palms engulfing them. "No, Tamsen. This is something I've got to think out for myself. You've always carried the load for everyone. I'm not going to let you do it for me. But thank you for asking."

He drew her close and placed his face against her cheek. "Just be there, Tamsen," he whispered, "No matter what happens. After Josie, you're my very special friend."

She lifted a hand, smoothing his sandy hair, now liberally sprinkled with silver, jerking back as a small pebble rolled from the top of the gorge. Sam looked upward and swore. Then he was running back the way they'd come, reaching the top in time to intercept the watchers who had spied upon them.

"Lani," he said. "Martha! Stop, right there!"

Martha fled, but Lani stood still, her face mutinous.

"What the hell do you think you're doing!" Sam took his daughter by the shoulders and shook her until her hair fell forward, covering her face.

"Answer me," he shouted. "What were you doing?"

243

"Watching my father make a fool of himself," she said, her voice mocking. "Something he seems to do very well."

He drew back his hand as if to slap her. Tamsen had caught up with him. "Sam, don't! You can't blame her! It must have looked like we—" She paused, flushing under Lani's contemptuous eyes.

"It certainly did," Lani said coldly. "And it isn't the first time. I've seen all I want to see, and it makes me sick! Now, if you'll let me go, I'll leave and you can continue where you left off."

"Lani!" Sam stepped back, his face twisted in agony. "Lani, you've got to listen—"

"I don't have to do anything," she said. "You've forfeited the right to give me orders. I'm going, and you can't stop me! I intend to go to *her* house and pack my things! Then I'll head straight for Lahaina, and David!"

"You'll keep away from that sonofabitch," Sam yelled, his face turkey-red.

But his daughter had already gone, running down the path to join Martha. In a few moments, they heard the sound of horses' hooves. Martha and Lani had gone.

"I won't try to catch them," Sam said grimly. "I'll try to talk some sense into the girl when we get back to the ranch house. Let's not let this spoil our day."

But it had already been spoiled. Tamsen sensed the tension in Sam as he deliberately tried to dawdle, knowing his basic need was to follow the girls and make Lani listen to what he had to say. As they returned along the trail, he paused at each and every landmark, studying it as though he might not pass this way again. At one point, he dismounted and led

244

Tamsen along a footpath to show her two ancient lava tubes.

They were known as the *Waiomao* and *Waianapanapa* Caves, he told her. In the second one, the Hawaiian Princess Popoalaea was supposed to have hidden from her jealous husband. He found her on an April day, swung her by her feet, and dashed her brains out against the roof of the cave. Each April, the waters of the cave were said to run red with her blood.

"You don't believe that!" Tamsen scoffed.

"Let's say I don't dis-believe it."

As they rode on toward the ranch, there seemed to be a shadow over the day. The old stories of incest and murder that formed the native beliefs crowded her mind. They did not fit with the picture of the smiling, friendly, generous people she had known.

They reached the ranch house to learn Martha and Lani had gone on toward home. They had taken the pack horse with them. Dan swore softly under his breath. They would ride after them.

Old Koma shook his head. In a mixture of Hawaiian, sign language, and pidgin, he told them that rain clouds were forming about the crown of Haleakala; and that soon the mountain would begin to weep, the low ground drowning in its tears.

"Flash floods," Sam explained. Lani and Martha would be through the worst of it, having left early. If not, Lani had sense enough to seek high ground.

They would have to wait until the morning.

When they finally resumed their homeward journey, it was clear the old man had known what he was talking about. Where they had forded easily, the stream beds were now rushing torrents. The roads were wet and muddy, strewn with leaves and debris where the waters from the mountain had roared down upon the land. It was slow going, the horses bogging down, and it was long after dark when they reached Maliko Bay where they had camped before.

Sam had brought emergency rations in his saddlebags. He made a small fire and boiled some water for coffee, making a stew of dried meat and vegetables. Alone in the darkness, Tamsen had a curious feeling of constraint, remembering she was a woman, he was a man, and they had been lovers on one night long ago.

He did not come near her, but spread his blankets to one side of the fire, hers to the other. He did, however, have a curious request.

"Take your hair down, Tamsen. I would like to just look at you for a while, and feel young again. It will give me something to remember."

26

Dan Tallant returned from his Honolulu trip, pleased with the way things were going. The figures he had already recorded in his survey were clear, concise, and entirely acceptable. His business, this time, had taken little more than a day. He took an extra day to talk with members of the American Party, weighing their tenets against the facts he had already ferreted out for himself. It was true that more of them were motivated by profit than by patriotism, but he was beginning to think as they did. Annexation was the only hope for the islands, caught as they were between west and east.

In addition, he found time to browse among the several streets of small stores, finding a richer selection of purchases than was available in Lahaina. He bought several lengths of material fit for court gowns. He hoped it would be possible to wangle an invitation to Kamehameha's palace when they moved their work to the island of Oahu—

He would enjoy showing this place to Tamsen. Honolulu was a mingling of barbarism and civilization. He looked at the island women, eyes and teeth flashing in unconscious invitation, their bodies mov-

ing seductively, sensuously. And the white women—
ladies dressed in cool pastel prints, wearing white
hats and gloves, an occasional one bending to the
local custom, wearing a necklace of fragile flowers.

Tamsen, he thought ruefully, would fit in neither category, but somewhere in-between.

Nevertheless, he plowed through stores of lace
and ruffles, his face red at the giggling of the clerks.
And he arrived home laden with surprises, slipping
into the room he shared with Tamsen, only to receive a surprise of his own.

The bed was empty.

Not wanting to wake Arab's children, he went
to the small house Nell and Dusty shared, banging
on the door. Nell answered, her drowsy face purple
with exasperation. The look faded when she recognized Dan, and was replaced by something akin to
fear.

"Hell," she growled, "It's you. Figgered we wudden see you fer a month a' Sundays. Whatsamatter?
They throw you back?"

"It looks like you're not the only one surprised
to see me home this early. If you don't mind telling
me, just where the hell is my wife?"

"Her an' Martha went visitin'," Nell stammered.
"Oughta be home purty soon."

"Pretty soon like when? My God, Nell, it's almost
morning. Where are they?"

Nell's mouth clamped shut and Dan stared at
her. "It's like that, is it? I'll wake Lani. She'll know
where Martha is, at least."

"Lani went too," Nell said grudgingly. "Aw-w,
hell, Dan, ain't no point in beatin' around th' bush.
They all went to Hana, with Sam Larabee. He ast
th' rest of us, but we turned down his invite." Seeing
the expression on his face, she said, "It ain't like you

think, you wrong-headed jackass! Just a gawdam picnic—"

"Is it, Nell?" His voice was weary. "Do you take me for some kind of fool? I know Tamsen's known Sam Larabee for longer than she admits to. I know she was involved in some kind of escapade in a dive in Lahaina. I also know that, somehow, Larabee was on the scene. And he seems to have been on the scene ever since. I've kept my mouth shut, waiting for Tamsen to tell me."

"She tried!" The old woman bridled. "I know, 'cause she tolt me."

"Go ahead," Dan said, his mouth grim, "Stand up for her. I'd expect you to. After all, you taught her all she knows."

He turned and strode away. Nell looked after him, her face flaming as his words penetrated her brain.

"Well, I'll be a sonofabitch!" she said. She slammed the door.

He returned to his room in the larger house. The gifts he'd brought Tamsen still lay on their bed. He lifted them off, tossing them into a corner, and began to prepare for bed, removing his boots and shirt.

To hell with it, he thought. He wasn't going to be able to sleep, anyway. He drew a chair to the window and sat looking out into the night. The moon made a path on the water. He stared at it, unseeing, as he pondered on the enigma that was his wife.

He was still sitting there at dawn when he heard the sound of approaching riders. Tight-lipped, he pulled on his boots and, through force of habit, thrust his gun in his belt. He was waiting, a shirtless, bronzed giant of a man, when Lani and Martha rode onto the premises, both girls half-fainting with fatigue.

"Where is Tamsen?" His voice was calm, but there was a deadly threat behind it.

The girls looked at each other uneasily. Irritated at their silence, Tallant seized Martha's wrist, pulling her from the saddle. "Where is she?"

Martha, unable to loose his implacable grip, tossed her head. "She'll be along later. Why don't you ask her? What she and Sam Larabee do is none of my business."

His grip tightened, hurting her. "It's sure as hell mine! Are they on the way? When did you see her last?"

"At Hana," Martha said, her eyes triumphant. "They sneaked off and left us. We caught them in a —a compromising situation, and Sam got mad. We came on home. They didn't need us, anyway. They had better things to do—"

Dan turned to look at Lani. The girl's face was pale, her eyes darkly circled, and she made no move to deny Martha's words.

Then it was true, he thought dully. It was true!

He left the girls and strode down the path toward the Larabee house, following a hunch that Sam and Tamsen weren't far behind the girls—that they might have stopped there for a final fond farewell.

The house was dark. He battered at the door. There was no answer. He'd been wrong. He stepped back seeing a faint glow appear at a window. A curtain twitched aside, and for a moment he glimpsed a face above a candle's light.

Josie! And her sweet, plain features were swollen, marred by a spreading purple bruise.

Good God! The man, Larabee, was a monster! No wonder he hadn't wanted his daughter to come home. "Mrs. Larabee! Josie! Let me in! I've got to talk to you."

There was no answer. The window framed nothing but darkness. It was if the apparition had been a figment of his imagination.

Perhaps it was.

Wearily, he made his way home—to wait for his wife. His only words were to Lani, packed and ready to depart. Josie was home. He had seen her. He advised the girl to wait. Her mother might need her.

Late the next afternoon, Sam Larabee and Tamsen Tallant reached the turn-off to the Larabee place. They would have arrived sooner, but Sam had stopped briefly in Lahaina, going into the mission house. Tamsen had no idea what transpired there, but he'd said little to her on the rest of the journey, seemingly immersed in his own thoughts.

"Do you mind riding the rest of the way alone?" he asked now. He'd been gone for some time. There would be things to do.

"Of course not," she replied. "Sam, Hana is beautiful. I enjoyed seeing it."

"I wish it might have been under better circumstances, with nothing to spoil it."

"Don't worry about Lani. I'll talk to her."

"She will be all right." He shouldered his mount close to Tamsen, reaching out to take her hand. He held it for a long moment, his eyes seeming to memorize her face. Then he jerked his horse's head around and disappeared down the trail.

Sighing, Tamsen rode on.

Her first impulse upon reaching home was to go to her room and change. Her hair was down, her gown disheveled from the night spent in the open.

But she would have it out with Lani first. It was clear Sam needed someone. With luck, she'd get some sense into the girl's head, and send her home.

She heard voices from the dining room. The family would be at the evening meal. She summoned a smile as she entered to greet them. "Hello—I'm back! I'll tell you all about it, but first, Lani—"

The faces that lifted toward her reflected a number of emotions. Lani's face was cold, blank; Martha's accusing. The others held something that looked like fear. Nell's jowls quivered as she said, "Tamsen—aw-w, hell!"

Tamsen didn't realize someone had appeared behind her until she was propelled into the room. She turned to face her husband, the glad cry on her lips dying as she saw death in his eyes.

"So you've finally decided to come home. Did he get tired of you? Or do you plan to wait until I'm gone again?"

"I don't know what you're talking about! If you think that Sam and I—"

"I don't think, I know."

"I don't know what you've got in your mind, Dan, but you're wrong! The girls jumped to some wrong conclusions and left. Then it rained, the water was up, we couldn't get through—"

"Floods?" Martha interrupted in an appalled voice. "Why, Aunt Tamsen! We didn't have any trouble!"

She didn't see the odd look Lani gave her, remembering the wall of water that had roared down the last stream just after their crossing.

"You can ask Sam," Tamsen said in a weary voice. "Now, Dan, I suggest we go to our room and talk this out. It's none of anyone else's business."

"Oh, but it is! I want it on record that I'm not the damn fool you've all taken me for. I know about your escapade in Lahaina! I also know about your previous relationship with Sam Larabee!"

She flinched, and he saw the guilt in her eyes.

Quivering with rage, he continued. "Sam Larabee's the one who came up with the rest of the stake for that whorehouse you ran in Frisco." It was a statement, not a question, and seeing her shrink, he knew it was true.

"You're still paying him back, I suppose. Or maybe you're paying for the roof over our heads. Whatever it is, I intend to wipe out the debt."

He shoved her away from him and turned toward the door.

"Dan! What are you going to do?"

"Do?" He laughed, mirthlessly. "You haven't given me much choice. I'm going to kill him."

The outer door slammed behind him.

Tamsen tried to follow, but Nell snatched at her skirt. "He'll be calmed down afore he gits down here. Hell, Tamsen, give 'im a chancet. Him an' Sam'll talk things over. He'll come runnin' back, his tail 'tween his legs, all ready t'kiss an' make up. If I'se you, I'd get myself gussied up." The old woman's eyes swept over Tamsen's disheveled condition. "You look like you had y'self a roll in the bushes."

"I know you didn't do anything wrong," Arab put in, her voice sweet and placating. "But you should have been honest with Dan, told him everything." She smiled up at the man beside her. "I would have told Juan—"

"Don't be so goddamned *smug*," Tamsen blurted. "You don't know what the hell you're talking about!" Tears pouring, she ran to her room.

She was furious at all of them! Dan for being such an idiot, shaming her like that before everyone, then striding off like an angry bull! The others for not coming to her defense. Martha! Oh, how she'd like to slap her face! She'd lied, deliberately! And she was the only one who could have told Dan about the fiasco in Lahaina! About Sam, though— no one knew of that early affair. Had Dan been guessing? Had he known all along?

Come to think of it, she was peeved at Sam, too. A man should be able to take charge of his own family problems and not let them spill over onto everybody else!

Which, she thought glumly, was exactly what Dan was doing now. He was settling his family affairs.

She dressed in a pretty gown that would be new to Dan, a Joseph's coat of colors, each hue blurring into the next in a shimmery weave. Her hands trembled on the buttons, and she fumbled with them, taking some time. And finally, she put up her hair, brushing it free of grass and leaves, seeing at last how she must have appeared to Dan.

Later, decently clad, she paced the floor, twisting her hands as she walked, wondering what was taking place in the meeting between her husband and Sam.

It was then she saw the packages Dan had brought home. She opened them, one by one, seeing the sheen of silk shot through with gold thread, and smoothing her hand over the richness of tawny velvet. Gifts from a loving husband.

It was she who had been wrong. Knowing Dan was jealous—and he had every right to be, considering her past, she should have found some way of mentioning that Sam was an old friend, then dismissing the subject. They shouldn't have accepted the offer of this house, nor taken Lani in, suspecting the girl was at odds with her father.

Though she loved Sam in a way that had nothing to do with her love for her husband, she owed her allegiance to Dan. Whatever Sam's problems, even if he were ill, as she suspected, she'd had no business meddling. Sam's problems should be resolved within his own family. And when Dan came back, she would tell him so, she would make him listen. It would be a public confession before the entire family—

Dear God, what was going on down there! Surely the two men would talk sensibly. But remembering the cold death in her husband's eyes, she was afraid—

Her first inkling that something was wrong came at the sound of a scream from the side porch. Lani's voice. She rushed downstairs to find everyone crowded outside, staring at a light in the sky. It glowed blood-red in the distance. Now and then, a tongue of flame licked upward through a column of black smoke.

Arab clutched Luka to her breast, protectively. "It's a volcanic eruption! I know it is."

"Shaddup, you gawdam fool," Nell growled. "It's th' Larabee place. I hope that jackass, Tallant, didden—" She broke off at sight of Tamsen and yelled, "Dusty, git th' lead out! Git down there an' see if anybuddy needs help—"

Bust Dusty was already gone. He and Juan were dragging their horses from the stable. They galloped full tilt down the trail.

Tamsen and Lani were not long in following.

Martha, looking white-faced at the holocaust, was trembling, the enormity of her own involvement suddenly more than she could bear.

Nell, too, was at the edge of her nerves. She turned on Martha. "Well, Miss Smartypants, you satisfied?"

"I didn't do anything," Martha mumbled.

"The hell you didden! Think I ain't seen you cosyin' up t'Tallant? You been tryin' t'cut Tamsen out ever since yer ma dumped you on us. If it hadden a-been fer you, she wudden a-got in that mess in Lahaina. Mebbe wudden of run into Sam agin." The big woman glared at the girl. "That Tamsen-girl's worth a dozen of you! How Em ever spawned a little bitch like you—"

"Tamsen's no good and you know it," Martha spat, her face crimson. "A cheap entertainer! She ran a brothel in San Francisco! Another one in the gold fields! Don't tell me I don't know what I'm talking about! I remember—"

"I know all that," Nell snapped. "I give her her first job; a green scared kid. And thank God, she smartened up quick, er Arab an' yer ma wudda starved t'death!"

"And did you give Mama her first job?"

Nell stared at her. "Em never worked in her life."

"Maybe she didn't think of it as work." Martha's lip curled. "Two men at a time! She doesn't even know which one my father was! I heard her say so."

Nell's flat palm caught her across the mouth. For a moment, the two women stared at each other, then Nell's anger faded.

"You'n me is goin' t'have us a tawk," the big

woman said quietly. "Er mebbe I'm gonna do th' tawkin', an yer gonna lissen."

In a low quiet voice, fairly free of her usual profanity, Nell told how Tamsen had taken a job at a Texas cantina, in order to support her orphaned sisters. Somehow, she managed to keep the truth of her work from the other girls, Arab and Em. She had to shoot a man to protect her virtue, and two of his friends had come to town seeking revenge. They discovered where Tamsen lived—but instead of Tam, they found gentle, innocent Em.

Em was brutally battered—raped. Dan Tallant had gone after her attackers, shooting them both, but the damage had already been done.

To protect her sister's good name, Tamsen had moved them to San Francisco. Martha was born along the trail. There, they'd tried to set up as seamstresses, but they were burned out in the Frisco fire. Tamsen had once more gone into the business.

"Then yer ma married Donald Alden. He went broke, shipped everbody off to Tamsen, who wuz married to Dan by then, and—"

"Don't, Nell," Martha sobbed. "I remember it! I remember it all, now! Oh, God, Nell! What have I done!"

"I dunno, girl. Less'n you want t'tell me."

Held in the big woman's matronly arms, Martha sobbed out the story of her rebellion at home, the way she'd come downstairs to apologize, what she'd overheard, and how—in her hurt—she tried to make life miserable for everybody. It was bad enough to think her mother was a loose woman. But to find she was a child of rape, it was no wonder her mother didn't love her.

"Think Arab loves Luka?"

Martha looked at her with wet eyes.

"Well, yer ma used to hold you and look at you the same way."

Martha burst into a spate of fresh weeping. Nell figured she had already done her good deed for the day. "Hell," she growled, "Yer drowndin' me. You got all that water t'waste, go down an' help put out that gawdam fire!"

27

Kimo, Larabee's young Hawaiian overseer, was on his way home from a hurried trip to Lahaina. He carried a miserable feeling of guilt on his shoulders. The Tallants, after all, had become his friends.

But yesterday, dropping in after the girls returned, he'd walked into a hornet's nest. Nell and Dusty seemed worried, and Juan was trying to sooth a cross Arab. Even little Luka was crying. Lani was white and withdrawn, and everyone seemed bent on ignoring Martha.

He'd tried to tease them into better humor, clowning, using the pidgin language he affected, and they'd disappeared, one by one, leaving only Martha, who turned on him.

Maybe, when the islands were annexed by the States, he would learn to speak properly, she told him angrily. And playing on her anger, he managed to draw out bits of information she had overheard.

Dan Tallant was more than just a surveyor, she boasted. He was instrumental in the purchase of Alaska. And he had the ear of the man who would be the next President! He was only here to make up

259

his mind if the islands were worth it. His was the final decision.

He didn't know how much of it to believe. Martha was an attractive girl, but still adolescent, immature. It was clear that she was at a rebellious stage. It was also plain that she had a crush on her aunt's husband. Therefore, she might be giving him more authority than he had.

But he had been forced to take action, alerting someone in Lahaina who would pass the word to Honolulu. Tallant would be watched, that was all. Still, it had seemed a betrayal of a friend.

He rode slowly, musing, chin on his chest, until he noticed the scent pervading the air. His head jerked up, and he saw the flames. He spurred his mount into a run.

Reaching the plantation, he could see small dark figures silhouetted against the towering blaze. His horse reared as he pulled it to a stop, leaping from his saddle in one fluid movement. He ran toward the burning house, shouting, "Sam!"

He skidded to a stop, seeing the faces of the fire-watchers: Tamsen, Lani, Dusty, and Juan.

Sam Larabee was not among them. Juan filled him in on the details. Evidently Sam and Josie had both been in the house. There was no way of reaching them, since the blaze had clearly swept the structure from all sides. Drawing Kimo to one side, he showed him a container he'd found. Kimo sniffed at it, his handsome features going hard.

Coal oil.

Forgetting his native role, Kimo cried, "But who would want to kill Sam? Good God! He was the finest, most honorable man I ever knew! He didn't have an enemy in the world!"

Combing the premises, they finally produced a

witness, a toothless, senile old drunken native. It had been a *lapu*, he quavered. A *lapu*, or ghost. One of those dangerous and malicious specters all living men feared. His face had the pallor of death. He was ten feet tall. He had poured a magic liquid on the earth around the house, setting it afire with his flashing eyes. He, 'Aukai, had run away to hide.

Pressed, he remembered one more item. The *lapu* had been clothed in un-lapu-like fashion. It had worn a blue shirt and trousers.

Crouched in the bushes, the smell of charred wood and fragrant blooms merging into a scent of decay, Martha buried her face in her hands. Sam Larabee and his wife were dead. They had died at Dan's hand. And it was all her fault. The evidence she collected to build up a case against Sam and Tamsen crumbled before her eyes. Even the scene at the pools, the one she described as *compromising*, hadn't been the act of passion she'd described it to be. It had been nothing more than a warm gesture of friendship, perhaps comfort.

She had not meant it to come to this! But she brought misery to everyone she ever loved.

Rising, she slipped back up the trail to where she'd left her mount. She lifted herself into the saddle and, instead of turning toward home, went sadly along the path that led to Lahaina.

At the entrance to the village, she slid from her horse, turned it toward home, and slapped its rump, hoping it would return. Then she went to the waterfront.

There was only one ship in port. She stood in the shadows, listening as two tipsy sailors talked. It was bound for Hong Kong, she discovered. It had been in port for some time, due to repairs. It would be leaving in the morning.

She walked along the beach until she found a native boy who had just come in with a load of fresh-caught fish. With deft fingers, she rearranged her gown before she approached him, sliding the shoulders down a little, hiking the skirt with an extra fold under her sash; finger-combing her hair into slight disarray before she approached him with a provocative, hip-swinging walk.

She had a lover aboard ship, she confided. And the bastard was trying to run out on her, leaving her in a delicate condition. She only wanted to talk with him once more, to persuade him to ask the captain to make it legal.

But she needed to get to the vessel. For the trip out, she would give this—

She proffered her single treasure, a nugget of gold that Duke Courtney had given her, attached to a slender chain.

A few moments later, wedged in among a cargo of gasping silver, Martha left the shores of Maui. She looked back only once, seeing the red hills of the island black against a lightening sky, and blinked tears away. She had the pitiful certainty that she would never return again.

She wasn't missed until the next morning. Tamsen had her hands full with a grieving Lani, and her own disbelieving shock that Dan would be capable of such an action. He would have to be insane! But if he hadn't done the deed, where was he?

At last, when Sam's daughter had cried herself sick, Tamsen laced a cup of tea with laudanum. She then led the dazed girl to the room she shared with Martha.

Martha's bed hadn't been slept in.

A search party was formed, all of them guilty that they hadn't thought of Martha sooner, especially Nell, who confessed she'd, "tolt the girl a few things that was hard t'swaller."

It was Dusty who found Martha's horse, still saddled. It indicated that she had fallen, perhaps been struck across the forehead by a tree limb. Even now, she might be lying somewhere along the trail.

Dusty and Juan set off toward the burned Larabee house. Nell and Arab searched the house and outbuildings once more. And Tamsen thought of the small beach at the foot of the cliff.

She made her way down the crooked path and stopped short. In a small curve of the beach, out of sight of the house, a bronzed man stood waist-deep in the water, vigorously scrubbing himself with sand.

Dan!

He didn't see her. She walked forward to where his clothes lay, neatly piled on a rock. They were permeated with an unmistakable smell.

"*Coal oil!*"

"Tamsen!"

He was coming toward her, smiling, sea water streaming from, silver against gold, as he stepped from the sea like some prehistoric god—

Or a *lapu,* she thought, stepping backward. A *lapu*—

"Tamsen, I'm sorry about last night. Sweetheart, forgive me—"

Sorry! Dear God! Sorry!

"You killed Sam," she said flatly.

"But I didn't—"

"You killed Sam! And Josie along with him! You were seen setting fire to the house!"

"And if I did?"

"Don't worry," she said, trembling with rage and grief. "Nobody's going to turn you in. They've all come to an agreement on that. But keep out of my sight! And don't come near me! Don't you ever touch me again!"

He stood still, as if considering her words. "That might be a good idea," he said slowly. "At least, for now."

By evening, Dan had his things moved into a small shed-like building. He insisted on taking his meals alone. His only concession to human companionship was during his work day, when Juan and Dusty pronounced him absolutely unchanged.

Sam Larabee's death was never mentioned, and Martha was never found.

BOOK III
HONG KONG

28

The ship *Mattie*, on a heading for Hong Kong with her cargo, was deceptive in appearance. Holystoned and gleaming above, she was rotten at the heart, the repairs made at Lahaina proving none too effective. It had been a choice of returning to California, or continuing on. The captain had chosen the latter course.

The man who walked the deck at night was equally deceptive. The western-style suit tailored for himself in Hong Kong covered the wiry frame of a street fighter. The small round cap he wore sat atop the brain of a tiger.

Feng Wu was one of the richest men in China.

His life began in quite another way. Born of a fisherwoman, taken, perhaps, by a member of one of the crews that plied the Hsi Chiang carrying opium to Canton in return for silks and tea, he had been thrust on the mercy of a small village from the moment he was born.

He subsisted on refuse from the dung heaps, squatted in evil-smelling tide-flats, scrabbling for shrimp. Then, as he grew older, stronger, he instituted a reign of terror among the smaller boys of his village, forcing them to steal for him.

Sly, intelligent, conniving—and dangerous—he went on to greater things, discovering the profits that derived from playing both ends against the middle. Simple banditry was not enough.

He became a member of a secret society with a strong anti-Manchu purpose. At the same time, he embarked on a course of self-improvement, mimicking his betters, and managed to insinuate himself into the imperialistic structure as an informer.

The supply trains of both factions were natural prey for Feng Wu and his own private band of outlaws, as wild and vicious as a pack of starving wolves.

He emerged from the T'ai Ping rebellion a rich man.

But for Feng Wu, riches were not enough. He had an insatiable yearning for power. He hated the British who occupied Hong Kong. Only once in his adult life had he been arrested; led to prison, the cangue resting on his shoulders; yoked like an ox!

He managed to bribe his way out, but not before seeing some of his compatriots—one-eyed Hsi among them—bound and kneeling, backs to a firing squad.

Therefore, when a Manchu had gone to England in the company of Robert Hart, director of the Imperial Maritime Customs Service, Feng Wu had made a study of the English tongue, had clothes tailored for himself in Hong Kong, and had gone to Washington with an eye to gathering information. There were no wars in China at this time. Perhaps he might be able to use something he learned in some manner. Again play both ends against the middle, and even his score with the British at the same time.

Unfortunately, his keen mind had been dazed by all he had seen. Great factories and machines. In

Washington, the great capital, there had been a woman. He had taken his own women with him, of course. His old wife, a hill woman he had taken pleasure in taming; his young wife, with Manchu blood in her veins; and two concubines. The people of America had stared as his retinue passed through the streets. At first, his heart swelled with pride. Then he realized it was because they were a curiosity in their heavily embroidered silks. They were shy before the gracious ladies of Washington.

He had them hidden away in a hotel. And when a fun-loving senator had offered to provide him with a woman, he was delighted. Her skin was not yellow, and she proved to be wanton and desirable as his women had never been. He paid her a tremendous fee.

His cheeks reddened beneath his amber skin as he recalled how he thought he had purchased her. She and the senator both laughed uproariously. "I don't mind sleeping with a Chink," the woman—her name was Flora—said. "But I'm not going to go home with one!" She patted his face, gave him a quick kiss, and said, "So long, dearie."

He soon found himself watching other women, his own now seeming ugly to him. He failed in the attempt to buy one, or even accord her the honor of becoming his wife. It just wasn't done, the senator said, shaking his head. Not in the States—

He finally realized that he, like his women, was only a curiosity. He, the great Feng Wu, who had descended on supply trains, slashing, killing, leaving no witness alive to tell the tale! Feng Wu, who had always found a way to get anything he wanted, was frustrated in his desire to have a white wife.

He looked at the lifeboat swung from the davits near where he stood, and smiled.

Until now, he thought. Until now.

He returned to his cabin. Not tonight, he thought. This was only the third night out. He had seen the girl climb into the lifeboat the night before they sailed. She would be growing hungry, thirsty, weak. Therefore her gratitude would be even greater when he rescued her.

He looked at the door to the adjoining cabin. The women would be waiting there, for him to make his choice of a partner for the night. T'zi, the old wife; Liang, the young one, and the concubines, Shui and Toy.

He wanted none of them. Removing his western clothing, he donned a robe, its wide sleeves heavily encrusted with red and gold embroidery. Sitting cross-legged on the floor, inscrutably Oriental despite his unknown blood, he reached for his pipe. And soon the air was thick with the sweetness of opium—the stuff of dreams.

Martha, huddled in the bottom of a canvas covered lifeboat was dreaming, too. A mist of hazy shifting scenes from the past appeared, disappeared, and was replaced by still others. There was a big house with lush carpets, and another place she had lived—shabby rooms in an office building in downtown San Francisco. Against both settings drifted the face of a distinguished white-haired man. Senator Donald Alden, the man she had known as her father. Then there was a confused image of shipboard, and Em crying—

Then she dreamed of a castle, a little house, and the rolling tawny waters of the Fraser River. And then she envisioned Duke Courtney, blond giant of a man—her new father, her guide, her God—

There were no tears, now, on her thin cheeks.

Three days under the canvas in the August heat had sapped the liquids from her body. Now she would even welcome the pool of perspiration that formed around her that first day. Dry tongue licked dryer lips as she thought of water.

Em's face appeared above her. "Did you want a drink, Martha?" There was a glass in the hand she extended to her daughter. Martha reached for it, her hand passing through the mirage that disappeared at her touch.

"Oh, God," she moaned, her mind clearing as she realized where she was. She lay pondering her alternatives. She could give herself up on the ship's crew—but the captain might insist on having her returned home when they reached Hong Kong. She couldn't face Tamsen or Lani again. She wouldn't go back to her mother and Duke. They were all well rid of her.

A second solution would be to just let herself over the side, slide down into the welcoming water, get it over and done with. But for now, she was too weak to remove the rope laced canvas from the hooks that held it. Perhaps—in the morning. after she'd rested a while—

Or she could just lie here and wait to die.

That night brought more frightening hallucinations. She was in a house, the Larabee house, and it was blazing. The flames crept closer until they encircled her. She could feel her flesh burning—

Mercifully, she lapsed into a coma.

On the night of the fourth day, Shui and Toy followed the instructions of Feng Wu, their master. Clad in dark, coolie-type garments, their faces blackened with ashes, they slipped like shadows to the railing. Shui slipped the ropes lacing the canvas

271

from their hooks and stood guard while Toy climbed into the lifeboat.

The little concubine lifted Martha so that Shui could reach her. Wrapping the girl's frail form in a dark blanket, they managed to drag her to the cabin the women of Feng Wu occupied.

There, T'zi and Liang waited to take charge. T'zi, once a hill woman, with fierce black eyes and hair drawn smooth against her skull, had known privation in her time. She knew exactly what to do. Water first, only a few drops at a time. The dehydrated body should be wrapped in damp cloth. Later, a minimum of strong, healing tea, then a broth of fish—

Martha opened her eyes.

Feng Wu's entourage traveled in style. His women had draped his quarters with tapestries of red, the color of happiness. For their own, they had chosen heavy gold brocade. It glittered like the sun, in the light of a scented candle. Over Martha's bed hung bits of paper, folded in mysterious fashion, each woman having contributed what was, in her opinion, good joss.

The two wives of Feng Wu bent over the girl on the bed. They were clad in snowy white embroidered coats, over long wrapped skirts. Behind them stood the two concubines, still clad in dark clothing, their faces smudged with blacking.

Angels, Martha thought. And the dark angels. I suppose they send them for people like me. She closed her eyes, and gave herself up to the rocking motion of the ship, drifting into a space where she was floating free.

When she woke, she had returned to lucidity. She was in a room, a strange room to be sure. The dangling papers that confused her earlier, spinning like planets above her bed, had resumed their true identity. Just paper. In a far corner, oddly garbed women were talking in whispers that sounded like the chirping of birds.

The ship rolled and Martha flung out a hand before she recalled that she was at sea. She frowned, wondering if this, too, were real, or if she would wake again in the lifeboat, dying of thirst.

Her movement caught the eye of the waiting women. Little Toy came toward her, grinning cheerfully. Of all the women, only she had a modicum of English. Feng Wu had found her in a brothel, to which her father had sold her at an early age. Her linguistic talents, such as they were, had been developed through contact with sailors who frequented the place.

"Heya," she said happily. "Goddam! Foreigndevil-lady wakeah! Werry much! Good joss, heya?"

Martha struggled to a sitting position. "Who are you? Where am I?"

"Elder sister, T'zi," the girl said ceremoniously. "Second sister, Liang." The two finely dressed women bowed, and Toy continued. "Shui," she pointed, "and Toy, my. You, heya?"

Martha realized she was asking for her name. She would never use it again. She didn't want to be Martha Courtney. Martha Courtney was dead in the flames that destroyed Sam and Josie Larabee.

"Lani," she said the only name that came into her mind. "Lani Larabee."

It wasn't until several days later, when she was strong enough to stand, that she was barred from going out on deck for a breath of air.

"You b'long Feng Wu, my," Toy said obstinately. "Heya?"

With rising horror, Martha recognized her position. She was considered the property of a mythical Chinese gentleman, whose women had rescued her. The tapestry-hung walls of the cabin closed in about her, like a gilded cage.

29

During the days that followed, the Chinese women made much of Martha, marveling over the length and luster of her dark hair. They insisted on brushing it with sweet, perfumed oils, surrounding her with warmth and affection until she almost lost her fears.

Though she could not communicate with T'zi Liang and Shui, they all seemed to be inveterate gossips and all eager to praise their benefactor, Feng Wu. Toy served as interpreter, passing their words on in her own inimitable fashion.

T'zi, she told Martha, had been a woman of the hills, of a fierce and warlike tribe of people. Then one day, Feng Wu and his followers had swept down upon them like a pack of wolves. They had fought back desperately, but they had been killed, men, women, and children. Only T'zi had been spared, carried off across the pommel of a saddle by none other than Feng Wu, himself.

T'zi kept nodding as Toy interpreted with extravagant gestures. Martha, stunned, recognized the expression on the older woman's face as one of pride. Dear God! The man had murdered her family! How could she feel this way?

Liang had been highborn, but her father, a gentle scholar, was too far gone in opium to care about anything but satisfying his craving. Feng Wu had purchased her for very little.

"Goddam lots good business mans, heya?"

Liang, too, was nodding with pride.

Shui had been an entertainer in a house of pleasure. "Not werry good," Toy said forgivingly, "Never mind." And Toy, herself, had been rescued from a brothel, thus owing Feng Wu her undying gratitude. "One man's dooa jig-jig, now," she said happily.

Martha didn't comprehend all she said, but it was clear this was one big happy family. She had no intention of becoming a part of it! When they disembarked at Hong Kong, she would run. She wanted no part of the mysterious Feng Wu, whom she had not yet seen. At night, she lay with her eyes fixed on the door that remained closed between the two cabins, fearing that a giant of a man would enter, carrying a bloodstained sword.

Two days out of Hong Kong, two light taps signaled T'zi to enter her master's room. When she returned she conversed with the others in their own tongue. They all put their hands over their mouths, politely, to giggle as they looked at Martha. Then they set to work, T'zi preparing scented water for Martha to bathe; Liang busily going through all their wardrobes, seeking the finest of clothing; Shui applied a touch of color to Martha's pale cheeks, and Toy, seeming to have forgotten any English words she knew, brushed the girl's hair, reverently.

As they helped her dress in a pajama-like coat with sleeves like wings, embroidered cuffs reaching to her fingertips, Martha knew they were preparing

276

her for the confrontation she dreaded. Now that the time had come, she felt too numb to be afraid.

Satisfied with their creation, the women chirped approval in their own language. Liang hobbled to the door on her bound feet, opened it and bowed, then stood aside as T'zi escorted Martha into the other cabin. There, Feng Wu's first wife burst into a musical introduction and would have knelt had the man not waved her aside. She backed into the next room, bowed, and closed the door.

Martha was alone with the man she had heard described as a wolf, a tiger.

She stood staring at him, struck dumb at his appearance. A wiry man, a little bit above medium height, dressed in a neat dark western-style suit. He had the yellow cast of the Chinese, but his features betrayed his mixed blood—the nose hawk-like, and a firm, slightly jutting chin. A small cap covered his shaven head, and the queue was coiled carefully beneath it.

Martha made herself meet his eyes. They were narrowed slits of liquid darkness, unreadable. She couldn't know that they were taking in every detail of her appearance, her slender figure, her flowerlike face, so like her Aunt Tamsen's, the long silken fall of hair. When he spoke, at last, it was in her own tongue, with a slight perceptible accent.

"I see that you, a woman, do not humble yourself before a man."

"In my country, women do not humble themselves." Her tone held an arrogance that frightened her. Dear God, this man was a murderer—

"Then we shall speak as they do in your land," he said, sounding amused. "Please to sit down." He gestured toward a chair, and Martha sat gingerly, feeling strange in unfamiliar clothing.

"What for did you hide away?" The question darted at her like a snake. "You have a lover aboard ship?"

"No," she said hotly. "I—"

"What for did you hide?"

Martha looked guiltily at her hands, trying to concoct a story. How could she say she had something evil within her; a thing that had brought trouble to everyone she loved—and death by fire to two innocent people? That she tried to break up a marriage, turning the man she thought she loved into a killer—

"You do a bad thing?" Feng Wu, with his cunning knowledge of human nature, hazarded a guess.

She shifted uneasily. "I—I suppose I did."

"You are a virgin maid?"

Her head jerked up, her cheeks flaming. "That is none of your business!"

His thin lips curved into a smile. Her reaction had answered his question. "You need not tell me of your crime," he said courteously. "I am prepared to offer you my protection."

Martha's eyes filled with tears. The man was only being kind, and he probably had no idea that his question had been an insulting one.

"You may return to the women," he said, inclining his head. "But first I wish to ask one thing. Would a woman of your race consent to marriage with a gentleman of China?"

"No!" The word burst from her. Dear God, he wasn't suggesting—! Then she tried to qualify her involuntary denial. "In my country, a man takes only one wife. It is the way we believe. I couldn't share a husband with other women. So, you see—"

For a moment, his eyes had been a glimpse into hell. Now, she was certain she'd imagined it. His features were smooth, composed, as he rose and led her to the door. She entered, and he beckoned to T'zi.

Feng Wu did not return to his chair, but seated himself, cross-legged, on the floor. T'zi knelt before him, her head bowed in humility, waiting as he took up his pipe, lit it, and puffed on it, reflectively, the sickly sweet smell of opium forming about the two of them, like a cloud. Finally, he spoke.

"You have been a good wife to me, T'zi. You have given me strong sons. It is in my mind to reward you."

She ducked her head even lower, a pleased flush spreading over her angular features.

"I took you from your hills," he said with a deadly softness. "I shall return you there, with much gold. You will be a rich woman, much sought after by many men."

The tough slender body that he had tamed with his own hands wilted at his words. She opened her mouth to speak, but no words came.

"Do not thank me," he said. "You may go. Send Liang to me."

Again, the scene was much the same. He felt he had cheated Liang's father of his most precious pearl. He would return her to him, forfeiting the bridal price. And she would go laden with gifts.

Shui was to return to the audience he was certain missed her as an entertainer. Toy, back to the brothel, where she would have the opportunity to pleasure many men.

Only Toy dared question his pronouncement. She leaped to her feet. "Goddam!" she shrilled. "W'at for? No like jig-jig, my?" Then her eyes narrowed. "Is foreign-devil-woman, heya?"

At the murderous mask that transformed his

features, she caught herself, bowed nervously, and escaped. The door closed behind her, she leaned against it and whispered, "Goddam!" Then she looked at her equally rejected sisters. They all wore expressions of sad resignation as they sat on their gold-brocade-covered beds, hands hidden in their sleeves.

They were accepting Feng Wu's commands in true Chinese female fashion, with dignity and grace. What was to be, would be. It was fate.

Only Toy, child of the streets, plaything of sailors, refused to bleed silently under the whip of her master's words.

"Goddam!" she said again, darting a look of hatred at the girl who claimed to be Lani Larabee. Finally, she joined her sisters-in-love, adding a fourth to the sorrowing group. Except that her mind was raging with ideas. There must be a way to change Feng Wu's mind, to get rid of the foreign devil. There must be *something* she could do.

30

More than a week later, the *Mattie* limped into Hong Kong's harbor and dropped anchor. It had been a grueling journey, the crippled ship wallowing like a beetle in waters with a greasy film that indicated a coming storm.

Luck had been with them, thought Captain Carnstead, puffing at his stubby pipe on the ship's bridge. Luck, and that young Aussie, Peter Channing. The boy knew engines. By God, he wished he had listened to him back in Lahaina and had the vessel more completely refitted instead of installing a few new parts that threw a strain on the rest of a worn-out engine.

But then, he, himself, had always preferred sails. With canvas aloft, one only had to wait for a good wind. And it was on a sailing vessel that he had stood as a lad, watching the British flag being raised for the first time over the thirty square miles of mountainous rock that was now Hong Kong—the Fragrant Harbour.

Eyes blinded with memories, Captain Carnstead didn't hear the young Australian's approach until he stood beside him. He took his pipe from his mouth and gave the newcomer a curt nod of greeting. "Channing," he said.

"Sir." Peter Channing returned his nod. They were both silent as the young man wiped grease from his hands, a smudge on his cheekbone making his eyes even more blue. At last, the Australian stuffed his grease-rag into a pocket.

"Well, Channing, what's the verdict?"

"Not as bad as I thought, sir. The fly-wheel bearings will have to be relined—the drive-shaft journals—"

"Drydock?"

Channing shook his head. "Just engine-room work. But it will probably take a couple of weeks."

The captain swore under his breath, then opened his mouth to voice another question, only to see that he lost the young sailor's attention. Peter Channing was gazing at his surroundings in fascination. The harbor was enclosed between two land masses, a six-mile stretch of water touching the north shore of Hong Kong and the mainland of the Kowloon Peninsula. The area swarmed with junks, with their high sterns, ribbed sails, and painted bows, their owners having sensed a coming storm and fled to the harbor for safety. Between them, like water beetles, the sampans plied, often manned by tiny black-clad women, with round hats woven of bamboo.

Beyond the exotic scene rose the island of Hong Kong, huge white British-style structures lining the shore; go-downs, or warehouses. Behind them, other buildings climbed the hills, transplanted flowers and shrubs already giving the place an aura of civilized living. Channing stared in awe.

"First time here?"

He nodded, and the captain launched into a description of the area. There was Pedder's Wharf, where they would go ashore. There was Dent and Company, Jardine Matheson and Company. In the background, the towers of the first Roman Catholic Chuch on Wellington Street were visible. The white mansion up there, he pointed out, where the flag flew, was Government House, on Upper Albert Road. And there—

"I had expected something more Oriental," Channing admitted.

Carnstead chuckled. "You will find it. Many of the sections are predominantly Chinese. There are barbers, cobblers, medicine-men plying their trade in the streets. You can only see the British structures from this distance, but all over the rock, in every nook and cranny, are little shacks and hovels occupied by Chinese. In the monsoons, they are often washed down the hillsides, the inhabitants buried in mud."

"My God!"

"Kowloon City," Captain Carnstead said, gesturing in the other direction, "is almost totally Chinese. It was leased to Britain in 1860, and annexed the following year. It is occupied to a great extent by a criminal element; smugglers, lawbreakers fleeing from British authorities, pirates. Unless a crime is a major one, affecting the well-being of Hong Kong, itself, the British tend to let well enough alone. I would suggest you confine your recreational activities to Hong Kong, itself—"

"I can assure you that I shall," Channing's words trailed off as he stared at a longboat, pulling away from the *Mattie*'s side. He had heard of the Chinese warlord who occupied the two main cabins aboard, and of his four women. This was the party now leaving the ship. But there were five women, not four. And though they were all clad in Oriental garb, one seemed to stand apart from the others. There was something undeniably Caucasian about her—and a look that was hauntingly familiar.

Captain Carnstead clapped a hand to his forehead. "Good lord! I forgot! I meant to do a little prying before they left the ship. But the girl is going willingly, don't you think?"

Seeing Channing's puzzled expression, he explained. A Chinese messboy had come to him as he was trying to maneuver the crippled ship into harbor, with a wild tale about a girl being held prisoner by his passenger, Feng Wu. The word had been delivered by one of Feng Wu's concubines, who asked the captain's intervention in rescuing the girl.

He hadn't quite believed the story, seeing it as the result of female jealousy. The warlord had probably sneaked some Hawaiian tart aboard at Lahaina, and his women wanted to be rid of her. He had meant to check it out, however, but now it was too late. The longboat had disappeared among the mass of junks surrounding them. He did have the girl's name, though, which he would hand over to the proper authorities.

He reached into his pocket and pulled out a slip of paper on which he'd scrawled the name. "Lani," he said. "That's Hawaiian, for certain. But there's an odd last name. Something like Lallabee."

"Larabee." Peter Channing's face was white as paper. "My God! Oh, my God, man! I know the girl! She was kidnapped, I can assure you! Her father is a planter on Maui, a fine family. The girl was a volunteer assistant at the mission, there. Lower another boat! I'm going after her—"

"Wait!" The captain caught his arm, pointing toward the waters. The longboat that had carried

Feng Wu and his women from the ship was returning. It was empty, except for members of the crew, and as it approached its mothership, the horizon grayed and disappeared, the rain that was a forerunner of the coming typhoon falling in heavy sheets, blotting out even the surrounding vessels.

An interrogation of the longboat's crew brought little information. Yes, there had been a girl who did not look Chinese, though her skin had a tinge of gold, and her hair was long and dark. She had not spoken, and her eyes had the look of one drugged, a user of opium, perhaps. The group had boarded a junk. Since they did not wish to land at Pedder's Wharf, they were evidently bound for Kowloon.

"Get me there," Channing grated. "Lower the boat!"

The captain caught his arm. "Don't be a fool, man! That place is like a warren. You'll never find him! And you'd most likely end up with a knife in your back. We'll go to the governor at Hong Kong, Sir Richard MacDonnell, and put it in the hands of the proper authorities!"

"To hell with the authorities!"

"Do you want the lady back alive?" Channing's striken face was answer enough. "Then you'd better take my advice."

The longboat was lowered once more, moving toward the coast of Hong Kong, invisible in the sheeting rain. Peter Channing sat hunched in misery, his mind going back to a luau at the home of Sam Larabee. He thought of Sam's honest, open features, of Josie's gentle hospitality. He realized he couldn't call Lani's face to mind, having been so engrossed in his conversation with the men present. But she was the daughter of his friends, and he couldn't abandon her to such a dreadful fate.

285

How had she fallen into Feng Wu's hands? And what was happening to her now?

At the moment, the girl he thought to be Lani Larabee lay on a silken bed aboard Feng Wu's own pleasure craft. Her eyes were opened, but dazed and dreaming as she drifted on a cloud of drug-induced illusion. The drape that bisected the vessel, dividing Feng Wu's private quarters from those of his women was at times a rainbow of iridescent ribbon, at others, the silver of falling water. Feng Wu's face seemed a golden moon, and she imagined herself falling into his eyes as he bent closer.

Fent Wu was jubilant. He had not touched the girl aboard ship, knowing that a single outcry would bring down the wrath of the ship's crew. The Americans and British had strange ideas about their women, putting a higher value upon them than his own people did. If her presence had become known, he would have explained that he had merely shown mercy to a stowaway. He could not have been condemned for that.

But now, she was his. His body ached to take her. But he wanted her to be conscious during the taking, to recognize him for the man he was. This would not be the brutal taking of a hill woman in a ditch, the blood of her people still wet on his hands. Nor would it be the dutiful compliance of a wife purchased from a highborn, poverty-stricken father. The concubines, Shui and Toy, he did not even consider. They had been used when he acquired them. They would be used again.

This one was different. When she was tamed, their love would be like a poem. He would teach her the art of love in his secret room in Kowloon. Then, having disposed of the other women, they would go to Macau, where the Pearl River ran yellow into the green China sea. They would enter the Tiger's mouth, moving into China until they came to the village where he had been scorned as a boy.

There they would live like a mandarin and his lady, envied and kowtowed to by all. Surely no warlord ever had a wife such as this—

The agony of his desire was almost impossible to bear. It gave him pleasure as well as pain. He was proud of the strong will that kept him from taking her on the spot. To prove himself further, he unfastened the braided frogs that held her brocade tunic in place, laying it open to reveal her gold-cream body, touched with rose.

With an indrawn, hissing breath, his fingers moved on to the wrapped skirt, putting it aside, marveling at the slim, smooth legs, her perfect proportions—

Then, to assure himself of his ability to endure torture, he knelt beside her, caressing her, his hands gentle though they trembled with the need to hurt, to bruise her tender flesh. That would come later—

She moaned and turned beneath his touch, and he buried his face against her breast with a choked cry. He was still holding her, shuddering with need, when the junk dropped anchor at the wharf in Kowloon.

Alerted to the fact that they had arrived, he called to Toy. "Dress her," he said curtly. Then he went out on deck, where he welcomed the cold and sobering rain.

31

Martha was still not aware of her surroundings when she was taken through the temple-like gate of the walled city of Kowloon. There, she was placed in a sedan chair, Feng Wu beside her, the other women following on foot as the vehicle—made of bamboo and consisting of a chair attached to long poles shouldered by bearers—sped through the rain.

The bearers turned off the main road, paved with huge square blocks of stone, and moved into a series of twisting alleyways. The sedan chair paused before a disreputable looking warehouse, and Feng Wu lifted Martha down and led her, with a supporting arm, into the empty building's echoing dimness.

A pressure at a certain spot, and a wall slid back, revealing a stairway leading down into an earthen tunnel. At the end of the tunnel was a door of gray, deteriorating wood. The warlord opened it, and, even in her daze, Martha blinked at the blaze of light and color that confronted her. Not until the next day would she be able to see the richness of her surroundings; the golden dragons entwined about vases of delicate, priceless porcelain; candlelight glittering on iridescent jade; walls hung with rich embroidered tapestries.

A manservant bowing obsequiously before him, Feng Wu carried Martha down a long hallway, where a light from golden sconces struck sparks from gem-studded swords, daggers, and knives that adorned the walls. Proceeding through a final doorway, he laid her gently on a scented bed. His women could care for her when they arrived. He had reached the limit of his endurance.

Martha was not fully awake until nearly noon the next day. She had gradually become aware of her strange surroundings, and sat up, dizzily, trying to focus on the room. She was no longer aboard ship. A wave of fear washed over her as she remembered. She had planned to go ashore at Hong Kong, to escape from the clutches of Feng Wu and his women. Yet she had no memory of disembarking from the vessel.

The woman, T'zi, had brought her a cup of tea—

Dear God, she had been drugged! Where was she? And why had they brought her here? It looked and smelled like the Chinese equivalent of a brothel!

She stood, and for a moment the room rocked around her. There was a sound of an opening door, and a bracing arm went about her waist. She was led to a chair.

When the wave of vertigo passed, she looked into the fierce dark eyes of T'zi.

"Why did you bring me here?" she cried. "What are you trying to do to me? Why can't you leave me alone?"

The woman seemed to understand her panic, if not her words. She made small comforting sounds, and brought a basin of water to lave Martha's face. When she left the room, Martha rose and stumbled to the door the Chinese woman closed behind her. It was locked, and she was trapped in this luxurious room.

For a time, she pounded on the door, calling to T'zi, to Liang, to Shui, to Toy. There was no answer. Then she went in search of windows, pulling aside the wall hangings in frantic haste. There were none. With a feeling of desperation, she realized she had no way of telling if it were day or night.

The air was thick with incense, too heavy to breathe. And she had never been so frightened in her life.

For a time, she wept. Then she sat down, drearily, trying to compose herself to wait for whatever might come. If T'zi returned, she might be able to overpower her and escape.

When the door opened after what seemed to be an eternity, it was not T'zi who entered, but a burly manservant. He carried a small tray with tea and cakes. Though she had no appetite, Martha realized she was weak with hunger, probably having eaten nothing since that fateful cup of tea the previous day. Fearful of being drugged again, she would not touch the food that was put before her.

Another eternity passed. The tea was cold and the cakes uneaten when the two wives and two concubines of Feng Wu entered Martha's room with great ceremony, carrying silken garments and a porcelain bowl of perfumed water in which floated a single white flower.

They did not speak as they set to bathing Martha, dressing her in a loose and flowing robe. Then T'zi began to speak in her own tongue, a long and ponderous admonition that ended with *"Fulfill your duties calmly and respectfully, reflect before you act, this shall win you honor and glory—"*

Her words were the time-honored Chinese axioms taught to every subservient wife, though Martha had no way of knowing what she said. The girl looked at Toy in a plea for an explanation, but the little concubine only turned her face away.

Bathed, gowned, her hair held back with a coronet of pearls, Martha was led by T'zi way down the long hall to another door. Martha looked wistfully at the weapons glittering on the walls, but she was unable to arm herself. Liang, Shui, and Toy followed on her heels. T'zi opened the door and entered, closing it behind her. Martha could hear her murmuring, Feng Wu's deep voice answering. Then T'zi emerged, Martha was thrust inside and the door closed behind her. She was alone in an alien, exotic atmosphere, thick with the smell of incense and opium—alone with Feng Wu—

He sat in a golden throne-like chair at the end of the room, his tunic encrusted with jewels that reflected the glimmer of his dark eyes. They were eyes that held her own with mesmeric effect.

"Come to me," he commanded.

She had moved one foot forward before she realized what she was doing. Then, with a little cry, she turned toward the door. This door, too, was a smooth surface, barren of knob or latch. Finally, she turned to face him—back to the carved panels that shut her in with him—shrinking before his gaze.

"When you are a dutiful wife," he said in a mocking tone, "I will show you how to open it. But for now," the note of command was back, "come to me. I order it!"

It's not a man, she told herself, but a mask. A yellow, metal mask. And this is a dream. Unable to speak, she managed to shake her head.

Feng Wu rose from his chair and advanced toward her. In his mind, he could see the woman in Washington, hear her laugh—laughing at him! He had been patient with this girl, too patient, waiting too long. Today, he had abstained from the soothing opium, drinking aphrodisiacal teas instead, and his desire was at a peak along with his anger. This woman would not refuse him, and she would have no opportunity to laugh at him. Their coming together would not be the poetic interlude he had planned, but he would tame her and satisfy himself. The poetry could come later.

Martha shrank before the purpose in his eyes, then his burning hands were on her shoulders, tearing away the silken robe. She began to struggle, and he laughed—a cruel sound without mirth—as he bent one arm behind her, tightening his grip until she sobbed with pain. Lifting her, he carried her to a curtained alcove where he threw her against satin pillows.

She lay numb with shock as he divested himself of his jeweled garments. This was what had happened to Mama, she thought dully, except that there were two of them. It had happened to Mama!

"Mama," she sobbed as he flung himself upon her. "Mama, help me!"

But there was only brutal, thrusting pain, the feel of wolfish teeth sinking into her bared shoulder, bruising fingers, clawing nails. She prayed she would die.

All night, he kept her there, applying schematic tortures to his brutal attempts at lovemaking: a pressure on a fingernail, until she was forced back into consciousness; hands on her throat, pushing her head back as he sought her mouth; a bitten lip, when she refused to cooperate.

By morning, he had still not forced her into willing compliance. He rose and stood looking down at her, at the black hair spread over the pillows, at the slender body, bruised and mutilated by tooth and nail.

He was certain that compliance would come. He considered himself a wolf, a tiger. He had never been one for poetry.

The women were called to return Martha to her room. There, her wounds were treated, her abused body bathed, and she was given a sleeping potion—a drug that could produce a shorter time-span sleep than opium. He would call for her again tonight.

Only T'zi was sent for her. It was clear that they thought her too weak to resist one lone woman. And, in truth, she was. She stumbled once, falling against the wall before T'zi caught her with a supporting hand. But the fall brought her out of her stupor; for in an instant she touched the cold blade of a jeweled sword. And she began to think again.

Another night such as she had already endured would be her last. Death would be a blessing now, but she did not intend to die alone. She would take Feng Wu with her.

Tonight, she would be tractable, letting him believe his attentions were welcome. And she would manage to conceal a weapon in her sleeve. The thought of vengeance brought her head up, and she walked the last few steps without T'zi's help. The door to Feng Wu's champers opened and she entered, forcing a smile.

As he took her, roughly, she set her teeth and

tried to respond. She would do what she had to do. No one in the world knew where she was.

And probably no one cared. She couldn't blame them for it, in any case.

32

Martha couldn't know she was the object of a desultory search, or that the girl the governor of the British colony sought was Lani Larabee.

It had taken a great deal of effort on Peter Channing's part to set the wheels of justice in motion. The Larabee girl was not a British subject. Sir Richard MacDonnell was not certain she didn't accompany Feng Wu of her own accord. He recalled a case where an American lady, a missionary at that, had—

Channing interrupted the governor. He knew Lani Larabee well. She was not the type.

Nevertheless, MacDonnell said stiffly that relations with the Orientals were touchy at best. Feng Wu was a powerful figure, and it wouldn't do to cross him. Perhaps if the Hawaiian government made a special request—

"I am an Australian subject," Channing said angrily. "We are under the Crown. I am making the request!"

The governor was beginning to lose his patience. His collar was chafing him, a typhoon was imminent, and he wished the confrontation to end.

"My dear fellow! You have no authority in the matter, I'm afraid. Now, if she were a relative—"

Peter Channing took a deep breath. "She is my wife," he said.

The two men he faced, Governor MacDonnell and Captain Carnstead, both wore expressions of incredulity. Channing thought quickly in order to compound his lie.

"I couldn't bear to leave her behind," he improvised. "I smuggled her aboard ship. Evidently, that sonofabitch found her and managed to carry her off. Now, I want to make my request once more." He glared at the governor. "I am a British subject. I am asking you to rescue my wife."

MacDonnell was profuse in his apologies, Carnstead stricken on Channing's behalf. "You should have confided in me," he kept saying. "Don't worry, son, we'll find her—"

The search was begun. One man, a Britisher, was assigned to cover Hong Kong; another to check out Kowloon. Peter Channing's heart sank. A spit-and-polish officer, searching the Oriental sections, had just about as much chance as a snowball in hell. MacDonnell could spare no more men to aid them. The rains had brought disaster, mudslides burying the hovels of the Chinese who had built them haphazardly on the slopes. Along with the hovels, whole families had been lost. Men in boots and slickers were out now, digging in the rain. MacDonnell had a duty to the people under his control. He could not call in the lifesaving squads to search for one kidnapped girl.

A week passed, with no results. In spite of Carnstead's warning, Channing crossed twice to Kowloon, wandering in the rain, speaking to anyone who would answer him in some form of English.

The few Britishers who had shops in Kowloon Chinese clad in western-type clothing; sailors of all nationalities.

It was one of the latter who carried the news to Toy. She had been returned to the brothel several days before. Finished with a customer, she sat nude before a mirror, brushing her long black hair, an act usually successful in selling a man another half-hour's time. Her sailor lay on the bed, watching her dark hair shining in the candlelight. It reminded him of something.

"Hey," he said, "You ain't by any chance the girl the Aussie's lookin' for?"

Toy's hand began to tremble. She put the brush down quietly. "W'at girl dis, heya? Tell me."

"Fergit it," he said, his face reddening. "It was a dumb idea. I think she's white, anyway, but he said she had long black hair, and yours made me think—"

She returned to the bed. Coaxing, cajoling, she got the story out of him. Some Aussie was staying at Government House on the island. Some Chink feller stole his girl, and she was looking for her. "Hell, he just come up to me on the street—"

As she submitted automatically to his eager arms, Toy's mind was working furiously. Somehow, she must find a way to cross to Hong Kong.

She insisted on a description of the Australian until her customer finally balked. "Hell, honey, whatcha want to know about him for? You've got me!"

Indeed she did. And she could hardly wait to get rid of him. All she wanted was to be back in the house of Feng Wu, where all that was necessary was to dooah jig-jig one man.

Hong King, waterlogged and reeking of death,

was girding itself for the coming storm. For a long time, the typhoon had stood out to sea. The talk among the British was rife with speculation. It would miss the island. It would turn away. It would hit it, dead center. Now the skies had darkened even more. The waters of the harbor were uneasy. And even more junks had crowded in, seeking a safe haven.

Peter Channing wandered to the porch of Government House, his face drawn with worry, his hands in his pockets as he stared moodily into the rain. Within a week, the *Mattie* would be repaired and ready to continue on her journey. He could not leave the daughter of Sam Larabee behind. Yet, he had signed on for the voyage. Perhaps, if he went once more to Kowloon—

"Meestah Chang-ying—?"

He jumped at the sound of a voice, like a small silver bell, finally locating the speaker in the shadow of a column. A tiny bedraggled creature in the clothing of a fisherwoman.

"You look find Lani Lallabee, heya? I help you, my!"

A sodden bit of paper was thrust into his hand, and the girl ran off into the darkness. "Wait," he called after her. "Wait!"

But she was gone.

He took the paper to his room, spreading it carefully, examining it by candlelight. It was a carefully drawn map, the word Kowloon at the bottom in block letters, street names laboriously written in English, Chinese characters beside them. He couldn't know the effort Toy had put forth in coaxing her sailor to aid her with translations.

He ran his finger along a line indicating an intersecting street he recognized. He had traversed

298

that one, too. But here, a wild profusions of lanes ran in a number of directions, sometimes curling back upon each other. Drawn in fine lines, they seemed to be alleys. At the convergence of two, there was a circle with a legend: "Warehouse. Below."

It might be a lead, and it might be a trap. The hair prickled at the back of his neck as he thought of walking into a warehouse in Kowloon where anyone or anything might be waiting for him. Despite the danger, he would go. And he would go alone.

His first problem lay in finding a way to cross the harbor. The Chinese boatmen had been the first to sense the coming blow, and they had no intention of being caught in the middle of the harbor. Finally, with a mixture of bribery and threat, making free use of the governor's name, he managed to commandeer a small sloop owned by a drunken Britisher.

The trip across the harbor was nerve-wracking. The pressure of the oncoming storm was heavy in the air; the waters were roiled and turgid. The wind began as they reached the other side, an advance warning of the tempest. The sloop slammed against the wharf and the Englishman secured it. He, too, was going ashore. The money the Aussie gave him assured him of a snug berth for the night. He pointed at the approaching wall of blackness.

"One way trip, matey. Ain't going back this night." With a cheery wave, the man stumbled off in search of a woman and a bottle, leaving Peter Channing alone in the ominous night.

The streets were dark, eerie, the houses boarded in anticipation of the storm, all lights extinguished in dread of fire. The inhabitants of Kowloon had prepared for this night. Carrying a lantern he appropriated from the sloop, Channing made his way through the dark streets, debris swirling around him. A singsong chanting sounded from a temple; prayers for safety, no doubt. When he reached the alleyways that turned and twisted, he pressed close to the rear of jerry-built, leaning structures as he made his way, one moment protected from the tearing wind, the next feeling its full force.

And all the time, he had a sensation of being watched. A spot between his shoulder blades ached with an imaginary pain. He was a bloody fool, coming alone like this at night to rescue a girl he hardly knew. He should wait until light to go to the magistrate.

But he didn't. Whatever came, he was in for it.

Pausing to check his map by the light of his lantern, he realized that he had reached his goal. The back of the warehouse was visible, just ahead. It was an enormous building, looming black against the raging sky. He blew out the lantern, and set it carefully down, taking a few tentative steps, feeling his way.

Then the furies of hell descended upon the area, with a roar of unbelievable violence. The wind slammed into Channing, knocking him to the ground. He rolled toward the shelter of a building, attempting to rise. But the flimsy structure gave before the wind's force. It's timbers screamed as they were wrenched apart, collapsing as the roof blew before the gale.

Struck by a bit of debris, Channing went down into darkness.

Sometime later, he had no idea how long, he woke to find himself lying in what appeared to be a rushing stream. The alleyway was flooded, the water moving with the wind. He tried to sit up, and realized he was trapped by fallen timbers. Battered, bruised, he finally managed to extricate himself. He stood dizzily, putting a hand to his head. It had a sticky dampness that he knew was blood.

Doggedly, he went on, fighting the wind. When he reached his goal, he was almost blown through its open door.

Moving away from the door, he put the shelter of a wall behind him and removed an oilskin packet from his pocket. It contained a number of matches and a small wax candle topped with phosphorus and sulphur, called a vesta by the English. Lighting one, he looked about.

The yawning structure was empty, warped and twisted by the gale. The door had been blown from its hinges. Advancing, Channing discovered the rear of the building had collapsed. Rubble lay across what appeared to be a set of stairs leading downward. At the foot was a square, dimly outlined with light.

There was no knowing who or what was down there. A hornet's nest of vicious criminals, no doubt. But there he would surely find Sam's daughter, if she were still alive.

Doggedly, he set to moving fallen timbers that blocked the way.

He was mistaken in his fears. Only two people occupied Feng Wu's exotic quarters on this storm-ridden night. True to his promise, the warlord had sent his other women away; T'zi to her village, Liang to her father, Shui and Toy to their respective occupations. The servingmen had been sent aboard the junk. All must be new, elegant in the Chinese way, a proper setting for his bride. As soon as the typhoon lost its force, they would sail for Macau and up the Pearl—into the Tiger's mouth—

Feng Wu smiled to himself as he donned a

robe of golden hue. He had tamed this girl. Last
night she had said she loved him. And the storm
blowing above, being shut in safety with this woman—the thought excited him. He had a feeling this
would be the night of all nights.

In her own chambers, Martha washed herself
with perfumed water and donned a cap of pearls.
She kept a careful eye on the ornate Chinese time-
piece she had been given. Tonight, she was to go to
him of her own free will, and on her knees as be-
fitted a humble wife.

And on the way to his chamber, she had something to do—

She was dressed, and there was still time. She
sat on the edge of her silken bed, her head in her
hands. If she failed in her intention, it was very likely she wouldn't live to see another day. She thought
of her mother, Em, who had endured brutality such
as she did and survived. She thought of Duke Courtney, who had indeed been a father to her. If she
could only talk to them both, tell them she was sorry
for the things she had done—get a message to them
—tell them she loved them.

And the people she had wronged: Tamsen,
Dan, the Larabees—

If she died at Feng Wu's hands, it would only
be what she deserved. If she lived, she would have
another man's blood on her hands.

It was time.

She touched the spot beside the door that T'zi
had shown her. It swung open. In the hallway, she
walked close to the weapon-hung wall, removing the
knife she'd previously selected with cold trembling
hands, sliding it deftly into her sleeve.

Before Feng Wu's door, she dropped to her
knees, tapping at it. "It is I, my lord," she called.

The opened door revealed him, a man of golden metal, arms crossed, legs straddled, looming over her.

She started to rise, but with a motion of his hands, he indicated she must crawl to him. She obeyed, hating him as he backed from her, step by step, prolonging the agony and humiliation.

Feng Wu had never felt more powerful in all his life. This was one of the women the Americans and English thought too good for him. He would show them. It was good, this taming of such a girl. T'zi was a mindless one, her body going to the strongest. But he had subdued this one, in both body and spirit. It had been necessary. His passion for her was so great that, should he not keep the upper hand, she would be the victor rather than he. He did not intend to let that happen.

He looked down at her, her forehead against his slippers, dark hair falling away to reveal an ivory neck that could be so easily broken in his two hands.

Reaching down, he drew her to a sitting position. She sat back on her heels as he cupped her face in his hands, shuddering at the expression of fanatic lust in his eyes.

"You are afraid?"

"Yes, my lord, I am frightened of the storm. The wind."

"The wind cannot reach us." He smiled, mirthlessly. "I have tamed it. Just as I have tamed you, little one. And tonight we will prove how well you have been taught. You will return to the doorway—" He lifted her to her feet and watched her walk across the room, turning to face him in confusion.

"Now, you will remove your robe. You will then come to me on your hands and knees once more. You will beg, you will plead for what I have to give you.

I have given up my wives, my concubines, for you. You must take the place of all of them, making me desire you. You know what to do. I have shown you—"

She still stood, staring at him, seeing his anger begin. "You will obey me," he snapped. "First—your robe—"

She began to tremble. The knife was hidden in her sleeve. And he was across the room. She had counted on his usual brutal behavior; the way he would grab at her, clutching her to him as he tore at her gown—

She couldn't cross the expanse of floor with a knife in her hand, nothing to cover it. Feng Wu was a strong man. She had reason to know! He would be upon her, breaking her wrist, perhaps turning the weapon on her instead. She let the knife slide down into her palm. Maybe if she ran to him, took him by surprise—

She licked her dry lips. "It is different in my country, my lord. There, you would come to me. It is the woman who is wooed—"

"You are in my country, now. Where women have their place. You will do well to remember that."

"But, my lord—"

She stopped, hopeless at his implacable features. She would do as he asked, leaving the weapon in the folds of the robe. Then, perhaps she could manage the deed later, when he slept. Tonight, the empty rooms, the storm raging without, was probably her only chance. In any case, she couldn't keep the knife. It would be missed from its place on the wall.

Her hands went to the front of her robe, and Feng Wu smiled.

At that moment, the wind reached a crescendo; the outer door of the ancient warehouse blowing inward with a crash. With a sound like a tremendous sigh, the rear of the building settled upon its haunches, beams crashing downward. Martha cowered, expecting the roof of the underground dwelling to cave in upon her, but Feng Wu stood firm in the knowledge that his home was a sanctuary. He lifted a beckoning hand.

There was a sudden sharp cracking sound behind him. He whirled, looking upward at a beam that began to buckle under the weight above, uttering a curse in his own tongue.

Martha, released from her panic at the sight of his fear, took advantage of the opportunity. She sprang forward, and plunged the knife into his back.

He stood still for a moment, his yellow features blank, all emotion washed away. His arms dropped to his sides, and he turned. Then, with an odd choked sound, he moved toward her, slowly, inexorably, step by step, only his eyes alive in a dead face.

Martha stood transfixed for a moment, looking into the face of hell. "No," she whispered. "No—"

A claw-like hand reached out, touched her. And the beam above crashed down as Martha ran, mouth open in a silent scream.

33

Peter Channing finally removed the last of the timbers that blocked his way. Gingerly, he climbed over the remaining debris and descended the stairs. The door at the foot, limned by light from behind it, had been warped by the force of the wind. There was no visible way of opening it, but a well-placed kick sent it crashing inward.

Channing blinked at the scene that confronted him. Golden idols, writhing dragons, a scent of incense, sickening to a man accustomed to the smell of sea air and salt spray. It was like walking into a dream world—

His dazed mind awoke at the sound of a scream. He barely had a glimpse of a small figure rushing from an open door when sections of the tunnel came crashing down as the warehouse above disintegrated in the gale.

The lights went out, and someone barreled into him, almost knocking the breath from his body. Instinctively, he reached out, grappling with the intruder, feeling the undeniable softness of a woman's flesh.

Martha fought back as he tried to hold her. "Let me go, damn you," she screamed. "Let me go!"

"Stop it, girl!" She'd heard that voice before, that accent! Dear God, who—

"It is Peter Channing. Remember me? I've come to help you—"

She went limp in his arms, fainting dead away. Behind her, the tunnel was still collapsing. He had to get her out of here.

He carried her up the steps, and to the rear of the building, where beams lay like crisscrossed jackstraws. Reasoning that they would afford protection from wind-driven projectiles, he crawled beneath them, searching for a spot that seemed secure, then pulled the girl's unconscious body into the haven he found.

His vestas had all been burned. He wished for one as he tried to make the girl comfortable, finding a place where her face would be free of the dripping rain. He felt the stickiness of blood on his hands, and wondered if it were hers, or his own. Though she was in shock, her heartbeat and pulse were good. His hands moved over her, finding no sign of injury.

He realized they were trapped until the storm subsided and there was light. She began to shiver and he spoke to her, soothingly, finally lying close beside her, holding her in his arms.

He awoke to hysterical screams.

Sitting up, painfully, bumping his head on a timber, he stared in confusion at the girl who had lain beside him. The storm had spent its fury. A dim watery light filtered through the fallen walls, and the girl cowered away, her eyes mad with fear.

Her hair was wild, her face bruised, and for a minute he didn't recognize her. All he knew was that this was not Lani Larabee.

"Stop it," he snapped. "Stop it!" Finally, he

slapped her, her head rocking back. Slowly, sanity replaced the mad look in her eyes.

"It is you," she whispered. "Peter Channing! I thought I dreamed it!"

Then she was in his arms, sobbing her heart out.

He finally pushed her away, studying the tear-stained face. "It's Martha, isn't it?" he asked. "Mrs. Tallant's niece?"

She nodded and he felt an obscure anger. He remembered the girl, now. He had the impression she was making a play for her aunt's husband, and catalogued her as a man-crazy little bitch. And she'd almost gotten him killed!

"I was looking for Lani Larabee," he said roughly. "What the hell—"

Martha bowed before the expression in his eyes. "I used her name," she said in a small voice.

"Why? And what in the name of God are you doing here?"

"Lani's was the only name I could think of," she said dully. Her gaze still lowered. "And I'm here because I ran away. I—I lied to Dan about Tamsen and Sam. He—he killed Sam and Josie. But I was really the guilty one, so I stowed away. Feng Wu found me—"

His shock and revulsion showed in his face. Sam Larabee, that smiling, friendly man! Josie, who had one of his opals—for protection against the eye of misfortune! Dan Tallant, whom he liked on sight—

Sam and his wife dead, the lives of Dan and Tamsen Tallant ruined, all on account of this conniving little troublemaker! She deserved anything she suffered at Feng Wu's hands! And he came flying like a damn fool to rescue her. True, she was a white woman in the hands of an unscrupulous Chinese, but if he knew the full circumstances, he wouldn't have bothered.

"We'll have to get you out of here," he said heavily. "Can you walk? And what about Feng Wu? Is there any danger?"

"I killed him," she said, pointing toward the stairs. "He's down there—"

He saw the rusty stains on her hands at the same instant she did. She tried to hide them in the folds of her robe. "I think I killed him," she amended, her eyes filling with tears. "Would you see?"

He left her and made his way down the steps, squeezing past fallen timbers; priceless objects smashed now, and beyond repair. Ancient porcelains lay in shards about his feet; a Buddha of jade and gold leaf tilted precariously, its head at its feet.

In a bedroom, rich with sumptuous tapestries and a silken bed, Channing found what he was searching for. There had been little damage here. Only a single beam had fallen, but it had found a mark. Beneath it lay a figure robed in bold, face down. A knife with a jeweled hilt protruded from its back.

Peter Channing, ashen, backed away.

He returned to Martha. Seeing her stricken eyes, he only told her that the man had been killed by a falling timber. Let her have one stain removed from her conscience, at least, was his grim thought. Now, he must get her out of here, and somehow across the harbor to Hong Kong before Feng Wu's henchmen discovered the body and tried to avenge the man's death.

He took her arm and led her, half-fainting, through the tortuous alleyways, and into the main streets. The streets, empty the previous night, were thronged with jostling Chinese, attempting to salvage what they could from the wreckage caused by the storm. When they reached the harbor, Channing found the wharf smashed, splintered by junks that had been dashed against it. The sloop he had chartered the night before was gone.

He led Martha to the magistrate's office. Here, he found the young officer set to search for the missing girl, asleep at a desk. He shook him awake.

The man rubbed his eyes. "Jove, what a night," he mumbled. "Though I've seen worse." He looked toward a window. "Don't tell me it's over!" His eyes came back to Channing then, opening wide at the sight of the girl beside him. "I'll be damned," he choked. "You've found your wife! Absolutely wizard, old chap! But she looks done up! I'll get some tea—"

He left the room on a run, and Martha stared at the young Australian, seeing for the first time the blueness of his eyes, accented by a lean, tanned, weather-beaten face; the blond, sun-streaked hair, like silk as it began to dry from the night's wetting; the bruise on his right temple, beginning to turn black; the cut that bisected the bruise—

"Your *wife?*" Her face was perplexed.

"The only way I could get the governor moving." His tone was sharp. "He refused to help unless he was searching for a subject of the crown. You will have to play the part, since we must ask for his protection."

"But I don't want—"

"What you want doesn't matter," he said rudely. "You got yourself into this mess, and I've gone to some trouble to get you out of it. You will do as I say."

The English officer arrived with a tea tray, his face beaming. "I say," he said, "we haven't been properly introduced. I'm Rogers."

Peter Channing nodded in acknowledgement. "I'm Peter Channing, of course, and this is—Mrs. Channing. And the tea is most welcome. Thank you very much."

Several hours later, Rogers had found a small government vessel to carry them to Hong Kong. As they left the devastated wharf, the boat nosed through the wreckage of the storm. Channing recognized the sloop that had brought him to Kowloon. It lay bottom side up, still afloat, but not for long. A junk had gone down, stern first. Its bow, dragon-painted, thrust above water, seemed to watch their departure with jeweled eyes. A dead man floated face down among the debris, an ancient Chinese woman in a sampan attempting to draw the body toward her with a pole.

Martha's nerves snapped and she leaned against Peter's shoulder in a state of half-consciousness. Channing, himself, was almost oblivious to his surroundings. His mind raced, considering all eventualities.

Feng Wu was dead, a knife in his back. It had probably been the true cause of his death, though the beam had completed the job. If the Chinese community wished to make a case of it, Martha might be tried for murder, an offense punishable by death. Her only defense lay in the fact that she had been kidnapped, carried away against her will. That, and being a subject of the Crown. He might have to swear, under oath, that she was his wife.

He approached the young officer in charge of the vessel after settling Martha comfortably. Before landing at Hong Kong, he first wished to go aboard the *Mattie*. Surely Captain Carnstead would be on his ship, surveying any damage the storm might have caused.

The *Mattie* listed to one side, a great hole gaping where a junk, torn from its anchor, had rammed her. And the captain was aboard as Channing had expected, a little irritable at being dragged from his duties for a private conference in his cabin.

Peter Channing told him a half-truth. First, he admitted he'd lied about being married to the girl, Lani Larabee. He had, however, compromised her in Lahaina, and she had stowed away on the *Mattie* without his knowledge, thus falling into the clutches of Feng Wu.

He had found her now, and wished to do the right thing by her. It was best that Governor Mac-Donnell not know the true circumstances, since she needed the protection she would receive as a subject of the Crown. Would Captain Carnstead perform a wedding ceremony?

The captain would, and did. Martha was brought to the cabin. In the presence of the captain, a Chinese messboy, and the ship's Negro cook, she became Mrs. Peter Channing. The words were pronounced, there was no ring; the bridegroom did not kiss the bride, who wore only a soiled and tattered brocade robe with nothing beneath it. But Martha wasn't aware of the missing elements.

She imagined she wore a full-skirted flowing gown and a misty veil. Duke Courtney was there at her side to give her away, Em smiling at the rear. It was the wedding of her dreams. She gave the appropriate answers in a soft, awed whisper, then turned to face the groom. He wore the face of Feng Wu—

She began to scream and Channing caught at her shoulders. Through the robe, he could feel her

312

burning flesh. Her eyes were glazed, two bright spots of fever burning her cheeks. The new young wife of Peter Channing was very, very ill.

He left the ship in haste, urging the officer in charge of the smaller vessel to hurry. Reaching Pedder's Wharf, Peter hired a sedan chair to carry his wife to Government House. She was babbling with delirium before they reached it.

Channing carried her inside, where a horrified Lady MacDonnell immediately took charge. She refused to let the girl occupy the small cell-like room where Peter had been staying, but led them to a large airy room with an enormous bed. She bent anxiously over Martha, whom she knew as Lani Channing. Lady MacDonnell was a gentle woman in a dark dress, her hair drawn back in smooth wigs. She called for servants to bring water to lave the girl's burning face, and soft, clean gowns from her own wardrobe.

Peter Channing would have none of it. Martha was muttering odd sentences about knives, blood. God only knew what she might confess to. He would care for her, himself.

Clearing the room of the lady and her female servants, he undressed Martha, bathing her bruised and ravished body, sickened at the signs of brutality he found. Poor child! How old was she? Seventeen? Eighteen? And to have endured this—

He kept trying to tell himself that she deserved some sort of punishment because she brought her predicament upon herself. He thought of Sam and Josie and what she had done to them; and of Tallant and his wife. He tried to steel himself against the tenderness that threatened to overwhelm him. He realized she had even killed a man with her own hand! His blood still stained it.

But as he washed the small hand, curled like that of an infant, feeling its burning heat that bespoke her fever, he could not hate her.

He looked at her for a moment before he slipped the soft gown that had been brought over her head. Her dark hair lay spread across a lacy white pillow; her dark eyes were closed, lashes long and curling against cheeks stained with rose. There was a look of purity about her; something untouched and defenseless that belied all he knew.

He bent, involuntarily, to kiss her cheek, and she smiled. "Duke," she said in a small, trusting voice.

His face crimson, Peter Channing backed away. He didn't know who the hell Duke was, and what's more, he didn't want to know.

He dressed her and took a seat beside the bed. Carnstead said it would be a week-and-a-half, now, before they could sail. What happened after that, after she came to her senses, was no concern of his. But for now he would keep her from incriminating herself.

He didn't expect the arrival of a doctor, sent for by the governor's wife. He could hardly refuse to allow the man entrance, and he knew that, upon examination, the physician would see the brutal marks that he himself had seen. He told him as much as he thought necessary before allowing him into the room.

His wife, whatever else ailed her, was possibly suffering from a brain fever. A sensitive girl, she had been abducted by a Chinese warlord—and raped.

On his way out, the doctor imparted the information to Lady MacDonnell, who wept with pity.

She had lived in many places, under varying

circumstances, her rigid British training replaced by a more liberal outlook on such things. Peter Channing, she told her friends, was a saint. Most men would have felt their wives degraded in such a circumstance, but not he. It was absolutely beautiful, the way he stayed at her side.

She had no way of knowing that as Peter sat, day after day, night after night, tenderly laving the girl's face, he was thinking of the friends she betrayed, murdered; and of a Chinese man in a gold robe, a timber across his body—and a knife in his back.

34

Martha's illness proved to be a combination of an Asiatic fever and nervous exhaustion. When she began to recover her senses, she found the handsome Australian sitting beside her bed. She had only the vaguest remembrance of a wedding. Had it taken place? He assured her that it did.

But there were other memories, hands touching her, turning her gently, a man's hands, tending her like a baby. This was something she dared not ask him. She turned away to hide her flushed face.

As soon as he was certain she was rational, he left her, returning to his work on shipboard. And she missed him, missed him terribly. There was no one there when she woke from a nightmare, to smooth back her damp hair, soothe her with a comforting hand. The nightmares were there whenever she closed her eyes, dreams of a burning house, of Feng Wu, with his face of yellow metal.

She would wake from those dreams, reaching out for Peter Channing, crying his name.

After a time, she was well enough to sit in a chair by a window. From her vantage point, she could see the *Mattie*, anchored in the harbor. All signs of the typhoon were gone, now. The green

China sea was quick to heal its scars. The junks had been repaired and were off to their fishing grounds, only a single rib-winged vessel crossing her view. But the *Mattie* had been more grievously wounded than had been thought at first. Weeks passed, a month, and she was still not under way.

Peter was out there now, working hard on the vessel that would take him away from her. She saw him infrequently, now that she was mending. He came just often enough to allay Lady MacDonnell's suspicions. Their visits were formal, once the door was closed against outsiders, with such conversations as "How are you?" "Quite well, thank you."

He was her husband and she was his legally wedded wife—and he had nothing but contempt for her. She didn't blame him. Oh, why hadn't God let her die—

Her cheeks were wet and she hastily brushed at them as someone tapped at her door. Lady Mac-Donnell entered, her smile instantly changing to a look of sympathy. "Poor child! You miss him very much, don't you?"

"I suppose I do," Martha said in a small voice.

"And you're not going with him when he leaves? I can't imagine—"

"He's afraid I'm not well enough, yet," Martha lied. In truth, Channing had wished to return her to Lahaina, there to be sent home to her parents. He was apparently upset when she refused. But how could Tamsen welcome her now? Or Dan? The others, knowing she'd brought about such tragedy? She was bad luck to everyone—

"Well, you are most welcome to remain here," her hostess said. "I've told your husband I enjoy your company."

"Thank you." Martha made no commitment.

When Peter was gone, she would quietly disappear. Perhaps find her way to England—

"The captain tells me they will be leaving in three days, as soon as they are provisioned," the older woman said with an arch smile. "In the meantime, I have a surprise for you—"

She halted. Martha had a surprise, herself. A wave of nausea swept over her. She was suddenly violently ill.

Lady MacDonnell supported her in her arms, washing her flushed face afterward. "My dear, why didn't you tell me? No wonder Peter insists on leaving you behind. Such a thoughtful man! I assure you, you will have the best of care! I look forward to having a baby in the house—"

Dear God! Oh, dear God! A baby! It couldn't be! It just couldn't be happening! A child by Feng Wu—She would die first!

Mistaking her pallor for weakness, her hostess insisted that Martha lie down. Tucking her in with loving hands, she asked, "And how long have you known?"

Martha's mouth was dry, stiff with shock, but she was able to give a proper answer.

"Since just before I was kidnapped," she whispered. "I knew then—"

"You're lucky you didn't miscarry," the older woman cooed. "You poor child! But don't you worry now, everything is going wonderfully well."

With a hasty peck on Martha's cheek, she left the room. Martha lay silent, her fists clenched upon her small flat stomach. Within her, something was growing. A child of the devil. She visualized a baby made of golden metal, with eyes like the black fires of hell.

History was repeating itself. The same thing

had happened to her mother, Em. She, too, had been taken against her will, by brutal lawless men. How had she felt when she found she was pregnant with a child of rape?

She thought of Nell's words, *"Think Arab loves Luka?"* Then, *"Well, yer ma used to hold you an' look at you th' same way."*

Her mother was a better person than she was. If she dared, she would get a knife and plunge it into her stomach, killing the thing that was growing within. But she wouldn't. Not because she was afraid to die, but because she'd broken enough of God's commandments already.

As Martha lay, sick with revulsion at her condition, a scowling Peter Channing made his way toward the house. Damn women for meddlers! Lady MacDonnell had approached Captain Carnstead earlier in the day with a request. Since the ship would be sailing shortly and Mrs. Channing would be remaining behind, perhaps it would be possible for Peter to get leave. The young couple could spend a few idyllic days together at Mountain Lodge, the small three-room cottage tucked away at the very top of Hong Kong. It was a form of hideaway, to which the governor retreated in the heat of summer. Here, garden parties were held, and tennis was played on the grass courts. It was not in use at this time, and the Channings would have privacy in which to say their farewells.

It was a romantic notion, and Carnstead went along with it. "All young couples should have a honeymoon," he said. Then he amended his remark. "A second one, I mean."

Peter Channing was summarily dismissed from all work and sent, reluctantly, to his wife.

It was a poor time to reside in the Mountain

Lodge. Though the building was sturdy, built to withstand monsoon and typhoon, it was a miserable place when clouds rested, as they did now, upon the peak. The small structure was blanketed in white fog as the young couple arrived in sedan chairs which the governor's lady had ordered to pick them up three days later. Inside, the fog had condensed, running down the walls and collected in pools on the highly polished floors. Only one bedroom had been prepared with linen kept in the hot-drying room. The other rooms were clammy with damp.

Lady MacDonnell had been most thoughtful. The room intended for the Channings' use contained a trunk of her own clothing, altered to fit Martha's slighter form. Peter's duffel had been brought from the ship and placed beside it. There were flowers on a low table, fruit, a picnic hamper packed with wine, bread and cheese. All this for a couple who were strangers to each other. Martha's eyes brimmed.

"You don't need to worry," Peter said gruffly. "You will have this room to yourself. I'll take the other." He took a book from the shelves, and disappeared. She didn't see him for the remainder of the day.

For the next two days, they met only at mealtimes. Peter looked tired, haggard. She was certain he was catching cold. He was exaggeratedly careful to avoid touching her.

She couldn't know how he woke from his dreams of her, groaning with need, or how often he walked into the swirling cloud-mist, outside, to settle his traitorous thoughts. He had no love for the girl, he told himself. It was only that he wanted a woman. Any woman! The way she was now, deceptively soft and humble, had gotten under his skin. The way the lamplight touched the smooth part in her hair, the defenseless look to the nape of her flowerlike neck—it would shake the resolve of a stronger man than he! If he only didn't know what she was like, inside—

On the last night, he congratulated himself. He'd resisted temptation. And soon they would be separated—forever.

He might have continued in his resolve, except for a dream. Martha went to bed that night, a twist of pain in her heart as she thought of what the morrow would bring. How she wished that things might have been different. If she and Peter Channing had met under different circumstances, had the opportunity to develop their relationship sweetly and cleanly, she would now be the happiest woman in the world. There was no chance for them. She knew it. She was bad, soiled, degraded. No decent man would want her.

She would tell him, in the morning, to forget their marriage vows. They had not been consummated, anyway. He could ignore them, find himself some other woman in his own land. Or perhaps the marriage could be declared void. She didn't know about such things.

She loved him. She knew that now. But in time, the hurt would go away. She had other things to do, Feng Wu's child to bear. She began to cry softly, and finally she slept.

In her sleep the dream came. A burning house turned into a dragon-twined brazier for incense. And behind the brazier stood Feng Wu. He came forward, moving mechanically, step by step, only his eyes glittering in a dead face. And she knew that he would turn, that there was a jeweled knife thrust to the hilt at the back of his golden robe—

Her scream was at first a strangled whisper,

then it rose to shatter the cloud-muffled stillness of the Mountain Lodge.

Peter Channing was beside her in an instant, shaking her into full wakefulness. "What is it?" he asked. "What frightened you?"

She began to sob. "Feng Wu," she said. "It was Feng Wu—"

"It was only a dream. Now hush. Just relax. I'll hold you." His soothing words turned into whispered endearments as he held her in his arms, feeling the shuddering cease, turning into something else, his own passions answering.

Her face, eyes petalled like flowers with wet lashes, turned upward, bright with wonder. And his mouth came down on hers, her body twisting to meet his, pressing against him with a throbbing warmth that set him trembling.

Still, he held to his resolve with a corner of his mind. He had no intention of seducing the girl. He only wished to comfort her, to calm her fears. "You will be all right now," he said, drawing away from her.

Her lips trembled. "Don't leave me—"

It would do no harm to stay awhile longer, now that he had himself under control. He lay down beside her, stroking her hair away from her tear-wet face. She opened her eyes and he looked into their dark depths, feeling himself falling, drowning in them. He knew it was time to go. Let her face her fears. He couldn't take much more of this—

"Ahhh—"

A groan burst from his lips as she turned, the bosom of her gown falling open, her beauty framed in lace. And suddenly they were both struggling to get closer, to become one. Still holding to the edge of sanity, he took her with gentleness until that last

322

moment when the cloud-shrouded room exploded into rainbows of pulsing light.

For a long time, they lay satiated, and he turned to her again. Except for words of love, they didn't speak. The past was forgotten, the future unthought of as they took pleasure in each other.

Peter was sleeping when dawn came. Martha sat up and looked down at him. What a foolish, childish concept of love she'd had before now. And this was all she would have of it. All of her life, she would have this one night to remember.

Sensing her eyes upon him, Peter Channing woke. He grinned up at her teasingly, sure that there had never been anyone so beautiful as this small girl, dark hair spilling over bare shoulders.

"There will be no more nonsense about staying behind, now. You're going with me?" It was half question, half-statement.

She shook her head, her eyes haunted. "No, Peter, I can't go. Our marriage was only a matter of convenience. Now you can consider it over."

He sat up, his face bewildered and angry. "What the hell? I thought—last night—"

"You didn't want me for a wife, Peter. You know the things I've done."

"You must have had your reasons," he said soberly.

She shook her head. "Not really. I've hurt a lot of people. And there's something else you don't know. I'm a—a bastard."

He was silent for a moment, then he shrugged his broad shoulders and grinned crookedly. "And there's something you don't know. My folks were both convicts, shipped off to Australia for crimes they won't mention. Guess we're even—"

"No, we're not. Peter," she took a deep breath. "Peter, I'm going to have a child."

He looked at first puzzled and then amused. "Of course you are. But it will probably take awhile. Good lord! One night? And even if you do, it's legal."

"The child," she said flatly, "will not be yours. It is Feng Wu's."

There was no answer, only a stunned silence. She put her face in her hands, hearing him get up, go into the other room, the sounds of a man dressing.

Peter Channing walked out into the cloud-shrouded morning. When the sedan-bearers arrived, he was halfway down the hill. Only one would be needed.

Martha was returned to Government House in time to watch the *Mattie* leave the harbor.

MOLOKAI

35

On the island of Maui, up the coast from Lahaina, Martha Courtney was very much in Tamsen's mind. She was involved in two projects. For one, she was moving, going back to the deserted collection of grass huts where they had been living when Sam found her. Christmas was over and done. It had been a dreary occasion, celebrated only for the sake of the children. There had been a tree, and Dan hadn't the grace to stay away.

He lingered on after the others left—despite her chill refusal to talk to him—and then had followed her to her room.

"We're going to have to stop this nonsense," he growled. "Tamsen, you're going to have to trust me!" He stepped toward her, his jaw jutting. "I'm not going to make any excuses or explanations. I just want you to say you believe in me! Then I want you to be my wife again—"

She looked at him, seeing the sincerity in his eyes, his arms half-extended in invitation. Then, superimposed, she could see the look of fury he wore when he flung himself out of the house with a threat to kill Sam Larabee.

He had been seen burning Sam's home. His

clothing had smelled of coal oil. And now he was asking for her trust. What did he take her for?

"I'm sorry, Dan. I can't." Her tone was flat, dull, final.

"I won't come to you again." He turned and left the room. After a while, she went to a rear window to watch him walk across the yard to the small house he occupied alone. Her heart ached, yearning after him. He had killed before their marriage. She knew that. He'd shot the two men who raped Em. But she had never thought of him as a murderer.

Now it was Sam who was dead at her husband's hands. Sam Larabee, her beloved friend and his gentle wife. Sam's daughter Lani was a casualty, too. She stayed along in one of the small huts on the Larabee property, the scent of the burned house in which her mother and father died, still lingering. She would see no one but Kimo. Even the Reverend David Selwyn had been turned away.

After that one episode on Christmas night, Dan hadn't tried to see Tamsen again. Shortly after the New Year, he, Dusty and Juan, having finished surveying the area near Lahaina, left for more remote areas. They would not return until the job on Maui was done.

It had been Tamsen's idea to move while they were away. Arab and Nell were reluctant to give up their comforts, but were forced to agree that they couldn't continue accepting a dead man's hospitality, especially when he had died at the hands of one of their own.

Everything was packed. Tamsen had moved all Dan's private papers into the small house that still held some of his things. She had paused there a long while, her hand smoothing the indentation on his pillow, picking up an old pipe he'd left behind, putting it down. Her eyes were dry. She had already shed too many tears. But her heart felt like it was bleeding.

It was all done. As she waited to leave, she was trying to accomplish her second goal; that of writing to Em, telling her that Martha had disappeared. In the days since the girl turned up missing, she'd begun to see her for what she was, a frightened rebellious child with runaway emotions that led her into the trouble. She surely knew she was responsible for two deaths! How she must have suffered! It was Nell's theory that she had done away with herself, perhaps leaped into the sea. Tamsen had walked the beaches for days, fearing to find some grisly reminder of the little girl she once loved.

But how to tell Em! She couldn't say, "Look, Martha goaded Dan into killing Sam Larabee, our old friend—and his wife died with him." Or, "Em, I'm afraid I mislaid your daughter, somehow." Perhaps just, "Em, Martha has been missing for some time and must be presumed dead. I'm sorry."

In the end, she wrote, *"Dan and the others are working away from home, and we're moving back to the area near Lahaina. I hope you had a merry Christmas. Arab and the children are well. How is that boy?"*

She managed a few more chatty lines, not mentioning Marth's name, or Sam's. There. It would have to do. She felt like a coward. Someday, she would have to tell Em the whole story. She prayed she would be able to face it when the time came. But for now, let Em be happy for a while in her ignorance of the events on Maui.

As they headed down the trail toward Lahaina, Tamsen asked the others to wait. She entered the path that led to the burned Larabee house, skirting

329

the ashes with a sick feeling in the pit of her stomach, and went toward the small house that Lani had taken for her own. The girl was on the porch and Tamsen called to her. Lani went inside and closed the door.

As Tamsen stood, hesitating, Kimo appeared at her side. He began to explain in his pidgin English that Lani didn't wish to see anyone, and Tamsen turned her anger on him.

"You can speak," she said, her eyes flashing. "I've heard you! Now go inside and tell Lani I want to see her."

"I'm afraid I can't influence her," he confessed. "I've tried. She thinks she had a hand in what happened to Sam and Josie. She knows now that Martha convinced her into believing something that was untrue. She's punishing herself. If Sam hadn't been such a damn fool—"

Tamsen stared at him. "What are you talking about?"

Kimo grinned painfully. "Never mind. It's all *pau*. Lani will be all right. Time will heal her hurts."

"I hope so, Kimo. I don't think it will heal mine."

His brows lifted questioningly and she hastened to say, "We are moving back to the compound near Lahaina. I left a note at the house, but if anyone should come here, Dusty or Juan, perhaps, I've moved all Dan's papers into the small house he sometimes used as an office. They are in two baskets beneath a bed."

Kimo's expression was bland, not revealing the plan working busily behind his dark eyes.

"I will tell them," he said. "Aloha."

"Aloha," Tamsen echoed, a lump in her throat. It seemed like such a final period to an episode that had brought both joy and grief.

Kimo watched until she was out of sight. After an interval, he went into Lani's little house. The girl's shoulders were bent, her eyes wet with tears.

"Do not cry, *Kanani*. If you believe in the mission God, you must know your father and mother live on."

"I do not believe in anything!" she raged.

He knelt beside her. "Then let me help you, my *Kealoha!* We will go far from here; perhaps back to Hana where there are others who love you. We will return to the old ways, to our own Gods. You will be my wife—"

"You're talking like a fool, Kimo! The old ways are gone! Aren't you ever going to wake up? I won't leave this place! It was Papa's, Mama's, and it's all I have left of them. I can't marry you. It wouldn't be fair to you—"

"It is still the Reverend Selwyn?"

Her eyes gave him his answer.

"Then go to him. The man loves you. I know it."

"I can't, Kimo. There is too much on my conscience now. And Papa wouldn't want it. He—for some reason—hated David."

"Now it is you who are the fool," Kimo flung at her, his dark eyes stormy. "It is our responsibility to keep the old ways! Our duty! If one wants something, nothing should be allowed to stand in the way! I intend to do my utmost to keep our country for our people. You should follow the dictates of your heart!"

"I don't want to discuss it, Kimo. Please go."

He bowed, mockingly. "*Lawa*, seestah! *Kala mai ia'u.*"

"It is not enough, Kimo! I am not your sister! And I do not wish to excuse you!" She began to sob.

"I love you Kimo! But just not enough! I know you want to help, but . . . Forgive me—"

He held her, trying to blink the tears that blurred his own vision. "Forgive you, Ipo? Do you think you need to ask me that, when I have loved you all my life. You are my sweetheart, my sister, my friend. Do not forget it!"

When Lani was calmed, Kimo left her, walking up the coastline toward the house where Sam's guests had lived. The place seemed so empty now, as if it had never been occupied. He skirted the structure that went to the rear to the small house where Dan had slept since that tragic night. He knew all about it. The Hawaiian grapevine left little to the imagination.

The door was locked, but Kimo carried Sam's ring of keys. He tried them until he found one that fit, and pushed his way inside.

Dan's papers were where Tamsen said they would be. He found the evidence he was looking for. There were copies of letters to Ulysses S. Grant, now President of the United States. He also found Grant's replies and letters to and from various senators and congressmen. They left no doubt that Daniel Tallant was playing a double role, and from the tone of his own messages, it appeared he was beginning to favor annexation.

Kimo set out for Lahaina.

The man he talked to there immediately embarked for Honolulu, the seat of the government, on the island of Oahu. There he spoke with one of the royal representatives, finally finding himself in the presence of King Lot, Kamehameha, Fifth. Princess Liliuokalani, wife of Governor John Dominis, stood by the king's side.

The man from Lahaina was awed by the appearance of the king. Kamehameha was clad in black trousers and white vest, with an elegant blue dress coat with gilt buttons. On his hands were immaculate white kid gloves. Portly, with dark, sensual features, he made an imposing figure.

He read the evidence the man from Lahaina had brought, passing it to Liliuokalani at his side. When he spoke, it was a disappointment. Despite his impressive size, he had a thin reedy voice.

"We have a problem here," he said, frowning. "I would like to have the man arrested, held until we can counteract his efforts regarding annexation. But it would create ill-will among the American Party—perhaps bring matters to a boiling point. I do not wish controversy or violence—"

"He is trying to take over our country," Liliuokalana interposed. "I say he should be tried as a traitor! Beheaded!"

The king waved a placating hand. "I fear you are more patriotic than diplomatic, my dear. I would prefer another way—"

Without speaking, Kimo's messenger handed another paper to the king. Kamehameha read it, his brows lifting. "Oho," he said, exultantly. "This is what we need—the very thing!" He turned to a guard at his side. "Take this to your captain. He will know what to do."

Two weeks later, Juan and Dusty arrived at the house where they had lived as guests of Sam Larabee. Tamsen, Arab and the children, and Nell were gone. They found Tamsen's note and made their way to the compound, where they stammered out their dreadful news.

They had been working near *Kahalui* when a company of the king's soldiers appeared. Dan was arrested, Dusty and Juan were taken along with him and interrogated regarding the death of Sam Larabee. They had perjured themselves.

Did they know of any bad blood between Tallant and Larabee?"

"No."

Had either of them heard Tallant threaten the life of Samuel Larabee at any time?

Again, "No."

Then they had been shown a paper, signed with the mark of one 'Aukai, who claimed to have seen Dan Tallant burn the Larabee home. Dan was in prison, and allowed no visitors. Juan and Dusty had been sent home.

Juan was pale, guilt-ridden by his attempted deception. Dusty was proud of his lie, and defiant. "It's a trumped-up charge, that's what it is! I recall hearing 'Aukai's tale. A lapu," he snorted. "A blasted ghost! I tell you, Tamsen, the man's a drunk!" He paused for effect, a typical alcoholic's contempt for another in his voice. "You're going to Honolulu, aren't you, Tamsen? You'll find some way to get Dan out—"

"I will do nothing." Tamsen's tone was dull, dead. "This is Dan's problem. He'll just have to prove he's innocent—if he can."

"My word, Tam! This isn't like you! We've got to fight!"

She looked at him steadily. "Dusty, can you honestly say Dan didn't set the fire that killed Sam and Josie?"

The old man began to stutter, his eyes stricken. "It isn't the way he'd do things, Tamsen. I admit, it looks bad, but—"

"Then prove it to me. When you do, I will go to Honolulu."

Tamsen rose, signaling the end of the conversation, and went into her own hut. There she lay on her bed mat, fists clenched against the agony that tore at her like the pangs of birth. The agony of a love that tore at her mind and heart, and refused to die.

36

The days that followed were unhappy ones for all of them. Tamsen was at the edge of her nerves. Always fragile, her strength deceptive, she lost weight, her dark eyes enormous and shadowed. The horror of Sam's and Josie's death haunted her dreams.

On a whim, she returned to the house above the ruins of Sam's home, feeling like an interloper. It was in her mind to search the small place where Dan had lived after the fire; perhaps to find something that would prove his innocence. Nothing had changed. The pillow still held the indentation of his head, his pipe still lay where she had found it.

She knelt, searching beneath his bed for the papers she had placed there. They were gone. Of course, they would have been found, taken to Honolulu to be searched for evidence.

They would find nothing that would prove his guilt. These only dealt with business. Her eyes widened as she realized what they *did* prove. She had gone over them before bringing them out here, trying to rid herself of any part of Dan. There were letters from Grant—

In the hands of the authorities, the papers would damn Dan Tallant as a spy, a traitor to the Hawwaiian government. Maybe Sam's murder wasn't the real issue after all. Someone had known of his purpose here! Dusty's words rang in her ears. "A *trumped-up charge—*"

Other than the accusations of *'Aukai,* known to be a disreputable character, she was the only one who had real evidence of Dan's involvement the night of the fire. Guilty or not, they couldn't hold him on the word of a drink-sodden native, not an American, here as an employee of the railroad interests. It had to be something more—

Someone had betrayed him. Someone who knew about his work, and where to find the papers! Who?

She heard herself telling Kimo, "I *moved all Dan's papers—They are in two baskets under a bed—*"

Kimo wouldn't have done this! But Kimo had loved Sam. He'd been like a son. It might have been his way of avenging Sam's death.

If it were, then *she* had been Dan's betrayer. And he would be crucified. It was one thing to be accused of a crime, another to be guilty of doing his duty for his country.

She left the small house and descended the twisting foot-trail leading down to the beach. The waters were blue and calm, splashing playfully on the rocks that were the horns of the crescent shaped sands.

There she had seen Dan on the morning after the fire, his beloved, tanned body gleaming in the sun as he scrubbed himself clean. And there, she looked toward the spot, and recalled his clothing,

337

reeking with the smell of fuel used in the burning.

She put her hands over her eyes to shut out the remembered sight.

Tamsen couldn't help Dan if he were being held for murder. But she would find out who had taken his papers and she would go to President Grant, herself, if necessary.

Climbing up the cliff path, she mounted her horse and rode as far as the entrance to Sam's plantation. There, she dismounted and walked the remainder of the way.

This time, Lani didn't see her. The girl sat on the grass, disconsolately weaving leis. They were hung from branches of a nearby shrub, evidently a method of helping time pass.

It won't help you, Tamsen thought. Poor child, it won't help!

She walked to where the girl sat. As Tamsen's shadow fell across her, Lani looked up. An expression of panic flitted across her face, and then she stood, the two women looking at each other with haunted eyes. Then, with a gasp of pain, Lani flung herself into Tamsen's arms, sobbing out her heartbreak.

Kimo, watching the two women, realizing that Tamsen was helping Lani as he never could. He withdrew into the cover of flowering shrubs and sat with his face in his hands.

Damn Sam! Damn him! Something would have to be done!

Tamsen stayed with Lani for a long time, trying to persuade her to come out of her shell, perhaps go back to her volunteer work at the mission. The girl was adamant in her refusal.

"You can't just stay here like this," Tamsen scolded.

"I know. I just need a while to think. Then I'm going to go away, leave the islands—"

"Where would you go?" Tamsen gasped.

"I don't know. Just somewhere far. It doesn't seem to make any difference."

Kimo, crouched in the flickering shadows, died a little. Lani had never mentioned going away to him. Despite the words that had passed between them, he'd thought Lani would always be here. He had a dream in which, someday, David Selwyn might dim in her thoughts, and she would turn to him.

He was Hawaiian. He loved his country. But with a surging pain, he knew that he loved Lani more, and that he would do anything to ensure her happiness.

Backing away from the scene, he reached a point that was out of earshot, then came toward the two women, making a great deal of noise to announce his approach.

He joined them, talking cheerfully, his language a mixture of erudite English and slangy pidgin in an effort to amuse them. Tamsen brought up the subject of Dan's papers. They were gone. Could anyone have taken them?

His face was bland as he lied to her. Who had a key? She had one? her husband? Then he might have returned before his arrest, and picked them up, himself.

It made sense. Nothing had been accomplished by her journey. Nothing had changed. Weary, drained by the emotional scene with Lani, Tamsen made her way down the coast to the collection of grass huts that was home.

At dusk, Kimo went to a spot on the beach where he kept a small boat. He pushed it into the water, and rowed for some distance before he hoisted a sail. He had made certain that Lani slept before he left, but he wished to take no chances. If she questioned him, however, he would say he had been doing some night fishing.

His errand took him longer than he thought. He was still not back in the morning. That evening, his heart sore, his massive shoulders aching, he beached the boat once more and found Lani waiting.

She had missed him, she said simply. She had looked for him, and finally come here to find his small craft gone. "I was frightened, Kimo," she said. "Don't leave me again—"

She came toward him, clad in a single length of cloth that wrapped her slim body in the Polynesian manner. There was a red hibiscus flower in her hair. His hopes returned, his pulse thundering at the sight of her, until he saw her eyes.

It was the welcome of a sister for a brother, that was all. Then just in time, he remembered.

"Don't touch me," he warned. "Stand back."

Her raised arms dropped, and she looked at him in confusion.

"It has to do with my Kahuna rites," he told her solemnly. "It is something a woman wouldn't understand. I am being trained to take my father's place, and the touch of a woman at this time is *kapu*."

"You are joking," she faltered. "Teasing me again."

"It is no joking matter, I assure you. Now there are other rites I must perform. I must ask you to leave me."

She stared at him for a moment in bewilderment, seeing that he meant what he said, then turned and went disconsolately toward the small house she now called home, out of sight of the sea.

When she had gone, Kimo stripped off the apron-like garment he wore in a twist about his loins and began to scrub himself with sand.

He felt he would never be clean again.

37

For the next few days, a hurricane flirted with the islands. Standing off to sea, never quite touching the land, it brought rain to Hilo on the big island, a steady downpour that filled the cups of exotic flowers to brimming, sending tree fern and liana into another spurt of luxurious growth.

Nearing Maui, it toyed with the waves, sending massive combers curling toward shore, lifting to show their green-glass undersides before they curved down to bury themselves in a thunder of foam.

Dusty and Juan were up-country, insisting on returning to work, despite Dan's absence. Nell and the little girls napped, and Arab was absorbed with Luka.

Restless, unable to keep herself occupied, Tamsen walked into Lahaina. She had given herself the excuse of purchasing needles, but she knew, in her heart, that wasn't her true reason. She went straight to the mission house.

Again, David Selwyn had a bad day. A child had drowned in the heavy surf and was brought to him too late to revive a spark of life. He tried to comfort the mother with God's word, only to find that she needed no comforting. Her family aumakua, was the shark-god who had taken the child's spirit to himself. In her sadness, she was honored.

He must leave this place, Selwyn thought furiously, before he lost his faith and his mind. He was attempting to hand-roll pills when Tamsen arrived, dropping one occasionally, hating himself for his clumsiness, trying not to think of Lani's deft fingers.

When Tamsen entered the dispensary, she stopped and swallowed hard. Instead of his customary suit and white coat, the young missionary was clad in blue shirt and trousers. His shoulders had filled out since she'd last been him, his face finally taking on a tan. With his scowl, he looked a bit like Dan, when he was angry.

"I'm sorry," she said, "I seem to have come at a bad time. Perhaps some other—"

He caught himself and forced a smile. "I've had a bad morning," he admitted. "Please sit down. How is the Narvaéz baby?"

"She still doesn't cry as she should. She hasn't tried to sit up—"

"Her limbs should be exercised. She should be forced to do things. Otherwise, she will be a vegetable."

"Arab still doesn't admit there's anything wrong with her—"

"Then make her see it," he snapped. "What the hell is wrong with her husband?"

Tamsen stared at him in shock. Realizing what he said, he flushed. "My apologies. But a child's life is important. This can't simply be ignored!"

"Juan loves Arab very much. He doesn't want to hurt her. He thinks, in time, she will see?"

"The time is now! The way that child is treated

343

now will determine her future development. You've got to make them realize that fact. And if they don't, then you take over!"

"I should have done something," Tamsen said distractedly, "but I've had problems—"

"Sam Larabee," Selwyn said, his face softening. "Your husband."

"You know about it?"

"A little," he said. "The plantation people talk, you know."

"Do you think Dan is guilty?"

He evaded her eyes. "I'm not a person to judge. There are times when I've felt like killing Sam, myself. Of all the stubborn, misguided—"

He stopped abruptly, and Tamsen cringed at the fury in his face. He meant what he was saying. This gentle man of God was capable of murder! And he was tall, dressed as Dan often was. There had been some altercation when Sam brought Lani to stay with them.

She realized that a faint hope had stirred in her breast; an insane, idiotic hope that Sam had died at someone else's hands. But all the time, she knew better.

Dully, she rose to leave, turning back as he ushered her to the door. "Reverend Selwyn—David —have you tried to see Lani?"

"I wrote her a note of sympathy," he said stiffly. "In return, I received word that I was not welcome to visit in person, that she had no need of me."

"I'm sorry."

"Don't be." There was a white line of pain about his mouth. "Do come again. And remember what I've said about the child."

Leaving the mission, Tamsen walked to the intersection of Front and Shaw streets. There she paused at the narrow causeway leading to the sacred island of Moku-ula. Here, she had come with Sam Larabee on a bright and beautiful day, soft with the fragrance of flowers.

She hesitated for a moment, then, recognizing the sentry as the same man who had allowed them to enter, went to greet him.

"I was here once before, with Mr. Larabee," she said.

He remembered. Without asking if she wished to enter, he smilingly waved her through.

Nothing had changed. She could shut her eyes and imagine Sam at her side, telling her the legend of the mo-o; the love story of Princess Nahienaena and Kamehameha, the Third. She could hear his voice as he said, *"When I come here, it makes me feel that there's something after death. It makes me feel peaceful—"*

It was odd that she could summon Sam to mind so clearly—when he was dead. Dan's living face was blurred in her brain.

Alone, on the island of the dead, Tamsen wept for Sam and Josie, for Dan, and for herself.

Leaving the island, feeling strangely cleansed, she went to see if there was any mail. There was none. She walked toward home, arriving at the compound, before she recalled that she'd forgotten the needles she'd planned to purchase.

Nell was gone, possibly having gone into town, herself. Romona and Missy were playing, making dolls of flowers and seeds. They stood them in a row, like ladies, in their ruffled hibiscus skirts.

With a touch of shock, Tamsen noted that the children once more looked neglected. She went in search of Arab, finding her in the hut, little Luka on her lap. Arab, too, looked unkempt, her bright hair

345

straggling, her gown soiled. Only the baby she held was freshly bathed, clean, sweet-smelling. Arab's face shone with adoration as she looked down at the little one. She looked up at Tamsen and smiled, a finger to her lips.

"I will take Luka now," Tamsen said firmly. "You will bathe Ramona and Missy. And do something about yourself. Would you want Juan to see you like that?"

Arab looked down, surprised, seeing her disheveled gown, and put up a hand to smooth the hair. "I've been so busy with the baby, I didn't realize," she said reluctantly. "Perhaps when she wakes—"

"She sleeps all the time," Tamsen said sharply. "It won't hurt her to miss a few minutes." She took the child from her sister. "You've forgotten that Missy and Ramona need you, too."

Arab flushed guiltily. All those months ago, she had made a promise to herself to remember that fact. But Ramona and Missy were such big girls. Little Luka was so helpless, just a baby. It was so good to hold her, to look down into the beautiful little face, that she sometimes forgot.

"Be sure to support her head," she sand anxiously as Tansem held Luka.

"For God's sake, Arab, she's more than a year old!"

Tamsen took Luka to her hut, hearing the glad cries of Ramona and Missy as Arab went to join them. She put the baby down on her sleeping mat, and laid back her soft blanket, removing the hampering clothes in which the little thing was swathed, despite the heat. Her body bared to the soft, scented air, Luka gave a small coo of surprise and delight. Tamsen's heart turned over. There was a degree of mind there after all, and Luka should have her chance.

She began to manipulate the small arms and legs, as David Selwyn had recommended, lifting the baby into a sitting position from time to time, supporting the small back with her hand.

"There! You're sitting up. Do you see how it feels? Do you like that?" The rosy mouth curled. The long silver eyes seemed to shine.

Absorbed in her task, she didn't see Arab enter. With a scream of anger, her younger sister snatched at the child, squeezing her against her bosom as she railed out at Tamsen.

"My God! What are you doing? You'll break her back doing that! Don't you ever touch my baby again!"

Luka began to cry, and Arab glared at Tamsen and left the hut in a huff. Tamsen sank back on the mat. There was nothing she could do, short of committing an act of violence. She could only talk to Juan when he came home.

She lay for a long time, unable to rest, her head pounding as she wondered if anything could possibly get worse. Then Nell poked her head in the door. She had picked up the mail, evidently while Tamsen was on her other errands. And she had a letter from Em.

Tamsen opened it, unable to summon any excitement until she saw the contents.

"*You haven't mentioned Martha in some time,*" Em wrote, "*not even answering my questions. Duke and I have been worrying about her. We think a trip to a warm climate would be good for the children, and, of course, we want to show off our boy. We'll be seeing you soon.*"

347

Dear God! Oh, dear God! Em was coming here! What could she tell her? What could she say? How long had the letter lain there? They hadn't picked up the mail for a long time. Perhaps she could stop them.

Hastily, she penned a note, saying that she received the letter, but now was a poor time to visit, since they were moving on.

She finished it, reread it, and tore it up. Martha was gone. It had been months now. At this point it was better to inform Em and Duke face to face.

That night, she couldn't sleep. She left the confining hut and sat outside, breathing the night's fragrance, trying to mend her shattered nerves. But it was still with her—in a sense of desperation—that something terrible was going to happen.

Kimo, up the coast, was in the same case. He walked the beach, feeling lost and alone. He hadn't cared to go near Lani in some days. He knew she was hurt and bewildered at the neglect of the only friend she had left.

And he couldn't even fulfill the task that had been set for him, not until the hurricane moved on its way and the waters were once more calm and serene.

38

Some distance at sea, the captain of a small charter ship scowled at the retreating back of the man who was employing him to deliver him and his family to the island of Maui. They had just exchanged harsh words.

"I am the captain of this vessel," he'd said, looking up at the big man, almost tiptoe in his indignation. "And I decide when it's safe to move. There's a hurricane in the vicinity. I've been watching the glass. We're going to sit it out until I'm convinced we should go on."

"Dammit," the enormous man growled. His red-checked shirt and corduroy pants tucked into mining boots belied his financial status. "Who the hell is hiring you, anyway. If you're scared—"

"I," the small captain spat, doubling his age-spotted fists, "am not afraid of anything, or *anyone!*"

To his surprise, the frown left the big man's face, to be replaced by a look of amused admiration. "Damned if I don't believe you," he said. "Go ahead, buster. Have it your own way."

He left and made his way to the rail, where his wife, Em, turned anxious flowerlike eyes on him.

349

"Did you talk to him, Duke? Can't we get up a little more speed?"

"Ain't a feller you can push," Duke Courtney grinned. "I reckon he knows what he's doing. We'll get there when we get there, Em. The kids asleep?"

"Sleeping like angels. Scotty's on his knees, bottom in the air, as usual. I can hardly resist spanking him. Cammie went off immediately. Victoria had her little tantrum first. I'll swear, that child reminds me of Martha—"

"Martha was a sweet kid when she was Vicky's age," Duke said.

Em interlaced her fingers, nervously. "I know, Duke. What happened to make her change like that? What did we do to her? I can't believe—"

"Calm down, Sweetheart." Duke Courtney put his arm about his small wife, pulling her blonde-brown head against his chest. "Maybe we'll find out when we get there. Honey, she'll be so damn glad to see us she'll forget we ever had any differences. She'll come running to meet us—probably knock you flat."

"I don't know, Duke." Em was pale, her eyes circled with worry. "I'm afraid—"

"Afraid of what," he scoffed. "What the hell is there to be scared of? Now, relax! You'll be seeing our kid in a couple of days."

"I don't think so, Duke. I—I just don't *feel* it. We haven't heard a word from her since she left, and Tamsen hasn't even mentioned her for a long time. Something's wrong, I know it."

Duke had some qualms of his own, but he wouldn't admit to them. He decided to try to tease her out of her concerns. "What could happen on an island, sweetheart? No snakes, no bears. She could run off with a native, but I don't think she could run too far. Not on a little speck of land in the middle of the ocean. Anyway, I think Tallant would stop her before she had a chance to compromise some poor defenseless Hawaiian."

"Duke, you idiot!" Em's cheeks were pink, but she was laughing.

He feigned a hurt expression. "I was only thinking. Like mother, like daughter, you know. Hell, you trapped me. Admit it!"

"I'll do no such thing." Em was blushing furiously now. He was hitting too close to the truth. It was she who proposed to him, not the other way around. And she had never been sorry for a minute. He'd been a good husband to her, a good father to Martha.

Martha.

At the thought of her oldest daughter, her worry began again. This time, Duke Courtney didn't try to divert her mind. There was no sense in trying. He knew his wife, and she would be a nervous wreck until Martha was safe in her arms. He hoped to God everything would turn out to be all right.

He was as crazy as Em to see Martha again. He looked forward to seeing all of them. Especially Tamsen, whom he had known first as the operator of a house on the Fraser. A gutsy mixture of tough and tender, steel and velvet, Tamsen was his kind of people.

Tamsen, on the island of Maui, was anything but the way Duke had pictured her. She had never felt so weak, so drained, so incapable of coping in her life. Finally, like a sleepwalker, she made her way to bed. She didn't sleep. The problems with Arab and the upcoming meeting with Em haunted her, prodding her into wakefulness.

Perhaps these worries were blessings. Her shock at Dan's behavior, her grief over Sam and Josie, were, for the moment, pushed to the back of her mind. Those indeed were the concerns that were too painful to bear.

The next day was even worse. Arab refused to come out of her hut. A worried Ramona carried her food to her. "Let her sulk," Tamsen told Nell, angrily. "I've had it with her! Let her sit in there until Juan comes home. If he's got a grain of sense, he'll slap the hell out of her!"

Despite her fury, she couldn't forget Selwyn's words. *"The time is now. The way the baby's treated now will determine her future development."*

She went to the door of Arab's hut. "Are you coming out, Arab? Or shall I come in?"

There was a moment's silence, and Arab called, "I'm coming." There were little shuffling sounds as she put Luka down. A cooing voice said, "Mommie will be back."

Then Arab crawled from the low doorway and stood to face Tamsen, her face flushed and defiant, her gorgeous hair tumbled about it. She looked no older than fifteen or sixteen, and she wore the same expression she did then: rebellious and defiant.

"I want to talk to you about Luka," Tamsen said in a steady voice.

"You're not to touch her again! You don't know how to handle babies. She fretted all night."

"Then why was I allowed to hold Ramona and Missy? I practically raised them."

"They're different." Arab flushed. "Luka is—sensitive."

"If Luka fretted, it was because her muscles hurt. And if they hurt, it's because she hadn't been

352

helped to use them. It has nothing to do with sensitivity!"

"She's just a baby."

"She isn't a baby any longer! She should be sitting up, standing, pulling up to things. You've got to face it, Arab! She's retarded! She needs help."

"She isn't! She's perfect! Anybody can see—"

"I've talked to Doctor Selwyn."

Arab's chin lifted. "What does he know? A man! He doesn't have any children!" She paused, then, her voice edged with spite, added "Neither do you, for that matter."

Tamsen fought to control her anger, and failed. "You always were the selfish one, Arab. Out to get what you wanted, no matter who you hurt. Well, this time, you're not going to get away with it! I'm going to talk to Juan—"

Arab's hand flashed out, catching Tamsen across the cheek. Both of them stood still, looking at each other with shock, then Arab burst into tears and fled to the shelter of her hut.

Ramona came running across the compound, her big eyes round as dollars as she caught at Tamsen's skirt. "Did she hurt you, Aunt Tamsen? Why did she hit you?" She began to cry. "I don't like Mommie any more."

Tamsen knelt to take the little girl in her arms. "Mommie isn't well, sweetheart. Sometimes she does things without thinking. She didn't mean to do that."

The child finally consoled, Tamsen went to her own hut. She had been deliberately cruel, hoping shock tactics would wake Arab to what she was doing to her whole family. But it hadn't worked. She wished she could get away for a while, everything was wearing on her nerves.

The opportunity came that evening. Kimo arrived. Lani wished to speak with her. It was very important, and, no, it wouldn't wait until morning. Soon, Tamsen found herself riding up the trail, but there was no sense of freedom. She seemed to have left bits and pieces of herself behind. She was as bad as Arab, she thought, wryly. But instead of concentrating on one child, she was trying to spread her love among too many.

Kimo was silent during most of the ride. Tamsen began to feel a faint twinge of alarm.

"Is Lani ill?"

His answer consisted of a single syllable. "No."

When they reached the turnoff to Sam's plantation, Kimo turned his horse in the other direction, slipping and sliding down the path to the sea. Tamsen followed, her mind whirling with speculation. Surely the girl could not be down here—unless something had happened, and she had been injured.

She kept her mouth shut, never having seen Kimo in such a surly mood.

When they reached the beach, he led her to his small boat, gesturing for her to climb into it. She obeyed. He did not touch her, though she could smell the scent of *awa* on his breath as he bent above the boat chanting an incantation in his own tongue.

"What was that for?" she asked as he joined her in the craft.

"A prayer to my gods, for our safe return," he said shortly.

"Where are we going?"

"You will see."

A little way from shore, he raised the sail. The waters were still choppy, and the small vessel seemed to swoop and dive as it rode the waves.

Within a few hours, a huge shape loomed black against the night sky.

Tamsen recognized it. She had seen its silhouette many times. It was clearly visible from the house above Sam's plantation.

The dread island of Molokai.

For the first time, it dawned on her that Kimo was mad. The hair prickled at the nape of her neck. "Kimo, isn't that the place where the lepers are?"

He didn't answer, and there was an edge of panic in her voice as she said, "Kimo!"

"We are not going to the leper colony. We are going there." He thrust his hand toward the left, and the boat began to veer in that direction.

"Kimo, why?"

"You will see."

They landed on a beach swept by a gentle, constant wind. The white beach, bordered by blue waters, stretched to meet treeless green slopes that extended into softly rolling hills. The full moon was echoed in the waters, lighting up the scene. It was nothing like Hilo, nothing like Maui. Tamsen's fears were allayed as she drank in the beauty of it.

Kimo built a small fire on the beach, and brought a curtain of bamboo from his boat, setting up a small shelter. "You will sleep there," he said.

"Kimo, I don't understand! What are we doing here?"

"Waiting."

Returning to his vessel, he took up his guitar and walked down the beach, disappearing around a bend. Soon, she heard him playing a sad and haunting song. It finally lulled her to sleep.

In the morning, she woke, feeling amazingly

rested in spite of her strange predicament. In the daylight, she would be able to face anything, even Kimo's peculiar behavior. She would find him and insist on going home.

Crawling from her shelter, she looked toward the direction in which he disappeared the night before. He was not in sight. Then her eyes came back to the waters directly before her and she gasped in shock.

There, waist deep in the blue sea, the sun touching a head crowned with hair like snow, glinting off wet brown shoulder, stood a man; a man who was almost as familiar to her as her own husband; a man in whose arms she had lain, all those years ago. Her onetime lover, her best friend, the man who had died at her husband's hand and now stood, resurrected, haloed in the morning light—

Sam!

39

She stood rooted to the sands, but only for a moment. Then she was running, splashing through the water, fully clothed, eyes blinded with tears that ran, salty, into her open mouth.

"Sam! Oh, dear God, Sam!"

He moved away, an insubstantial figure in the glimmering light. "Don't touch me, Tamsen, please—"

"I will touch you, Sam Larabee! Ah, God! I thought you were dead! I've got to touch you, hold you—"

Her arms were around him as she laughed and cried at the same time. He flinched away for a moment, then he gripped her, savagely returning her embrace. "Tamsen, my love! My friend!"

For a time, her joy at seeing him blotted out all thought. Then a measure of sanity returned. "Dan! Then he didn't—Oh, my God, Sam, what have I done—"

"It's what I've done, Tamsen. I did what I thought was best. But I didn't know what a mess I'd made of things until Kimo came a few days ago, to tell me."

"I don't understand—"

"That's why he brought you here, so I could explain. But first, Tamsen, wash yourself thoroughly, every part of you that might have touched me. I— I'm probably unclean. I'll wait for you on shore, and then we'll talk."

She obeyed as he built up the fire on the sand before the shelter where she had spent the night. As she scrubbed her arms with sand, a horrible thought began to form in her mind. Sam had had an almost morbid preoccupation with death and disease. Now he was here on Molokai, the island of the lepers. She thought of Manu, the obscene, evil-smelling thing that was less than human; Manu, whom someone must have loved at one time.

She was trembling when she left the water and approached the fire, seeing the head that had turned white in a few short months; the face that lifted to her lined; the hot blue eyes now filled with an infinite weariness.

"Sam, do you have leprosy?"

He tried to smile, his mouth twisting as if in pain. "Not yet, Tamsen. But Josie does."

She dropped to her knees beside him. "Sam!"

He shied away. "Don't touch me. You mustn't take any chances. I meant to talk to you from the water. Now, I want you to listen. I don't want to leave her any longer than I have to, and I have a lot of wrongs to right."

Quietly, he began to tell her his story. Some time ago, he had begun to worry about his wife. Her problem had begun with a numbness in her feet. Her eyes had taken on a glassy look at times, the flesh on her cheeks assuming a transparent look that she attempted to hide with a lotion she concocted.

She had all the classic symptoms of beginning leprosy. He had not wished to recognize it as such, but had searched for other complaints that might produce the same symptoms. Then the purple bruises of the leper's mask had begun to appear, her features beginning to coarsen—

He paused, choked with emotion for a moment, and then went on. David Selwyn had hit upon the truth. He had gone to his office at his request, and heard the awful diagnosis. He would have to report it to the authorities, Selwyn said. He could let him have a month—

He had wanted to hit out, to blame everything and everyone else for his predicament. David Selwyn, God—and then he would come to terms with it. His only wish was to make it easier for Lani.

"You think it was easier to believe you were both dead?" Tamsen couldn't control her bewilderment.

"Lani worked in David's mission, remember. She knows what leprosy can do. And she knows the conditions in the colony; the way the lepers are dumped offshore, having to swim or drown; the privations, lawlessness, lone women raped by rotting horrors—"

"Sam, no!"

"It's like that, Tamsen." He went on to describe the filth and degradation that existed among the lepers of Molokai. Knowing Josie would be sent here, he made his own arrangements. He came to Molokai, found several lepers who were dependable, who seemed to have an arrested stage of the disease. He had armed them, and set them to guard the necessities of life he brought here. But he delayed bringing Josie, as long as he could. The trip to Hana had been, in effect, a farewell.

"And—Dan?"

"He wanted to kill me when he came that night." Sam grinned ruefully at the memory. "And he might have, if he hadn't seen Josie. Then he helped me clear out the last of our things. He left Josie and me on the boat, then burned the house. He brought us here, to Molokai, then returned the boat."

"Dear God, why didn't he tell me?"

"He gave me his word. Don't you see—I didn't want Lani in that house again, for fear of contagion. And it was better for her to think we were gone, to make a new life for herself."

"Do you think what she has now is a new life? Sam, she thinks Dan killed you both! And she feels guilty, because she accused you falsely. She just sits there, grieving. She won't see David Selwyn, because she thinks you two were at odds! It's killing her!"

"I know," he said wearily. "Kimo's terrified of leprosy. Yet he walked right into the colony a few days ago, to tell me what a damn fool I've been, how much trouble I've caused. I also know about Dan. Tamsen, I've written a letter to the king. Josie managed to sign it, with my help. Maybe it will help your husband, I don't know. I don't think my death was the real issue. I've also written a letter to a priest, called Father Damien."

Tamsen nodded. "I know him."

"If anybody can help us here in this godforsaken place, he will. But I don't know what to do about Lani." His eyes were filled with agony as he spoke.

"I think I do, Sam. Do I have your permission to use my own judgment?"

"You do."

"How is Josie? Has the disease progressed to a great degree?"

"Her appearance has deteriorated. You wouldn't

360

recognize her, I'm afraid. But, thank God, she still retains some of her strength."

"Could she make the trip here—as you did?"

He looked startled. "Why, I don't know. It's a rough trail over the peaks. But, yes, I suppose so. I brought along a mule."

"Then have her here one week from today. I'm bringing someone to see her."

Sam's face paled. "Lani can't see her mother like she is, Tamsen."

"It's that bad?"

"I'm afraid so."

She reached out to him in sympathy, but he drew away. To hide her emotions, she stood and walked a little way down the beach. Her eyes fell upon the bamboo screen that had been her shelter for the night. An idea sparked in her brain, and she whirled to face the second-best-loved man in her life.

"The screen! You can set it up, and Josie can talk from behind it. Please, Sam! You've got to do it for Lani's sake!"

"I don't know, I just don't know!" he sat in thought for a moment, and then smiled. "We'll do it your way," he said decisively. "Looks like my way's done nothing but worry the hell out of everyone."

"Sam!" This time, she didn't give him time to avoid her, but ran straight into his arms, hugging him. "I've got to kiss you, Sam, for old time's sake! And don't worry about giving me anything. I'm not afraid."

When they finally parted, his eyes were wet. "I wish I could turn the clock back to a night in San Francisco, Tamsen. Things might have been different."

361

"But then, you wouldn't have met Josie?"

"No, I wouldn't have met Josie. And I wouldn't trade my life with her for anything in the world. Not even what's left of it."

He finally left her, walking up the grassy slopes, standing tall upon a grassy knoll, his hair blowing in the wind as he lifted a hand in farewell. It was not a final good-bye. They would see each other once more, one week from this day, at dawn—if all went well.

After that, it was highly probable that they would never meet again.

Kimo had appeared beside her like a shadow. He took her arm, and she followed him, numbly, to the small boat waiting to carry them back to the land of the living.

40

Tamsen had recovered her senses by the time they reached the island of Maui. It was late evening, and the sun was setting above Maui's red hills. During the journey, her mind had swung in wild arcs, between sympathy for Sam and Josie—to elation that Dan was innocent of the terrible deed she had accused him of. Elation mixed with a dreadful guilt, because she hadn't believed in him.

How could she, knowing his hot temper, his jealousy that she had fed with her own actions; seeing the proof in his fuel-soaked clothing?

It made no difference. She had turned him away, when he had asked for her trust. Perhaps she would have stood by him in any case, if it had been anyone but Sam. If it were possible, she loved two men, each in a different way. The fault had lain in her.

She wanted to go to Dan, to beg his forgiveness. But he was allowed no visitors. The important thing was to get the letter directly into the hands of Kamehameha, bypassing his advisers. Kimo would handle that, he told her. But it would take time.

While she waited, she would see what she could

do for Lani to ensure her happiness. Time was something Josie didn't have.

When they landed at the small beach, a distance from Sam's burned home, Tamsen went directly to the place where Lani lived. She knocked, and Lani opened the door. She would have closed it again, but Tamsen hurled her small body against it, the girl falling back into the room.

Inside, Tamsen shut the door firmly behind her, and turned to face her friend's daughter.

"Lani," she said, "I have something to tell you. Something that will hurt, and make you happy at the same time. I would advise you to listen."

A short time later, Tamsen set out on the ride down the coast to Lahaina. A weeping Lani was beside her, having to be restrained from galloping all the way. It seemed an eternity before they reached the mission. It had been quiet there, and David Selwyn was catching a few winks of sleep when the door flew open and he was engulfed in a small whirlwind.

"David," Lani said, laughing through her tears, "Oh, David, why didn't you tell me! Why!"

He didn't answer, still dazed at finding the girl he'd been dreaming of in his arms. His eyes were filled with wonder. And finally, he did the only thing he knew to do. He placed his mouth on hers, shutting off the spate of words, and they clung together in an embrace, oblivious to Tamsen in the doorway.

She backed away, quietly closing the door behind her. All was well, now, with these two. She was certain that David Selwyn would go along with the plan she and Lani had discussed on the journey down the coast. Now, all she wanted to do was get back to the compound, stretch out on her woven mats, and think of Dan. Nothing else seemed to matter now.

Lani had her David; Sam and Josie, despite their tragic circumstances, still had each other. She could not be responsible for Luka. That job belonged to Arab and Juan, no matter how they botched it. And as heartbreaking as Martha's disappearance would be to Em, she had Duke to lean upon and console her.

Now it was her time to be selfish. She needed a few minutes to review her own life, to discover where she and Dan had failed in their communication. She needed a little while alone.

Approaching the compound, she heard the sound of voices raised in anger; a child crying, an expletive from Nell. Tamsen kicked her horse into a trot, and sped into the clearing where a strange sight met her eyes.

Nell, Arab, the children, were all in the center of the compound, facing an irate giant of a man. A woman stood at his side, a child in her arms; flanked by children at either side.

As Tamsen reined in her mount and leaped to the ground, the man turned to face her, taking a step in her direction.

Duke Courtney! Em!

"Tamsen! Now maybe we can get some goddam sense out of someone. *Martha*—Tamsen, where the hell is she?"

Tamsen hadn't had the period of quiet her nerves required. She stared at her brother-in-law, her eyes blank as she tried to hold to what little control she had remaining. "I don't know, Duke," she said finally. "I honestly don't know."

Em had braced herself, expecting the worst. So it was Tamsen, not Em, who crumpled to the ground.

Arab took charge, directing Duke to carry Tamsen to her hut. She handed Luka to Nell. The children were to all sleep in the larger structure, Duke and Em to have the house that had been Martha's. Nell was in charge of Ramona, Missie, Em's twins, and the two babies for the night.

Nell looked helplessly down at Luka, whom she'd never been allowed to touch. "Gawdam," she said, weakly. "Well, Gawdam!"

Em worked with Nell to get the little ones settled. When they were all abed, the women crept from the house of woven grass and into the night air. Duke waited for them, his arms folded across his chest.

"All right, Nell, let's have it. What has Tamsen done now?"

The old ex-madam set her jaw and assumed a pugnacious stance. If Em and Duke thought they could send Tamsen their problem child and then blame her for what happened, they had another think coming! Duke wanted the truth, by God, he was going to get it! In her own inimitable fashion, she poured out the whole story; the way the little bitch had chased Dan; the act she had driven him to do; the details of their last conversation the night the house burned.

"She ain't—*wasn't*," she amended, "a bad girl. Jes' overheered she was a bastard, and done her best t'act like one."

Em had flinched at every word. Now, she sagged against Duke's arm, her flowerlike face gone old and gray. When she spoke, her voice was calm.

"Thank you, Nell."

"Don't thank me. Hell, I ain't done nuthin'." Nell eyed her suspiciously.

"Yes you have. You told us what we've done wrong. If—if she's found, maybe we can make it up to her."

366

"Make it up, hell! All she needed was her butt blistered," Nell growled.

Em began to cry. Without knowing it, in those few harsh words, Nell had given her back her little girl. Not a rebellious, flirtatious, troublemaking child-woman, but a naughty child whom a spanking would cure. A spanking, with hugging to follow. She could see Martha's face in her mind now, impish, irrepressible. She couldn't be dead. They would find her—

Em flung herself into Nell's arms, much to the old woman's consternation. Holding the sobbing woman, Nell could only look beyond her at Duke, her eyes bulging. "Well, gawdam!" she said foolishly. "Gawdam! Git yer wife t'bed, man."

"I'm not going to bed," Em said, finally drawing away. "You go on, Duke. I'm going to Tamsen."

Tamsen had revived. Arab didn't allow her to talk, and gave her a sedating drink. When Em joined her, Arab was considering sending to the mission for Doctor Selwyn. She feared Tamsen had suffered a breakdown. She had kept insisting that Sam was alive, that she was trying to get an audience with the king, and that Dan was coming home.

Finally, Em lay down on one side of Tamsen, Arab on the other, the three sisters together at last, each with her own private heartache, their three heads close together, Gold-brown, silken-black, and red-gold. And Tamsen, comforted in the knowledge that the two people she loved and cared for most in the world, her sisters, finally slept.

Outside, Duke Courtney was hunched over a small fire, thinking of Martha, the daughter he loved most of all. She wasn't the child of his body, but she was most certainly the child of his heart. He watched the dawn come up, still mulling over the things Nell had told him. He would find Martha, dead or alive. Tomorrow, he would begin to comb the island.

Nell, too, was wakeful. Though she wouldn't admit it to herself, the responsibility for all these kids scared the hell out of her. With the morning sun, little Scott began to whimper. Nell moved to where he lay, and thrust a seeking hand beneath his light blanket. "Oh, no," she groaned.

She finally managed an awkward, bulky diaper, and Luka stirred. Again, she checked. "Migawd," she scolded, "Not you, too!" She hoped their folks would get things straightened out today. She couldn't take much more of this. That damn Martha seemed to cause about as much trouble gone as she did when she was around.

In a smaller hut, Tamsen stirred, waking her sisters as she sat bolt upright.

"We've got to get a wedding dress," she said, distractedly, "and a white suit—with white gloves. He can give her away—"

Em and Arab looked at each other in horror. Tamsen's mind had surely snapped.

41

Tamsen wasn't too certain of her own sanity as she fought her way out of her drugged sleep and recognized Em. The final events of the previous night came back to her, slowly, and she clutched at her sister.

"Oh, Em, I'm sorry! I'm so sorry!"

Em held her sister close. "It's all right, Tamsen. Nell told us the whole story. About Dan—Sàm." Her voice broke. She still remembered Sam Larabee after all these years with fondness. In the San Francisco fire, he had saved their lives, hers, Martha's, Tamsen's. And through Martha's mischief, he had been poorly repaid.

"But it isn't true, what Nell told you." Tamsen launched into the story of what she'd discovered on Molokai. Em's cheeks were wet with tears of relief. Dead or alive, Martha hadn't been the cause of a man's death. That knowledge helped, somehow.

The three sisters left the hut, emerging into bedlam. The small cousins, having discovered each other at last, were running helter-skelter in glee. Nell, Luka in her arms, looked as distracted as a mother hen with a hatching of ducklings. Duke was attempting to cook breakfast over the open fire, and keep an eye on a small boy who was exploring the premises, staggering on chubby legs. Seeing Em, the child came toward her, laughing, catching her skirt as he fell.

Em picked him up. "This is Scott," she laughed as he gripped a handful of her hair. She pried his plump fingers away, kissed his red cheek, set him down and gave him a smack on the bottom. He chuckled, and made his unsteady way back to his father.

Arab watched him go, her face ashen. The boy was younger than Luka. Luka, who lay stiff and docile in Nell's arms. She went cold all over.

Finally, she moved to Nell and took the baby, leaving the old woman wiping her brow in relief. With determined steps, she walked back to where Em stood, supporting a still shaky Tamsen.

"This is Luka," she said, seeing the look of shock that turned to pity as Em looked down at the bundle in her arms.

"She's—She's lovely," Em said in a stifled voice.

"She's retarded." There, she'd said it! "It was a difficult birth. Tamsen—Tamsen has started her on a series of exercises that may help. I want to learn to handle it, myself. The girls, too. It's something we can do together—as a family."

Tamsen's heart swelled with happiness. At last, everything was working out for the best. Martha's disappearance and Sam's tragic plight were the only clouds on her horizon.

The morning was spent in joyous reunion. The arrival of Dusty and Juan added ot the happy confusion. The children, zooming everywhere, giggling and screaming, delighted with their newfound relatives, kept Em busy. She was grateful for that. It kept her from thinking.

Only Duke was quiet, withdrawn. He had drawn Juan and Dusty aside, and discussed the scope of their search for the missing girl. There seemed little hope that she would be found.

The one man in the world who knew where she was, stood at the rail of a ship in the roadstead of Lahaina, only a short distance away. After a struggle with his conscience, wondering if his intervention would be a betrayal of the girl who now bore his name, Peter Channing had decided they should be informed of her whereabouts. Yesterday, he'd hired a horse and ridden up the coast to where the Tallant and Narvaéz family had lived. The house was empty.

He should have known. Of course they would be gone. Leaving the house on the cliff, he rode down to the Larabee home. Here, too, all was deserted. Where the house had stood, the island had already begun to reclaim its own, a soft-furred grass creeping to cover ashes, a flowering vine concealing the remains of a chimney. Plants and trees, untended, had flourished in a tangle of jungle growth. The bamboo chairs and table beneath the poinciana tree, where Josie had spent much of her time, had been tipped, upended, perhaps by wind. Her throne-like chair was broken.

Channing righted it, attempting to press its broken parts into place, to no avail. The chair, like its owner, was dead.

Leaving, he turned once more to look at the place where he had been the guest of a happy family. Desolate and overgrown, it would help him remember Martha's true nature when he weakened, as he had so often since he left her.

Now, leaning on the rail of the *Mattie*, the scene

was still vivid in his mind as the coastline of Maui, with its red hills, receded into the distance.

He chided himself for the way he left Martha on that last day at the Mountain Lodge at the top of Hong Kong. She wasn't able to prevent the condition she was in, though she'd certainly brought it upon herself. But to let him make love to her as he did that night, and then to spring something like that on him! That yellow bastard's get already growing inside of her! It had made a joke of something beautiful. A stupid, dirty joke.

He could see her now, lying against the pillows, her hair spread in a waterfall of silk, her mouth still bruised with his kisses. Groaning, he slammed his fist against the railing. He would have to keep the devastation she had caused fresh in his kind, remember it when he saw her again. As for Feng Wu's little bastard, he would have no difficulty in remembering that. He had already received a notification of the child's birth.

"A little daughter," Lady MacDonnel had written, effusively, "with dark hair that turns red in the sun. She is going to be dark, I think. Her complexion has a creamy-yellow look. She has her mother's lovely eyes, and the dearest tiny hands—"

He had crumpled her letter and tossed it overboard. He didn't mention the baby in the letter he wrote to Martha, as a dutiful husband should. Nor did she say anything about it in her answer. But the child would be there when he reached Hong Kong, he was certain of that.

It would make it easier to work out some plan by which they could go their separate ways. Though what Martha would do, he had no idea. There was no one to care what happened to her—except himself.

The island of Maui, where Duke Courtney sat mapping out a plan of search, was soon left far behind.

A few nights later, two more vessels left the coastline of the island. The first, leaving several hours earlier, held Tamsen, Kimo, a liberal supply of disinfectant from the mission dispensary, a white linen suit, and a pair of men's white gloves. Kimo's boat went ashore at Molokai, where a tall man paced the sands. The bamboo screen that had been Tamsen's shelter at an earlier time stood at a distance, fastened between supports formed by branches that Sam must have carried for some distance.

Behind the screen, crouched the thing that Josie had become.

Sam rushed to meet them, stopping short as they stepped onto the beach. His eyes were stricken as he searched the empty craft behind them, hope dying.

"Lani?"

"She's coming, Sam. But first, there's something we have to do."

While Sam, at Kimo's direction, stripped off and doused himself liberally with disinfectant, getting into the fresh clothing Tamsen and Kimo had brought, Tamsen walked to within a few feet of the bamboo screen. A muffled sound of warning stopped her. She realized that Josie could no longer speak. Her skin crawled at the memory of Manu, but she managed to keep her own voice calm.

"Josie, I'm sorry you are ill. But you are a very lucky woman, having a man like Sam. We've brought you something. I think I can promise you this will be the happiest day of your life."

When the other boat arrived, it held Em, Duke, Arab, Dusty, and Juan. Nell, forced to choose between leprosy and staying at home with the children, selected what she considered the lesser of the two horrors.

"Kids is jes' ez bad," she said distastefully, "But they ain't so permanent."

Sam's eyes widened as he saw Em step from the vessel, then he forgot her. His daughter stepped from behind big Duke Courtney's shelding bulk. Lani! Lovely Lani, in a white gown and flowing veil, her eyes shining with happiness, David Selwyn beside her. At the rear was an elderly man. Sam couldn't recall his name, but he had been Lani's teacher at the mission school. He was clad in dark clothing, and carried a Bible.

It was obvious what was going to take place. Sam buried his face in his hands, his body racked by hoarse, choking sobs.

Lani put her arms around him. "Don't, Papa," she begged. "Please don't. You do want this, don't you?"

Sam squared his shoulders and fought for control, managing to summon his old, cocky grin. "Hell yes," he said. "Let's get on with it."

Lani turned uncertainly toward the bamboo screen, knowing what was behind it. Knowing she wanted to go to her mother, Sam caught at her arm. Kimo, at one side, struck up the Hawaiian wedding song on his guitar, and the old minister moved to stand with his back to the screen.

Selwyn, his face white with emotion, took his place before him, and a little to one side. Lani, drawing a deep breath, placed her hand on her father's extended arm and moved forward, her eyes on her bridegroom's face.

The morning sun rose as she neared him, touching the bridal couple with a halo of light. The winds of Molokai lifted Lani's filmy veil, giving her an ethereal appearance. And on the shore, the blue waters whispered in cadence with Kimo's playing, spreading the sands with frothy lace.

"Who gives this woman's hand in marriage?"

"Her mother and I do." Sam's voice was firm and clear, carrying. From behind the screen came a sound of muffled weeping.

The solemn words continued, ringing in the clear morning air. When they were finally pronounced man and wife, David Selwyn kept a tight grip on his young wife's arm, urging her toward their transport after the nuptial kiss. For a moment, she followed docilely, then turned, tossing her bridal bouquet. It fell just short of the screen. She moved to grip her father's hand for a long moment, then put her tear-wet cheek against Tamsen's.

"I'm sorry, Tamsen," she whispered. "I'm so sorry!"

Tamsen understood.

Then it was the groom's turn. He had considered Tamsen a fallen woman. He had learned humility and gratitude and was beginning to see there were gradations between black and white. He said the only words that came to his mind: "God bless you."

Tamsen and Kimo were the last to go. Sam, overcome, clung to Tamsen's hands with his gloved ones, thanking her. She explained that she'd gotten her own satisfaction from the wedding. She only wished Dan could have been here.

"You've heard from him? He's going to be released?"

She glanced toward Kimo, waiting in the boat. Kimo was seeing to the details. He had delivered Sam's letter into the right hands. To her surprise, Sam's face went bleak.

Kimo was Hawaiian to the core, he told her. If Dan's arrest had political overtones, the boy could not be trusted. Though he was like a son to him—

Sam paused, seeing the fear in Tamsen's eyes. "It may be all right," he said doubtfully. "Wait a week, two—then go to Honolulu. I wish I could help you—"

"And I wish I could help you." Stifling a sob, she said, "Keep well, Sam." And then she fled.

With a jaunty gesture of confirmation, he went on, not looking back, stopping only to pick up Lani's bouquet to place in the disease-ravaged arms of his wife.

She could do nothing more for Sam. She knew she would never return to the beautiful, tragic island behind her, and this was most probably, a final good-bye. She kept her eyes straight ahead, thinking of Dan. It had been Kimo, who took his papers. She was sure of that now. Unless she could find a way to help him, Dan was as doomed as Josie.

She looked at Kimo, studying his impassive features, and knew that any appeal to his sympathies would be fruitless. Any moves she made must be done on her own . . .

But right now, she couldn't think. Not with the other things that plagued her mind. She shut her eyes against a vision of Manu; seeing Josie's features superimposed over his decaying ones, imagining tall clean-cut Sam lifting a living object with disfigured limbs and oozing sores; placing it on a mule and leading it over the top of the world; the rotting ruin of a woman, with Josie's heart inside, and Lani's bouquet clutched to her dying breast.

Finally she buried her aching head in her arms.

She would return home and write letters to President Grant, to the senators who had been urging annexation, asking that they use their influence on Dan's behalf. Within the week, she would write to King Kamehameha, himself, requesting an audience.

In the meantime, she would stand by the Courtney's in their fruitless search for Martha.

HONOLULU

42

A week passed—two weeks. A letter arrived from Father Damien, stating his interest in the lepers at Molokai. He had seen the effects of leprosy; indeed he had conducted services on the island. It was his utmost wish to go there and offer comfort to his ailing people. The strictness of the new board of health regulations had caused priestly visits to cease. But through the grace of God, and his bishop, Maigret, perhaps some arrangement might be made where he could go to live among them.

"Jove, the man's a saint," Dusty said piously, upon hearing the letter.

"He's a damn fool," Nell snorted.

Tamsen failed to comment. She was too shaken by another message that arrived. Written and signed by one of Kamehameha's aide's, it was short and to the point.

The prisoner, Daniel Tallant, accused of the murder of one Samuel Larabee and his wife, was at present in restraint, and would be allowed no visitors. The statement of Mrs. Tallant, denying the death of the alleged victims, would be considered prejudiced, and therefore invalid in court.

As to her request for an audience, His Majesty

was busy with affairs of state. An attempt to see him would only result in disappointment.

Daniel Tallant, she was assured, would be given a fair trial, once all the evidence was at hand.

In orther words, Tamsen thought bitterly, they had locked him up and thrown away the key!

No word arrived from political figures in the United States. She had to face the bitter truth. In Dan's profession, there was always praise when he succeeded. Caught out, he became a man without a country, expendable. No one would dare bring pressure to free him, for fear of destroying the delicate balance of diplomatic relationships.

Finally, at the end of her nerves, an idea began to form in her mind.

She visited Lani often, encouraging her to talk about the society of the royalty who reigned over the islands. Kamehameha was a monarchist, dedicated to keeping his country free of entanglements. Believing in freedom and equality for his people, he particularly distrusted the United States. He and his brother, now dead, had visited there. They had been taken for Negroes, rather than princes of royal blood, and suffered some rather embarrassing slurs.

As a man, he was quite handsome in a portly way. He had never married. It was said that he loved his brother's widow, Queen Emma, a beautiful woman. He had proposed and she rejected him. It was known that he liked a pretty face. There was a good deal of drinking and dancing at court, as there had been during the reign of the last several monarchs, much to the consternation of the mission group.

Though Kamehameha was very much a man, perhaps the most profound influences upon him were women. It was said that the wife of Governor Dominis, a woman almost fanatic about Hawaiian independence, was one of his chief advisers—off the record, of course. Another was the wife of Charles Bishop, a banker. Her main interest lay in educating the children of Hawaii. A forward-looking woman, she seemed to view annexation as inevitable.

And then there were rumors that the king obeyed the commands of a female Kahuna named Kamaipuupaa.

Tamsen listened, trying to sift fact from rumor. In addition, she enlisted Em's aid in stitching gowns fit for a princess. "What are you planning to do," Em teased, "Take over the throne?"

"I just might at that," Tamsen smiled, mysteriously. She intended to keep her plans to herself, lest word of her trip to Honolulu reached Kimo's ears. She had already had to squelch Juan's and Dusty's plans to rescue Dan, even if it must be done by force. If anyone else wound up in prison, it would be Tamsen herself. It wouldn't be the first time . . .

The days passed. The edge of Em's grief over Martha had dimmed, giving way to resignation. Duke had tramped doggedly over every inch of terrain where she could possibly be found. He went to the docks with Tamsen, and they interrogated the captain of every vessel plying back and forth between the islands. Martha had not taken passage on any of them. It was as if she had disappeared from the earth.

One thing of value came from their visit to the harbor. A shabby, sea-worn ship had just landed part of its cargo of Chinese immigrants. The remainder were to be delivered to Honolulu on the morrow. The half-caste captain was surly. No, he had not seen such a girl. It was his first time in this port, and the last time, if he had any say in the matter. He had been blown off course. His crew lived on stagnant water and spoiled beef for a month. From Honolulu, he was heading home. He'd stick with his own waters after this.

That night, Tamsen wrote a note saying she was going to Hilo on Dan's business; that she would be back when it was completed. Then she packed her new gowns, tying her baggage to the back of her horse, and walked beside it to the harbor.

When the ship sailed for Honolulu, Tamsen went with it. If her people looked for her, it would be in the wrong direction. The captain of this vessel wouldn't be available for comment. If he returned to Lahaina at all, it wouldn't be for a long, long time.

The trip was not unpleasant. Though the vessel was rank and smelly, the captain who had been surly with Duke Courtney was honored to have a lady aboard. He gave her his own small cabin, sending a Gôa steward with fresh fruits that had been brought aboard at Lahaina. For a time, she was concerned that he might expect payment, other than in coin, for his gallant hospitality, and was grateful for being proved wrong. In the morning, the steward brought hot water and towels, and she was able to bathe, dressing herself in an elegant new traveling gown.

When she stepped off the weathered craft at Honolulu, she was the center of all eyes.

Her first glimpse of Honolulu, from the ship's deck, had been a view of gray housetops, hidden among masses of verdant green, with a backdrop of volcanic mountains towering behind them. The smooth harbor had been filled with small craft, men-of-war, flags flying. It had been colorful, but not as colorful as the sight that met her eyes upon landing. As Dan had been, she was dazed by the bustle, the hodgepodge of nationalities, each wearing some type of apparel native to his country. Squat Hawaiian girls glided through the streets, graceful despite their bulk, dressed in gaudy colors, festooned with flowers. Slim-legged Polynesians walked saucily, making male heads turn. And here and there, a planter would be seen with his lady, whip in hand as he guided a trap through the crowded byways.

Leaving the vicinity of the wharf, Tamsen found a small store. There, she asked where a trap could be rented, and where lodgings for a lady might be found.

A short time later, she drove in style to the Hawaiian Hotel, newly built; pausing to admire the edifice of three stories and a cupola; a double stairway sweeping in an arc to an entrance on the second floor; a veranda on each floor, with a white fence running its length. There was a green lawn, and tall trees before the structure provided a shaded, home-like atmosphere.

Tamsen smiled with satisfaction. It provided exactly the kind of background she was looking for.

The startled clerk was a little dubious about renting a room to a lone woman, but her imperious attitude awed him. When she started to sign the record, she seemed to hesitate, but only for a space.

It must be a ladylike name, she thought. She wrote *Emmeline* in a firm hand, following it with her maiden name, *McLeod*. With a sad smile at the clerk, she added *Widow*.

Shown to her room, she reveled in the luxuriousness of it, after these last months in a grass hut. There was even a fan, operated by pulling a cord.

She bathed again, brushed her traveling costume, and called for her carriage once more, asking the directions to the Bishop residence. In her bag, she had a note prepared, in which she requested an audience with Bernice Pauhi Bishop, apologizing for her unannounced arrival.

The Bishop home was a magnificent edifice. Tamsen felt her courage fail at the sight of it. With a sharp, mental reprimand, she pulled herself together. A woman who sought the company of kings shouldn't shy away at the sight of a banker's house.

She went to the wide front door, where she was greeted by a tidily dressed servant to whom she gave her message. She stood nervously adjusting her gown until the servant reappeared. She was followed by a small woman in a dark gown with lace at the throat. She had beautiful, kind dark eyes, a gentle face, and her skirts swirled beneath a tiny waist. Tamsen smiled and extended a hand as the woman looked at her questioningly.

"Do forgive me! I know this is an imposition, but I'm in need of help. And I did recall my friend, Josie Larabee, mentioning your name."

"Josie Larabee?" Mrs. Bishop looked started. "Ah, that would be Josie Kalama. I haven't seen her since she married. Surely you've heard—"

"We were at their home just two years ago, my husband and I. They mentioned that they were thinking of moving to Honolulu. Then when I arrived at Lahaina and found their house had burned—"

Bernice Bishop's sweet face was filled with

sympathy. "My dear woman, they're dead, Josie and her husband, too. Murdered. I'm so sorry—"

Tamsen wavered, putting a hand to her forehead, and the woman moved quickly to her side, leading her to a chair. Tamsen looked up at her with dazed eyes. "Dead! Josie? Sam? And now, my husband! Everyone I loved—"

Her hostess clapped her hands, summoning the servant once more. "A cup of tea," she ordered. "And lace it with brandy. Hurry."

Soon the two women were sitting across from each other, Tamsen, still appearing shaken, unfolded the tale she had contrived. Her husband had died a year ago. On his deathbed, he'd made her promise to go to Sam and Josie, a more temperate climate than their Boston home. She took considerable time in leaving, due to the disposal of their property. And then she arrived in Lahaina to find—nothing. She came to Honolulu, hoping to find some trace of the Larabees. Now she was alone in a strange country and had no friends.

She wiped delicately at her eyes as the woman made small incoherent sounds of sympathy. "Don't, my dear. You will have a host of friends! I will see to it, myself."

At last, Tamsen rose reluctantly. "I must go," she said. Leaving, she passed a pianoforte. Reaching out, she touched the wood with loving fingers. "It is like mine," she murmured. "Do you play?"

Bernice Bishop obliged with a few chords of an old song, and Tamsen began to sing in her husky whisper. Her hostess listened, a bit confused. It was certainly not a trained voice, but there was something haunting in the way it broke, slipping into a minor key. She had never heard anything like it.

"Thank you," Tamsen said wistfully. "For a moment, I almost forgot . . ." She left the sentence hanging in the air as she smiled wanly at Bernice Bishop. "Thank you for making me feel so at home. And forgive me for coming here with my problems."

"Do let me know how things go. By the way, where are you staying?"

"At the Hawaiian Hotel. It's quite genteel. Thank you again, Mrs. Bishop. And good-bye."

Her hostess escorted her to the door and stood watching as she drove away. She looked again at the note she'd dropped on the small table beside the entrance. *Emmeline McLeod,* she read. A nice-sounding name. And certainly, a lovely woman, despite her present sadness. Perhaps she could do something for her, get her introduced into some friendly circles. She would certainly be a welcome addition to their small local society.

Her face brightened as she thought of Queen Emma's garden party. She looked at her small calendar in the table's drawer. Tomorrow night. A perfect time to introduce her new frind, if Emma didn't mind.

Writing a hasty note, she called her servant and dispatched it to the Winter Palace, as Emma's home was known. She frowned a little. Liliuokalani wouldn't like it, an American being included in their select group. Probably, Emma would invite the girl for that very reason—

Tamsen, leaving the Bishop home, felt a curious mixture of elation and guilt. She felt she had accomplished her mission. But only because her hostess had been so infinitely warmhearted and kind. Tamsen had taken advantage of that kindness. She returned to the hotel, her face flushed with shame at her actions.

That night, the ache of her conscience was healed when a letter arrived; an engraved invitation on thick, creamy paper, bearing Queen Emma's seal.

She went to bed, but not to sleep. For, somewhere in Honolulu, Dan was sleeping. In these last months, she had tried to shut her mind against him, trying to fit the man she had known and loved into the picture of a cold-blooded killer.

Now memories of the real Dan were coming back to her. His teasing eyes, his strong brown hands that could be gentle—or urgent—as they aroused her.

"Dan," she whispered, "I'm here!"

She would set him free, no matter what she had to do, no matter what the price would be. She would have her man back!

43

The next evening, Tamsen was a bundle of nerves as she alighted from her carriage. She had taken great pains in choosing her gown, going through her entire wardrobe, discarding garments one by one. Her first thought was to be conspicuous, wearing perhaps the deep crimson silk, with its low cut neckline that bared her shoulders. And with it, perhaps a long fringed shawl.

It did not suit the character she had chosen for herself. She must go slowly—

In the end, she selected a dress styled with utmost simplicity. Of a soft white material, it buttoned to her throat, a fold of material like a cowl draping her shoulders. Long nun-like sleeves went to her wrists. The only trim was a girdle of braided ribbon, emphasizing her tiny waist, the ends falling gracefully to her hem.

She looked like a child, she thought ruefully. But a child wouldn't have the curves that filled the dress—however innocently—nor the darkly shadowed eyes of a woman who had lain awake all night, thinking of her man . . .

She approached the home of Queen Emma, a

small figure, alone in the amber twilight. The Winter Palace was a large shady abode, rather like a New England house in appearance. It had two sweeping verandas, the entrance on the upper, which was pleasantly comfortable in the English fashion. The lower floor consisted of space for servants and offices. It was neither overly large nor imposing, but to Tamsen arriving alone to a group consisting of strangers the whole effect was overwhelming. She was impressed with the spreading lawns with benches set beneath wide spread trees, and people standing in small clusters or promenading as the royal band played.

She stood, hesitant. The garden was suddenly illuminated with Chinese lanterns, taking on the appearance of a tropical fairyland. A feeling of panic fluttered in Tamsen's breast. Her idea wouldn't work! She had been presumptuous in coming here. She had an impulse to flee.

"There you are!" Mrs. Bishop had seen the small figure at the edge of the lights, and sensed her reluctance to enter. She moved toward her with a welcoming gesture. Tamsen put her fright, surely visible, to good use.

"I haven't attended a social function since my husband's death," she confessed. "I was accustomed to an escort."

Of course! Bernice Bishop chided herself for not having sent a driver for Mrs. McLeod.

Apologizing for her thoughtlessness, she led her to greet their hostess, Queen Emma, widow of the present king's dead brother.

Remembering Lani's gossip; that the present king was in love with this woman, and she had refused him, Tamsen studied her carefully.

Below average height, she seemed very young, and was very graceful in her movements. Her expression was one of dignity mingled with gentle sweetness. Dressed simply in black, her attendants about her, she sat to receive her guests, turning her charming smile on each with impartiality.

Tamsen had only a moment with her, and then moved on, guided by Mrs. Bishop's hand on her arm. "Lydia," the woman called. A woman turned to face them. Straight-backed, stern-faced, there was no welcome in her eyes as she looked at Tamsen.

"Mrs. Emmeline McLeod," Bernice Bishop introduced her. "And this is Lydia Dominis, also known as Princess Liliuokalani."

The princess acknowledged the introduction with severe dignity. "You are an American?" she asked. At Tamsen assent, she slowly unfurled a fan, as if to clear the air of an obnoxious presence. The hatred in her eyes scarcely veiled, she excused herself.

The royal band stopped in the middle of a rendition to strike up a fanfare. The king had arrived.

He stood on another lawn, presentations being made to him by his chamberlain. Simply dressed in a well-made dark suit, his only ornament the star of the Austrian order of Francis Joseph, he managed to dominate the scene. His courtiers were resplendent in uniforms that glittered with epaulettes, cordons, and a prodigious display of gold lace, all enhanced by the lantern light.

Tamsen held back a little as Bernice Bishop drew her along. Soon, she was standing face to face with the man she had come to see. Her name was given, and he murmured a perfunctory word of welcome, his eyes passing over her to the next in line—someone known to him.

He was already extending his hand to his friend as she rose from her curtsy.

She found herself once more in Mrs. Bishop's charge, introduced into a small friendly group, an ice in her hand. She withdrew to the edge of the festivities, despising herself. She had come here for only one purpose, to gain an audience with Kamehameha. She had no idea how to proceed from there. But she could have thrown herself on her knees, disclosed her true identity, and begged for Dan's release. She might not have an opportunity to come in contact with him again—

She set her jaws and started forward, looking up to catch the eye of Lydia Dominis, Liliuokalani, and faltered. She had behaved quite correctly, she told herself. This was not the place or time.

Tamsen had been too intent on her own thoughts to notice the impression she had made on the young men present. There were officers of the King's Guard, at least forty ship's officers from vessels at present in the harbor. In addition, there were members of the royal family, distant cousins of the king; big, barrel-chested, thick-bodied men who eyed the slender young widow with approval.

When the music began, Tamsen was captured by a smiling dark man in splendid trappings. His name was Leke, he informed her as he whirled her down a lane to join couples dancing on the lawn. The upper suite of the house had been thrown open to those who chose to dance there, but most preferred the gardens, the shaded lawns. Here, there was more leeway for flirtation.

Amused, Tamsen fended off her would-be suitor's flowery comments, only to meet with more of the same with the next man who captured her. She found all the Hawaiian men to be extravagant

393

in their compliments, amorous in their attentions. Except for Leke, who was proving himself a serious contender for her affections, they meant no harm.

The officers from the various ships were a different story. Believing her to be of mixed heritage, due to the darkness of her hair and eyes, her creamy skin, some of them treated her with an irritating condescension, as if they were favoring her with their presence, expecting her to come to them at the crook of a finger.

It was maddening, especially when she thought of Josie and Lani who had probably been subjected to the same treatment at times.

Still, it was exciting to be once more the center of things, to be courted and flattered, spun from one pair of masculine arms to another, to be told she was the most beautiful woman in the gathering.

At eleven, supper was served on the lawns. A number of men vied for the honor of sitting at Tamsen's—Mrs. Emmeline McLeod's—side.

Unknowingly, she was the focus of at least three pairs of eyes. Bernice Bishop's were smiling. The pretty young widow would not be lonely long, from all appearances. Princess Liliuokalani frowned. There was something about the newcomer that bothered her. The Americans were not above using a woman with this girl's obvious charms to infiltrate the court. She must talk to Leke, who was making a fool of himself over her.

From his royal table, set apart from those of his subjects, King Kamehameha, Fifth, found it difficult to concentrate on the discussion begun by one of his honored guests. Introduced to the girl in white, a press of people waiting, he must have overlooked her somehow. But he had been watching her all evening. There was something about her that set her apart from the others. Even in her simple gown, she seemed to glow like a candle.

Who was she, and where did she come from?

Following the late supper, tables laden with delicacies, there was entertainment. The historical hula, lately revived, was performed by a bevy of young ladies, clad in discreet long gowns, garlanded with flowers. Their movements brought painful memories of Josie. Josie, who would never dance again.

After the hula, there was music and singing. Liliuokalani and her brother David Kalakaua sang together, a medley of their own compositions. Hearing the songs, seeing the way the woman's face softened as she sang of her native land, Tamsen felt she could understand her a little better. But it was her love for her country that made her a deadly adversary.

A laughing boy, reminiscent of Kimo, made everyone laugh with his antics as he played a guitar, singing nonsense songs. Then Bernice Bishop made her way to Queen Emma, whispering something in her ear. Emma beckoned to Tamsen.

"Oh, I couldn't," Tamsen said, startled at the request the royal personage made. "I don't think—"

"It is my wish." It was no longer a request, but a royal command.

Alone, unaccompanied, Tamsen sang a song in her husky, breaking voice. Where before the audience had listened only to the music, their attention was now riveted on an electric presence; the very essence of womanhood, her voice touching on ecstasy, skirting the edge of heartbreak. The purple of the night sky seemed to deepen, the scent of flowers become a sweeter fragrance. As she stopped on a final note, her arms half-lifted, there was a breathless hush before a thunderous applause.

Lot Kamehameha, King Kamehameha the Fifth was thirty-nine years old. At one time, he had been betrothed to Bernice Pauahi, now Mrs. Charles Bishop. Throughout his life, he had loved one woman, his sister-in-law, Queen Emma. He was busy with affairs of state, the governing of a country torn apart by dissenting factions, on the verge of being swallowed up by some larger power. He had no time for women.

Yet there was something about this girl that intrigued him. True, she was beautiful, but there was a kind of pulsing power beneath her beauty. For a whole space she had held the ruling class of Hawaii in her small hand.

The party had lasted overlong, and he must leave so that the others would be free to go. He made his bow to Emma, smiled at Mrs. Bishop, his good and lasting friend, then turned to Princess Liliuokalani.

"You are holding a luau for our guest, the Duke of Edinburgh, next week. Please add the young woman who sang to the guest list and ask that she contribute to the entertainment."

"Don't be a fool, Lot! I don't think—"

"Madam, you forget yourself. And it doesn't matter what you think."

He moved away, and she looked after him, her face black with anger. They shared the same desires for their country's welfare, she and Lot. She had been close to him, advised him in many matters. She did not intend to allow him to be swayed by an American woman with a pretty face.

Tamsen returned to the hotel with a sense of euphoria. As she finished her song, she looked straight into the eyes of the king. She knew she sparked his interest, even though she hadn't reached his ear, tonight. But she would in time. Something told her to take it slowly, that this was only the beginning.

Her blood still coursing with the feeling of power her success had generated, she turned her carriage over to a footman and walked for a time in the dark lanes beneath the shadowing trees. Finally, turning to enter the hotel, she looked up at the structure, looming against the purple sky, the wooden spindles of its verandas gleaming like lace in the moonlight, a faint glimmer showing through a window here and there.

To use Nell's words, it would make one helluva house!

An impish smile curving her lips, she entered the hotel; a former cantina entertainer, an ex-madam. But tonight, she had cut a swath in royal society.

She went to bed, to dream of her enchanted evening. In her dream, she ended her song, stretching her arms toward the king. Then the face of Kamehameha faded, and in his place stood Dan . . .

44

Kamehameha had spent a most unkingly night, a reminder that he was not an immortal being, but a man, with a man's needs. The royal bed from which he rose was rumpled, his appearance showing signs of strain as he went to his desk to face the problems awaiting him.

He viewed his calendar with distaste. For one thing, the Kaona-trouble had surfaced again. Several years before, a native named Kaona, graduate of Lahainaluna school, a former member of the house of representatives, a district judge at Honolulu, had gone mad, beginning to have visions that the end of the world was at hand. He had collected followers whom he dressed in white robes and formed his own church. He had been arrested, placed in an asylum, and was there when the volcanoes began to erupt.

His divine voices told him the volcanoes would engulf the islands, except for a single spot. Released, he appropriated someone else's land at South Kona for himself and his followers. In an attempt to evict them, a constable was dragged from his horse, his head split open with an ax—and then R. B. Neville, the sheriff of the district, had been killed, his brains beaten out with a club, his head cut off and displayed on a pole.

Kaona was in prison, now, sentenced to ten years at hard labor. But a member of his own cabinet was suspected of being a Kaonite. This morning, he must see this man, talk to him—

And there was the case of Zephaniah Spalding. He arrived in Honolulu in December, 1867, supposedly carrying messages for United States Minister McCook. He'd stayed on, with some vague excuse of starting a cotton plantation. Then it was discovered he was writing annexationist letters to his father, a member of congress. The man was most definitely a spy, but the hands of the Hawaiian Government were tied. He was now assigned to the United States consulate at Honolulu. And he had the gall to request an audience for today.

King Kamehameha sat for a time, his head in his hands. His kingdom was being infiltrated from within and without. Kaona, Spalding, American planters, who had formed a coalition to work for annexation; and finally, the American, Daniel Tallant.

He turned all correspondence concerning the man over to Princess Liliuokalani. There was no real proof that he had murdered the Larabee people, but until the case was brought to trial, the man could be held indefinitely. This was the plan the king, himself favored. But Liliuokalani had been pressing him to set a date for the hearing. He knew her well enough to know that, with her dislike for Americans, and especially for those who sought to disrupt her beloved country, she would manage to produce incontrovertible evidence of his guilt. The man wouldn't stand a chance.

Still, the princess was his old friend and trusted

adviser. He had treated her badly last night, speaking sternly as he did. Reaching for pen and paper, he ordered the trial of Daniel Tallant to take place within one month from the present date. He signed it with a flourish. It was his first act of the day.

The remainder of the morning was an exercise in frustration. The cabinet member denied the accusations placed against him. There was no visible proof to convict him. Spalding's information was that he was returning to the States as soon as his replacement arrived, news which proved either good or bad. At least Spalding was a known quantity. His coming replacement was not.

For some reason, it didn't seem to matter. At noon, the king turned the remainder of his work into the hands of his chamberlain. Claiming an indisposition, he returned to his bed where he lay, trying to concentrate on state problems. The face of a small girl-woman kept getting in the way, blotting them out, most effectively.

Cursing himself, he called for a cup of tea, laced with brandy. Another. And finally, he sank into an alcohol-induced stupor plagued with disturbing dreams.

He and the young American widow were on the royal barge; the scenery about them shimmering, finally settling into a recognizable scene. It was the Wailua river, the place of Sacred Waters, where the immigrants of Tahiti had first landed and the descendants of the great Chief Puna had settled; Wailua, where all true high chiefs must be born; place of the seven sacred *Heiaus*—

The guardsmen at the oars were clad in ceremonial regalia, his own attire was his dress uniform, glittering with his decorations and badges of office.

The nameless girl he had seen last night at the garden party wore a wedding gown.

He reached for her, his fingers passing through gossamer, like spider webs, as she faded into nothingness.

He woke, his head aching. The dream still seemed very real. He called for pen and paper and wrote a brief note to Bernice Bishop, sent it to her address, then sat back to wait.

Tamsen, unable to rest in her hotel room, that morning had called for her carriage. Driving alone, she set out in the cool dawn, driving along roads shaded by arched trees that flecked the road with rainbows of gold as the sun rose higher. Umbrella trees, caoutchouc, alligator pear, monkey pod, coco, and date palms lined the lanes. From houses hidden by dense foliage, drifted the fragrance of gardenia, roses, lilies, tuberoses, and great trumpet flowers with open, gold-dusted throats.

The architecture, concealed by jessamine and passionflowers overwhelmed in masses of bougainvillea, was of varied construction. There were structures of clapboard, painted white and green, houses of coral, grass, bamboo, sun-dried brick—of one, or two stories—growing from the earth as if they'd been nurtured into being. There were houses on stilts. Lawns were of incredible greenness, and in other spots, only the edge of a veranda lost in a forest of flowering tree and vine, indicated a dwelling.

Nowhere did she find a structure that resembled a prison, and she dared not ask. She finally returned to the hotel, and went to her room. The door opened upon a surprising scene.

The entire room had become a bower of blossoms and fern. A large basket occupied the center of a table. It held a variety of perfect Hawaiian fruit. Tucked among the fruit was a message bearing Kamehameha's seal.

The note, written in the king's own hand, welcomed Mrs. Emmeline McLeod to Honolulu. He would take pleasure in showing her the sights of his country. She would please be in readiness at nine, on the morrow.

Her hands went to her face as she stared, unseeing, at the munificent gifts. She would have her opportunity at a private audience with the king!

Her joy was dimmed the next morning when Kamemeha appeared with a full retinue.

The moment he despatched the gifts and message, he began to have second thoughts. For the ruler of a country to behave like a schoolboy over a woman he barely met was ridiculous. It was unbefitting a direct descendant of Kamehameha the Great. He recalled the scandal of Princess Victoria Kamamalu, a scant few years before. She had fallen in love with a married man, an Englishman, an auctioneer by the name of Monsarrat. Lot, himself, had been appalled. As Kuhina-Nui of the land, Victoria had to sign the papers that would banish her lover from the islands.

She had died at the age of twenty-eight.

As Princess Liliuokalani—Lydia—had pointed out, just a few moments after he had issued his unfortunate invitation, he knew nothing about this woman, except that she was American, and a widow. It would be a dangerous undertaking if he chose to pursue the relationship.

A small, pigtailed Chinese houseboy tapped at Tamsen's door, to say the king had called for her, his tongue stumbling over the English words in his excitement. He escorted her to a side door where she was taken in tow by a glittering footman and escorted to a vehicle that waited with uniformed guardsmen on horseback before and behind.

It was not a coach, but more of a wagon, in the English style, a large bed, with two seats facing each other, a canopy over all. To her dismay, Tamsen found herself seated beside Liliuokalani, facing the king and his chamberlain. The entourage moved out.

As they rode, the princess plied Tamsen with questions. Where did they live in Boston? And what did her husband do?

Tamsen invented a background, an ancestral home near the city, but not of it. Her husband dabbled in the arts. Was a patron, in fact. He was a man of independent wealth, spending his time in worthy causes; education, for example, and—she was careful to maintain an innocent expression—prison reform.

Kamehameha had been silent through all the conversation, his heart thudding as he watched his guest's artless face. Truly, she was a jewel among women. The dark traveling dress she wore had a frill of lace that framed her face, giving it a look of unearthly purity. Beside Liliuokalani, with her heavier features and stern eyes, the girl had an appearance of evanescence. He had been wondering if he leaned forward to touch her, she might disappear as she did in his dream, leaving a cobweb of nothingness in his grasp.

He had not merely been sitting in haughty, royal silence—as it appearaed. He had been virtually tongue-tied, wondering how to enter the conversation. When Tamsen mentioned prison reform, he seized upon it.

"Then you will be interested in seeing our prison. We pride ourselves on the institution. It faces the Nuuanu Valley, and has a fine view of Honolulu from its rooftop."

He directed a rider alongside to change the direction of the cavalcade.

Tamsen clasped her hands to stop their trembling. Her confusion went unnoticed as they passed through the streets. The king was the recipient of cheers and greetings. Young women held their children high, so that Kamehameha's eye might fall upon them. Old people, remembering the days of *kapu* cast their eyes down as the august personage passed in his carriage.

When they reached the prison, Tamsen learned the king intended to allow her to tour the place. Her heart was in her throat as she prayed that she would see her husband—and that she wouldn't. If he saw her, and made some sign of recognition, what would happen? She would have to throw herself on the king's mercy then and there . . .

The interior of the prison was as Kamehameha said it would be. The rooms were clean and spacious. They were also empty. During daylight hours, the convicts were sent out to work on the roads.

Murderers? They were executed. One did not allow rabid dogs to live. Those awaiting trial? They were kept in another, less pleasant place.

Tamsen dared ask no more questions. She dutifully admired the view from the roof. Then, Liliuokalani commenting on her pallor, Tamsen Tallant, known in Honolulu as Emmeline McLeod, widow, pleaded fatigue.

They returned to her hotel, Kamehameha, himself, stepping from his carriage to assist her to the door. The touch of her small hand on his arm had been too much. And he was away from Liliuokalani's listening ear. They had not seen much of the

404

area's natural grandeur. The pali, for example. Did she ride? Tomorrow, would she care to accompany him—alone?

Tamsen looked disbelievingly into the dark eyes of the big man who was king of the islands, recognizing what she saw there. It was the same expression that had appeared in the eyes of many lesser men.

She thanked him for the outing, and accepted his invitation, going to her room with a thoughtful frown.

Her new knowledge gave her another string to her bow. Tomorrow, she would wait and watch, playing it by ear. The king's attraction to her opened the door to new possibilities. Perhaps she could lead him, unknowingly, into doing what she wished him to do.

All else failing, there was always blackmail. A king couldn't afford to have any scandal attached to his name. Why was it, she wondered forlornly, whenever her loved ones were in any kind of trouble, she began to think like a madam?

45

True to his word, the king appeared alone, mounted on a magnificent horse, leading a slim chestnut mare behind him. They left at dawn, thus were able to ride through the streets of the small city without exciting the attention of Kamehameha's subjects. Evidently the king felt a sense of freedom. At the edge of Honolulu, he spurred his mount into a gallop. Tamsen, laughing, followed suit. When they finally stopped, the ruler's dark face was stained red with exertion; Tamsen's hair fallen into disarray. They smiled at each other, easily falling into a camaraderie that erased the stiffness of their first meeting.

They climbed a well-worn path through a green paradise. Along the trail, hibiscus greeted the morning with its yellow bloom. Streams sang and fell in small waterfalls over stones that glistened with rainbows in the sun. Around them, grey hills of rock soared to a height of four thousand feet or more.

Reaching the pali, they tethered their horses and walked through a rift to come upon a heart-stopping view. Miles of improbably pinnacles stretched in the distance; a carpet of green velvet below; a view of toy houses and gardens with white-lace coral and blue sea beyond.

Tamsen looked at the view, unable to tear her eyes away. Kamehameha looked at the woman, her gown and hair wind-whipped, her cheeks bright with excitement at the wonders before her.

Tamsen was too filled with the awesome sight to speak as they left the pali and rode down the trail. At a certain spot, Kamehameha turned his horse from the path, pushing through hibiscus and candlenut growth until he reached a clearing. Here a liveried footman stood. A cloth was spread on the ground, set with porcelain dishes; a feast of bread, wine, fruit, and cheese carefully covered with monogrammed linen. At their approach, the footman obligingly disappeared.

"Your Majesty, how thoughtful!"

"Please call me Lot—it is my name."

Becoming Lot and Emmeline, they settled to their meal. Tamsen, without appetite since the Larabee house burned, was suddenly hungry. It was a good feeling. Lot watched her with enjoyment. She ate as greedily as a child, licking her fingers after a particularly delicious morsel. She felt his eyes on her and blushed.

"I was starving," she said frankly. "It must be the exercise, the morning air—and the surroundings."

"You like my country, then?"

"Very much. I've never seen a place so beautiful."

"And it will remain that way as long as I am king. There are those who would see it change." He rose and walked restlessly away, then turned to face her. "The pali you just saw—many years ago, my ancestor, Kamehameha the Conqueror, took this island. He attacked the forces of the King of Oahu in the Nuuanu Valley, and drove them over the precipice where we stood. Their bones still lie below. I can promise you, anyone who tries to take over my islands will join them there."

A chill touched Tamsen's spine and she tried to keep her voice even. "But who would do this? I can't imagine—"

His eyes held the same fanatical gleam she'd seen in Liliuokalani's. "The English have tried. And now, your fellow-Americans."

"That can't be true!"

"I'm afraid it is. The American party here is agitating for annexation. And we're holding a fellow now. His trial for murder comes up in a few weeks. He—" He stopped. "This cannot be of interest to you."

"But it is. If he's an American, perhaps if I saw him, talked to him—"

"Forget it," Lot said. "It isn't a subject for a lovely day. Look, there are several small cakes left." He gestured toward them with a teasing smile.

Tamsen swallowed. She had suddenly lost her appetite.

As far as Lot was concerned, the subject was closed. The rest of the day was spent in, what was for him, foolish and altogether enjoyable play. They wandered over the lower slopes, Tamsen gathering her arms full of flowers. And once, they removed their shoes and waded in a small, clear stream, Tamsen holding her skirts above the water, revealing a glimpse of slim ankle from time to time; the portly ruler a ludicrous but somehow endearing sight with his trouser legs rolled to the knee.

Finally it was time to straighten their disheveled

garments. Tamsen managed to pin her hair into place. Dignified, sober-looking, but with eyes that danced as they looked at each other, they rode back into town to receive homage due to the king as they wended their way toward the hotel.

Tamsen spent the next three days in Lot's company. There was much to see: the Punchbowl, a perfect extinct crater, with its striations of color; a climb to the seven-hundred-sixty-foot eminence of Diamond Head, so called for the calcite crystals found on its slopes; the royal school; the compound, *Pohukaina*, in which the palace known as *'Iolani Hale* stood. A structure of coral blocks and stone, standing six feet above the ground with a half-cellar below, it had a shingled roof held up by slender pillars. Cool verandas surrounded it. The roof sloped at a steep angle, crowned by a widow's walk from which one could view the beauty of the area from all sides.

He did not live in the Palace, Lot pointed out, but in one of the other buildings that crowded the compound, some of them with roofs of grass. The Palace was used for public ceremonies and affairs of state. There were those who believed the structure to be too modest to serve its purpose; who wished to build an edifice more appropriate to its function. But it would not be within his lifetime, he assured her.

A black mood seemed to descend on him as he looked at the Palace he intended to preserve. He had suddenly been reminded of his duties; the battle, so hard fought, to keep things from changing, slipping out of his grasp. Not that he needed the Palace to jog his memory. He had returned to his home the previous evening to find a nervous chamberlain and Liliuokalani waiting. She had looked pointedly at his disheveled attire, and suggested that now, with the *Galatea* soon to arrive in port, the Duke of Edinburgh aboard, he should consider giving up childish pleasures. Surely the American woman had been entertained sufficiently.

He had the uncomfortable feeling that Liliuokalani, Lydia Dominis, could see into his heart and mind.

Returning Tamsen to her hotel, Lot was unusually reticent. He had been pleased to escort her, he said politely. He hoped to see her at the luau to be given for Prince Alfred, Duke of Edinburgh, at the Dominis home, known as Washington Place.

His attitude was one of dismissal. Tamsen went to her room, wondering how she had offended him. For several days, she had sought for ways to bring up the subject of Dan's innocence. She painstakingly copied a page from David Selwyn's records, confirming Josie's leprosy, before leaving Lahaina, and she'd carried it tucked into the bosom of her gown as proof, should the proper moment arrive.

Somehow, she had erred in judgment. Tonight's farewell had seemed so final—

Her mouth set in determination. She would not let it be.

Lot, leaving Tamsen at her abode, returned to his own home. It had been a pleasant interlude, he told himself. But it was over. He had indulged in a few days of temporary madness, but it had done no harm. After all, he was only human. The little American widow had seemed to return his attentions, and he'd been flattered. What man wouldn't be?

He reviewed his portly self in a long mirror, with distaste at what he saw. If he only had the lean body of David Kalakaua, his wit and charm—! He did not wish a woman to love him only because of his royal lineage, but for himself.

He went to his couch, resolute in his determination to put the McLeod woman from his mind. But his dream returned; the royal barge, the sacred river, and the girl in her wedding gown eluding his touch, disappearing. He woke, his forehead covered with a cold sweat. The dream meant something, he was sure of it.

Calling an orderly, he sent for the female Kahuna, Kamaipuupaa. He would insist that she interpret his dream.

When she arrived, he found himself unable to put it before her, fearing it would indicate a royal weakness. Instead, he confined himself to asking his same timeworn question, one she had, as yet, been unable to answer. Would the Americans succeed in annexing this country?

Kamaipuupaa retired to a small hut used for sacred ceremonies. Here, she kept the human bones, wrapped in kapa, that served as her unihilili. There, she surrounded her grisly possession with the appropriate gifts. Squatting before it, she downed a cup of awa, and began the necessary incantations.

At dawn, she returned to the still sleepless king, her eyes carefully blank to hide what lay behind them. "I have been given a message of the future, Your Majesty. And it is good. This thing, if it happens, will not come about within your lifetime."

That his life was almost ended, she did not say. It had not been his question.

46

Tamsen spent several lonely, fretful days. And finally, the day arrived for the festive luau to be held at Washington Place, the home of the Dominis family.

The luau was to begin at eleven in the morning. Tamsen was dressed long before, wearing the nun-like gown of white she'd worn to the garden party at Queen Emma's home. She waited impatiently for the time to pass, and for her escort to arrive.

Due to her expeditions with Kamehameha, the earlier part of the week had been filled. During the last several days, she'd been unable to escape the attentions of an adoring Leke. Hoping until the last moment to receive some word from the king, she had finally accepted Leke's invitation to attend the luau at his side.

He arrived at last, assisting her into his carriage where she was forced to listen to his effusive compliments and, more than once, tap a wandering hand across the knuckles with her fan. He took it in good grace, as a natural part of courtship. She felt if he tried to touch her, intimately, again, she would scream.

They arrived at Washington Place without incident. The home of Liliuokalani, Lydia Dominis, was a mansion, built along the lines of the finer southern plantation homes. The lawns were well kept, the flowering trees and shrubs exquisite. And the guest list contained only the most important of Kamehameha's people, along with Major J. H.Wodehouse, Ambassador of Great Britain, and his wife; the Queen Dowager, Kalama, widow of Kamehameha, Third, and Princess Miriam Likelike, sister to Liliuokalani.

Leke led Tamsen forward and they went through the ceremony of greeting the king. Tamsen made a deep curtsy, and Lot extended his hand to touch her fingertips. His own were cold, through his white gloves. She could feel them trembling. There was agony in the dark eyes that met her own, a chill as he turned his gaze on Leke.

She couldn't subdue a glow of triumph. He was suffering from jealousy! He hadn't forgotten her, then. Perhaps government affairs had become pressing, or—there had been pressure put on him from some other source.

She turned. Liliuokalnai was watching, her mouth set in a straight line. In her hostess, Tamsen found her enemy.

The meal was delicious, cooked and served in traditional Hawaiian fashion, Kamehameha and Prince Alfred placed a little apart from less royal personages. Gleaming in their uniforms, leis draped about their shoulders, they conversed politely with the British Ambassador, Lot scarcely able to conceal his lack of attention as he watched the young American widow, seated a great distance away.

Following the meal, there was entertainment. Liliukalani had deliberately spaced her singers and dancers for the greatest effect. Prince Alfred smiled his appreciation of the hula dancing by lovely girls, hand-picked for their grace and beauty. Beneath a nearby tree, a troop of guitarists played a medley of native songs. A large woman with a glorious soaring voice sang at some distance from the royal party. Then, in the center of the lawn, a group of Maori dancers, imported for the occasion, entertained.

The afternoon wore on. The guests, replete with food, began to yawn through the entertainment. Then, from the far edge of the drive where carriages waited, their drivers clad in plumed capes of yellow feathers, Liluokalani announced the last performer. Tamsen, fighting tears of anger, knew her small voice wouldn't carry to the royal party. It wasn't intended to.

A piano had been brought to the lawn. Someone struck up an opening chord. Tamsen stood trembling, a small figure at the end of a vast expanse of lawn. She forced her body to stop its trembling and opened her mouth to sing.

The king was on his feet, a staying hand upraised. "Wait! I wish our guest to hear this."

Tamsen stood rooted as he led the royal party across the grass, halting it a few feet away. "Now," he said. "Listen."

There was a moment's hush, the pianist confused. Then the chord sounded again. Tamsen moved effortlessly into her song, words that she had composed herself, setting them to the tune of an old ballad. A song of a young white girl coming to an enchanted island, meeting a man of the islands, finding love and heartbreak. Into her voice, she put the sound of the sea washing against moonlit shores, the cadence of the waves; the magic of love, and in the end a poignant plea to her lover, her arms out-

414

stretched as she sank to her knees, head bowed before his silence.

There was a long pause, then the young Duke said, "My word!" It was an awed whisper, but it served to pull Lot, King Kamehameha, the Fifth, back to his senses. Stepping forward, he removed his lei and draped it over the girl's bowed shoulders. Prince Alfred followed suit, adding his own. He lifted her to her feet.

"Amazing," he said fervently. "I do hope you are scheduled to entertain at the other gala events!"

The king's lips parted in a smile of incredible sweetness. "Of course she is," he said gently. "It is my command."

When Tamsen reached the hotel that night, fending off the amorous Leke, she found a tray on her small table. It contained a number of engraved invitations, each bearing an impressive seal.

Lot, King Kamehameha, the Fifth, had spoken. His people had heard and obeyed.

Tamsen attended a veritable round of picnics, parties, and balls. At all of them, she sensed the king watching her. Leke, unaccountably, had been dispatched to another of the islands on the king's business. But for each event, a vehicle with a liveried footman called for her. At the various functions, she did not lack for male attention. At one point, seeing all the eager masculine faces around her, she was struck by a horrifying thought.

Dear God! Next year she would be forty years old!

The notion haunted her until she stood to sing, feeling the power flow into her body, seeing her listeners mesmerized, each man certain that she was singing directly to him.

She need not begin to worry for a little while.

415

One date after another was lined through on Tamsen's calender. The final event was held at the home of Prince Alfred, the house he had been given to use during his stay. Tamsen was nervous about attending alone. Picnics, garden parties, teas, were one thing. A ball was quite another. She dared not miss it. Tonight would be her last tie with King Lot. She must make him want to see her again.

Tonight, she would wear the crimson silk. She had been discreet long enough.

Attired in the brilliant gown, she placed a shawl over her creamy shoulders, then discarded it. She would carry it over her arm. She wore her hair down. It swung to her waist, smooth, straight and long. For ornament, she wore only a slender gold chain.

Advised that her carriage waited, she hurried downstairs where a footman assisted her to a small, curtained vehicle. As she stepped inside, she stopped, her eyes going wide. There was some error. It was already occupied, and by a man—

A gloved hand reached out to her, as the gentleman drew her to a seat beside him. She could see his features now, in the dimness. The King! Lot, himself, had come to fetch her to the ball.

That evening, he divided his attention solely between Tamsen and his royal guest, dancing until dawn, surprisingly light on his feet for such a heavy man. Tamsen found herself having a wonderful time, despite the fact that thoughts of Dan were, at all times, in the back of her mind.

Liliuokalani, regal and dignified, moved from guest to guest in an attempt to make up for Lot's neglect. Her face was impassive, but her eyes sparked with anager. She would have a few words to say to the king, tomorrow. Bernice Pauahi Bishop watched the proceedings with concern. It was clear that Lot was smitten with the American. It was equally clear that Liliuokalani was furious. She hoped, that introducing the nice young widow into their circle, she hadn't created a problem.

When the party finally ended, Lot had little time to change and return for the farewell ceremonies aboard the *Galatea*. In spite of it, he insisted on seeing Tamsen—his beloved Emmeline—to her hotel. Once inside the curtained carriage, he slipped a glove off and took her hand in his. It was so small in his large palm, like a trembling bird. He was trying to get up courage to declare himself. This was the one girl he wanted in all the world. Evidently she guessed his intent. She appeared nervous and frightened.

He couldn't know that she was trying to get up courage, too. Enough to go down on her knees in the carriage floor and beg him for her husband's life.

"Emmeline?"

"Lot?"

They had each said the other's name at the same moment. They both laughed, awkwardly, and tried again, with the same results.

"We'll have to talk one at a time," Tamsen said. "You first."

"No, you. I insist."

As they quibbled, a pack of dogs rounded a corner in pursuit of one small female. She shot straight at the nervous, finely bred team, veering only at the last instant. The horses reared, their driver cursing as he tried to control them. Then there was a gentling hand at their heads. Eyes rolling, mouths foaming, they settled down.

"Send that man to me," Lot called. "Tell him the king wishes to thank him."

Tamsen leaned to see their rescuer as Lot opened the curtain to speak. Clad in a crimson gown, her hair about her shoulders, in an enclosed carriage with the king of the islands—she looked down, and into the startled eyes of Kimo.

His gratitude conveyed, Kamehameha gave the order to drive on. He owed the man more thanks than just for stopping the carriage, he thought. He had also stopped him from making a fool of himself. It was clear that Emmeline was tired. Her face was as white as a ginger flower. This hour between an all-night ball and a departure ceremony wasn't auspicious for a proposal. For that, one needed moonlight, solitude. Tonight they would walk on the beach together, far from human intrusion.

But for now, "When the horses took fright, you were about to say something?"

"It was nothing, nothing at all." It was hard to see Kimo as a villain, but Sam had warned her. Tamsen was hard put to control her trembling. Maybe it hadn't been Kimo, but someone who resembled him. Or if it had been, perhaps he didn't recognize her. She seized on the last thought with a fierce hope.

47

It had, indeed, been Kimo, who Tamsen had seen. Though the dog pack that swept in front of the king's carriage had been accidental, Kimo was there by design. He had been sent for by no less a person than the Princess Liliuokalani, and questioned thoroughly as to what he knew about Daniel Tallant, his family, his work, his friends.

He described all areas as accurately as he could. The woman's eyes narrowed. "His wife. Describe her once more, please?"

He did so, and she asked, "Do you know an Emmeline McLeod?"

Dan's wife's sister was named Emmeline. He believed McLeod to have been their maiden name.

"Describe her."

He did. A flowerlike woman with gold brown hair and blue eyes. Liliuokalani shook her head. "The other one, his wife, she is still on Maui?"

She had gone to Hilo, on some sort of business, he said.

The princess looked triumphant, but she said nothing more on the subject. She talked of the weather on the other islands, of the work still going on at Hilo to repair the earthquake's damage. She asked him to remain within call for a few days, since she might have need of him.

He was happy to oblige. Though he had aided Lani in her marriage to David Selwyn, the experience had left him embittered. Too, Sam Larabee, before his planned disappearance had deeded Kimo a large amount of land. It only served to make him more of a nativist than he was, this owning of so much of his own island. He planned to use only Hawaiian labor, to divide it into small farms, the only stipulation being a return to the old ways.

He had been shocked to learn Dan Tallant was to go on trial. He had thought the man would just be held for a time and let go. It hurt to have a man's death on his conscience, but it was a small price to pay if it prevented annexation to the United States.

Lydia Dominis, the Princess Liliuokalani, shared his beliefs. If she needed his aid, she would receive it.

Late last night, he had received a message. He was to wait at this spot, a short distance from the Hawaiian Hotel. A small carriage with drawn curtains would pass by. If possible, he was to get a look at the person who accompanied the king, and see if he felt any note of recognition.

The dog pack had been sent by the gods. He had seen that person almost face to face. There would be no error in his identification.

It had been Tamsen Tallant who sat beside the king. Tamsen Tallant, in a rich gown of crimson silk. The king had looked at her with adoring eyes. It was unbelievable that she could insinuate herself into his royal favor in such a short time. Did he know her true identity? If he did, the situation was beyond hope. In this case, the female was deadlier than the male.

He made his way back to Washington Place. The guests were gone, the servants clearing the premises, but Liliuokalani waited, a slightly heavy woman, her waist tightly laced, still in her evening wear. She looked like a queen as she received him and heard what he had to say.

"I knew it," she said on a soft note of exultation. "I have a nose for American intrigue." She inclined her head toward Kimo. "You will be well rewarded."

"I ask no reward, Your Highness. It is enough to do something for my country."

Her stern eyes smiled their approval and he took his leave. He had liked Dan Tallant, and he had admired his wife. But a man did what he had to do.

The princess, behind him, opened her fan, thoughtfully, and snapped it shut again. She was tempted to go to Lot's home and face him with what she had heard when he returned. But it would be more effective later. Not when he had just come from the girl.

She could wait.

She waited until all the fanfare that set the *Galatea* on its way had faded. The ship moved out to sea, the royal party standing on the shore to watch its leaving. King Kamehameha wore an unmistakable expression of relief. The hubbub was over and done. He had scarcely been able to keep his mind on the ceremony, the flowery speeches. The face of a small dark girl kept appearing before his eyes, clouding his thoughts, turning them into different channels.

He turned to leave. Lydia Dominis stood before him. He made a sweeping gesture, as though to move her from his path, but she stood her ground.

"I have something to say to you, Your Highness." She bore down on his title, making a mockery of it. "And this time, you are going to listen."

His face lost its mahogany darkness as she spoke, turning a sickly yellow. "It is a lie," he said, his words stumbling a little. "A dastardly lie! Someone is trying to blacken the lady's name! Lydia, I swear, if you—"

"I am merely telling you the truth," she said with dignity. "Believe it or not, as you choose. But if you don't try to prove it one way or another, you are not the sovereign I think you are."

"Lydia, my dear friend, forgive me. But if I've ever prayed that someone would be wrong in her judgment, it's now."

"I wouldn't have come to you with this, Lot, if I were not sure. You know me well enough for that."

His eyes tortured, he studied her steadfast features. "Yes, Lydia, yes. God help me, I do."

Tamsen chose her nun-like gown for the walk the king suggested. She was well aware of the appearance of innocence it gave her, and tonight she would need all the help she could get.

When he declared his love—and she was certain he would—she would not mention her relationship to Dan. Instead, she would pretend to return Lot's affections, and ask him to prove his for her— by releasing the American who was her fellow countryman. After Dan was out of the country, Kimo could do his worst.

For a while, she paced the floor, trying to rehearse the coming conversation. It wouldn't come clear in her mind. She had a heavy feeling, as if something terrible were going to happen. What if Lot had already discovered the truth?

She thought of the small pistol among her things; a weapon she learned to use so well in her early days. It might be wise to carry it from now on. But it should be very well concealed. She looked thoughtfully at the full sleeves of her gown. Finding a ruffled silken garter, she slid it up her wrist, and placed the weapon against her inner arm.

It would do very well.

His Royal Majesty was punctual, as usual. She smiled to herself as a small Chinese brought the news that her carriage waited. She had been foolish to let herself get so concerned. It had not been Kimo, after all. This man had worn a linen suit, and to her knowledge Kimo didn't own one. It was true that the boy was more intelligent than he pretended to be. But to serve as a spy, to make his way into royal circles, brown Kimo—in his scrap of bright print cloth—just didn't fit the picture.

For a moment, she considered removing the gun from her sleeve, then decided against it. She might need it sometime in the days to come. She might as well get used to it.

Lot had dismounted to assist her into the carriage, himself. The moon fell on his face, and she paused in consternation. The man was ill!

He was only fatigued, he told her at her anxious questioning. There had been the all-night ball, then the farewell ceremonies. Following that, he had some affairs to attend to. He had no opportunity to rest.

Still she worried. The hand he extended to aid her was cold. Inside the covered vehicle, she couldn't see his features, but sensed that he was suffering. Perhaps they should postpone their walk for another night? She wouldn't mind—

He gave a great moan, and reached out, taking her into his arms. He made no attempt to go farther, but only held her like a child against his chest. She could feel the trembling of his muscles, hear his great heart beating. For a moment she lay passive wondering what to do. This was not the formally romantic approach she expected. And she must remember that she was supposed to be a young widow who would be shocked at finding herself in this predicament, no matter what her feelings toward him were.

"Your Majesty!" she said in a gently chiding voice. "Please!"

He released her, and she sat up, rearranging her rumpled gown. "Forgive me," he said. "I'm not King Kamehameha tonight, but a very troubled man. If I've offended you, if you wish to return to your hotel—"

She reached for his hand, taking it in both of hers, stroking it gently. "Don't be foolish, Lot. I wasn't offended—just surprised. If you'd like to discuss your troubles?"

"Not now," he said heavily. "Later, perhaps I will."

Tamsen pushed the curtains aside and looked out. He had said they were going to walk along the beach at some secluded spot. But the waters were nowhere in sight. For a moment, she was disoriented. Then she realized they were moving inland. A small bird of panic began to flutter in her breast.

"Lot, where are we going?"

Life seemed to return to the bulky body beside her. His hand gripped hers, strongly. "The walk will come later, perhaps. Since I met you, I've longed to give you everything you wanted. It came to me, to-day that you made a request I haven't fulfilled. That will come first. And afterward, I may have something to ask of you."

She tried to recall something she had mentioned, and couldn't. She could only think how kind this man beside her had been, and that she was intending to use him. Her voice was sincere as she smiled at him in the darkness. "Please don't think I'm a wanton woman, Lot. But if you want to hold me, I don't mind."

She went willingly into the bearlike arms, and he held her as they continued their journey in companionable silence.

They reached their destination, and he helped her to the ground. They stood in a small compound set in a cocoanut grove. The moonlight revealed a number of small houses, built of coral. Certainly not a romantic atmosphere. Not a place for an assignation.

"Come," Lot said. He led her forward to a building, produced a key and unlocked the door. Sensing her reluctance, he smiled down at her, that incredibly sweet smile she had seen so rarely. "There is nothing to be afraid of."

Her misgivings allayed by his attitude, she stepped inside.

The room was square, containing only a bed, a chair, a table. And at the table, by the light of a single candle, a man was writing. A shirtless man, his brown shoulders gleaming in the light.

"Dan!"

The name burst from her lips. Lot's hand dropped from her arm, his big body seeming to sag as if the life had gone out of him.

"You are acquainted, I see." It was not a question, but a statement.

Dan had leaped to his feet at the sound of her voice, his face a mixture of joy and bewilderment. Now it turned ugly. He looked at the couple in the doorway with loathing.

"I never saw this woman in my life!"

"I am not a fool, Tallant." Kamehameha's voice was cold, deadly. The portly man faced Dan with dignity, looking every inch a king. "I am not a fool, and I do not intend to be taken for one, by you—or your wife."

Tamsen knelt before him, taking his hands, holding them to her tear-wet face. "Your Majesty —Lot—I beg you, forgive me for pretending to be someone else. I—I've grown very fond of you. Let him go! Send him away—back to the States. I'll do anything, be anything you want—"

He pushed her from him, his face a mask of pain and fury. "Daniel Tallant will go on trial, as scheduled. I promise you that you will watch him die. After that, I will decide what is to be done with you."

"Keep your hands off her!" Dan had rounded the table, Kamehameha reached for the sword at his side. Tamsen, flung against the wall, moved instinctively. The small gun was out of her sleeve in a single motion, pointed at the king's heart.

"Don't move," she said in a deadly voice, "or I'll shoot."

Dan reached her side and together they backed toward the door. "Give me the gun," Dan snarled, "I'll kill the bastard."

"No you won't. We will lock him in. You go see to the man driving the carriage—"

Tallant went out into the darkness, and Tamsen faced the king of all the islands. "I didn't lie to you about everything," she said in a small voice. "When I said I'd grown fond of you, I meant it. Forgive me, Lot."

He didn't answer. He just stood, his arms folded, his face impassive. Tamsen stepped outside and closed the door.

Arms went around her, pinning her own to her side. A rough hand wrested the pistol from her grasp as she fought in silence. Then there was a blaze of light as torches were lit all over the compound. Dazedly, she saw the place swarmed with the king's guards. Dan stood, his hands tied behind him, armed guardsmen at either side.

Her own hands were tied, and she was pushed to stand beside her husband. Kamehameha emerged from the coral house and stood before them in regal dignity, his face cold and judging.

"As I said earlier," he told them quietly, "I am not a fool."

Tamsen closed her eyes. She knew instinctively that they were going to die, she and Dan. In her heart, she said a silent farewell to those she loved; Arab and Juan, Em and Duke Courtney, Nell and Dusty, the children—

There was no need to say good-bye to Dan. They would go together. She moved closer to him, straightening her shoulders, and they stood, two proud, figures, waiting for whatever might come.

48

On Maui, at the compound near Lahaina, Tamsen's small group of family and friends had grown increasingly worried. Arab and Juan had been upset from the beginning, the morning when Tamsen's letter was found. They could think of no business she would have on Hilo—unless she'd got some word of Martha. Then she would have certainly told Duke and Em.

Nell was disturbed, too, though she didn't say so. "Hell, you know Tam. She's a big girl. She knows whut she's doin'. She's got herself in some messes, sure, but she allus comes out a-smellin' like a gawdam rose."

Comforted by Nell's confident words, Arab settled herself to wait for Tamsen's return. Days passed, and she came awake in the night with the sensation that something was terribly wrong.

She confided her fears at breakfast, and was surprised to find Nell agreeing with her. Em and Duke, too, had become concerned. Involved in their search for Martha, they'd had little time to worry about anything else. Now it appeared she would not be found, and another of their loved ones had disappeared.

After breakfast, without a word of his intentions, Duke Courtney set off to Lahaina. The small steamer, *Kilauea*, made regular trips between the islands. It would have been the transportation to take Tamsen to Hilo. He checked the passenger lists. She had not gone aboard.

Doggedly, he retraced the steps he'd taken in his search for Martha. He found no record of Tamsen's departure anywhere. Like Martha, she seemed to have disappeared from the earth.

He was white-faced and silent when he returned. There was no point in worrying the others. The whole affair was beginning to take on sinister overtones. He never was an overly imaginative man, but there was sure as hell something peculiar going on.

That night, he held Em in his arms, surprising her with the force of his passions. He held her so tightly her moan of pleasure turned to one of pain.

"Duke! You're hurting me! What's gotten into you?"

"I'm sorry, sweetheart," he whispered against her hair. "It's just—if anything ever happened to you, I'd die."

"Nothing's going to happen," she said softly. "I'll always be here."

"I hope so. Oh, God, Em, I hope so!"

He was thinking of Martha. Em tasted tears in her throat.

In the weeks they'd been here, he'd roamed the island like a madman. The sooner they faced the fact that Martha might never be found, the better.

"Let's go home, love. Back to Barkersville. As soon as Tamsen returns, let's go home."

He held her close, his eyes staring into the darkness over her head. "Sure," he said. "That's what we'll do." He didn't dare tell her that he was beginning to doubt she would ever see her sister again.

The days dragged by, the members of the small group keeping their concerns to themselves in order to protect each other. Only the children were frank in their admissions. They missed Tamsen, who played games with them. The sober atmosphere that haunted the compound made their lives pretty dull.

They were delighted when Kimo rode into the compound. He'd always been a favorite with his teasing and his magic guitar. They ran to him, screaming with excitement. Hurt as he passed them by, they returned disconsolately to their games.

Kimo had come from the mission house. Finding Lani alone, he stayed only a short time. It was clear that she was happy, her face shining. He watched her, fixing the image of her in his memory, as she prattled on, telling him he should find himself a wife.

One day, he would. But there would never be another Lani.

Sensing his morose mood, Lani stopped in mid-sentence. "Is something wrong, Kimo? You—You haven't heard from my father? Mama—" her face was suddenly gray.

"A'ole!" he said. Then he shrugged and summoned a grin. "Kimo come along mission, get black sin wash away, 'ae?"

"Kimi, you fool!" She laughed, her color returning. "As if you had any! I've never known you to hurt anyone in my life."

"Suppose I did," he said, suddenly sober. "Suppose I did a wrong thing, because I thought it was right?"

She looked at him in confusion, seeing his troubled eyes. "I don't think anyone could answer that,

430

but you," she said, carefully. "What have you done?"

He wavered for a moment, then assumed his old, humorous expression. "It isn't what I've done, but what I'm going to do. I'm going to kiss another man's wife good-bye."

He swept her into his arms and kissed her soundly, then moved toward the door. Alarmed, she called after him. "Where are you going, Kimo?"

"Aloha," he called back. Then he was gone.

When David Selwyn arrived a few minutes later, he found his young wife in a disturbed state. She told him the story of Kimo's visit, what he had said and done.

"What do you suppose he was talking about?" he asked.

"I don't know, David. I just don't know!" For no known reason, she began to cry, and was finally comforted in her husband's arms.

From the mission house, Kimo went to the compound. The enthusiasm with which he was welcomed did nothing but increase the ache in his heart. Lani had informed them of his trip to Honolulu. He was evasive in answering their questions. Finally, the silences becoming awkward, he rode away.

His betrayal of the Tallants would always be around his neck, like a lei of thorns. Their kindness to Sam had made them his friends. But his country came first. He must always remember that.

He would go to Lahaina, and from there he would take ship to Hilo, moving down the coast to where dark and brooding jungle-growth cast shadows on beaches of black sand. There, in a place of ancient graves, his father lived in the old way. There, he would learn at his father's feet. He would

431

collect the human bones, wrapped in *kapa*, that would serve as his *unihilii*. And he would cast the spells that would keep his islands free. He would find himself a native woman—not Lani, ah, not Lani! But one who would bear him sons who in turn would learn the old arts. And they would preserve Hawaii forever.

When he had gone, Nell was the first to speak. "What the hell was eatin' him?" she boomed. "Didden even ask after Dan er Tam."

Duke Courtney was silent. Kimo knew more than he was telling. He'd seen it in his face. And it was logical that Tamsen might have gone to Honolulu, since Dan was there.

If she did, she would have had to swim! He'd talked to every sea captain who plied the waters between the islands, to everyone from whom she might have chartered a smaller boat—

Something stuck in his mind, something out of place that didn't seem to fit—

The shabby little boatload of Chinese immigrants, with its surly captain! It was bound for Honolulu, then returning to the China seas. For Tamsen to board a tub like that! Why would she take such a risk, and why wouldn't she tell them she was going to Honolulu? Why did she mislead them, giving Hilo as her destination?

Because she was Tamsen, that was why! She had planned to do something foolhardy, and she didn't want to get the rest of them involved.

The next morning, Duke Courtney set off for Honolulu with a vague statement about turning the search for Martha to the authorities there. He thought they might be more efficient than the locals at Lahaina.

Not wishing to be conspicuous, Courtney didn't

stay at the hotel, going instead to a mission where Selwyn had given him a written introduction. Dressed in rough garb, he might have been a sailor ashore for a time. He walked the streets of the small city, gloomily searching every face he saw. He searched in vain.

Deciding that it had been a wild goose chase, he made up his mind to return to Em. He would not go, however, without some kind of news.

He went to the office of the magistrate, asking for word of the American, Tallant. Apparently, the office had never heard the name. Courtney demanded to see their records. The ledger he was shown was conspicuously new. There was no entry of Dan's name in its pages of carefully copied script.

Duke Courtney knew a runaround when he saw one. His big frame fairly vibrated with the desire to tear the place apart, breaking a few heads in the process. The old exultant fighting yell rose in his throat as he squared away. He swallowed it. He was no longer a bully-boy, ready to take on the world. He was a family man, an English subject with Canadian citizenship, looking for an American on a Hawaiian island.

They'd have him slammed so far back in the pokey he'd never be heard of again. They didn't need any more mysterious disappearances.

He left the offices, glowering, his head down. Hell, he might as well get his gear together and head back to Em. He should have stayed in the hotel. At least the beds would have been better than those at that damn mission. He slept on a slab meant for a midget, his feet thrusting out over the end.

The hotel! He hadn't checked there, and where else would a woman stay? In a few short minutes, he'd reached the building. The clerk frowned at sight of the big man in his rough garb. Common sailors were not encouraged here.

No, a Tamsen Tallant had never registered here. Nor a Mrs. Daniel Tallant.

Duke thought for a moment. Tamsen had never done anything in a simple manner. He tried to think of another name she had used in the past.

"See if you have a Poppy Franklin," he ventured.

The clerk was getting irritable. Since he didn't know the lady's name, he said bitingly, he might describe her appearance.

Duke held his palm on a horizontal level with his heart. "About this high," he said, considering. "And built like—you know." He made curving motions with his hands. "Black hair, big eyes, coloring about like—" he looked around, helplessly, then pointed at a flower in a vase, its petals creamy gold. "Like that," he finished.

The clerk was smiling now. "That would be Mrs. Emmeline McLeod. I regret to say that she's no longer here. She—"

He stopped, gasping as Duke gripped his collar, hauling him half across the desk. "Where is she," he raged. "Dammit, tell me!"

A few minutes later, he left, not much wiser than before. The clerk, terrified out of his wits, had babbled all he knew. The lady in question was known to be a favorite of the king. She had left with him one night and not returned. Rumors were rife about the hotel for several days. Then her baggage had been sent for, her bill paid. The lady was leaving the islands and returning home.

Folding a sum of money into the dazed clerk's fingers, Duke slammed out of the hotel and made his way to the Palace. There, he demanded an audience with the king.

His Royal Majesty was away at the moment. His request would be filed. Perhaps in several months—

Duke Courtney balled his fists and looked at the guards standing by, their hands tense on their weapons. He contented himself with a four-letter expletive and made his way back to the wharf, where he took ship for Maui.

Emmeline McLeod. Tamsen had used his wife's first name and her own maiden name. Why? What in the hell had she been up to, and where was she, now? Maybe even in the king's goddam bed! He smashed his fist against the ship's rail, his anger turned on Tamsen. The pain it inflicted brought him back to his senses. If Tamsen had seduced Kamehameha, it would only be for one reason. And that reason's name was Dan Tallant. Maybe she'd got him to set Dan free, and they'd both taken off for the States, leaving the rest of them here to sweat it out—

That didn't sound like Tamsen, or Tallant, either. And where in the hell was Martha—?

RETURN TO
HONG KONG

49

Martha was very much on Peter Channing's mind as his ship moved into Hong Kong harbor. He wondered if she would still be there at Government House, now that he was so long overdue. Captain Carnstead had decided to change course, making for Tokyo. They had been there for some time, engaged in trading, contracting materials for the next journey. Then they had skirted the Ryukus, returning after many long months to the familiar harbor.

Today, it was not so familiar. A few more structures had been added along the shoreline, but the real changes were due to a gala atmosphere. A visit from the Duke of Edinburgh was pending. Flags flew in profusion from every vessel in the harbor waters. Store fronts were festooned with banners, hung with gilded lanterns. An ornate triumphal arch had been erected at Pedder's Wharf.

In seeking to welcome an English prince, the city of Hong Kong had managed to look more Oriental than ever.

In spite of his ambivalent feelings toward the girl to whom he was, unfortunately, married, his pulse was thudding as he made his way through the streets thronged with busy Chinese, working like ants as they gilded buildings and hung streamers. He made himself stop to survey a store front where a bamboo framework had been erected to display chandeliers and puppets in the duke's honor. He stared at it, head tilted in interest, but his eyes blank and unseeing. Finally, he moved on.

He climbed the long hill to Government House, noting with dismay that the same confusion existed there. Excited servants ran about, flapping dust mops and shaking small rugs. A man teetered on a ladder, hanging paper lanterns. The entry to the building was being scrubbed.

He had come at a bad time. It was a good excuse to postpone his meeting with Martha. No, it wasn't! After all she was supposed to be his wife! She had a child the MacDonnells thought to be his. Sir Richard, due to his office, would immediately learn the *Mattie* was in port. They would be shocked that he didn't come at once to his wife and baby. He was trapped—

Trapped was the word for it. He'd hoped to find the Tallants, to return Martha into their keeping. He would give her grounds for divorce; desertion, adultery, whatever she wished, and he would be rid of her.

The Tallants were gone. The Larabee home had burned, and there was no one on the premises. Now, he knew that he should have gone to the mission. Selwyn might have known where the Tallant and Narvaéz families were. He suspected they had gone back to the States. If he'd only had more time—

But he didn't. And Martha, if she were still here, had no place to go—except with him. The MacDonnells had cared for her far too long. They would expect him to make other arrangements now. He didn't want to take Martha home with him. Yet he couldn't leave her here. He was between the devil and the deep blue sea!

There was no more time to speculate on his condition. The governor's lady, as harried as she was in preparing for the royal visitor, spotted him. Adjusting her lace morning cap, she sped down the walk. "Peter Channing! Richard told me your ship was in port! Of course I haven't told Lani. I'm sure you wish to surprise her! I'll have one of the servants call her—"

She turned in happy distraction, but Peter stopped her in time. "Forgive me, but I would like to meet her—alone. Can't I just go up to her room?"

Her face softened into understanding. "Of course! How silly of me. Do go right along. She's been so *worried*."

Peter climbed the steps that led to another floor, then followed the hallway to the door of the room Martha occupied. The face of the girl who opened the door at his knock had changed. It was fuller, softer, sweeter, somehow, with a kind of glow about it. He had to restrain himself from snatching her up. But then her expression changed as she recognized him, sharpening as she stared at him, defiance in her eyes.

A number of maids were on their knees, scrubbing the hall floors. He sensed their eyes on them. "Lani," he cried, "Sweetheart! I'm back."

"Peter," she echoed dutifully in a voice that fell short of enthusiasm. He pushed in, and closed the door behind him.

"You might at least try to play your part, Martha! For God's sake—"

"I've played it for months now," she shot back. "I've been here, remember! You haven't been under any strain!"

"Let's not quarrel," he sighed. "Fighting won't solve anything. I can't leave you here indefinitely. I'll only be in port a week or so. And I've got to figure what to do with you."

Martha was shivering. The sight of the tall young man who was her husband—his stern, honest face, and the way his broad shoulders blocked out everything beyond him—brought back that night at Mountain Lodge too vividly. She found herself wanting nothing more than to fly into his arms and cry herself to sleep; to wake there, close and warm—

But he wanted no part of her. The way he had left her before proved that. She tried to keep her anger whipped up to cover her confusion.

"You needn't worry about me. I can go back to Maui."

He shook his head. "That's out of the question. They have all gone, and I haven't a clue as to where. I suppose I'm committed to taking you home to Australia—"

He looked so desperate at that eventuality that Martha's fury exploded.

"You needn't worry. I can always find work in Hong Kong! A brothel, perhaps. Chinese men like white-skinned women, I know that!"

"Don't be a fool!"

"Fool! I'd stoop to anything before I would be forced on you!"

They glared at each other. "Speaking of brothels," Peter Channing growled, "I think I will go out and find one. I feel the need of a real woman."

"Go to Kowloon," she said, sweetly informative, naming an address. "I understand there's a particularly interesting one there. Oh—ask for Toy."

He left the room, still seething. As he dashed past Lady MacDonnell, he paused to tell her that he'd only been allowed a few minutes ashore, and that he would return.

By the time he reached the harbor area, he regretted his harsh words to Martha. And, like an idiot, he hadn't even asked about the baby. He had no desire to see the thing, but Martha had given birth, alone, in a strange country, dependent on Lady MacDonnell's charity. He had no wish to be cruel.

He thought about her last words. How did she know the address of a brothel in Kowloon? And who the hell was Toy?

That night, because he was expected to, he returned to Government House. Martha played her part to the hilt before the MacDonnells, so sweetly happy that he was almost fooled. When Lady MacDonnell discovered he hadn't seen his child on the earlier visit—she was napping, Martha explained—she insisted upon going to the nursery with them for the joy of viewing the face of a father seeing his baby for the first time.

Peter Channing knew nothing about babies. He had never been close to one. Yet he was expected to play the part of proud parent to a child that wasn't even his. Lady MacDonnell picked up the squirming little bundle and held it toward him. Startled, he retreated. He sensed the women were laughing at him. Evidently he had performed as expected.

"Touch her," Lady MacDonnell urged. "She won't break."

He extended a tentative finger, and the baby clasped it, opening huge dark, long-lashed eyes.

"She's very nice," he said uncertainly.

"It takes a while with fathers," their hostess told Martha with a condescending amusement. Peter's ears were red as his wife guided him from the

443

room. Behind him, he could hear Lady MacDonnell still cooing to the child. "Very nice, indeed! You're a perfect little angel, aren't you, Petra?"

He stiffened. *Petra!* Martha had named the kid after him! Of all the goddam nerve!

The young couple made their excuses and retired early that night, Martha blushing under the older woman's knowing look. It had been difficult maintaining their charade. All that saved them was Sir Richard's interest in Peter's travels. Once that subject was exhausted, it was wise to flee.

Peter opted to spend the night in the chair. He might as well share the bed, Martha said indifferently. It was clear he had no misguided intentions as to their relationship. He certainly didn't, he told her, stiffly. But he had no desire to give her the impression it was otherwise.

He turned his back while she prepared for bed, and then moved the chair to a far corner of the room. The door to the nursery where a small gaslight was kept burning stood partly opened. There was just enough glow so that he could see Martha's face, her eyes closing quickly in a calm, serene sleep.

Damn her! To go to sleep so quickly, and to look so beautiful in the process! He shifted uncomfortably, his muscles aching, trying to make himself remember that this girl was responsible for the death of Sam and Josie Larabee. Most likely, the marriage of Dan Tallant and Tamsen was a dead issue. They had probably broken up and gone their separate ways. Martha said Feng Wu kidnapped her. He had no way of knowing that for sure. She had chased Dan Tallant, egged him into murder. She might have thought it exciting to be a warlord's mistress.

She had even managed to seduce him. There

444

was a name for girls like Martha. He wasn't certain what it was, but—there was a name.

He finally slept, trying to hunch his tall form into a shape to fit the chair. He woke, suppressing a groan, at the sound of a baby's cry.

The bed creaked. Martha was sitting on its edge, feeling for her slippers. He closed his eyes to slits, pretending sleep as she stood and glided toward the nursery door. For a moment, her slim form was visible through the thin material of her nightdress, warm, glowing—

He swallowed hard. Then she was out of the doorway. He heard her talking to the child in soothing tones. When she didn't return, he got to his feet and tiptoed to the door.

Martha sat in a small white rocker, the baby cradled in her arms, her face soft with a maternal love as she bent over her baby. It was an expression Peter Channing had never seen before. His own mother had been a hard-bitten, sun-scorched woman of the Outback.

He returned to his chair, his emotions raveled. He wished to God little Petra had been his child.

50

The MacDonnells had the impression that their young charge would be leaving them, taking the baby that had become a part of their lives. Neither Martha nor Peter made any attempt to relieve them of their concern. After all, Martha thought miserably, I can't stay here forever. She found herself thinking more and more of Peter's notion to take her to Australia, to take her to his home.

Then she would recall the look of desperation with which he had made that statement. She would not force herself and her child on someone who didn't want them; who considered the baby a shameful thing. Peter Channing had come to her rescue. She was indebted to him for that. But the debt was cancelled when he took her in what she thought was love—then left her as he would leave a prostitute who made further demands on him. He was tied to a fallen woman, and he despised the thought.

Confused at her own feelings, Martha accepted the hugs and sad sighs the busy Lady MacDonnell doled out whenever she had time to think.

"I can't bear to have you leave! I suppose you must. It's selfish of me—but I will miss you so!"

"I can't stay here forever," Martha answered, blushing.

"I know you can't! And I'm sure you can't wait to be alone with that handsome husband. But to have you go at a time like this, when everything's such a turmoil! If I just had time. No, Chen!" Lady MacDonnell rushed distractedly to show a Chinese houseboy how some particular job should be done.

Martha, relieved, returned to her room. Peter had gone to assist the governor with some chore, and she had these few moments alone. He had told her his ship would sail in three days, the morning after the ball that was to be held for the Duke of Edinburgh. She had to come to some kind of decision.

Sitting on her bed, her hands twisted in her lap, she considered her situation. She couldn't remain dependent on the MacDonnell's charity forever. True, Peter Channing had sent money for her keep. But she couldn't expect him to go on doing that forever. He would want to go home, settle down, perhaps marry if he could rid himself of her. The thought stabbed at her, a very real pain.

He had gotten her into this situation, she thought angrily. It was he who insisted on a stupid shipboard ceremony when she was too dazed to know what she was doing. Maybe he considered himself some kind of hero, then grew tired of the game. Whatever his reasons, they were stuck with each other. She would accompany him to Australia, but there she would leave him. Someway, she'd get back to the States and try to make some kind of life of her own. She would tell him the next time they were alone.

Petra, in the next room, began to whimper. Martha rose and went in to her, holding her in an

447

agony of love. Her mother, Em, must have felt like this when Martha herself was an infant. In return, Em had nothing but heartbreak over a girl whose own good blood had been mingled with bad. Martha shuddered, recalling Feng Wu. Little Petra—if a baby inherited the sins of its father, as the Bible said—had little chance. All Martha could do was love her—and hope. If Petra broke her heart, well, she deserved it.

But Emmeline Courtney did not. She didn't deserve a bastard for a child—nor one for a grandchild. One thing for sure, Martha would never go home.

Peter Channing, returning from aiding the governor—one of the fountains in the garden had ceased to flow, and no one knew what to do about it but himself—was thinking, too. Sir Richard, as broken up as his lady over the prospect of losing their almost-adopted daughter and her baby, took it upon himself to give Peter a stern lecture on his responsibility to his little family.

"You really should give up this wandering, old man! Settle down! You have a fine girl there. Two of them, in fact. They must be your first concern."

Channing had a hunch the governor considered him not quite good enough for his wife.

Good God! If the man only knew! If he knew the girl he and his wife had such affection for was an impostor, a home-wrecker, responsible for the death of two fine people—a murderess—

And he had to stand there and take the man's insufferable advice! He was supposed to give up his life and devote it to the welfare of a conniving little bitch with an illegitimate child—

The scene that greeted his eyes when he entered the room he shared with his wife did little to ease his boiling emotions. Martha stood by the window, the baby in her arms. Peter's heart thudded for a moment, seeming to turn over. To cover his feelings, he spoke in a harsher voice than he'd intended.

"This isn't a nursery. Put the kid back where it belongs. I want to talk to you!"

Martha threw back her head and returned his gaze. Then she obeyed quietly, returning to face him.

"What is is?"

"I'm giving you an ultimatum. The MacDonnells think I'm taking you with me, and by God, I am. I don't know what the hell I'm going to do with you in Australia, but I'm not going to have Sir Richard instructing me in my duties! Get your gear packed!"

"And if I don't choose to?"

"You're legally my wife. You don't have a choice!"

Feeling his anger begin to cool, he turned and slammed out of the room. Martha watched him go, her eyes hot with fury. Damn him! Oh, damn him! Just when she'd made up her own mind, he'd had to storm in like this! And his reference to Petra—"Put the kid back where it belongs."

She would do as he said, but she'd make sure he knew it was under protest. And she had no intention of making it easy for him!

Finally, Petra asleep under the eye of a watchful Chinese servant, Martha went down for tea. Lady MacDonnell insisted on preserving all amenities, despite the flurry of preparing for their royal guest. Clad in a pale blue tea gown, she poured while a servant passed trays of scones and bite-sized sandwiches. She looked up as Martha entered, approving the girl's dress, one of her own old ones, resewn to fit. Of dusky rose, it gave a touch of color to Martha's cheeks.

Peter Channing, awkwardly balancing a fragile porcelain cup and wishing he were anywhere else in the world, felt an odd pang. No wonder the girl didn't wish to leave. She looked as if she were born to this kind of life. There would be none of this ahead for awhile. If she stayed with him, she would face a rigorous life. He was beginning to understand Sir Richard's attitude a bit, and he didn't feel too happy about it.

"You look lovely, Lani," Lady MacDonnell said. "And how is Petra doing?"

"Fast asleep," Martha smiled.

"Such a healthy child! I do hope she takes well to a sea voyage." The lady happily embarked into a discussion of children, childhood diseases, proper upbringing. Martha let her words flow over her. Her own attention was caught by the conversation of the men. Peter was discussing the vegetation of his country; the almost tropical growth in the Darwin area of the north, and down the east coast from Cape York to Brisbane. The giant gum trees of the southwest, sometimes reaching a height of two hundred feet; mixed forests with hoop and bunya pine in the warmer regions of the north. Then there were forests of eucalyptus where there was a lesser amount of rainfall, degenerating into mallee and mulga toward the interior as the climate became dryer.

He talked of the grass trees, some of them bearing spikes of flowers, resistant to fire, as were the acacia which often germinated when a rain followed a forest fire.

It all sounded fascinating and unreal, especially when Peter went on to describe the animal life of the country; the marsupials of different types, wolf, mole, cat, anteater—the koalas, and the wombats. He went on to tell of the birds, the cassowary and emu; and of the reptiles, such as the water-holding frog that distends its body with water, burying itself, sealing itself into a tiny room made of mud and mucus. Then there was the black and yellow corboree frog in the higher altitudes with ability to survive beneath the snow for four months. In Victoria, there was an earthworm that grew to lengths of ten feet or more—

Martha watched his face as he spoke, seeing his serious blue eyes luminiscent in his tanned lean face; the way he leaned forward, every muscle of his broad shoulders vibrant as he described the country he loved. Sir Richard was enthralled.

And finally, Peter reached into his pocket with a familiar gesture, withdrawing the opals that remained.

Martha shut her eyes, sickly. Just so had he removed the packet on a long ago night, shaking the jewels into the palm of his hand. They had all been friends, then, Dan and Sam, Tamsen and Josie. And she had spoiled it. Sam and Josie were dead; the others—Dan and Tamsen; Arab, Juan, and their family—were God knows where!

Martha rose. "Please excuse me. I think I'll go to my room."

Peter looked up, his eyes going cold as he looked into her mind, seeing what was there. Only Lady MacDonnell protested her leaving, but then apologized. "I beg your pardon. I forgot you have packing to do."

"I don't—"

Peter Channing interrupted Martha. "Indeed she does. Our plans are to go on board tonight."

Their hostess refused to accept his words. "You can't leave before tomorrow night. There's the ball for Duke Alfred—Lani has a new gown. Why, it will be a farewell party. I won't hear of it!"

They were all looking at Peter, as if he had committed a crime, Sir Richard, his lady, his own wife. He dug in his heels. "Our ship sails early the following morning."

"And you will be aboard," Sir Richard said stiffly. "I shall see to it, myself. I intend to tell Carnstead, in case he offers any objections. I will have you delivered to the wharf in my own carriage. My word, old chap! Any man who would deprive his wife of an event like this—"

Channing threw up his hands in a gesture of angry helplessness. "I do not intend to deprive my wife of anything. It is her decision."

"Then we will be most happy to attend."

We? Peter's face reddened. He would be miserable at such an affair. Miserable and out of place. He wouldn't be forced into such a spot.

"I have business to take care of," he stammered. "If Mar—Lani attends, it will be alone. Now, if you will excuse me—I must get back to the ship."

Three pairs of accusing eyes watched him leave. When Martha had gone to her room, Sir Richard took a reflective draw at his pipe. "Can't quite make this Channing out," he said. "He seems a surly chap at times. Yet at others—"

"He can be charming," his wife finished for him. "But our little Lani and the child—D'you think he'll be good to them?"

"He'd better," Sir Richard said grimly. "I had a fatherly chat with him today."

His face reddened with pleasure as his lady placed an affectionate hand on his knee. "You *are* a love, dear Richie." The name was a pet one, out of the past.

He put his pipe down and patted her clumsily on the back. "Let's not get carried away, old girl. I only did my duty. And about the ball—I think he'll come around."

51

Peter Channing, upon reaching his ship, indeed had second thoughts. Sir Richard MacDonnell and his wife had stood by the girl they thought to be Lani Larabee Channing. They had no true idea of her past, or that the baby had been sired by the Chinese criminal who had kidnapped Martha. They had every right to express their opinions. In their eyes, he probably seemed an insensitive brute.

They showed a deep affection for Martha. Grudgingly, he admitted to himself that she did have endearing qualities at times. It would not be fair to leave them worrying about how he would treat her—and the baby.

He would go to the goddam ball. But in order to do so, he would have to have some dress clothes. He looked at his sun-bleached, salt-stained working garb. He had nothing else, and there was little time.

He went to Captain Carnstead. The older man rubbed his chin in thought. Less than twenty-four hours. It gave him no leeway. But there was a hole-in-the-wall shop he had patronized in Kowloon, the small Chinese tailor who owned it was most obliging and did good work—if he were still there. He went to his cabin and returned with a name and address. Channing frowned as he studied it. The street name seemed familiar.

He took a small boat to Kowloon City and, following the captain's directions, found himself on a narrow street. Rickety buildings lined it, opening directly onto the roadway. Narrow alleyways between the structures had been roofed over to form small roadside businesses, and here Peter found the little tailor Carnstead recommended.

The shop was not enclosed. The tailor plied his craft in full view of the street. An admiring crowd gathered to watch him take the measurements of the tall, red-faced Australian, carrying on a singsong of comments in their own tongue as they discussed his proportions.

The tailor did not speak English, but his young son did. The most revered gentleman's suit would be done, chop-chop. His father would stitch all night. But the honored one must return in the morning, to assure the fit. Their humble abode was forever grateful for his patronage, and they guaranteed satisfaction. They did much business with sailing men, getting much patronage from the business next door.

Escaping the boy's effusive thanks, Peter Channing left. He glanced at the sign on the adjacent structure, took another step and stopped short.

Someone had written a number he could read on the gilded board beneath the Chinese characters. Twelve! It was a number he remembered, and now he knew why the street had a familiar ring.

"*Speaking of brothels,*" he'd said, "*I think I will go out and find one. I feel the need of a real woman.*"

455

"Go to Kowloon," Martha had answered. "I understand there's a particularly interesting one there. Oh—ask for Toy."

He'd wondered how she knew the address of a brothel in Kowloon—and who Toy was. Well, hell, he might as well find out. He had nothing else to do. He entered the building and went down a long, dark hall that stank of incense and perspiration. At the end, a beaded curtain closed off a doorway. Pushing it aside, he found himself in a tawdry room decorated with shabby hangings, and soiled paper ornaments. A bench along one wall was lined with shoddy-appearing men; waterfront riffraff. A table faced the curtain. Behind it sat a heavy-featured woman; her shrewd eyes skimming over Channing, cataloguing him. He asked to see Toy.

Toy was busy with a customer. There were others waiting. Perhaps another night? Her eyes opened wide as he pressed a wad of money into her hand. She waved him to the head of the line.

Toy was having her own problems. Her only hope these days was to find another wealthy protector. Chun Li, the rat-faced youth with her now, didn't fit into that category. He had become a nightly customer, and she had his credentials checked. Despite his bragging, he was nothing but a scavenging little thief. He wanted her to be his wife. If she spurned his love, he would kill himself. If she came with him, he would give her the world.

The time alotted him was over. She would lose another customer and Madam Chang would beat her.

"Goddam," she said wearily. "Go to hell, heya?"

He beamed at the sound of his beloved's voice, continuing his liquid flow of poetic Chinese, praising her beauty, begging her favor. The man couldn't even speak English! Sighing, she guided him to the door, telling him in her own tongue that he must go before her passions were aroused once more; that she would die a thousand deaths until he came again.

The door finally shut behind him, she leaned against it. Chun Li was weak, but his very weakness made him dangerous. One day she would have to kill him, she thought dismally. Madam Chang would be angry at losing a paying customer, but she would see to it that the body was spirited from the premises and dumped into the harbor—

Hearing footsteps on the stairs, she opened the door a little and went to the bed, arranging her robe around her attractively, letting it slip from one shoulder, the color of yellow ivory, fixing a smile on her painted lips as she awaited the coming of her next customer.

Peter Channing pushed the door open, gingerly, every muscle tense. Everything about this dive spelled danger. The little Chinese who slipped by him as he mounted the stairs had looked at him with an evil malevolence that chilled his blood. He'd been a fool to come here, money in his pockets, not knowing what he'd find.

The small, delicate flower of a girl who faced him was a definite surprise. Toy's eyes widened as she looked at her new customer in appreciation. Tall, lean, handsome, he was quite a man! Maybe she could persuade him to buy up her time for the remainder of the night.

When he didn't move, she rose and came toward him, letting the robe fall open as she reached to clasp her arms about his neck. "Big man, werry," she purred. "Jig-jig goddam good, heya?"

Sickened, Peter pushed her from him, the

strong scent she wore making him dizzy. "No, please. I just want to talk to you."

She retreated to sit on the bed, her mouth pouting, her lovely liquid eyes filled with suspicion, her mind working like lightning. The men who came here could want only two things; a girl—or information about a relative or friend who had disappeared from these premises. She would say nothing. And then she would try to seduce him and send him happily on his way. Maybe she'd be able to get a reward from Madam Chang.

Channing drew up the one chair in the room and sat down, facing her. "Do you know a girl named Martha Courtney?" he asked.

The name produced no reaction, other than bewilderment. Toy shook her head.

"Then—Lani Larabee?"

This time, he knew he'd touched a nerve. The girl stiffened. "Lani Lallabee?" she asked cautiously.

"The girl staying at Government House," he said with impatience. "You do know her. I can see that. So don't try to lie to me! Where did you meet her? What do you know about her? Has she come here?"

Toy's mind raced behind her impassive face. She'd hoped the girl had died in the rubble that accompanied the typhoon. She didn't. She was alive, and at Government House. This man could be one of two things; her lover—or a British policeman sent to investigate.

"Lani Lallabee, you like werry much?"

Channing thought her question over. There was something between him and Martha, but it certainly had nothing to do with liking her. "Not very much," he answered honestly.

The girl rose, her robe swishing around her as she paced the room like a small tiger cat. Finally she turned to face him. "Lani goddam werry bad. Steal mans, my! Deaded he, werry!" She spun behind Channing, and he felt something slam into his back. He stiffened, then relaxed. It had only been her fist, not the knife he had somehow expected.

What was she saying? He tried to make some sense from the spate of words. Shui was killed in the typhoon. She and the others had found Feng Wu's body, the knife in its back. T'zi had taken poison. She didn't know what happened to Liang. Lani had killed Feng Wu. It could be proven. She should be taken to prison, executed—"

It finally dawned on him that she was asking him to accomplish this for her. That she thought he was a representative of British law. He held up a staying hand. "I'm not a policeman, Toy. I have no authority. I—I suppose I just needed some answers."

He turned to leave and the girl was suddenly beside him, clutching at him, pressing her body to his. "No go," she said invitingly. "Jig-jig, now. Goddam werry good—"

He put her away from him with gentle hands. "No need for that. Here, this is for you."

She clutched avidly at the money he handed her and stood watching as he walked to the door. Then, "Mans!" He turned to look at her. "Lani Lallabee, never mind. She deaded werry soon, heya?"

He felt a sudden chill at her expression. Closing the door, he hurried down the stairs and out into a night illuminated by dragon-lanterns, and filled with slinking, furtive shadows. He intended going back to the ship for the night—but not now. In Toy,

Martha had a deadly enemy. He had a hunch the Chinese girl hadn't known where Martha was—until he told her.

He did not breathe easily until he landed once more at Pedder's Wharf on the Hong Kong side. As he walked up to Government House, so eminently civilized, he was able to laugh at himself. The sinister atmosphere of the place he visited had gotten to him. His imagination had done the rest.

Because of it, he had committed himself to another night in that goddam chair!

Entering their room, he found Martha already abed, her silken hair spread about her, her eyes closed in sleep. He felt a sudden surge of protectiveness toward her. She looked so small, so defenseless—and so lovely.

He didn't know that her looks were also deceptive; that, inside, she was a seething mass of emotions. For she recognized the scent that still clung to his clothing. He had come from Toy.

52

Channing spent a miserable night, finally wedging himself into a more comfortable position near morning. When he woke, stiff and aching, the sun was shining brightly. Martha was not in the room, and the door to the nursery was closed.

Dammit, he had to talk to her—

He pushed the door open. The baby kicked and cooed under the eye of a Chinese maid. Martha was nowhere to be seen. The Chinese girl put a hand to her mouth and giggled. He had an uncomfortable feeling that she knew he had spent the night in a chair.

He went downstairs to find tables being set for the evening to come, heavy silver, crested china against fine linen. In the flurry of activity, he learned that the MacDonnells and Martha were taking breakfast on the rear terrace, leaving the house free for last minute preparations. He was to join them.

Like hell, he would! He was tired of people directing what he should or should not do. Especially when they didn't have all the facts in the case. He'd let them think he had no plans of showing up tonight. Then, they'd change their tune. Right now, he had an appointment to keep with a Kowloon tailor.

Again, he crossed the harbor. The small back street that seemed so ominous in the dark was merely shabby in the day. The door to the brothel was closed, the shades drawn. He grinned to himself as he recalled his impressions of the previous night; the bead curtain, the narrow dark hallway that set his nerves on edge. The scent of the place. It was implanted so strongly in his memory that he could smell it now.

In the day, it was only a pathetic place where pitiful lonely men went in search of something that resembled love.

The suit was ready, except for minor details. Peter was forced to try it on, his only barrier between himself and the watching Chinese who thronged about the open shop, a ragged curtain at the rear. Bared to the knees, his shoulders protruding above, he was certain that the comments bandied in a foreign tongue were salacious. He dressed in haste. After much measuring and pinning, he was forced to endure the ordeal again. The lad who spoke English was gone. The old Chinese held up four fingers. Peter was to return at four.

Channing had not seen Toy, but she saw him. Standing at an upstairs window, unable to sleep because of what she learned the previous night, she saw him pass. She wondered at his relationship with the girl she knew as Lani. She hoped it wouldn't bother him too much when the girl was "deaded." She already decided how that task was to be handled. It would be at a great cost to herself, but it would be worth it. Maybe, she thought hopefully, Chun Li would be trapped after he'd committed the deed. Then she could go on working, her conscience clear, waiting for a rich man to come along and find her—another Feng Wu—

At eight o'clock that night, a tall, handsome man, impeccably dressed, presented himself at the door of Government House. Lady MacDonnell failed to recognize Peter Channing for a moment, then her lips curved in a broad smile. Lani was not yet down. She tried to lead him toward a group of dignitaries, but he waved her away. He would wait for Lani—and surprise her, since she didn't expect him.

He found an alcove where, partially hidden by a plant, he could watch the stairs. When Martha descended, he found it hard to swallow. She was so beautiful it made his chest hurt. In a sweeping gown of apricot that bared her shoulders and creamy throat, she looked as if she belonged in these rich surroundings.

He stood, something like pride swelling within him. This girl was his *wife!* He would go to meet her—

He stopped himself in time. His were not the only eyes that noted her appearance. A young man broke from a group of beribboned officers. "Lani! I was afraid you had gone—"

"Sir Cecil!" Martha was apparently as glad to see the man as he was to see her. He gallantly took her hand as she came the last few steps, her other hand holding her skirts in a graceful way. When she reached the floor, he gripped them both as he went into a series of pretty compliments that she fended in a practiced way. Then there was another man at her side. Another—

Peter Channing was stunned. He had not considered this. For some reason, he'd thought of Martha as living a quiet, lonely existence here while he was away. He'd been a fool! A damn fool! He'd pegged her as man-crazy when he met her. And girls like that never changed. No wonder she'd balked when he charged in here, a self-styled hero, to take her away from all this—

He had no idea that Martha had been seething all day, knowing that he'd been with Toy—or that she had spied him in one heart-stopping moment, from the stair.

"But I'm not going. Sir Cecil," she was saying, now. "I've changed my mind. I'm staying."

"And your husband?" another officer broke in.

Martha drooped, her fan coming up to cover a trembling mouth. "That's—over. It was a mistake from the beginning, Bruce."

"Jove! The chap hasn't treated you badly, has he?"

The fan moved higher, her shining head bent, concealing brimming eyes. "I'd prefer not to discuss it," she said.

Peter Channing, in his hiding place, was livid with anger, not unmixed with admiration. It was one helluva act she was putting on! And it released him from any responsibility. She had no intention of going to Australia. All he had to do was walk out of here, and never see her again. He didn't have to worry about what would happen to a lonely waif in a strange country. Hell, she would manage.

Peter left his place of concealment and strode from the house. He would not return again. He would go to the ship, change clothing, wad this monkey suit up and throw it into the harbor. He wanted nothing to remind him of any of this when he sailed in the morning.

He left the porch of Government House, and

paused. Something moved in a shrub in the shadows. He saw a face, a Chinese face with ferret features. A servant watching the arrivals, no doubt.

He was almost to Pedder's Wharf when that face came alive in his mind. He had seen it before—on a dark stair in Kowloon City. He had been going up, this man coming down. He thought of Toy's threat. *"Lani Lallabee, never mind. She deaded werry soon—"*

He turned on his heel and, cursing himself, went back to Government House to stand in the darkness outside.

Within the house, Martha was surrounded by admiring men. Word had spread quickly that Lani Channing and her husband were going their separate ways. Unattached white females were scarce in Hong Kong, most officers reduced to courting a senior's buck-toothed visiting relative. This girl, despite the fact that she was encumbered with a child, was a real catch. So lovely—and the governor's ward—

Martha should have been flattered at their attentions. Instead, she was only unutterably weary. She had burned her bridges, cut off all avenues of escape. The governor and his lady wouldn't mind her staying for a while. She would tell them her husband had been less than affectionate when he returned. They would have noticed that. And then she would say it was because he had another woman. Certainly no untruth—

She would offer to help with official correspondence to pay for her keep. Then, well rid of a husband who did not want her, perhaps she would marry Sir Cecil—or Bruce—or Rodney. At least, she would give her child a father.

Then why did she hurt so? Why couldn't she get the memory of a night at Mountain Lodge out of her mind—

Soft strains of music drifted through the room, and people began to separate into couples except for two small knots in which a central figure commanded attention. In the middle of one stood Martha Channing, known as Lani Channing in Government House. At the other end of the ballroom, the honored guest, the Duke of Edinburgh held forth. He paused in conversation, and stared, his eyes slightly glazed. "My word! I can't believe—"

Sir Richard followed his gaze. The crowd about Martha had shifted, and for a moment she stood exposed, the clothing of the young officers around her a perfect foil for her bright gown.

"My ward," the governor said proudly. "Pretty, isn't she?"

But the Duke had gone. He crossed the room in haste, his mind fumbling for a name. Jove, how had the woman got here so soon!

"Mrs. Emmeline McLeod," he said, reaching her side. "So good to see you again!"

The eyes that turned to him were blank with shock; the face the same as he recalled, yet different. He backed away, reddening. "My apologies," he stammered. "I was certain you were a young widow I met in Honolulu. Forgive me."

He bowed himself away. Martha stood stiff, his words ringing in her head. Emmeline McLeod—Her mother's maiden name—A widow. Mama had come to search for her! But—a widow! Duke dead? Oh, dear God, no!

She excused herself for a few moments, pleading a headache, and went to her room where she stood for a moment in confusion. Em in Honolulu, a

466

widow! No mention of her sisters, her new baby brother. Perhaps there had been some disaster—

Her mother needed her!

Peter Channing would help her. She must get to him before his ship sailed. Snatching Petra up, she hurried out a rear entrance, rounding to the front, only to pause at a new thought. The royal personage could not have mistaken her for her mother. They were not alike, at all. Em was softly fragile, her hair a drift of brown-blonde. It was Tamsen she resembled. Aunt Tamsen, who must have had some reason for masquerading under another name —and had chosen a familiar one.

She did not see Peter Channing standing tall in the shadow of a pillar—nor the small crouching figure that scuttled spiderlike from the bushes to one side, something glinting in his hand. But Channing saw him.

Peter stepped out with a shout of warning. Martha froze, poised to flee as he ran toward her. Then she turned, stumbling, a yellow hand driving a knife home as Channing reached her attacker, knocking him to the ground.

53

Leaving Martha's assailant to the houseboys who came running at Martha's scream, Peter Channing caught at his swaying wife. "My God, Martha! Are you hurt?"

"No, it's the baby! Peter, it's the baby! Look at her! Look!"

The blanket in which the small body was wrapped was splotched hideously.

Shouting at a houseboy to bring his wife, Peter took the little one and ran to a rear entrance. Entering a kitchen, he shoved twittering servants away and placed the blood-spattered bundle on a table. If that slimy little wharf rat had killed his child—

He folded the blanket back with fearful hands. Petra looked up at him with solemn, interested eyes. He turned the small body, seeing no wounds, suppressing a sob of relief. Then a new horror struck him. This was Martha's blood.

He turned toward the entrance. Martha stood there, swaying, supported on the arm of a guard. Her face was white, her eyes enormous as he went toward her.

"She's all right, Martha. Petra's not hurt."

468

With a little sigh, Martha Channing crumpled to the floor.

A servant went for Lady MacDonnell as Channing carried his wife upstairs, a Chinese maid following with the baby. Putting his wife gently on her bed, Peter cut her gown away. Martha had been struck twice, once in the underarm as she stumbled, and her hand was pierced as she attempted to ward off a second blow. That would account for the blood-spattered blanket—

Lady MacDonnell arrived with a physician in tow, and Peter was promptly banished from the room. He waited in the nursery, where the Chinese maid cooed over his daughter, his anger rising. Dammit, that was his wife in there! He had a right to be with her. And this was his child—

He dismissed the maid. He would take over the baby's care. The little servant looked at him doubtfully, but fled before the look in his dark face. Petra was quiet, but he picked her up, walking with her, feeling her warmth and the scent of rose petals peculiar to babies.

Lady MacDonnell found him thus when she entered to tell him the doctor had gone. Lani had been sedated. While her cuts were superficial, she should not be moved for a few days. She was horrified that this should take place on the very lawn of Government House. She hadn't the slightest idea why—!

"A common thief, no doubt."

Finally, the governor's lady pulled herself together. She must return to see to her royal guest. She would send two maids, one to watch over Lani, the other to care for the baby.

"We need no one," Channing said positively. "I prefer to look after them myself."

Her arguments had no effect, even when she

pointed out that Lani mustn't be disturbed. He would have to sleep in a chair. He began to laugh, laughing so hard and so long that she wondered, going back downstairs, if the doctor should have sedated the husband, too.

Peter Channing spent the remainder of the night, changing from a hard-bitten adventurer who had never known the softness of love in his life, into a husband and father. In that moment when Martha's assailant struck, he had realized that he loved this girl, that he wouldn't want to live without her. Seeing the baby's blanket stained with blood, thinking it was dead, he had forgotten the circumstances of its birth. Then when Petra had looked at him, solemn and trusting, he capitulated. She was his own, and would never learn otherwise—as Martha did.

Looking down at his sleeping wife, he knew there was much about her he didn't understand. But she was little more than a girl, herself. A little girl, carrying a lifetime of guilt on her shoulders. Maybe she deserved the blows she received, maybe not. Whatever had happened, it was in the past. The future was what counted.

He tucked the baby into her bed and watched over her for a long time. Then he returned to his chair, now drawn close to Martha's side. Tonight, it didn't seem quite so uncomfortable, though he didn't sleep. Every soft movement from the nursery brought him to his feet.

At dawn, he changed Petra, awkwardly, and held her in his arms as he stood at the window, watching the *Mattie* leave the harbor. It would be sailing toward Australia. Home—

He turned to find Martha watching him. "It's

morning isn't it? Your ship is gone." It was a statement, not a question.

"It's leaving now. We were watching it, Petra and I—"

"I'm sorry." Her eyes were glassed with tears.

"Don't be sorry. It's my own fault." He explained that he had seen Toy, and that the girl had sworn vengeance; that he'd inadvertently told her where Martha was staying.

"I knew you'd been with her. I smelled her scent that night."

He saw what she thought in her face. "It wasn't like that," he explained. "Believe me, Martha. Things aren't always what they seem—"

"I know," she said in a small voice. His heart ached for her. He wanted desperately to touch her, to hold her. He shifted Petra from one arm to another, feeling ludicrous. Then he marched into the nursery and put her down. "Mind your own business for a little while," he ordered. "I've got better things to do."

The small face crinkled into a smile, and he couldn't resist kissing a petal-soft cheek as he left her, to drop to his knees at Martha's side. There, holding her unbandaged hand, he told her that he loved her. That, unknowingly, he had loved her since that night at Mountain Lodge. He had been wrong in leaving as he did, and his guilt haunted him all the days they were apart. Last night, thinking the baby had been stabbed, he'd known he loved her as his own.

He talked on, the tears that streaked her pale cheeks giving him his answer. Finally, he took her gently in his arms, careful not to hurt her. His ship had gone. From this time, he would do as she wished to do. They could take the next vessel to Australia, or—

She clung to him, weeping. She had a father for her child, now. No one in the family need ever know. She would like to go back to Lahaina, to see if there was anything she might set right. If not, perhaps the sight of the Larabee's burned house, now ashes, might erase the horror of its flames from her mind. She would like to find her Aunt Tamsen, see if her marriage was in ruins. And then she would like to go home to see her mother, and Duke, to beg their forgiveness.

She had done so much that needed forgiveness; caused so many hurts.

She cried it all out, all the tears she had been hoarding for so long. And even with her wounds, and the fact that it would be long days before their love could be consummated, they were closer than they had ever been before.

KAUAI

54

Lot, Kamehameha the Fifth, studied the analysis sent to him by his representative in Washington. The tone of it should have done much to raise his spirits, but he hadn't felt well of late. Last night, he'd slept little, after a recurring dream. Thoughts of Tallant's wife, imprisoned in one of the small coral buildings in the compound, continued to plague him.

He closed his mind against her and reread the missive. The American President, Grant, had made a number of mistakes. One of them was an attempt to negotiate a treaty through which Santo Domingo would be annexed; handling the situation through his private secretary. Charles Sumner and his followers had sent the plan down to defeat. Annexation was no longer a popular issue. In addition, Grant was suspected at the moment of involvement with Jay Gould and James Fisk in an attempt to corner the New York gold market. In the writer's opinion, this was nonsense, but the President had his hands full at present. The talk of annexing the islands that had flared so ominously at one time had died away, perhaps forever.

As Kamaipuupaa had said, it would not happen in his lifetime.

Liliuokalani would be pleased.

Laying the report aside, he reached for the two other papers that held his attention this morning. These troubled him. The first stated that Daniel Tallant had been tried and found guilty of murdering Samuel Larabee and his wife. A date of execution had been set. It needed only the king's signature to put it into effect.

The other missive contained a threat. It had been delivered to a sentry in the night, and Lot, sleepless, coming early to his desk, had been the first to see it.

Taking his handkerchief and a letter-opener, he managed to spread the thing without touching it with his hands, reading it once more. It stated that, unless Daniel Tallant were freed, the lepers still able to travel would leave Molokai and throng about the palace gates. It was signed, *Sam Larabee.*

Sighing, Kamehameha dropped the letter into a basket, along with his handkerchief, then washed his hands with brandy. He felt the paper meant just what it said. After all, these were dying people. They had nothing to lose. He could, of course, set patrols and blow their boats out of the water before they arrived. But wholesale murder did not appeal to him.

Neither did the death of an innocent man.

Resting his huge head in his hands, he considered the facts in the case. Daniel Tallant had not committed murder. He was guilty of being a spy, sending information to the United States. Now, apparently, that information was useless.

If he allowed the man to die on a trumped-up charge, it would be only for one reason. Because he

476

loved that man's wife. It would be so simple to simply sign his name to Tallant's death warrant. So simple.

Sighing heavily, he rose, calling a sentry to burn the contents of his basket, another to deliver the Washington report to Lydia Dominis. He donned a black, somber coat, folding the third paper into his pocket, and called for his horse. A few minutes later, he rode into the compound where Daniel Tallant and his wife were held in small coral buildings, apart from each other.

Tamsen, as usual, was writing. She had soon learned that her every wish was obeyed. Her cell-like room, in contrast to Dan's, was bright and cheerful, with fresh flowers and fruit every day. Her own clothing had been brought to her, along with a good supply of books. Too nervous to read, she had asked for pen and paper, writing to Arab, to Em, to Nell. She had no idea that her messages would ever be delivered, but it was her last chance to tell them how much she loved them all.

Intent on her writing, she scarcely looked up when the door grated open. It would be the guard with her breakfast tray. The door closed again, and there were no further steps. Tamsen's head jerked up.

In the doorway of her prison stood the king.

It was the first time she'd seen him since the night she held him at gunpoint. He did not look angry. Just—sad, and ill. Tamsen rose to her feet to face him, her shoulders stiff, her eyes wary.

"Your Majesty," she said.

Kamehameha drew off his riding gloves and tossed them to a table. "The name is still Lot."

"I'm glad you came, Lot," she said in a small voice. "I want to tell you again—I'm sorry."

477

"Do you expect that to help you—or your husband?"

"No," she said hopelessly, "I don't."

"Aren't you going to beg? Cry? Ask for my forgiveness? Pretend something for me that you do not feel?"

"It's a little late for that, isn't it?" She looked at him, steadily. "You know I am Dan Tallant's wife. I love him, more than life itself."

He growled, deep in his throat like a wounded bear. "You may get a chance to prove that." He drew the papers that stated Tallant's guilt, demanding his death, from his pocket and spread them on the table. Tamsen's eyes filled with tears as she stared at them.

"I willl make one request, Lot. When we die—let us die together."

"Em—"

"The name isn't Em," she said tartly. "It's Tamsen. Tamsen Tallant."

"Tamsen, then! Don't be a fool! You can save yourself! I can make you a queen! Queen of these islands—"

"And Dan? My husband?"

Lot's eyes slid away. It was answer enough. A woman could not become a queen when she already had a husband. The only logical answer would be to rid the world of him.

"I don't believe we have any more to say to each other," Tamsen said, honestly. "I only ask that you honor my request. Let me die with him."

Kamehameha turned toward the door, then back again. "Do you remember the day we rode to the pali? When we picnicked on the slopes, you gathered flowers, and we waded in the stream?"

She nodded.

"That was the happiest day of my life," he said. "I was not a king, but a man. And do you remember the story I told of the pali? How my ancestor drove his enemies over the rim?"

Again she nodded.

"This is the unhappiest day of my life," he said. "I must remember I am not a man, but a king."

He looked at her for a moment, his sad eyes devouring her face as though he might never see it again, then he was gone.

Tamsen sat down at the table, put her face on her folded arms and cried. She cried for Dan, and for herself, separated by a few yards of alien soil. They would die here, perhaps without the chance of seeing each other again. And she cried for a sad king who had loved two women too much, and neither of them had loved him enough.

When she finally lifted her head, the pages of her letter were blotched with tears. It didn't matter. No one would ever receive them. She wiped her eyes and doggedly continued her letter to Em.

Kamehameha returned to the royal compound, the trip seeming to take an eternity. A pain bloomed in his chest, opening and closing like a giant fist. He was weak and soaked with perspiration when he reached his destination, sliding from his horse into the arms of one of his guards.

Bernice Bishop had been awaiting his arrival. Alarmed, she took over, calling her own physician. Too ill to protest, Lot submitted to her tender ministrations. When the doctor arrived, he listened to the royal heart and took the royal pulse, his expression growing graver by the moment. The king was not stupid, and he was a sensitive man.

"How long do I have to live?"

The physician jumped at his words, his mouth

beginning to form assurances. Kamehameha raised a quelling hand.

"In my position, I have to know," he said quietly.

The doctor turned away from him, putting his equipment back into a satchel. "A year, two, perhaps three with luck," he muttered.

Kamaipuupaa, too had known. He should have guessed. His poor country—

Kamehameha, fifth king of all this beauty, was the loneliest man in the world.

The medication he was given helped him sleep, but it did not keep him from dreaming. It was his same dream of the royal barge, himself in dress uniform—and his bride, as they moved up the Wailua River, birthplace of kings. He did not reach for her, knowing she would slip away. But she turned toward him, wearing the face of death.

He woke in the morning with only a dull memory of pain. For the first time in weeks, his mind was crystal clear. Perhaps it would be that way for the rest of his days, a consolation for having so little time left.

There was something he must put an end to, and he would do it. He called a guard.

55

All through the night after Lot's visit, Tamsen suffered the tortures of the damned. Dan was going to die, and for a crime he didn't commit. Lot knew he wasn't guilty, but he was allowing this absurd farce to continue to the end. It was her own fault. If she'd only done as she intended, petitioned the king on that first meeting, he might have listened.

Now, it was painfully clear that he intended to eliminate her husband, either because of his love for her—or because she had injured his royal pride.

Whatever it was, her interference had only compounded the problem. Dan didn't have a chance.

She remembered Lot's words, on that night he'd taken her to the place Dan was held prisoner: *"I promise you, you will watch him die. After that, I will decide what is to be done with you."*

Please God, let her die with him!

For the first time, she understood why Sam Larabee had gone into exile with is beloved Josie, knowing he faced a similar fate, in all probability; caring for a loved one who had become a horror— yet was still Josie. Dan would have chosen to go with his wife, she with him—

When it came to the end, nothing else mattered. Why, then, did people let smaller things come between them? Suspicion, jealousy: those lost years when she had tried to overcome her past, to become someone else? Her own family, whom she had regarded as children, needing her. All these had stood as barriers, blurring the edges of their love—

Em and Duke would have to bear their grief over losing Martha, alone. Arab and Juan, together, would be responsible for whatever happened to little Luka. Ramona, Arab's least-favored child, whom only Nell thought beautiful, would have to grow up as best she could. Except for Nell and Dusty, too old to cope with grief, the world would go on without her if she were gone—

If she were gone. If only Lot would accede to her request. If she could stand beside her husband, touching him, at the moment of death.

A note arrived for Tamsen after a long night and a longer day. It merely said, "Request granted."

It was signed with Kamehameha's seal.

That night, she was able to sleep. The guards came for her the next morning before she was fully awake, courteously withdrawing to give her a moment to dress. She chose the simple off-white gown that reminded her of her wedding dress. She brushed her long black hair, her face dreaming as her mind went back to that wedding; a hurry-up affair, taking place on a wharf in San Francisco. She could hear the minister's sonorous words, "Do you take this man—" In the background, for music, there had been the lapping of the waves below.

A glow had appeared in the east as the minister pronounced them man and wife. It had been an omen, she thought then. Finally, they had stepped into a small boat that waited to carry them to their ship; its oars cutting through lace-frothed waters in a spray of silver. Dan had pointed to a last faint star lingering in the lightening sky—

Perhaps death would be like that; setting out in a small craft, moving toward a shadowed ship that would carry them to an unknown destination.

It didn't matter, as long as they went together.

Her face serene, she signaled the guards that she was prepared for whatever might come, her only feeling one of surprise that she felt no fear.

She was put into a closed carriage, and driven through the still-silent streets. When they reached their destination, a guard aided her in alighting. She looked about with dismay, seeing the harbor, night-fishing vessels coming in.

"I don't understand. What are we doing here?"

The guards appeared to be deaf and mute as they hurried her into a small craft which they rowed to a waiting ship. There, she was helped aboard and taken to a small cabin.

With its plush appointments, it was fit for a king. And it was empty, except for its luxurious furnishings.

She turned like a spitting cat. "Where is my husband? I demand to know where we're going!"

Hands seized her, not ungently, and she was pushed inside, the door closed and locked against her.

Frantic thoughts coursed through her mind. Lot would not kidnap her. He wouldn't dare! He'd promised her request—to die with Dan—would be fulfilled. Still, she had no knowledge of the working of his mind! He was all-powerful, here. It would be so easy to execute Dan, and—

Her heart stopped beating. Perhaps Dan was already dead. He couldn't be! She would know—

Weeping, she beat on the locked door. Nobody answered her sobbing calls.

Finally, conscious that the ship was moving, she sank into a heap on the floor, sick with frustration, dazed—

Then she heard the tapping. It came from an inner wall. She listened for a moment, not daring to believe. There was a peculiar sort of rhythm to it—a bawdy song she used to sing at the cantina.

Dan! It was Dan! Lot had kept his promise, after all!

Taking off her shoe, she used it to echo his signal. She could hear his voice, but not his words. Frantically, she searched the wall. It was papered in rich velvet. Running her fingers over it, she felt the imprint of a knothole at its base.

She hammered at the spot with her small, dainty heel, feeling the place give. And finally, it fell away. She tore at the worn velvet with her fingers, and there was a small opening.

"Dan!"

"Tamsen, sweetheart! It is you! Oh, God!"

Tears streaming, she thrust a finger through the aperture, feeling his hand close about it; his dear, familiar hand. She wanted to stay like that forever, just touching, but they must talk—

"Dan, where are they taking us?"

"Back to Maui, I suppose. Perhaps to the scene of the crime. I don't know how they arrange these things." His voice had a hopeless note. "That thing about making you watch—I prayed he wouldn't go through with it."

"I'm not watching, Dan. I'm going with you."

There was an indrawn breath of horror. "Tam! My God! *Why!*"

She tried to adopt a light tone. "I invited myself, that's why. And King Lot was kind enough to go along with my request."

The only answer was a despairing groan. "No! Ah-h-h, no!" It was followed by the harsh racking sobs of a man weeping.

"Dan," she said desperately, "Sweetheart, listen to me! Please listen!"

After a long moment, he managed to get himself under control. "I'm listening, Tam."

"I love you," she said in a passionate whisper, "I love you! Can you understand that? I've never loved anybody else." She stopped and swallowed. This was a time for honesty.

"That's not true, Dan. I love Sam Larabee, but not in the same way. I guess I went out of my mind a little bit when I thought you'd killed him—and Josie. I should have known better. But I was shocked, sick with grief. I couldn't think. I should have listened to you, stood by you, and I didn't. Now it's too late. I know they're alive, and saying I'm sorry doesn't mean anything."

"That doesn't mean you have to die with me. You don't have to prove anything—"

"I'm not trying to prove anything. I haven't been a good woman at times in my life." She overrode his sound of negation. "I haven't, and you know it. A lot of the time, I haven't even been a good wife. But I'm not afraid of dying. I'm more afraid of living without you. Please—"

Dan Tallant closed his eyes in agony at her last plaintive word. He had heard it so many times before. But then it had been whispered in the depths of passion, a sound of need. And he had answered, holding her, his own desires burning pure and bright—

His Tamsen had always been hell-bent on liv-

485

ing. Now, she was hell-bent on dying. Nothing he could say would stop her.

They talked for a long time, Dan seeing the small face beyond the partition in his mind's eye. Her black hair would be down, he knew it; her eyes luminous, smoky with love. She, in turn, saw a tanned face, dark hair, with a sprinkling of silver at the sides, falling boyishly over eyes that could be deep and dark, the color of warm honey, or as cold as death.

Death! She shivered. Sensing a change, Dan asked, "Tam?"

"I was just thinking how much I love you," she lied.

"And I love you. I'm a damn poor excuse for a man, getting you into this mess."

"It's not your fault, it's mine!"

"Dammit, Tamsen! You know that I—"

Tamsen giggled. "Dan, do you realize we're arguing? At a time like this?"

He was quiet for a moment, then he laughed. "I guess that's part of loving. At least it is for us. Sweetheart, can you try to rest? No telling what's coming, or when. Whatever it is, let's face it with as much courage as we can."

By mutual agreement, each pulled the mattresses from their beds and put them on the floor. Tamsen put her finger through the knothole, and Dan clasped it. Holding each other in the only way they could, they finally slept.

56

Long before morning, Tamsen felt a gentle pressure on her finger, followed by the touch of Dan's lips against it. For a moment she was dazed. Then, "What is it, Dan?"

"We've stopped moving, sweetheart. We're at anchor. Can't you tell?"

There was no feeling of motion, only a gentle rocking. "Where do you suppose we are?"

"I don't know where the hell we are. I don't think it's Maui. The time isn't right. But I have a hunch they'll be coming for us soon."

They dragged their mattresses back to their beds. Tamsen took a moment to smooth her rumpled gown into some semblance of order. There were toilet articles on a built-in dresser with a mirror. She used them. She looked at her reflection in the lamp-lit mirror, seeing a small white figure, surprisingly neat for having slept in her gown. She might be dressed for a garden party, or a walk on a beach with a king . . .

She returned to the small aperture in the wall that separated them. "Dan?"

"I'm here, sweetheart."

"Dan, tell me you're not sorry that I'm—going with you."

"I'm not sorry, love."

But he was. Inside, he was raging at their predicament. He'd been in tight spots before, but nothing like this. It was his own damn fault! He'd arrived at Sam Larabee's, prepared to beat the hell out of him. Sam had gone to carry a last crate of possessions to a waiting boat when he got there, but of course he didn't know that. What he found was a cloaked figure sitting on a bamboo chair, looking at the house and weeping.

He went toward it. "Josie?" The figure rose and tried to flee in a sort of hobbling walk. "Josie!"

He caught her, her hood falling away in the process. And he had looked into a nightmare face. He recognized it for what it was.

He had seen leprosy before. He let her go.

Sam returned, shaken to find their secret had been discovered. He made him vow to keep it safe, and told him his plan. It was better for Lani to think they were both dead, rather than know Josie was committed to a slow, dreadful dying in the horror colony of Molokai, and that he was with her, risking his own health. "But I couldn't let her go alone! I love her!"

Ashamed of his jealousy, Tallant bowed his head before the luminscence of Sam's blue eyes. He understood that kind of love.

He helped get Josie to the boat, reckless of contamination. Then he told them to go. He would take care of the burning It was too much for a dying woman to watch her home go up in flames.

And afterward, when Tamsen believed him to be guilty of murder, it had hurt. It had hurt like hell. But then he had convinced himself it was a good idea to keep apart from her until he knew he hadn't contracted Josie's disease.

They had wasted so much time. And now, there was so little left!

"What are you thinking, Dan?"

He jerked himself back to the present. "How I got myself into this by keeping quiet about Sam."

"Sam's death wasn't the real issue," she reminded him. "I left your papers in the cottage, and told Kimo where they were. It's because of your work here. And it's my fault they found proof—"

"It doesn't really matter, now. Why we're here, where we are, what they intend to do with us. The important thing is that we love each other. Tamsen, I fell in love with you the first time I saw you. You were bending over a campfire, your black hair swinging—an Indian, or a gypsy—"

"I don't know when I first knew, Dan," she said honestly. "But I feel like I've loved you all my life."

There was a far away rapping sound. "They're at my door," Dan said hoarsely. "I'll see you, sweetheart." Then there was the sound of his footsteps moving away, a mumble of voices. Tamsen rose, absently smoothing her gown, her eyes on her own door as she waited, a small girl-woman, back straight and shoulders stiffened to face whatever might come.

She waited for a long time. Thirty minutes? An hour? She didn't know. And finally she knew, with a dull feeling of hopelessness, that Lot did not intend to keep his promise. In all likelihood, she would never see her husband again.

When the door finally opened, it framed a footman in Kamehameha's livery. Tamsen's heart shrank. She could feel it, cold and marble-hard in her breast. Numbly, she followed him, to be helped

In the stern, beneath a canopy, on a seat woven of down a portable stair into a gaily decorated barge. bamboo, cushioned with velvet, sat Lot, Kamehameha, the Fifth. The sun glinted off the decorations of his dress uniform. She was led to sit beside him. Dan was nowhere to be seen.

Tamsen sat stiff and silent as the barge moved away from the larger vessel. At either side, sturdy native men manned the oars. In the center, another strummed a guitar while a trio of girls sang a medley in their own tongue. Tamsen was grateful for the entertainers. Their music ruled out the need for conversation. She was too angry, too sick at heart, to even pose a coherent question.

They had crossed the channel and moved into a river's mouth before Lot spoke. The singing had ceased, the guitar only a soft cadence, a background for Kamehameha's words. His high and not-too-pleasant voice was soft now, blending with the music.

"This is the river, *Wailua*," he said reverently. "The most beautiful and sacred of all our rivers. It is known as The King's Highway, since once only the highborn, or alii, were allowed to enter here."

He pointed out a spot at the river's mouth. There, once was a city of refuge. There, where tall palms shaded a spot strewn with giant stones.

My God, Tamsen thought, panicked, it's those early days in Honolulu all over again! He's choosing to ignore Dan! To pretend the situation doesn't exist! She turned on him, furiously. "Where is my husband! You promised me—"

"All in good time," he said stiffly. "I do not allow anyone to leave my islands—in any way—without an appreciation of them. You will sit quietly, and you will listen."

490

It was a royal command.

In another instant, his tone had softened, changed. "There is the *Malae Heiau,* once the most important religious place on Kauai—until Queen Kapule became a Christian and turned it into a cow pasture." There was a note in his voice that indicated he did not wholly agree with her decision.

On the left was *Mount Kapu.* On the right, *Nounou Mountain,* known as the sleeping Giant. Once Nounou had been an odd little fish with great red eyes. Pleading with a man to take him to his village, he ate all the food the villagers had, turning into an immense giant. The people fed him lots of Maia to make him sleepy, and a Kahuna, with the help of a magic song by a young girl, put him to sleep forever. It was still forbidden for young girls to play or sing near the giant, since he might wake—

"Lot, please—"

"It is only a legend," he said modestly. "There is another, which is associated with the *menehunes* —the little people of our islands. It is said—"

A table was brought and set before them, spread with a variety of delicacies. Tamsen could only think of that other day, the visit to the pali, when they had found a similar spread waiting as they returned. The audacity of Kamehameha amazed her. He was deliberately being cruel—or he was mad.

There had been no breakfast. She had not eaten since yesterday. But she knew she would choke on any of the king's fare. She pushed it all away. He didn't seem to notice.

He pointed out the spot where the King's Path ran along the brow of a hill. The small grass house at the lower end, in front of a coconut grove was *Holo-Holo-Ku Heiau,* or the Birthplace.

491

He told her of the *Bell Stone;* the story of *Hina and Kuohu, the turtle;* He pointed out the *hau* trees, seemingly growing from the water, telling of their uses and that, many years ago, Hi-Hi-Aka-La-La-Ha a powerful man in love with Princess Poliahu had agreed to climb Poliahu Cliff to prove himself worthy of her hand. He failed to reach his goal by a set time, and Princess Poliahu turned him into a tree. Then there was the *Sister Rock—*

His stories had gone on for several hours, almost three. Stories contrived to amuse and entertain her as they drifted along a blue gray river running like a wide ribbon between pandanus and hau trees. He was not the king of the islands. He was her friend, Lot, at his most charming. Her every attempt at questioning was skillfully evaded. Dear God, did he think she was made of stone?

Finally her nerves stretched to the breaking point. She turned on him, striking out with both small fists, tears streaming. "Stop it," she screamed. "Where is my husband! Where are you taking me? I've got to know!"

He caught both wrists, holding her, looking into eyes that were wild with frustration and grief. His own filled with wonder. I've touched her, he thought, and she didn't fade away!

Ignoring the first part of her question, he said, calmly, "We are going to a spot I think to be the most beautiful place on earth. The place I selected for a ceremony if I should ever marry."

She shrank back. Marry! Oh, dear God! Then Dan was dead!

"We call it *Mama-Akua-Lono,*" he said.

She sank back limply, not hearing the voice that went on and on. If he had what she suspected in mind, she would drown herself. Dan! Oh, Dan!

The late evening sun shone through the trees, dappling the water with splashes of gold and shadow as the royal barge drew up to a small wooden landing. Another boat had preceded them. Empty, it rocked in the wash created by the newcomer.

Tamsen lifted her eyes, unable at first to sort out the waiting figures in the play of light and shadow.

And then she saw him. Her beloved husband. His hands were fastened behind his back, his eyes blindfolded, but her heart gave a surge of joy.

Kamehameha was going to keep his promise, after all. She and Dan would die together.

57

No one stopped Tamsen as she scrambled from the boat, throwing her arms about the prisoner. After a moment, Lot said, "Take him away."

A guard pulled Tamsen forcibly from her husband, holding her pinioned as she watched Dan being led down a leafy path. Then her own hands were tied, and a strip of cloth covered her eyes.

"I will take her," Lot said gently. An arm about her, he steered her along the path that Dan had taken. She could feel the hau branches catching in her hair. The trail was uneven, and she often stumbled and would have fallen without Lot's support. There was a steep incline, and finally she was placed firmly in a standing position, sensing that someone was at her side.

"Dan?" she whispered.

"I'm here, sweetheart."

She moved closer to him, feeling his warmth, touching her arm to his. "I'm not afraid, Dan."

"Neither am I, love. But I'm mad as hell!"

His answer was so typical that she almost laughed. She lifted her face, feeling the softness of the island air against her mouth, smelling the fragrance of blossoms and green leaves. It was not a bad way to die.

"Captain of the guard!"

It was Lot's voice. The voice of King Kamehameha, the Fifth, ringing from a distance away. Tamsen braced herself for a sound of guns. Did one hear the bullet that struck, she wondered. Let their aim be true!

Lot, at the rear of the small glade, looked at the couple standing before him. The slender, wide-shouldered, hard-muscled man; the woman, so fragile, little more than a drift of white at his side. He, himself, felt suddenly old, a fat man in a dress uniform designed to hide his bulk. The pain in his chest began to blossom.

"Remove their bonds," he said quietly. "Then the blindfolds. Turn them about."

Their eyes no longer covered, Dan and Tamsen looked at each other. His hand went out to seize hers. And then they saw the panorama that lay before them. A faint light sifted into an enormous shallow cave, its exterior completely festooned with overlapping fern; an enchanted place. From above, before the cavern's mouth, a slender wisp of water fell like a spun-silver ribbon into a declivity that seemed a pool of gold. There was an awesome hush about the place.

They stared for a moment, in wonder, then turned to face Lot and his guards, their eyes filled with confusion and bewilderment.

"Daniel Tallant," Lot's voice rang out, splintering into a million echoes as the cave's natural amphitheater caught his words and amplified them. "I have here a stay of execution, and the king's pardon. Sam Larabee, the supposed victim, and his wife have been found to be living on the island of Molokai."

"Dear God!" Tamsen's knees buckled, and Dan caught her waist, supporting her.

"This does not mean that you are free," the king said harshly. "You are also guilty of spying on my country. You might have been executed. Maybe that fact will open your eyes to the beauty around you. You are going to be left here. I want you to imagine the beautiful Wailua lined with tall buildings and teeming with commerce, the sacred places of my people destroyed."

He paused, looking at the grotto, at the surrounding scenery, as if he were seeing it for the last time. "In the morning, a small boat will await you at the landing. It is my hope that you will leave the islands, a changed man."

He turned his fierce gaze on Tamsen. "Mrs. Tallant—" he stopped, the pain in his chest suddenly too great. He settled for a dignified bow. "Aloha."

Dan and Tamsen stood rooted to the spot as the remainder of the party marched back down the trail. Dan Tallant's face was white, his eyes stunned.

"Good God! I don't believe it!"

Tamsen threw her arms around him, laughing and crying at the same time. "I do, Dan! Oh, what a wonderful place! What a wonderful man!"

Still skeptical, he insisted she stay behind while he followed the trail the others had taken to the landing. The royal barge and the other large vessel were gone. A small rowboat with a single pair of oars bobbed at the landing.

Dan grinned as he saw it. King Kamehameha, the Fifth, in a grandiose gesture had given him both his life and his wife. But he didn't believe in making it easy for him. It was a long way to the river mouth.

He returned to Tamsen. "You were right. They're gone."

"And we're here! We're here and we're alive! Oh, Dan!"

For a time, they were merely content to hold to each other, unable to believe in their own private miracle. Then, like children, they wandered, hand in hand, exploring the grotto in the last dim light. They found a bamboo basket filled with food, a bed of fragrant leaves already prepared. The thought that had plagued Tamsen's mind; that Lot had saved them with a last-minute decision, was erased.

The dim light faded. For a time, they stood watching the fall of water against the darkening sky. Then Dan's voice took on a new note.

"Tamsen," he said huskily. "Oh, Tam!"

She felt his hands at the neckline of her gown, fumbling at its fastenings. They were trembling, and she reached to help him. Finally, the off-white gown she'd thought would be her shroud slithered to the earth.

His mouth found hers, burning there, his hard hands gliding over the small body he knew so well, until she shuddered with the urgency of her need. He carried her gently to the leafy, perfumed bed, and lowered her into its depths.

"Say it," he said in a broken voice.

"Dan—please—"

He took a long time in arousing her to the kind of passionate madness they'd once known together. When she protested, clinging to him like a wild thing, he said, "Tamsen! Tamsen! We have all the time in the world—"

Finally, their love was consummated. Two pagans, in a cavern lost from the sight of man. Outside the grotto, the falling ribbon of water made its own music, dew dropping from the ferns making an accompaniment that echoed through the cave in a bell-like splintered sound.

In the morning, Tamsen woke first. Slipping from Dan's encircling arms, she looked down at his sleeping face, at the miracle of his beautiful, breathing body. More than anything she wanted to wake him. But—it must be in a very special way. Her mouth quirked in an impish grin, and she tiptoed away.

Dan Tallant woke to the sound of his name. A mere whisper, it was echoed and re-echoed by the cave.

"Dan—Dan—Dan—"

Disoriented, still in a dream, he leaped to his feet. And then he saw her—his love.

A golden shaft of morning light gilded the creamy body, hip-deep in the shallow pool beneath the waterfall. Tamsen's hair hung almost to the water, a yellow hau flower tucked into its dark cascade. She smiled at him, hands beckoning, as she began a provocative love song, her small, husky voice vibrating with invitation that sounded all around him. Behind her, the hau forest was a burst of yellow bloom, the trail dappled with sun.

He made his way toward her, afraid that this was a dream; that the picture she made would shimmer and disappear. She scooped up a handful of water, and splashed him, her song turning to joyous laughter.

Then he was beside her, holding her hair back with one hand while he kissed her warm mouth. The waterfall poured over them, wetting their faces, as if in benediction.

It was a long time before they left paradise for the small boat in which they were to journey down the Wailus together.

BACK OF BEYOND

58

At the small compound on the outskirts of Lahaina, there was a turmoil of indecision. Duke
Courtney had finally felt it necessary to reveal his
findings in Honolulu. Tamsen had been there—under another name. She had disappeared, following an
outing with the king. Someone had picked up her
things, saying that she was leaving the islands. He
had gone to the magistrate's office, and found no
record of Dan. It was his hope that she managed to
get him free, and they sailed for home.

Nell was the first to react. "It ain't so!" she bel-
lowed. "It ain't so! Tamsen wudden run off an' leave
us in th' lurch! Migawd!" Her beady eyes opened
wide. "He's done kilt 'em! That there high-muckety-
muck finished 'em both off! They's dead! I know it!
Oh, gawdam! gawdam!"

She began to cry. Nell, in tears was an alarming
sight. Her face was splotched red and white. Sobs
shook her huge frame, setting it all in motion as she
rubbed at her nose with a pudgy hand, snuffling
loudly.

Dusty moved to her side, his frail arm trying
to subdue her shuddering frame. "There, Nell! Don't

take on so! Jove! I am certain there is an explanation—"

Nell refused to be comforted. Finally, he led her toward the hut they shared.

The others sat in an uneasy silence, Em finally dissolving in tears. "Maybe she's right," she whispered. "First Martha, then Dan—and now, Tam—"

Despite her agitation, Nell had heard. She turned about, her face crimson. "Won't wash," she roared. "None of them things is related. On'y one who'd wanna kill Martha would be Tam. An' I wudden blame her."

Em flinched. "I know Martha caused a lot of trouble," she admitted. "I'm sorry."

Arab put a comforting arm about her older sister. "Hush! It doesn't matter, now. All that matters is finding her."

"We won't find her, you know that." Em's lovely eyes were sunken, shadowed with her long trial. "It's been too long, and we've looked everywhere. And if Dan and Tamsen were coming back, they'd be here now. I—I can't stand any more." She turned to her husband. "Duke, I want to go home."

He put his arms around her. "Give it another day or two," he begged.

The next day brought yet another blow. A letter came, addressed to Daniel Tallant and Company. It bore the seal of the President of the United States.

Juan opened it. It stated that their employment as surveyors for possible railroad sites was discontinued as of the letter's date. No mention was made of their pleas to intercede on Tallant's behalf.

"Gawdam rats, a-leavin' a sinkin' ship," Nell swore.

Juan tried in vain to explain that Dan had

known the dangers when he came here. That accepting responsibility for his own safety was a vital part of his job. He finished, to find Arab looking at him with frightened eyes.

"Does the same hold true for you?"

"I don't know," he said in exasperation. "I suppose so."

"That settles it! We're leaving immediately for home."

Two women began to pack. Two men held back. Nell was too worried and grief-stricken to think, Dusty too occupied with Nell. The children, sensing the unrest that plagued their elders, were grave and quiet, except for little Scott. He delighted in running away from his new playmate, a little blonde girl with long silver eyes. Luka had finally learned to stand on her own two feet.

Em and Arab, determined to bring matters to a head, finally walked into Lahaina. They intended to book passage for their various destinations. Em, Duke, and their family to Victoria, where they would make their way home; Arab, Juan, and their daughters to the States. Upon landing in San Francisco, they would have to decide where home would be.

Duke and Juan didn't know of their plans. After passage was arranged and paid for, there would be little they could do but comply. Em felt that home would ease her heartache, or at least make it bearable. Arab wanted to get her man to safety.

Passing the mission on the way to the wharf, Arab stopped still, her mouth open. "T—Tamsen?" she said, stammering a little, her face gone white.

Em followed her gaze. A couple stood at the mission door, their backs to the sisters. A tall man, a baby's face peeping over his broad shoulder; a small woman standing beside him. It was the woman who caught Arab's eye. She was dressed in traveling costume, skirts belling from a tiny waist. A small bonnet of lacy straw covered her hair, concealing her face. But there was something in the way she stood facing Reverend Selwyn and his wife who were saying farewell from the doorway. Then she spoke, in a voice choked with tears.

"Thank you, Lani! We'll go there. I'm so sorry about your folks! But I'm glad—I'm glad—"

Em swayed and Arab put out a steadying hand. But her sister tore herself from her grasp and was running.

"Martha! Oh, God! Martha!"

Martha whirled, her eyes round. Lani had told her where to find the others. But she hadn't mentioned *this!* "Mama," she whispered, "Mama!" Then she, too, was running. They met in the middle of the street. There they held each other tightly, the mother who had thought her daughter was dead, the daughter who had been through hell because of her own actions; who had thought she would never see her mother again, to beg forgiveness.

Lani and David Selwyn joined Arab in separating the two, leading them into the mission house, Peter Channing following, his eyes suspiciously moist as he watched the reunion.

Recalling the Duke of Edinburgh's story about meeting Emmeline McCleod, widow, Martha suddenly gasped, "Papa! Is he—?"

"He's fine. A little worn out from looking for you, but—"

Martha buried her face against her mother's shoulder. "Oh, Mama, what have I done to you? Do you think they'll let Dan go? Do you think Tamsen will ever forgive me?" She burst into wild weeping, again.

Em tried to soothe her. "Of course she will! There's more to it all than you know. Stop crying!" Finally, she stamped her foot, speaking in mock anger as she had when Martha was a child. "Stop it this minute, Martha Courtney!"

"The name is Channing, ma'am."

Em whirled to face the tall man who stood in the background, his face wreathed with a smile. "Who—?"

He shifted the baby to a more comfortable position and held out a strong, brown hand. "Peter Channing. You seem to know my wife, Martha. And here's someone else you may want to meet. Our daughter, Petra. Petra, this is your grandmother."

Em reached out to the child, her hands shaking, her heart too full for expression.

There was too much to assimilate all at once. And Duke was waiting. Duke, who had combed this island inch by inch, refusing to believe that his adopted daughter was dead; fearful of what he would find behind every stone, every shrub, every hill. They must go to him at once. Then, there would be time for talking—

Their return to the compound created a furor. The children saw them first, and came running to meet them. The squeals of delight from Martha's young sisters were equaled by Arab's daughters at seeing Martha return. Behind the bevy of girls, small Scott came at his toddling run, Luka, with precarious balance, behind him. Martha went to her knees to hug the little brother she'd never seen, her other arm going around Luka. Luka, walking! It had been so long—

Duke, rounding the corner of a hut to check

on his offspring stopped, his mouth open. That girl looked like Tamsen. But it wasn't—Oh, my God! He ran toward her and she flew into his arms, her bonnet falling back. He smoothed her hair, distractedly, as he blinked hard. "Martha," he kept saying, "Goddam! Well! Goddam!"

Only Nell stood aloof and angry. This was the girl who made a mess of her Tamsen's life, and Nell didn't intend to forget it. Martha wilted before the big woman's glare, all her guilts returning.

"Where's Aunt Tamsen?" she asked.

Em's heart sank. She wasn't going to have her daughter's homecoming spoiled. She looked steadily at Nell. "Tamsen's away," she said. Tomorrow would be time enough to tell her.

The remainder of the day was spent in rejoicing. Martha told her carefully revised tale of her disappearance. Knowing she was at fault, she'd fled the night of the fire, stowing away on the *Mattie*, Peter's ship. He had rescued her, and they were married by the captain. A baby coming, she had stayed with friends in Hong Kong while he completed his tour of duty. They had decided to come here—"

"Dunno why!" Nell growled, subsiding at a frown from Em.

Martha faltered for a moment, then went on. Then they were going to Barkersville to visit her folks, before going to their home in Australia.

"As to why I came back," Martha faced Nell, her mouth trembling, "I wanted to right any wrongs I could. I wanted to say I was sorry for hurting everybody I loved—" She stopped, her voice breaking.

She looks like Tamsen, Nell thought. Like Tam, when she knows she's done wrong. Standing there

506

like that, her eyes all big and scared, but trying to tough it out—

She enveloped the girl in a bear-hug. "Hell," she rumbled, "It's awright. Ain't nobuddy never made a mistake er two."

She backed off, her own eyes wet, but unable to totally concede. "A-course, they's allus them what makes more mistakes than others." She stamped off to her hut. It was as close as Nell had ever come to making a concession.

That night, alone in their hut, Em lay beside her husband. She was suddenly surprised to find Duke's hand on her bare shoulder, turning her to face him. His mouth, through years of expertise, found hers in the dark. For a moment, they clung to each other, feeling desire begin to build. It had been a long time. Duke had been fatigued from his search for Martha, Em frantic with worry. But now all was well with them—

Em surrendered to the emotions aroused by his caressing hands, knowing how the face above her own would look; his eyes gentle, his mouth, so recently bracketed by worry, tender with love—

Then, with one swift movement, his hand was at the neckline of her nightdress, the soft material giving to his strength.

"Duke! Duke Courtney! What in heaven's name are you doing?"

"Never made love to a grandmother, before," he said, a lilt of laughter in his voice. "Don't want to miss a thing."

He hadn't, she thought, wryly, when he finally slept, his arm thrown across her as if she might escape. He'd missed nothing! For a while, she thought of their years together, how wonderful they'd been.

How lucky she was in finding him; her second husband, and the only man she ever loved. Em McLeod, the quietest of the three sisters; an unwed mother, a widow, and again a wife. And now, a grandmother—

She thought of little Petra. Such a sweet weight she had been in her arms. Her granddaughter! She was certain of that, though there were other things in Martha's story that puzzled her. She had known her daughter long enough to know when she was lying. No—not a lie—But there had been factors missing from her story; something that Martha did not choose to tell. Perhaps she, Em, would never know the full truth.

The baby, Petra, didn't resemble Peter in any way. There was an Oriental cast to the lovely little features. Em had often seen such children in the arms of Chinese mothers in San Francisco.

Whatever the situation, it was clear that Peter Channing worshiped both mother and child. So it really made no difference. All that counted was Martha's happiness, and that Petra was an adorable, heavenly little bundle to hold.

She wondered if Duke would consider moving to Australia . . .

59

Duke Courtney took it upon himself to tell Martha the remainder of the news the next morning. He led his daughter to a spot where a fallen palm made an arch, its tip caught and held in the crotch of another tree. Beyond the arch was a strip of beach, the blue waters lazily caressing the sand.

Putting both hands at Martha's waist, Duke swung her to a seat high on the trunk as he did when she was a little girl. Indeed, her feet dangling, her hands spread to brace herself, her bright smile, she looked like a child.

He stood before her, the wind ruffling his blond hair with its recent streaks of gray; his blue eyes serious. "Martha, I've got to talk to you."

He repeated what he'd been told of the night of the fire, and the developments that followed; most of which Martha already knew. Sam Larabee and his wife were believed dead. Tallant arrested for their murder. As she knew, now, Sam and Josie were on Molokai. Attempts to free Dan had failed, since the murder charge was not the real issue. Tallant had been an agent, here at the request of the President of the United States, in the guise of railroad surveyor. Someone had leaked the information, and his papers had fallen into the wrong hands.

His soft voice went on. Martha closed her eyes. She could hear her own voice, bragging to Kimo, telling him—oh, God, what had she told him! It was a minute before she could comprehend what Duke was saying.

He had gone to Honolulu. There were no records at the magistrate's office regarding Dan. Tamsen had been there, but she had disappeared—in the company of the king. Her clothing had been sent for, and the hotel told she was returning home.

"Papa, you don't think—"

"I don't know what to think, Martha."

"But what are you going to do?"

"Wait awhile, I suppose. Then take your mother home to Barkersville."

She slid from the tree, and he caught her. She extricated herself from his arms and leaned her forehead against the smooth bark of the tree. "Papa, how can you and Mama love me after all I've done! I've done such bad things! More than you know!"

"What you've done is past, Martha. The important thing is why—"

Her head still bowed, she told him how it had been in Barkersville: how she had strange, wild feelings she didn't understand; that she wanted to be beautiful and glamorous like her aunt; Mama had been ill, then pregnant. She hadn't seemed to be able to talk to her, anymore—

"You could have talked to me."

She flushed. "I didn't think you would understand."

"I know young boys get mixed-up sometimes. I figure girls do, too—"

"I was mad at you the night you made me come

510

home," she said. "And then I was sorry. I came downstairs and heard you and Mama talking. What I heard made me think—" She stopped, her cheeks flaming.

"Think what, Martha?"

"That Tamsen was bad. That you'd been lying to me all those years, to make her look good. That Mama—that Mama was bad, too. I didn't know Donald Alden wasn't my real father. I didn't know I was a bastard—"

She began to cry, and he took her in his arms. "Do you believe all that now?"

She shook her head, still shivering. "Not all of it. But I do know I have bad blood! That's what made me the way I am! Oh, Papa—"

He glared at her. "Of all the goddam stupid things to think! And you with a kid of your own! I can see how what you heard that night shook you up, but hell! Bad blood? There's no such thing! There's only babies. Like a clean slate. Give 'em enough love, and they turn out all right. Bad blood, hell! There's only bad parents. Which me and Em must have been—"

"No, Papa! No!" She looked at him, her eyes big, shocked at his sudden attack.

"We did the best we could," he said simply. "Guess it wasn't enough. Keep on thinking the way you are, and you'll be watching Petra, to see if she inherited any meanness from you. Then you're in for a helluva lot of trouble."

Somehow, he had hit on the very source of her worry. Poor little Petra had bad blood on both sides. But there was no such thing—

She threw her arms about his neck. "I love you, Papa."

On the way back to the compound, watching

her fly ahead of him, anxious to be with her husband and child, Duke Courtney smiled to himself, a little smugly. There was a lot Martha wasn't telling about her jaunt to Hong Kong. That baby had Chinese blood, or he'd eat his hat! And he figured Channing knew it, and didn't care. Of all his children, he guessed he probably loved Martha the most. It was Em who had suffered, watching for unpleasant traits inherited from an unknown father.

Maybe he got Martha started out on the right track.

Meanwhile, he got it off his chest about Tamsen and Dan. He was not a praying man, but he stopped beside a flowering tree and offered an inarticulate unspoken thought to the heavens. They had to return, for their own sakes, and for Martha's.

The days passed, melting one into another, held together by a thread of joy at Martha's return, and concern over the missing loved ones.

Little Petra throve, chuckling as she was passed from one pair of loving arms to another. Martha and Em spelled Arab with Luka's exercises, giving her time with Ramona and Missy. Small Scott dogged his father's heels, managing to be included in all the male conversations which dealt variously with what they should do, when they should give up and return home—and opals.

The gemstones Peter still carried were taken out a dozen times a night, pored over, discussed. Even old Dusty had caught the fever.

"Like a beautiful woman," he said, with a covert glance at Nell. "They shine from within."

Nell would make a harrumphing sound, but it was clear she was pleased.

Duke was definitely interested in what Peter

had to say of opal mining, and especially of the ruggedness of Australian life. Hell, Barkersville was beginning to be a city. It was getting pretty crowded there and he had already made his pile in gold. He always wanted to live near his grandchildren, he confessed to Em. Maybe they could work something out.

Juan Narvaéz was not a talker, but a listener —a thinker. Neither was he a wealthy man in his own right. For years, his fortunes had been tied in with Dan Tallant's—Dan, whom he loved like a brother. Of pure Spanish descent, reared like a young prince in his own homeland, he had little to offer in the way of skills. Once, long ago in San Francisco, he had tried to find work; had seen his golden wife living in poverty. He did not want to face that again.

Still—Australia? It was an unknown. Yet with such riches to be taken from the land! He looked at the opal in his palm, at the smoky fire of promise it contained. Did he dare venture such a course? A rough life, Peter said. Ramona and Missy would thrive in it. But Arab—and Luka? His eyes went to his daughter, seeing her golden hair, her slanting silver eyes; the little girl who would always be a child.

He couldn't chance it. If only Dan and Tamsen were there! His lips quirked in a self-mocking smile. Like everyone else, Juan Narvaéz, born and groomed to head the *cortes* of Spain, was dependent on the leadership of those two.

He said nothing to Arab. He would wait and see.

Only between Dusty and Nell was there honest communication. Dusty figured he could find his fortune in Australia. Nell was all for it. "Hell," she said enthusiastically. "Peter says they's a damn sight more men than wimmen. Mebbe I could start me up a house—Ef I ain't too gawdam old."

"You'll always be young, Nell," Dusty offered gallantly.

Nell slapped him between the shoulder blades. "You oughta know, you sonovabitch!"

Nothing was resolved, no decisions firmed up. The climate of Maui was soft and warm, only enough breeze to set up a dreaming stirring of leaves; the fragrance of the flowering bushes and trees was narcotic, an opiate to the senses. The compound nestled in greenery at the foot of red hills, held close in Maui's palm. The inhabitants moved like sleepwalkers, their senses drugged by the gentleness of the days.

The nights were especially soporific. The dark sky, spangled with stars; the hush—

It became a time to wait for.

On one such evening, the entire group brought their sleeping mats out of doors. It was early yet, but a mist had formed over Maui, obscuring the sunset. The same mist made the small grass huts untenable, a moist heat, unusual for this island, making it difficult to breathe.

Outside, however, it was perfect. The perfection was shattered with Peter Channing's pronouncement that he and Martha must be leaving soon. They must think of returning to Australia and building a life together.

Duke Courtney was expecting it, but it was still a shock. "But, hell, man—!" he began. Then he fell silent. Martha was no longer his daughter, but a wife and mother. Em began to weep softly, and he put his arm about her.

"Peter's right," he growled. "It's something we've

514

got to think about. We can't just sit here on our backsides."

"Duke!" Em chided, "The children!"

He subsided with an angry, "Well, dammit, we can't!"

For a moment, all was quiet, then Martha pointed, with an indrawn breath. "Look!"

A ray of light had broken through clouds of mist, pointing from heaven to earth; a shimmering Jacob's ladder of gold. It brought a sigh of appreciation from everyone, even the pragmatic Nell. It seemed to move through the atmosphere, coming toward them, breathtaking in its splendor. When it reached the edge of the compound where the trail to Lahaina began, it outlined two figures in its glow.

Two figures; one large, one small, but both seeming unnaturally elongated, transparent and ethereal, smiling faces gilded with magic.

The watchers were spellbound. It was Martha who broke the silence. With a small inarticulate cry, she began to run on stumbling feet. The name on her lips was Tamsen.

Tamsen didn't recognize the faltering figure in a modish traveling gown until they were face to face. Her mind went from numbed disbelief to relief. Martha! Alive! Dear God! She stood for a moment in confusion, the stiff face of the young woman before her was like a wall between them.

Then that face began to break up, ice melting beneath a flood of silent, drenching tears. Martha's quivering mouth was that of a little child. A three-year-old Martha, who had been naughty, and had come to her Aunt Tamsen for forgiveness and consolation. She raised her hands in a helpless, childish gesture.

"Tamsen?"

It was a voice out of the past. Tamsen reached out to her, and the two women clung together, weeping, as the rest of the party converged.

The golden light above them held, illuminating the faces of the sisters, their husbands, and children —friends. When little Luka toddled into the circle, her hair a halo of gilt, her silver eyes filled with recognition, Tamsen's heart was filled to overflowing.

She knows me, she thought. She remembers me!

With an incoherent sound, she fell to her knees, hugging the child. Dan Tallant looked at his wife, a small dark girl in a soiled white gown, with loving eyes.

So small, so fragile—childless, yet mother to them all; the bond that held them together. He had never loved her so much.

The group stayed up more than half the night, but they did not get down to practicalities until the next day. It was Duke who first announced his plans. If Peter and Martha had no objections, he, Em and the children would accompany them to Australia. Look into the situation there. Hell, there was nothing to hold him in Barkersville. And while his own kids were passable—he swatted little Scott affectionately, and made a face at his giggling daughters—he'd always had a hankering to be a grandfather.

His speech was interrupted as an ecstatic Martha threw her arms around his neck. When he freed himself, Peter Channing was there, grinning, pumping his hand.

"Looks like it's settled then."

Two families knew their destination. The other members of the group looked at Dan. He had brought them here. Their work had been discontinued by order of the government of the United States. Dan had read that letter without comment.

Now, he turned away from the questioning eyes. The hazards he'd faced were part of his job. The governmental order didn't lessen his love for his country. But it set him free. Free from having to make a recommendation he didn't want to make.

He was certain the islands would be annexed one day, but it would be through no choice of his. He wanted to go now, before it was too late. Before tall buildings fringed the shores. Before the lovely Wailua, the King's Highway, was opened to curious eyes. Before the grotto with its silver ribbon fall—where he had found both his life and his love again—was contaminated by civilization. He had no wish to see the changes that would come to the beautiful islands with their brown and gentle people.

"I understand they need surveyors in Australia," he said. "Good God! All that land,—"

After the initial backslapping and hilarity had quieted, Dan found a minute alone with his wife.

"I should have asked you first," he admitted. "If you have any objections—"

"None at all." Somehow, it was something she had expected. Always before them, there would be a new life, a new frontier. And she would be with the man she loved—every step of the way.

60

Within a few days, the ship *Warwick* sailed from Lahaina Roadstead at dawn, bound for an Australian port. The Tallant, Narvaéz, and Courtney families were aboard, along with the Channings, and their old friends, Nell and Dusty. They had boarded the vessel the previous night, but only Dan and Tamsen Tallant had risen to witness their departure.

The little town of Lahaina lay sleeping in its bower of flowers and trees. The rising sun touched on red hills soaring high above the city, robes of verdant green about their feet. Even at a distance, there was a fragrance of flowers mingling with the scent of the sea.

It was a sight to hold the eyes. But Tamsen's turned away, looking into the distance toward the shadow of Molokai.

"Don't worry about Sam," Dan said gently, pulling her close. "He's doing what he wants to do. You know that."

"Yes," she whispered. "I do."

She couldn't tell him that she hurt inside. That here in the islands, she was leaving small pieces of her heart. Sam Larabee was her beloved friend; the man she loved second-best to Dan. And now there was a name to put in third place; that of a king, who had been human for a little while; who had shown her the view from the pali, and waded with her in a stream.

"What are you thinking?"

Tamsen searched for an answer. Sometimes a woman had thoughts it wasn't wise to share.

"I don't know, Dan. About the islands, I suppose. I love them, in spite of all the things that happened. The big island—in spite of the earthquakes, the eruptions—it was so beautiful; the tree ferns, the flowers. Maui, with its beaches, its red hills. Molokai—" She stopped. In her mind, Molokai would always be a place where a wedding was held on the sands. Where she last saw Sam.

Swallowing, she went on. "Honolulu on Oahu." Again, she could go no further. "Or Kauai."

"I'll settle for Kauai," he laughed. The memory of a golden girl beneath a silver waterfall, a hau flower in her hair, was vivid in his mind. He would carry that picture forever, never seeing Tamsen in any other way.

"Dan—do you feel like you've failed here?"

The laughter left his face, and he turned somber eyes to the view before him. "Failed? No. I'm just—relieved that it's over. I've always felt there was something blocking my way. As if I wasn't meant to succeed this time." He forced a wry grin. "I'm not expecting you to understand."

Tamsen thought of a grass hut in a clearing high above Hilo; of a big man, naked except for a twist of cloth, the firelight flickering on his mahogany features, a bowl in his cupped hands. A man

519

who had summoned his aumakua, who controlled the wind. A man who followed the old ways. Who would not welcome change.

Understand? "I think I do," she said. "I think I do."

Their idyll was interrupted, the others sleepily joining them. They lined the rail, Dan's arm about Tamsen, Peter Channing's about Martha. Tamsen and Martha exchanged affectionate glances, their differences forgotten. Juan hugged Arab to him. Em clung to Duke Courtney, encumbered by Petra, the only child to wake at this ungodly hour.

Finally, Nell appeared, towed along by Dusty, like a ship with pink sails in her feather trimmed-negligee. "Didden wanna git up," she grumbled, "But, hell!"

Even she was silenced at the view, the outlines of the town dimming in the distance, becoming only a mass of cloud, the sun glinting on one red pinnacle pointing skyward.

We're all together, Tamsen thought, surprised. For the first time, they had left no one behind. Perhaps it was a good omen.

They watched Maui become a cloud of whipped cream resting on the sea. As day broke, the ship's wake sent spume flying into the air; glittering droplets of water that had the look of opals shining in the sun.

Get the whole story of
THE RAKEHELL DYNASTY

The bold, sweeping, passionate story of a great New England shipping family caught up in the winds of change —and of the one man who would dare to sail his dream ship to the frightening, beautiful land of China. He was Jonathan Rakehell, and his destiny would change the course of history.

THE RAKEHELL DYNASTY—
THE GRAND SAGA OF THE GREAT CLIPPER SHIPS
AND OF THE MEN WHO BUILT THEM
TO CONQUER THE SEAS AND CHALLENGE THE WORLD!

Jonathan Rakehell—who staked his reputation and his place in the family on the clipper's amazing speed.

Lai-Tse Lu—the beautiful, independent daughter of a Chinese merchant. She could not know that Jonathan's proud clipper ship carried a cargo of love and pain, joy and tragedy for her.

Louise Graves—Jonathan's wife-to-be, who waits at home in New London keeping a secret of her own.

Bradford Walker—Jonathan's scheming brother-in-law who scoffs at the clipper and plots to replace Jonathan as heir to the Rakehell shipping line.

BEST OF BESTSELLERS
FROM WARNER BOOKS

__**RAGE OF ANGELS**
by Sidney Sheldon (A36-214, $3.95)
A breath-taking novel that takes you behind the doors of the law and inside the heart and mind of Jennifer Parker She rises from the ashes of her own courtroom disaster to become one of America's most brilliant attorneys. Her story is interwoven with that of two very different men of enormous power As Jennifer inspires both men to passion, each is determined to destroy the other—and Jennifer, caught in the crossfire, becomes the ultimate victim.

__**SCRUPLES**
by Judith Krantz (30-531, $3.95)
The ultimate romance! the spellbinding story of the rise of a fascinating woman from fat, unhappy "poor relative" of an aristocratic Boston family to a unique position among the super-beautiful and super-rich, a woman who got everything she wanted—fame, wealth, power and love.

__**LOVE'S TENDER FURY**
by Jennifer Wilde (D30-528, $3.95)
The turbulent story of an English beauty—sold at auction like a slave—who scandalized the New World by enslaving her masters She would conquer them all—only if she could subdue the hot unruly passions of the heart.

ESPECIALLY FOR YOU
FROM WARNER

PERSPECTIVES ON WOMEN FROM WARNER BOOKS

__**GLASS PEOPLE**
by Gail Godwin (92-089, $2.25)
Godwin's protagonist, Francesca, is a cameo figure of perfect beauty, but she is her husband's possession without a life or depth of her own Francesca travels East, to home, to find answers to her own life in her own way.

__**THE ODD WOMAN**
by Gail Godwin (91-215, $2.50)
Jane Clifford must decide the meaning and place of love in her own life She must search within herself and within the lives of the women who have touched her life, family and friends, to find her own form of independence.

__**THE PERFECTIONISTS**
by Gail Godwin (A92-207, $2.25)
The relentless sun of Majorca beats down upon a strange group of vacationers: a brilliant English psychotherapist, his young American wife, his small, silent illegitimate son and a woman patient They look at one another and themselves and see the unsavory shadows that darken their minds and hearts.

ROMANCE...ADVENTURE...DANGER

DAUGHTERS OF THE SOUTHWIND
by Aola Vandergriff   (D30-561 $3 50)

The three McCleod sisters were beautiful virtuous and bound to a dream
—the dream of finding a new life in the untamed promise of the West
Their adventures in search of that dream provide the dimensions for this
action-packed romantic bestseller

DAUGHTERS OF THE WILD COUNTRY
by Aola Vandergriff   (D30-562 $3 50)

High in the North Country, three beautiful women begin new lives in a
world where nature is raw, men are rough and love, when it comes,
shines like a gold nugget Tamsen, Arab and Em McCleod now find themselves in Russian Alaska, where power, money and human life are the
playthings of a displaced, decadent aristocracy in this lusty novel ripe
with love, passion, spirit and adventure.

__DAUGHTERS OF THE FAR ISLANDS
by Aola Vandergriff   (D30-563, $3.50)

Hawaii seems like Paradise to Tamsen and Arab—but it is not. Beneath
the beauty, like the hot lava bubbling in the volcano's crater, trouble
seethes in Paradise. The daughters are destined to be caught in the turmoil between Americans who want annexation of the islands and native
Hawaiians who want to keep their country. And in their own family, danger looms .and threatens to erupt and engulf them all.

__DAUGHTERS OF THE OPAL SKIES
by Aola Vandergriff   (D30-564, $3.50)

Tamsen Tallant, most beautiful of the McCleod sisters, is alone in the
Australian outback. Alone with a ranch to run, two rebellious teenage
nieces to care for, and Opal Station's new head stockman to reckon with
—a man whose very look holds a challenge. But Tamsen is prepared for
danger—for she has seen the face of the Devil and he looks like a man.

ESPECIALLY FOR YOU
FROM WARNER